ACCLAIM FOR RAYMOND CHANDLER

"Chandler wrote like a slumming angel and invested the sun-blinded streets of Los Angeles with a romantic presence."
—Ross Macdonald

"[Chandler] wrote as if pain hurt and life mattered."
—*The New Yorker*

"Chandler seems to have created the culminating American hero: wised up, hopeful, thoughtful, adventurous, sentimental, cynical and rebellious."
—Robert B. Parker,
The New York Times Book Review

"Raymond Chandler invented a new way of talking about America, and America has never looked the same to us since."
—Paul Auster

"Philip Marlowe remains the quintessential urban private eye."
—*Los Angeles Times*

"[Chandler]'s the perfect novelist for our times. . . . He takes us into a different world, a world that's like ours, but isn't."
—Carolyn See

"Raymond Chandler was one of the finest prose writers of the twentieth century. . . . Age does not wither Chandler's prose. . . . He wrote like an angel."
—*Literary Review*

"Raymond Chandler is a star of the first magnitude."
—Erle Stanley Gardner

"[T]he prose rises to heights of unselfconscious eloquence, and we realize with a jolt of excitement that we are in the presence of not a mere action tale teller, but a stylist, a writer with a vision."
—Joyce Carol Oates, *The New York Review of Books*

RAYMOND CHANDLER

▼

THE SIMPLE ART OF MURDER

▼

VINTAGE CRIME

VINTAGE BOOKS

A DIVISION OF RANDOM HOUSE

NEW YORK

First Vintage Books Edition, August 1988

Library of Congress Cataloging-in-Publication Data
Chandler, Raymond, 1888–1959.
The simple art of murder.
1. Detective and mystery stories, American.
2. Detective and mystery stories—Authorship.
I. Title.
PS3505.H3224S56   1988   813'.52   87-45923
ISBN 0-394-75765-3 (pbk.)

The stories in this book appeared in *The Simple Art of Murder*,
Houghton Mifflin, 1950. The material in that edition originally
appeared in the following magazines: *Black Mask, Dime
Detective, Detective Fiction Weekly, The Saturday Evening Post,
Atlantic Monthly* and *The Saturday Review of Literature*.

Manufactured in the United States of America

Book design by The Sarabande Press

CONTENTS

▲

THE SIMPLE ART
OF MURDER

▼

AN ESSAY

Fiction in any form has always intended to be realistic. Old-fashioned novels which now seem stilted and artificial to the point of burlesque did not appear that way to the people who first read them. Writers like Fielding and Smollett could seem realistic in the modern sense because they dealt largely with uninhibited characters, many of whom were about two jumps ahead of the police, but Jane Austen's chronicles of highly inhibited people against a background of rural gentility seem real enough psychologically. There is plenty of that kind of social and emotional hypocrisy around today. Add to it a liberal dose of intellectual pretentiousness and you get the tone of the book page in your daily paper and the earnest and fatuous atmosphere breathed by discussion groups in little clubs. These are the people who make best sellers, which are promotional jobs based on a sort of indirect snob appeal, carefully escorted by the trained seals of the critical fraternity, and lovingly tended and watered by certain much too powerful pressure groups whose business is selling books, although they would like you to think they are fostering culture. Just get a little behind in your payments and you will find out how idealistic they are.

The detective story for a variety of reasons can seldom be

1
▼

promoted. It is usually about murder and hence lacks the element of uplift. Murder, which is a frustration of the individual and hence a frustration of the race, may have, and in fact has, a good deal of sociological implication. But it has been going on too long for it to be news. If the mystery novel is at all realistic (which it very seldom is) it is written in a certain spirit of detachment; otherwise nobody but a psychopath would want to write it or read it. The murder novel has also a depressing way of minding its own business, solving its own problems and answering its own questions. There is nothing left to discuss, except whether it was well enough written to be good fiction, and the people who make up the half-million sales wouldn't know that anyway. The detection of quality in writing is difficult enough even for those who make a career of the job, without paying too much attention to the matter of advance sales.

The detective story (perhaps I had better call it that, since the English formula still dominates the trade) has to find its public by a slow process of distillation. That it does do this, and holds on thereafter with such tenacity, is a fact; the reasons for it are a study for more patient minds than mine. Nor is it any part of my thesis to maintain that it is a vital and significant form of art. There are no vital and significant forms of art; there is only art, and precious little of that. The growth of populations has in no way increased the amount; it has merely increased the adeptness with which substitutes can be produced and packaged.

Yet the detective story, even in its most conventional form, is difficult to write well. Good specimens of the art are much rarer than good serious novels. Second-rate items outlast most of the high-velocity fiction, and a great many that should never have been born simply refuse to die at all. They are as durable as the statues in public parks and just about as dull.

This fact is annoying to people of what is called discernment. They do not like it that penetrating and important works of fiction of a few years back stand on their special shelf in the library marked "Best-sellers of Yesteryear" or something, and nobody goes near them but an occasional shortsighted customer who bends down, peers briefly and hurries away; while at the same time old ladies jostle each other at the mystery shelf to grab off some item of the same vintage with such a title as *The Triple Petunia Murder Case* or *Inspector Pinchbottle to the Rescue*. They do not like it at all that "really important books" (and some of them are too, in a way) get the frosty mitt at the reprint counter while *Death Wears Yellow Garters* is put out in editions of fifty or one hundred thousand copies on the newsstands of the country, and is obviously not there just to say goodbye.

To tell the truth, I do not like it very much myself. In my less stilted moments I too write detective stories, and all this immortality makes just a little too much competition. Even Einstein couldn't get very far if three hundred treatises of the higher physics were published every year, and several thousand others in some form or other were hanging around in excellent condition, and being read too.

Hemingway says somewhere that the good writer competes only with the dead. The good detective story writer (there must after all be a few) competes not only with all the unburied dead but with all the hosts of the living as well. And on almost equal terms; for it is one of the qualities of this kind of writing that the thing that makes people read it never goes out of style. The hero's tie may be a little out of the mode and the good gray inspector may arrive in a dogcart instead of a streamlined sedan with siren screaming, but what he does when he gets there is the same old futzing around with timetables and bits of charred paper and who trampled the jolly old flowering arbutus under the library window.

I have, however, a less sordid interest in the matter. It seems to me that production of detective stories on so large a scale, and by writers whose immediate reward is small and whose meed of critical praise is almost nil, would not be possible at all if the job took any talent. In that sense the raised eyebrow of the critic and the shoddy merchandising of the publisher are perfectly logical. The average detective story is probably no worse than the average novel, but you never see the average novel. It doesn't get published. The average—or only slightly above average—detective story does. Not only is it published but it is sold in small quantities to rental libraries and it is read. There are even a few optimists who buy it at the full retail price of two dollars, because it looks so fresh and new and there is a picture of a corpse on the cover.

And the strange thing is that this average, more than middling dull, pooped-out piece of utterly unreal and mechanical fiction is really not very different from what are called the masterpieces of the art. It drags on a little more slowly, the dialogue is a shade grayer, the cardboard out of which the characters are cut is a shade thinner, and the cheating is a little more obvious. But it is the same kind of book. Whereas the good novel is not at all the same kind of book as the bad novel. It is about entirely different things. But the good detective story and the bad detective story are about exactly the same things, and they are about them in very much the same way. There are reasons for this too, and reasons for the reasons; there always are.

I suppose the principal dilemma of the traditional or classic or straight deductive or logic and deduction novel of detection is that for any approach to perfection it demands a combination of qualities not found in the same mind. The coolheaded constructionist does not also come across with lively characters, sharp dialogue, a sense of pace, and an acute use of observed detail. The grim logician has as much atmosphere as a drawing board. The scientific sleuth has a nice new shiny laboratory, but I'm sorry I can't remember the face. The fellow who can write you a vivid and colorful prose simply will not be bothered with the coolie labor of breaking down unbreakable alibis.

The master of rare knowledge is living psychologically in the age of the hoop skirt. If you know all you should know about ceramics and Egyptian needlework, you don't know anything at all about the police. If you know that platinum won't melt under about 3000° F. by itself, but will melt at the glance of a pair of deep blue eyes if you put it near a bar of lead, then you don't know how men make love in the twentieth century.

And if you know enough about the elegant *flânerie* of the pre-war French Riviera to lay your story in that locale, you don't know that a couple of capsules of barbital small enough to be swallowed will not only not kill a man—they will not even put him to sleep if he fights against them.

▼

Every detective story writer makes mistakes, of course, and none will ever know as much as he should. Conan Doyle made mistakes which completely invalidated some of his stories, but he was a pioneer, and Sherlock Holmes after all is mostly an attitude and a few dozen lines of unforgettable dialogue. It is the ladies and gentlemen of what Mr. Howard Haycraft(in his book *Murder for Pleasure*) calls the Golden Age of detective fiction that really get me down. This age is not remote. For Mr. Haycraft's purpose it starts after the First World War and lasts up to about 1930. For all practical purposes it is still here. Two thirds or three quarters of all the detective stories published still adhere to the formula the giants of this era created, perfected, polished, and sold to the world as problems in logic and deduction.

These are stern words, but be not alarmed. They are only words. Let us glance at one of the glories of the literature, an acknowledged masterpiece of the art of fooling the reader without cheating him. It is called *The Red House Mystery*, was written by A. A. Milne, and has been named by Alexander Woollcott (rather a fast man with a superlative) "one of the three best mystery stories of all time." Words of that size are not spoken lightly. The book was published in 1922 but is timeless, and might as easily have been published in July, 1939, or, with a few slight changes, last week. It ran thirteen editions and seems to have been in print, in the original format, for about sixteen years. That happens to few books of any kind. It is an agreeable book, light, amusing in the *Punch* style, written with a deceptive smoothness that is not so easy as it looks.

It concerns Mark Ablett's impersonation of his brother Robert as a hoax on his friends. Mark is the owner of the Red House, a typical laburnum-and-lodge-gate English country house. He has a secretary who encourages him and abets him in this impersonation, and who is going to murder him if he pulls it off. Nobody around the Red House has ever seen Robert, fifteen years absent in Australia and known by repute as a no-good. A letter is talked about (but never shown) announcing Robert's arrival, and Mark hints it will not be a pleasant occasion. One afternoon, then, the supposed Robert arrives, identifies himself to a couple of servants, is shown into the study. Mark goes in after him (according to testimony at the inquest). Robert is then found dead on the floor with a bullet hole in his face, and of course Mark has vanished into thin air. Arrive the police, who suspect Mark must be the murderer, remove the débris, and proceed with the investigation—and in due course, with the inquest.

Milne is aware of one very difficult hurdle and tries as well as he can to get over it. Since the secretary is going to murder Mark, once Mark has established himself as Robert, the impersonation has to continue and fool the police. Since, also, everybody around the Red House knows Mark intimately, disguise is necessary. This is achieved by shaving off Mark's beard, roughening his hands ("not the hands of a manicured gentleman"—testimony), and the use of a gruff voice and rough manner.

But this is not enough. The cops are going to have the body and the clothes on it and whatever is in the pockets. Therefore none of this must suggest Mark. Milne therefore works like a switch engine to put over the motivation that Mark is such a thoroughly conceited performer that he dresses the part down to the socks and underwear (from all of which the secretary has removed the maker's labels), like a ham blacking himself all over to play Othello. If the reader will buy this (and the sales record shows he must have), Milne figures he is solid. Yet, however light in texture the story may be, it is offered as a problem of logic and deduction.

If it is not that, it is nothing at all. There is nothing else for it to be. If the situation is false, you cannot even accept it as a light novel, for there is no story for the light novel to be about. If the problem does not contain the elements of truth and plausibility, it is no problem; if the logic is an illusion, there is nothing to deduce. If the impersonation is impossible once the reader is told the conditions it must fulfill, then the whole thing is a fraud. Not a deliberate fraud, because Milne would not have written the story if he had known what he was up against. He is up against a number of deadly things, none of which he even considers. Nor, apparently, does the casual reader, who wants to like the story—hence takes it at its face value. But the reader is not called upon to know the facts of life when the author does not. The author is the expert in the case.

Here is what this author ignores:

1. The coroner holds formal jury inquest on a body for which no legal competent identification is offered. A coroner, usually in a big city, will sometimes hold inquest on a body that *cannot* be identified, if the record of such an inquest has or may have a value (fire, disaster, evidence of murder). No such reason exists here, and there is no one to identify the body. Witnesses said the man said he was Robert Ablett. This is mere presumption, and has weight only if nothing conflicts with it. Identification is a condition precedent to an inquest. It is a matter of law. Even in death a man has a right to his own identity. The coroner will, wherever humanly possible, enforce that right. To neglect it would be a violation of his office.

2. Since Mark Ablett, missing and suspected of the murder, cannot defend himself, all evidence of his movements before and after the murder is vital (as also whether he has money to run away on); yet all such evidence is given by the man closest to the murder and is without corroboration. It is automatically suspect until proved true.

3. The police find by direct investigation that Robert Ablett was not well thought of in his native village. Somebody there

must have known him. No such person was brought to the inquest. (The story couldn't stand it.)

4. The police know there is an element of threat in Robert's supposed visit, and that it is connected with the murder must be obvious to them. Yet they make no attempt to check Robert in Australia, or find out what character he had there, or what associates, or even if he actually came to England, and with whom. (If they had, they would have found out he had been dead three years.)

5. The police surgeon examines a body with a recently shaved beard (exposing unweathered skin) and artificially roughened hands, but it is the body of a wealthy, soft-living man, long resident in a cool climate. Robert was a rough individual and had lived fifteen years in Australia. That is the surgeon's information. It is impossible he would have noticed nothing to conflict with it.

6. The clothes are nameless, empty, and have had the labels removed. Yet the man wearing them asserted an identity. The presumption that he was not what he said he was is overpowering. Nothing whatever is done about his peculiar circumstance. It is never even mentioned as being peculiar.

7. A man is missing, a well-known local man, and a body in the morgue closely resembles him. It is impossible that the police should not at once eliminate the chance that the missing man *is* the dead man. Nothing would be easier than to prove it. Not even to think of it is incredible. It makes idiots of the police, so that a brash amateur may startle the world with a fake solution.

The detective in the case is an insouciant amateur named Anthony Gillingham, a nice lad with a cheery eye, a nice little flat in town, and that airy manner. He is not making any money on the assignment, but is always available when the local gendarmerie loses its notebook. The English police endure him with their customary stoicism, but I shudder to think what the boys down at the Homicide Bureau in my city would do to him.

▼

There are even less plausible examples of the art than this. In *Trent's Last Case* (often called "the perfect detective story") you have to accept the premise that a giant of international finance, whose lightest frown makes Wall Street quiver like a chihuahua, will plot his own death so as to hang his secretary, and that the secretary when pinched will maintain an aristocratic silence—the old Etonian in him, maybe. I have known relatively few international financiers, but I rather think the author of this novel has (if possible) known fewer.

There is another one, by Freeman Wills Crofts (the soundest builder of them all when he doesn't get too fancy), wherein a murderer, by the aid of make-up, split-second timing and some very sweet evasive action, impersonates the man he has just killed and thereby gets him alive and distant from the place of the crime. There is one by Dorothy Sayers in which a man is murdered alone at night in his house by a mechanically released weight which works because he always turns the radio on at just such a moment, always stands in just such a position in front of it, and always bends over just so far. A couple of inches either way and the customers would get a rain check. This is what is vulgarly known as having God sit in your lap; a murderer who needs that much help from Providence must be in the wrong business.

And there is a scheme of Agatha Christie's featuring M. Hercule Poirot, that ingenious Belgian who talks in a literal translation of school-boy French. By duly messing around with his "little gray cells" M. Poirot decides that since nobody on a certain through sleeper could have done the murder alone, everybody did it together, breaking the process down into a series of simple operations like assembling an egg beater. This is the type that is guaranteed to knock the keenest mind for a loop. Only a halfwit could guess it.

There are much better plots by these same writers and by others of their school. There may be one somewhere that would

▼

really stand up under close scrutiny. It would be fun to read it, even if I did have to go back to page 47 and refresh my memory about exactly what time the second gardener potted the prize-winning tea-rose begonia. There is nothing new about these stories and nothing old. The ones I mentioned are all English because the authorities, such as they are, seem to feel that the English writers had an edge in this dreary routine and that the Americans, even the creator of Philo Vance, only make the Junior Varsity.

This, the classic detective story, has learned nothing and forgotten nothing. It is the story you will find almost any week in the big shiny magazines, handsomely illustrated, and paying due deference to virginal love and the right kind of luxury goods. Perhaps the tempo has become a trifle faster and the dialogue a little more glib. There are more frozen daiquiris and stingers and fewer glasses of crusty old port, more clothes by *Vogue* and décors by *House Beautiful,* more chic, but not more truth. We spend more time in Miami hotels and Cape Cod summer colonies and go not so often down by the old gray sundial in the Elizabethan garden.

But fundamentally it is the same careful grouping of suspects, the same utterly incomprehensible trick of how somebody stabbed Mrs. Pottington Postlethwaite III with the solid platinum poniard just as she flatted on the top note of the "Bell Song" from *Lakmé* in the presence of fifteen ill-assorted guests; the same ingénue in fur-trimmed pajamas screaming in the night to make the company pop in and out of doors and ball up the timetable; the same moody silence next day as they sit around sipping Singapore slings and sneering at each other, while the flatfeet crawl to and fro under the Persian rugs, with their derby hats on.

Personally I like the English style better. It is not quite so brittle and the people as a rule just wear clothes and drink drinks. There is more sense of background, as if Cheesecake Manor really existed all around and not just in the part the camera sees; there are more long walks over the downs and the characters don't all try to behave as if they had just been tested by MGM. The English may not always be the best writers in the world, but they are incomparably the best dull writers.

▼

There is a very simple statement to be made about all these stories: they do not really come off intellectually as problems, and they do not come off artistically as fiction. They are too contrived, and too little aware of what goes on in the world. They try to be honest, but honesty is an art. The poor writer is dishonest without knowing it, and the fairly good one can be dishonest because he doesn't know what to be honest about. He thinks a complicated murder scheme which baffled the lazy reader, who won't be bothered itemizing the details, will also baffle the police, whose business is with details.

The boys with their feet on the desks know that the easiest murder case in the world to break is the one somebody tried to get very cute with; the one that really bothers them is the murder somebody thought of only two minutes before he pulled it off. But if the writers of this fiction wrote about the kind of murders that happen, they would also have to write about the authentic flavor of life as it is lived. And since they cannot do that, they pretend that what they do is what should be done. Which is begging the question—and the best of them know it.

In her introduction to the first *Omnibus of Crime*, Dorothy Sayers wrote: "It [the detective story] does not, and by hypothesis never can, attain the loftiest level of literary achievement." And she suggested somewhere else that this is because it is a "literature of escape" and not "a literature of expression." I do not know what the loftiest level of literary achievement is: neither did Aeschylus or Shakespeare; neither does Miss Sayers. Other things being equal, which they never are, a more powerful theme will provoke a more powerful performance. Yet some very dull books have been written about God, and some

▼

very fine ones about how to make a living and stay fairly honest. It is always a matter of who writes the stuff, and what he has in him to write it with.

As for "literature of expression" and "literature of escape" —this is critics' jargon, a use of abstract words as if they had absolute meanings. Everything written with vitality expresses that vitality: there are no dull subjects, only dull minds. All men who read escape from something else into what lies behind the printed page; the quality of the dream may be argued, but its release has become a functional necessity. All men must escape at times from the deadly rhythm of their private thoughts. It is part of the process of life among thinking beings. It is one of the things that distinguish them from the three-toed sloth; he apparently—one can never be quite sure—is perfectly content hanging upside down on a branch, not even reading Walter Lippmann. I hold no particular brief for the detective story as the ideal escape. I merely say that *all* reading for pleasure is escape, whether it be Greek, mathematics, astronomy, Benedetto Croce, or The Diary of the Forgotten Man. To say otherwise is to be an intellectual snob, and a juvenile at the art of living.

I do not think such considerations moved Miss Dorothy Sayers to her essay in critical futility.

I think what was really gnawing at Miss Sayers' mind was the slow realization that her kind of detective story was an arid formula which could not even satisfy its own implications. It was second-grade literature because it was not about the things that could make first-grade literature. If it started out to be about real people (and she could write about them—her minor characters show that), they must very soon do unreal things in order to form the artificial pattern required by the plot. When they did unreal things, they ceased to be real themselves. They became puppets and cardboard lovers and papier-mâché villains and detectives of exquisite and impossible gentility.

The only kind of writer who could be happy with these properties was the one who did not know what reality was.

Dorothy Sayers' own stories show that she was annoyed by this triteness; the weakest element in them is the part that makes them detective stories, the strongest the part which could be removed without touching the "problem of logic and deduction." Yet she could not or would not give her characters their heads and let them make their own mystery. It took a much simpler and more direct mind than hers to do that.

▼

In *The Long Week End*, which is a drastically competent account of English life and manners in the decades following the First World War, Robert Graves and Alan Hodge gave some attention to the detective story. They were just as traditionally English as the ornaments of the Golden Age, and they wrote of the time in which these writers were almost as well known as any writers in the world. Their books in one form or another sold into the millions, and in a dozen languages. These were the people who fixed the form and established the rules and founded the famous Detection Club, which is a Parnassus of English writers of mystery. Its roster includes practically every important writer of detective fiction since Conan Doyle.

But Graves and Hodge decided that during this whole period only one first-class writer had written detective stories at all. An American, Dashiell Hammett. Traditional or not, Graves and Hodge were not fuddyduddy connoisseurs of the second-rate; they could see what went on in the world and that the detective story of their time didn't; and they were aware that writers who have the vision and the ability to produce real fiction do not produce unreal fiction.

How original a writer Hammett really was it isn't easy to decide now, even if it mattered. He was one of a group—the only one who achieved critical recognition—who wrote or tried to write realistic mystery fiction. All literary movements are like this; some one individual is picked out to represent the whole movement; he is usually the culmination of the movement. Hammett was the ace performer, but there is nothing in his work that is not implicit in the early novels and short stories of Hemingway.

Yet, for all I know, Hemingway, may have learned something from Hammett as well as from writers like Dreiser, Ring Lardner, Carl Sandburg, Sherwood Anderson, and himself. A rather revolutionary debunking of both the language and the material of fiction had been going on for some time. It probably started in poetry; almost everything does. You can take it clear back to Walt Whitman, if you like. But Hammett applied it to the detective story, and this, because of its heavy crust of English gentility and American pseudogentility, was pretty hard to get moving.

I doubt that Hammett had any deliberate artistic aims whatever; he was trying to make a living by writing something he had firsthand information about. He made some of it up; all writers do; but it had a basis in fact; it was made up out of real things. The only reality the English detection writers knew was the conversational accent of Surbiton and Bognor Regis. If they wrote about dukes and Venetian vases, they knew no more about them out of their own experience than the well-heeled Hollywood character knows about the French Modernists that hang in his Bel-Air château or the semi-antique Chippendale-cum-cobbler's bench that he uses for a coffee table. Hammett took murder out of the Venetian vase and dropped it into the alley; it doesn't have to stay there forever, but it looked like a good idea to get as far as possible from Emily Post's idea of how a well-bred débutante gnaws a chicken wing.

Hammett wrote at first (and almost to the end) for people with a sharp, aggressive attitude to life. They were not afraid of the seamy side of things; they lived there. Violence did not dismay them; it was right down their street. Hammett gave murder back to the kind of people that commit it for reasons, not just to provide a corpse; and with the means at hand, not hand-wrought dueling pistols, curare and tropical fish. He put these people down on paper as they were, and he made them talk and think in the language they customarily used for these purposes.

He had style, but his audience didn't know it, because it was in a language not supposed to be capable of such refinements. They thought they were getting a good meaty melodrama written in the kind of lingo they imagined they spoke themselves. It was, in a sense, but it was much more. All language begins with speech, and the speech of common men at that, but when it develops to the point of becoming a literary medium it only looks like speech. Hammett's style at its worst was as formalized as a page of *Marius the Epicurean;* at its best it could say almost anything. I believe this style, which does not belong to Hammett or to anybody, but is the American language (and not even exclusively that any more), can say things he did not know how to say, or feel the need of saying. In his hands it had no overtones, left no echo, evoked no image beyond a distant hill.

Hammett is said to have lacked heart; yet the story he himself thought the most of is the record of a man's devotion to a friend. He was spare, frugal, hard-boiled, but he did over and over again what only the best writers can ever do at all. He wrote scenes that seemed never to have been written before.

▼

With all this he did not wreck the formal detective story. Nobody can; production demands a form that can be produced. Realism takes too much talent, too much knowledge, too much awareness. Hammett may have loosened it up a little here, and sharpened it a little there. Certainly all but the stupidest and most meretricious writers are more conscious of their artificiality than they used to be. And he demonstrated that the detective story can be important writing. *The Maltese Falcon* may or may not be a work of genius, but an art which is capable of it is not "by hypothesis" incapable of anything. Once a detective story can be as good as this, only the pedants will deny that it *could* be even better.

Hammett did something else; he made the detective story fun to write, not an exhausting concatenation of insignificant clues. Without him there might not have been a regional mystery as clever as Percival Wilde's *Inquest*, or an ironic study as able as Raymond Postgate's *Verdict of Twelve*, or a savage piece of intellectual double-talk like Kenneth Fearing's *The Dagger of the Mind*, or a tragi-comic idealization of the murderer as in Donald Henderson's *Mr. Bowling Buys a Newspaper*, or even a gay Hollywoodian gambol like Richard Sale's *Lazarus No. 7*.

The realistic style is easy to abuse: from haste, from lack of awareness, from inability to bridge the chasm that lies between what a writer would like to be able to say and what he actually knows how to say. It is easy to fake; brutality is not strength, flipness is not wit, edge-of-the-chair writing can be as boring as flat writing; dalliance with promiscuous blondes can be very dull stuff when described by goaty young men with no other purpose in mind than to describe dalliance with promiscuous blondes. There has been so much of this sort of thing that if a character in a detective story says "Yeah," the author is automatically a Hammett imitator.

And there are still a number of people around who say that Hammett did not write detective stories at all—merely hard-boiled chronicles of mean streets with a perfunctory mystery element dropped in like the olive in a martini. These are the flustered old ladies—of both sexes (or no sex) and almost all ages—who like their murders scented with magnolia blossoms and do not care to be reminded that murder is an act of infinite cruelty, even if the perpetrators sometimes look like playboys or college professors or nice motherly women with softly graying hair.

There are also a few badly scared champions of the formal or classic mystery who think that no story is a detective story which does not pose a formal and exact problem and arrange the clues around it with neat labels on them. Such would point out, for example, that in reading *The Maltese Falcon* no one concerns himself with who killed Spade's partner, Archer (which is the only formal problem of the story), because the reader is kept thinking about something else. Yet in *The Glass Key* the reader is constantly reminded that the question is who killed Taylor Henry, and exactly the same effect is obtained—an effect of movement, intrigue, cross-purposes, and the gradual elucidation of character, which is all the detective story has any right to be about anyway. The rest is spillikins in the parlor.

▼

But all this (and Hammett too) is for me not quite enough. The realist in murder writes of a world in which gangsters can rule nations and almost rule cities, in which hotels and apartment houses and celebrated restaurants are owned by men who made their money out of brothels, in which a screen star can be the finger man for a mob. and the nice man down the hall is a boss of the numbers racket; a world where a judge with a cellar full of bootleg liquor can send a man to jail for having a pint in his pocket, where the mayor of your town may have condoned murder as an instrument of money-making, where no man can walk down a dark street in safety because law and order are things we talk about but refrain from practicing; a world where you may witness a holdup in broad daylight and see who did it, but you will fade quickly back into the crowd rather than tell anyone, because the holdup men may have friends with long guns, or the police may not like your testimony, and in any case the shyster for the defense will be allowed to abuse and vilify you in open court, before a jury of selected morons, without any but the most perfunctory interference from a political judge.

It is not a fragrant world, but it is the world you live in, and certain writers with tough minds and a cool spirit of detachment can make very interesting and even amusing patterns out of it. It is not funny that a man should be killed, but it is sometimes funny that he should be killed for so little, and that his death should be the coin of what we call civilization. All this still is not quite enough.

In everything that can be called art there is a quality of redemption. It may be pure tragedy, if it is high tragedy, and it may be pity and irony, and it may be the raucous laughter of the strong man. But down these mean streets a man must go who is not himself mean, who is neither tarnished nor afraid. The detective in this kind of story must be such a man. He is the hero; he is everything. He must be a complete man and a common man and yet an unusual man. He must be, to use a rather weathered phrase, a man of honor—by instinct, by inevitability, without thought of it, and certainly without saying it. He must be the best man in his world and a good enough man for any world. I do not care much about his private life; he is neither a eunuch nor a satyr; I think he might seduce a duchess and I am quite sure he would not spoil a virgin; if he is a man of honor in one thing, he is that in all things.

He is a relatively poor man, or he would not be a detective at all. He is a common man or he could not go among common people. He has a sense of character, or he would not know his job. He will take no man's money dishonestly and no man's insolence without a due and dispassionate revenge. He is a lonely man and his pride is that you will treat him as a proud man or be very sorry you ever saw him. He talks as the man of his age talks—that is, with rude wit, a lively sense of the grotesque, a disgust for sham, and a contempt for pettiness.

The story is this man's adventure in search of a hidden truth, and it would be no adventure if it did not happen to a man fit for adventure. He has a range of awareness that startles you, but it belongs to him by right, because it belongs to the world he lives in. If there were enough like him, the world would be a very safe place to live in, without becoming too dull to be worth living in.

SPANISH BLOOD

ONE

Big John Masters was large, fat, oily. He had sleek blue jowls and very thick fingers on which the knuckles were dimples. His brown hair was combed straight back from his forehead and he wore a wine-colored suit with patch pockets, a wine-colored tie, a tan silk shirt. There was a lot of red and gold band around the thick brown cigar between his lips.

He wrinkled his nose, peeped at his hole card again, tried not to grin. He said: "Hit me again, Dave—and don't hit me with the City Hall."

A four and a deuce showed. Dave Aage looked at them solemnly across the table, looked down at his own hand. He was very tall and thin, with a long bony face and hair the color of wet sand. He held the deck flat on the palm of his hand, turned the top card slowly, and flicked it across the table. It was the queen of spades.

Big John Masters opened his mouth wide, waved his cigar about, chuckled.

"Pay me, Dave. For once a lady was right." He turned his hole card with a flourish. A five.

Dave Aage smiled politely, didn't move. A muted telephone bell rang close to him, behind long silk drapes that bordered the very high lancet windows. He took a cigarette out of his mouth and laid it carefully on the edge of a tray on a tabouret beside the card table, reached behind the curtain for the phone.

He spoke into the cup with a cool, almost whispering voice, then listened for a long time. Nothing changed in his greenish eyes, no flicker of emotion showed on his narrow face. Masters squirmed, bit hard on his cigar.

After a long time Aage said, "Okey, you'll hear from us." He pronged the instrument and put it back behind the curtain.

He picked his cigarette up, pulled the lobe of his ear. Masters swore. "What's eating you, for Pete's sake? Gimme ten bucks."

Aage smiled dryly and leaned back. He reached for a drink, sipped it, put it down, spoke around his cigarette. All his movements were slow, thoughtful, almost absent-minded. He said: "Are we a couple of smart guys, John?"

"Yeah. We own the town. But it don't help my blackjack game any."

"It's just two months to election, isn't it, John?"

Masters scowled at him, fished in his pocket for a fresh cigar, jammed it into his mouth.

"So what?"

"Suppose something happened to our toughest opposition. Right now. Would that be a good idea, or not?"

"Huh?" Masters raised eyebrows so thick that his whole face seemed to have to work to push them up. He thought for a moment, sourly. "It would be lousy—if they didn't catch the guy pronto. Hell, the voters would figure we hired it done."

"You're talking about murder, John," Aage said patiently. "I didn't say anything about murder."

Masters lowered his eyebrows and pulled at a coarse black hair that grew out of his nose.

"Well, spit it out!"

Aage smiled, blew a smoke ring, watched it float off and come apart in frail wisps.

"I just had a phone call," he said very softly. "Donegan Marr is dead."

Masters moved slowly. His whole body moved slowly towards the card table, leaned far over it. When his body couldn't go any farther his chin came out until his jaw muscles stood out like thick wires.

"Huh?" he said thickly. "Huh?"

Aage nodded, calm as ice. "But you were right about murder, John. It *was* murder. Just half an hour ago, or so. In his office. They don't know who did it—yet."

Masters shrugged heavily and leaned back. He looked around him with a stupid expression. Very suddenly he began to laugh. His laughter bellowed and roared around the little turretlike room where the two men sat, overflowed into an enormous living room beyond, echoed back and forth through a maze of heavy dark furnure, enough standing lamps to light a boulevard, a double row of oil paintings in massive gold frames.

Aage sat silent. He rubbed his cigarette out slowly in the tray until there was nothing of the fire left but a thick dark smudge. He dusted his bony fingers together and waited.

Masters stopped laughing as abruptly as he had begun. The room was very still. Masters looked tired. He mopped his big face.

"We got to do something, Dave," he said quietly. "I almost forgot. We got to break this fast. It's dynamite."

Aage reached behind the curtain again and brought the phone out, pushed it across the table over the scattered cards.

"Well—we know how, don't we?" he said calmly.

A cunning light shone in Big John Masters' muddy brown eyes. He licked his lips, reached a big hand for the phone.

"Yeah," he said purringly, "we do, Dave. We do at that, by——!"

He dialed with a thick finger that would hardly go into the holes.

TWO

Donegan Marr's face looked cool, neat, poised, even then. He was dressed in soft gray flannels and his hair was the same soft gray color as his suit, brushed back from a ruddy, youngish face. The skin was pale on the frontal bones where the hair would fall when he stood up. The rest of the skin was tanned.

He was lying back in a padded blue office chair. A cigar had gone out in a tray with a bronze greyhound on its rim. His left hand dangled beside the chair and his right hand held a gun loosely on the desk top. The polished nails glittered in sunlight from the big closed window behind him.

Blood had soaked the left side of his vest, made the gray flannel almost black. He was quite dead, had been dead for some time.

A tall man, very brown and slender and silent, leaned against a brown mahogany filing cabinet and looked fixedly at the dead man. His hands were in the pockets of a neat blue serge suit. There was a straw hat on the back of his head. But there was nothing casual about his eyes or his tight, straight mouth.

A big sandy-haired man was groping around on the blue rug. He said thickly, stooped over: "No shells, Sam."

The dark man didn't move, didn't answer. The other stood up, yawned, looked at the man in the chair.

"Hell! This one will stink. Two months to election. Boy, is this a smack in the puss for somebody."

The dark man said slowly: "We went to school together. We used to be buddies. We carried the torch for the same girl. He won, but we stayed good friends, all three of us. He was always a great kid . . . Maybe a shade too smart."

The sandy-haired man walked around the room without touching anything. He bent over and sniffed at the gun on the desk, shook his head, said: "Not used—this one." He wrinkled his nose, sniffed at the air. "Air-conditioned. The three top floors. Soundproofed too. High-grade stuff. They tell me this whole building is electric-welded. Not a rivet in it. Ever hear that, Sam?"

The dark man shook his head slowly.

"Wonder where the help was," the sandy-haired man went on. "A big shot like him would have more than one girl."

The dark man shook his head again. "That's all, I guess. She was out to lunch. He was a lone wolf, Pete. Sharp as a weasel. In a few more years he'd have taken the town over."

The sandy-haired man was behind the desk now, almost leaning over the dead man's shoulder. He was looking down at a leather-backed appointment pad with buff leaves. He said slowly: "Somebody named Imlay was due here at twelve-fifteen. Only date on the pad."

He glanced at a cheap watch on his wrist. "One-thirty. Long gone. Who's Imlay? . . . Say, wait a minute! There's an assistant D.A. named Imlay. He's running for judge on the Master-Aage ticket. D'you figure——"

There was a sharp knock on the door. The office was so long that the two men had to think a moment before they placed which of the three doors it was. Then the sandy-haired man went towards the most distant of them, saying over his shoulder: "M.E's man maybe. Leak this to your favorite newshawk and you're out a job. Am I right?"

The dark man didn't answer. He moved slowly to the desk, leaned forward a little, spoke softly to the dead man.

"Goodbye, Donny. Just let it all go. I'll take care of it. I'll take care of Belle."

The door at the end of the office opened and a brisk man with a bag came in, trotted down the blue carpet and put his bag on the desk. The sandy-haired man shut the door against a bulge of faces. He strolled back to the desk.

The brisk man cocked his head on one side, examining the corpse. "Two of them," he muttered. "Look like about .32's— hard slugs. Close to the heart but not touching. He must have died pretty soon. Maybe a minute or two."

The dark man made a disgusted sound and walked to the

23
▼

window, stood with his back to the room, looking out, at the tops of high buildings and a warm blue sky. The sandy-haired man watched the examiner lift a dead eyelid. He said: "Wish the powder guy would get here. I wanta use the phone. This Imlay——"

The dark man turned his head slightly, with a dull smile. "Use it. This isn't going to be any mystery."

"Oh I don't know," the M.E.'s man said, flexing a wrist, then holding the back of his hand against the skin of the dead man's face. "Might not be so damn political as you think, Delaguerra. He's a good-looking stiff."

The sandy-haired man took hold of the phone gingerly, with a handkerchief, laid the receiver down, dialed, picked the receiver up with the handkerchief and put it to his ear.

After a moment he snapped his chin down, said: "Pete Marcus. Wake the Inspector." He yawned, waited again, then spoke in a different tone: "Marcus and Delaguerra, Inspector, from Donegan Marr's office. No print or camera men here yet . . . Huh? . . . Holding off till the Commissioner gets here? . . . Okey . . . Yeah, he's here."

The dark man turned. The man at the phone gestured at him. "Take it, Spanish."

Sam Delaguerra took the phone, ignoring the careful handkerchief, listened. His face got hard. He said quietly: "Sure I knew him—but I didn't sleep with him . . . Nobody's here but his secretary, a girl. She phoned the alarm in. There's a name on a pad—Imlay, a twelve-fifteen appointment. No, we haven't touched anything yet . . . No . . . Okey, right away."

He hung up so slowly that the click of the instrument was barely audible. His hand stayed on it, then fell suddenly and heavily to his side. His voice was thick.

"I'm called off it, Pete. You're to hold it down until Commissioner Drew gets here. Nobody gets in. White, black or Cherokee Indian."

"What you called in for?" the sandy-haired man yelped angrily.

"Don't know. It's an order," Delaguerra said tonelessly.

The M.E.'s man stopped writing on a form pad to look curiously at Delaguerra, with a sharp, sidelong look.

Delaguerra crossed the office and went through the communicating door. There was a smaller office outside, partly partitioned off for a waiting room, with a group of leather chairs and a table with magazines. Inside a counter was a typewriter desk, a safe, some filing cabinets. A small dark girl sat at the desk with her head down on a wadded handkerchief. Her hat was crooked on her head. Her shoulders jerked and her thick sobs were like panting.

Delaguerra patted her shoulder. She looked up at him with a tear-bloated face, a twisted mouth. He smiled down at her questioning face, said gently: "Did you call Mrs. Marr yet?"

She nodded, speechless, shaken with rough sobs. He patted her shoulder again, stood a moment beside her, then went on out, with his mouth tight and a hard, dark glitter in his black eyes.

THREE

The big English house stood a long way back from the narrow, winding ribbon of concrete that was called De Neve Lane. The lawn had rather long grass with a curving path of stepping stones half hidden in it. There was a gable over the front door and ivy on the wall. Trees grew all around the house, close to it, made it a little dark and remote.

All the houses in De Neve Lane had that same calculated air of neglect. But the tall green hedge that hid the driveway and the garages was trimmed as carefully as a French poodle, and there was nothing dark or mysterious about the mass of yellow and flame-colored gladioli that flared at the opposite end of the lawn.

Delaguerra got out of a tan-colored Cadillac touring car that had no top. It was an old model, heavy and dirty. A taut canvas formed a deck over the back part of the car. He wore a white linen cap and dark glasses and had changed his blue serge for a gray cloth outing suit with a jerkin-style zipper jacket.

He didn't look very much like a cop. He hadn't looked very much like a cop in Donegan Marr's office. He walked slowly up the path of stepping stones, touched a brass knocker on the front door of the house, then didn't knock with it. He pushed a bell at the side, almost hidden by the ivy.

There was a long wait. It was very warm, very silent. Bees droned over the warm bright grass. There was the distant whirring of a lawnmower.

The door opened slowly and a black face looked out at him, a long, sad black face with tear streaks on its lavender face powder. The black face almost smiled, said haltingly: "Hello there, Mistah Sam. It's sure good to see you."

Delaguerra took his cap off, swung the dark glasses at his side. He said: "Hello, Minnie. I'm sorry. I've got to see Mrs. Marr."

"Sure. Come right in, Mistah Sam."

The maid stood aside and he went into a shadowy hall with a tile floor. "No reporters yet?"

The girl shook her head slowly. Her warm brown eyes were stunned, doped with shock.

"Ain't been nobody yet . . . She ain't been in long. She ain't said a word. She just stand there in that there sun room that ain't got no sun."

Delaguerra nodded, said: "Don't talk to anybody, Minnie. They're trying to keep this quiet for a while, out of the papers."

"Ah sure won't, Mistah Sam. Not nohow."

Delaguerra smiled at her, walked noiselessly on crêpe soles along the tiled hall to the back of the house, turned into another hall just like it at right angles. He knocked at a door. There was no answer. He turned the knob and went into a long narrow room that was dim in spite of many windows. Trees grew close to the windows, pressing their leaves against the glass. Some of the windows were masked by long cretonne drapes.

The tall girl in the middle of the room didn't look at him.

She stood motionless, rigid. She stared at the windows. Her hands were tightly clenched at her sides.

She had red-brown hair that seemed to gather all the light there was and make a soft halo around her coldly beautiful face. She wore a sportily cut blue velvet ensemble with patch pockets. A white handkerchief with a blue border stuck out of the breast pocket, arranged carefully in points, like a foppish man's handkerchief.

Delaguerra waited, letting his eyes get used to the dimness. After a while the girl spoke through the silence, in a low, husky voice.

"Well . . . they got him, Sam. They got him at last. Was he so much hated?"

Delaguerra said softly: "He was in a tough racket, Belle. I guess he played it as clean as he could, but he couldn't help but make enemies."

She turned her head slowly and looked at him. Lights shifted in her hair. Gold glinted in it. Her eyes were vividly, startlingly blue. Her voice faltered a little, saying: "Who killed him, Sam? Have they any ideas?"

Delaguerra nodded slowly, sat down in a wicker chair, swung his cap and glasses between his knees.

"Yeah. We think we know who did it. A man named Imlay, an assistant in the D.A.'s office."

"My God!" the girl breathed. "What's this rotten city coming to?"

Delaguerra went on tonelessly: "It was like this—if you're sure you want to know . . . yet."

"I do, Sam. His eyes stare at me from the wall, wherever I look. Asking me to do something. He was pretty swell to me, Sam. We had our trouble, of course, but . . . they didn't mean anything."

Delaguerra said: "This Imlay is running for judge with the backing of the Masters-Aage group. He's in and the gay forties and it seems he's been playing house with a night-club number called Stella La Motte. Somehow, someway, photos were taken of them together, very drunk and undressed. Donny got the photos, Belle. They were found in his desk. According to his desk pad he had a date with Imlay at twelve-fifteen. We figure they had a row and Imlay beat him to the punch."

"You found those photos, Sam?" the girl asked, very quietly.

He shook his head, smiled crookedly. "No. If I had, I guess I might have ditched them. Commissioner Drew found them —after I was pulled off the investigation."

Her head jerked at him. Her vivid blue eyes got wide. "Pulled off the investigation? You—Donny's friend?"

"Yeah. Don't take it too big. I'm a cop, Belle. After all I take orders."

She didn't speak, didn't look at him any more. After a little while he said: "I'd like to have the keys to your cabin at Puma Lake. I'm detailed to go up there and look around, see if there's any evidence. Donny had conferences there."

Something changed in the girl's face. It got almost contemptuous. Her voice was empty. "I'll get them. But you won't find anything there. If you're helping them to find dirt on Donny—so they can clear this Imlay person. . . ."

He smiled a little, shook his head slowly. His eyes were very deep, very sad.

"That's crazy talk, kid. I'd turn my badge in before I did that."

"I see." She walked past him to the door, went out of the room. He sat quite still while she was gone, looked at the wall with an empty stare. There was a hurt look on his face. He swore very softly, under his breath.

The girl came back, walked up to him and held her hand out. Something tinkled into his palm.

"The keys, copper."

Delaguerra stood up, dropped the keys into a pocket. His face got wooden. Belle Marr went over to a table and her nails scratched harshly on a cloisonné box, getting a cigarette out of it. With her back turned she said: "I don't think you'll have any luck, as I said. It's too bad you've only got blackmailing on him so far."

Delaguerra breathed out slowly, stood a moment, then turned

away. "Okey," he said softly. His voice was quite offhand now, as if it was a nice day, as if nobody had been killed.

At the door he turned again. "I'll see you when I get back, Belle. Maybe you'll feel better."

She didn't answer, didn't move. She held the unlighted cigarette rigidly in front of her mouth, close to it. After a moment Delaguerra went on: "You ought to know how I feel about it. Donny and I were like brothers once. I—I heard you were not getting on so well with him . . . I'm glad as all hell that was wrong. But don't let yourself get too hard, Belle. There's nothing to be hard about—with me."

He waited a few seconds, staring at her back. When she still didn't move or speak he went on out.

FOUR

A narrow rocky road dropped down from the highway and ran along the flank of the hill above the lake. The tops of cabins showed here and there among the pines. An open shed was cut into the side of the hill. Delaguerra put his dusty Cadillac under it and climbed down a narrow path towards the water.

The lake was deep blue but very low. Two or three canoes drifted about on it and the chugging of an outboard motor sounded in the distance, around a bend. He went along between thick walls of undergrowth, walking on pine needles, turned around a stump and crossed a small rustic bridge to the Marr cabin.

It was built of half-round logs and had a wide porch on the lake side. It looked very lonely and empty. The spring that ran under the bridge curved around beside the house and one end of the porch dropped down sheer to the big flat stones through which the water trickled. The stones would be covered when the water was high, in the spring.

Delaguerra went up wooden steps and took the keys out of

his pocket, unlocked the heavy front door, then stood on the porch a little while and lit a cigarette before he went in. It was very still, very pleasant, very cool and clear after the heat of the city. A mountain bluejay sat on a stump and pecked at its wings. Somebody far out on the lake fooled with a ukulele. He went into the cabin.

He looked at some dusty antlers, a big rough table splattered with magazines, an old-fashioned battery-type radio, a box-shaped phonograph with a disheveled pile of records beside it. There were tall glasses that hadn't been washed and a half-bottle of Scotch beside them, on a table near the big stone fireplace. A car went along the road up above and stopped somewhere not far off. Delaguerra frowned around, said: "Stall," under his breath, with a defeated feeling. There wasn't any sense in it. A man like Donegan Marr wouldn't leave anything that mattered in a mountain cabin.

He looked into a couple of bedrooms, one just a shake-down with a couple of cots, one better furnished, with a make-up bed, and a pair of women's gaudy pajamas tossed across it. They didn't look quite like Belle Marr's.

At the back there was a small kitchen with a gasoline stove and a wood stove. He opened the back door with another key and stepped out on a small porch flush with the ground, near a big pile of cordwood and a double-bitted axe on a chopping block.

Then he saw the flies.

A wooden walk went down the side of the house to a woodshed under it. A beam of sunlight had slipped through the trees and lay across the walk. In the sunlight there a clotted mass of flies festered on something brownish, sticky. The flies didn't want to move. Delaguerra bent down, then put his hand down and touched the sticky place, sniffed at his finger. His face got shocked and stiff.

There was another smaller patch of the brownish stuff farther on, in the shade, outside the door of the shed. He took the keys out of his pocket very quickly and found the one that unlocked the big padlock of the woodshed. He yanked the door open.

There was a big loose pile of cordwood inside. Not split wood—cordwood. Not stacked, just thrown in anyhow. Delaguerra began to toss the big rough pieces to one side.

After he had thrown a lot of it aside he was able to reach down and take hold of two cold stiff ankles in lisle socks and drag the dead man out into the light.

He was a slender man, neither tall nor short, in a well-cut basket weave suit. His small neat shoes were polished, a little dust over the polish. He didn't have any face, much. It was broken to pulp by a terrific smash. The top of his head was split open and brains and blood were mixed in the thin grayish-brown hair.

Delaguerra straightened quickly and went back into the house to where the half-bottle of Scotch stood on the table in the living room. He uncorked it, drank from the neck, waited a moment, drank again.

He said: "Phew!" out loud, and shivered as the whiskey whipped at his nerves.

He went back to the woodshed, leaned down again as an automobile motor started up somewhere. He stiffened. The motor swelled in sound, then the sound faded and there was silence again. Delaguerra shrugged, went through the dead man's pockets. They were empty. One of them, with cleaner's marks on it probably, had been cut away. The tailor's label had been cut from the inside pocket of the coat, leaving ragged stitches.

The man was stiff. He might have been dead twenty-four hours, not more. The blood on his face had coagulated thickly but had not dried completely.

Delaguerra squatted beside him for a little while, looking at the bright glitter of Puma Lake, the distant flash of a paddle from a canoe. Then he went back into the woodshed and pawed around for a heavy block of wood with a great deal of blood on it, didn't find one. He went back into the house and out on the front porch, went to the end of the porch, stared down the drop, then at the big flat stones in the spring.

"Yeah," he said softly.

There were flies clotted on two of the stones, a lot of flies. He hadn't noticed them before. The drop was about thirty feet, enough to smash a man's head open if he landed just right.

He sat down in one of the big rockers and smoked for several minutes without moving. His face was still with thought, his black eyes withdrawn and remote. There was a tight, hard smile, ever so faintly sardonic, at the corners of his mouth.

At the end of that he went silently back through the house and dragged the dead man into the woodshed again, covered him up loosely with the wood. He locked the woodshed, locked the house up, went back along the narrow, steep path to the road and to his car.

It was past six o'clock, but the sun was still bright as he drove off.

FIVE

An old store counter served as bar in the roadside beerstube. Three low stools stood against it. Delaguerra sat on the end one near the door, looked at the foamy inside of an empty beer glass. The bartender was a dark kid in overalls, with shy eyes and lank hair. He stuttered. He said: "Sh-should I d-draw you another g-glass, mister?"

Delaguerra shook his head, stood up off the stool. "Racket beer, sonny," he said sadly. "Tasteless as a roadhouse blonde."

"P-portola B-brew, mister. Supposed to be the b-best."

"Uh-huh. The worst. You use it, or you don't have a license. So long, sonny."

He went across to the screen door, looked out at the sunny highway on which the shadows were getting quite long. Beyond the concrete there was a graveled space edged by a white fence

32
▼

SPANISH BLOOD

of four-by-fours. There were two cars parked there: Delaguerra's old Cadillac and a dusty hard-bitten Ford. A tall, thin
man in khaki whipcord stood beside the Cadillac, looking at it.

Delaguerra got a bulldog pipe out, filled it half full from a
zipper pouch, lit it with slow care and flicked the match into
the corner. Then he stiffened a little, looking out through the
screen.

The tall, thin man was unsnapping the canvas that covered
the back part of Delaguerra's car. He rolled part of it back,
stood peering down in the space underneath.

Delaguerra opened the screen door softly and walked in long,
loose strides across the concrete of the highway. His crêpe soles
made sound on the gravel beyond, but the thin man didn't turn.
Delaguerra came up beside him.

"Thought I noticed you behind me," he said dully. "What's
the grift?"

The man turned without any haste. He had a long, sour
face, eyes the color of seaweed. His coat was open, pushed
back by a hand on a left hip. That showed a gun worn butt to
the front in a belt holster, cavalry style.

He looked Delaguerra up and down with a faint crooked
smile.

"This your crate?"

"What do you think?"

The thin man pulled his coat back farther and showed a
bronze badge on his pocket.

"I think I'm a Toluca County game warden, mister. I think
this ain't deer-hunting time and it ain't ever deer-hunting time
for does."

Delaguerra lowered his eyes very slowly, looked into the back
of his car, bending over to see past the canvas. The body of a
young deer lay there on some junk, beside a rifle. The soft eyes
of the dead animal, unglazed by death, seemed to look at him
with a gentle reproach. There was dried blood on the doe's
slender neck.

Delaguerra straightened, said gently: "That's damn cute."

"Got a hunting license?"

"I don't hunt," Delaguerra said.

"Wouldn't help much. I see you got a rifle."

"I'm a cop."

"Oh—cop, huh? Would you have a badge?"

"I would."

Delaguerra reached into his breast pocket, got the badge out, rubbed it on his sleeve, held it in the palm of his hand. The thin game warden stared down at it, licking his lips.

"Detective lieutenant, huh? City police." His face got distant and lazy. "Okey, Lieutenant. We'll ride about ten miles downgrade in your heap. I'll thumb a ride back to mine."

Delaguerra put the badge away, knocked his pipe out carefully, stamped the embers into the gravel. He replaced the canvas loosely.

"Pinched?" he asked gravely.

"Pinched, Lieutenant."

"Let's go."

He got in under the wheel of the Cadillac. The thin warden went around the other side, got in beside him. Delaguerra started the car, backed around and started off down the smooth concrete of the highway. The valley was a deep haze in the distance. Beyond the haze other peaks were enormous on the skyline. Delaguerra coasted the big car easily, without haste. The two men stared straight before them without speaking.

After a long time Delaguerra said: "I didn't know they had deer at Puma Lake. That's as far as I've been."

"There's a reservation by there, Lieutenant," the warden said calmly. He stared through the dusty windshield. "Part of the Toluca County Forest—or wouldn't you know that?"

Delaguerra said: "I guess I wouldn't know it. I never shot a deer in my life. Police work hasn't made me that tough."

The warden grinned, said nothing. The highway went through a saddle, then the drop was on the right side of the highway. Little canyons began to open out into the hills on the left. Some of them had rough roads in them, half overgrown, with wheel tracks.

Delaguerra swung the big car hard and suddenly to the left,

shot it into a cleared space of reddish earth and dry grass, slammed the brake on. The car skidded, swayed, ground to a lurching stop.

The warden was flung violently to the right, then forward against the windshield. He cursed, jerked up straight and threw his right hand across his body at the holstered gun.

Delaguerra took hold of a thin, hard wrist and twisted it sharply towards the man's body. The warden's face whitened behind the tan. His left hand fumbled at the holster, then relaxed. He spoke in a tight, hurt voice.

"Makin' it worse, copper. I got a phone tip at Salt Springs. Described your car, said where it was. Said there was a doe carcass in it. I—"

Delaguerra loosed the wrist, snapped the belt holster open and jerked the Colt out of it. He tossed the gun from the car.

"Get out, County! Thumb that ride you spoke of. What's the matter—can't you live on your salary any more? You planted it yourself, back at Puma Lake, you goddamn chiseler!"

The warden got out slowly, stood on the ground with his face blank, his jaw loose and slack.

"Tough guy," he muttered. "You'll be sorry for this, copper. I'll swear a complaint."

Delaguerra slid across the seat, got out of the right-hand door. He stood close to the warden, said very slowly: "Maybe I'm wrong, mister. Maybe you did get a call. Maybe you did."

He swung the doe's body out of the car, laid it down on the ground, watching the warden. The thin man didn't move, didn't try to get near his gun lying on the grass a dozen feet away. His seaweed eyes were dull, very cold.

Delaguerra got back into the Cadillac, snapped the brake off, started the engine. He backed to the highway. The warden still didn't make a move.

The Cadillac leaped forward, shot down the grade, out of sight. When it was quite gone the warden picked his gun up and holstered it, dragged the doe behind some bushes, and started to walk back along the highway towards the crest of the grade.

正常

SIX

The girl at the desk in the Kenworthy said: "This man called you three times, Lieutenant, but he wouldn't give a number. A lady called twice. Wouldn't leave name or number."

Delaguerra took three slips of paper from her, read the name "Joey Chill" on them and the various times. He picked up a couple of letters, touched his cap to the desk girl and got into the automatic elevator. He got off at four, walked down a narrow, quiet corridor, unlocked a door. Without switching on any lights he went across to a big french window, opened it wide, stood there looking at the thick dark sky, the flash of neon lights, the stabbing beams of headlamps on Ortega Boulevard, two blocks over.

He lit a cigarette and smoked half of it without moving. His face in the dark was very long, very troubled. Finally he left the window and went into a small bedroom, switched on a table lamp and undressed to the skin. He got under the shower, toweled himself, put on clean linen and went into the kitchenette to mix a drink. He sipped that and smoked another cigarette while he finished dressing. The telephone in the living room rang as he was strapping on his holster.

It was Belle Marr. Her voice was blurred and throaty, as if she had been crying for hours.

"I'm so glad to get you, Sam. I—I didn't mean the way I talked. I was shocked and confused, absolutely wild inside. You knew that, didn't you, Sam?"

"Sure, kid," Delaguerra said. "Think nothing of it. Anyway you were right. I just got back from Puma Lake and I think I was just sent up there to get rid of me."

"You're all I have now, Sam. You won't let them hurt you, will you?"

"Who?"

"You know. I'm no fool, Sam. I know this was all a plot, a vile political plot to get rid of him."

Delaguerra held the phone very tight. His mouth felt stiff and hard. For a moment he couldn't speak. Then he said: "It might be just what it looks like, Belle. A quarrel over those pictures. After all Donny had a right to tell a guy like that to get off the ticket. That wasn't blackmail . . . And he had a gun in his hand, you know."

"Come out and see me when you can, Sam." Her voice lingered with a spent emotion, a note of wistfulness.

He drummed on the desk, hesitated again, said: "Sure . . . When was anybody at Puma Lake last, at the cabin?"

"I don't know. I haven't been there in a year. He went . . . alone. Perhaps he met people there. I don't know."

He said something vaguely, after a moment said goodbye and hung up. He stared at the wall over the writing desk. There was a fresh light in his eyes, a hard glint. His whole face was tight, not doubtful any more.

He went back to the bedroom for his coat and straw hat. On the way out he picked up the three telephone slips with the name "Joey Chill" on them, tore them into small pieces and burned the pieces in an ash tray.

SEVEN

Pete Marcus, the big, sandy-haired dick, sat sidewise at a small littered desk in a bare office in which there were two such desks, faced to opposite walls. The other desk was neat and tidy, had a green blotter with an onyx pen set, a small brass calendar and an abalone shell for an ash tray.

A round straw cushion that looked something like a target was propped on end in a straight chair by the window. Pete Marcus had a handful of bank pens in his left hand and he was flipping them at the cushion, like a Mexican knife thrower. He was doing it absently, without much skill.

The door opened and Delaguerra came in. He shut the door and leaned against it, looking woodenly at Marcus. The sandy-haired man creaked his chair around and tilted it back against the desk, scratched his chin with a broad thumbnail.

"Hi, Spanish. Nice trip? The Chief's yappin' for you."

Delaguerra grunted, stuck a cigarette between his smooth brown lips.

"Were you in Marr's office when those photos were found, Pete?"

"Yeah, but I didn't find them. The Commish did. Why?"

"Did you see him find them?"

Marcus stared a moment, then said quietly, guardedly: "He found them all right, Sam. He didn't plant them—if that's what you mean."

Delaguerra nodded, shrugged. "Anything on the slugs?"

"Yeah. Not thirty-twos—twenty-fives. A damn vest-pocket rod. Copper-nickel slugs. An automatic, though, and we didn't find any shells."

"Imlay remembered those," Delaguerra said evenly, "but he left without the photos he killed for."

Marcus lowered his feet to the floor and leaned forward, looking up past his tawny eyebrows.

"That could be. They give him a motive, but with the gun in Marr's hand they kind of knock a premeditation angle."

"Good headwork, Pete." Delaguerra walked over to the small window, stood looking out of it. After a moment Marcus said dully: "You don't see me doin' any work, do you, Spanish?"

Delaguerra turned slowly, went over and stood close to Marcus, looking down at him.

"Don't be sore, kid. You're my partner, and I'm tagged as Marr's line into Headquarters. You're getting some of that. You're sitting still and I was hiked up to Puma Lake for no good reason except to have a deer carcass planted in the back of my car and have a game warden nick me with it."

Marcus stood up very slowly, knotting his fists at his sides.

His heavy gray eyes opened very wide. His big nose was white at the nostrils.

"Nobody here'd go *that* far, Sam."

Delaguerra shook his head. "I don't think so either. But they could take a hint to send me up there. And somebody outside the department could do the rest."

Pete Marcus sat down again. He picked up one of the pointed bank pens and flipped it viciously at the round straw cushion. The point stuck, quivered, broke, and the pen rattled to the floor.

"Listen," he said thickly, not looking up, "this is a job to me. That's all it is. A living. I don't have any ideals about this police work like you have. Say the word and I'll heave the goddamn badge in the old boy's puss."

Delaguerra bent down, punched him in the ribs. "Skip it, copper. I've got ideas. Go on home and get drunk."

He opened the door and went out quickly, walked along a marble-faced corridor to a place where it widened into an alcove with three doors. The middle one said: CHIEF OF DETECTIVES. ENTER. Delaguerra went into a small reception room with a plain railing across it. A police stenographer behind the railing looked up, then jerked his head at an inner door. Delaguerra opened a gate in the railing and knocked at the inner door, then went in.

Two men were in the big office. Chief of Detectives Tod McKim sat behind a heavy desk, looked at Delaguerra hard-eyed as he came in. He was a big, loose man who had gone saggy. He had a long, petulantly melancholy face. One of his eyes was not quite straight in his head.

The man who sat in a round-backed chair at the end of the desk was dandyishly dressed, wore spats. A pearl-gray hat and gray gloves and an ebony cane lay beside him on another chair. He had a shock of soft white hair and a handsome dissipated face kept pink by constant massaging. He smiled at Delaguerra, looked vaguely amused and ironical, smoked a cigarette in a long amber holder.

Delaguerra sat down opposite McKim. Then he looked at

the white-haired man briefly and said: "Good evening, Commissioner."

Commissioner Drew nodded offhandedly, didn't speak.

McKim leaned forward and clasped blunt, nail-chewed fingers on the shiny desk top. He said quietly: "Took your time reporting back. Find anything?"

Delaguerra stared at him, a level expressionless stare.

"I wasn't meant to—except maybe a doe carcass in the back of my car."

Nothing changed in McKim's face. Not a muscle of it moved. Drew dragged a pink and polished fingernail across the front of his throat and made a tearing sound with his tongue and teeth.

"That's no crack to be makin' at your boss, lad."

Delaguerra kept on looking at McKim, waited. McKim spoke slowly, sadly: "You've got a good record, Delaguerra. Your grandfather was one of the best sheriffs this county ever had. You've blown a lot of dirt on it today. You're charged with violating game laws, interfering with a Toluca County officer in the performance of his duty, and resisting arrest. Got anything to say to all that?"

Delaguerra said tonelessly: "Is there a tag out for me?"

McKim shook his head very slowly. "It's a department charge. There's no formal complaint. Lack of evidence, I guess." He smiled dryly, without humor.

Delaguerra said quietly: "In that case I guess you'll want my badge."

McKim nodded, silent. Drew said: "You're a little quick on the trigger. Just a shade fast on the snap-up."

Delaguerra took his badge out, rubbed it on his sleeve, looked at it, pushed it across the smooth wood of the desk.

"Okey, Chief," he said very softly. "My blood is Spanish, pure Spanish. Not nigger-Mex and not Yaqui-Mex. My grandfather would have handled a situation like this with fewer words and more powder smoke, but that doesn't mean I think it's funny. I've been deliberately framed into this spot because I was a close friend of Donegan Marr once. You know and I know that never counted for anything on the job. The Commissioner and his political backers may not feel so sure."

Drew stood up suddenly. "By God, you'll not talk like that to me," he yelped.

Delaguerra smiled slowly. He said nothing, didn't look towards Drew at all. Drew sat down again, scowling, breathing hard.

After a moment McKim scooped the badge into the middle drawer of his desk and got to his feet.

"You're suspended for a board, Delaguerra. Keep in touch with me." He went out of the room quickly, by the inner door, without looking back.

Delaguerra pushed his chair back and straightened his hat on his head. Drew cleared his throat, assumed a conciliatory smile and said: "Maybe I was a little hasty myself. The Irish in me. Have no hard feelings. The lesson you're learning is something we've all had to learn. Might I give you a word of advice?"

Delaguerra stood up, smiled at him, a small dry smile that moved the corners of his mouth and left the rest of his face wooden.

"I know what it is, Commissioner. Lay off the Marr case."

Drew laughed, good-humored again. "Not exactly. There isn't any Marr case. Imlay has admitted the shooting through his attorney, claiming self-defense. He's to surrender in the morning. No, my advice was something else. Go back to Toluca County and tell the warden you're sorry. I think that's all that's needed. You might try it and see."

Delaguerra moved quietly to the corridor and opened it. Then he looked back with a sudden flashing grin that showed all his white teeth.

"I know a crook when I see one, Commissioner. He's been paid for his trouble already."

He went out. Drew watched the door close shut with a faint whoosh, a dry click. His face was stiff with rage. His pink skin had turned a doughy gray. His hand shook furiously, holding the amber holder, and ash fell on the knee of his immaculate knife-edged trousers.

"By God," he said rigidly, in the silence, "you may be a damn-smooth Spaniard. You may be smooth as plate glass— but you're a hell of a lot easier to poke a hole through!"

He rose, awkward with anger, brushed the ashes from his trousers carefully and reached a hand out for hat and cane. The manicured fingers of the hand were trembling.

EIGHT

Newton Street, between Third and Fourth, was a block of cheap clothing stores, pawnshops, arcades of slot machines, mean hotels in front of which furtive-eyed men slid words delicately along their cigarettes, without moving their lips. Midway of the block a jutting wooden sign on a canopy said, STOLL'S BILLIARD PARLORS. Steps went down from the sidewalk edge. Delaguerra went down the steps.

It was almost dark in the front of the poolroom. The tables were sheeted, the cues racked in rigid lines. But there was light far at the back, hard white light against which clustered heads and shoulders were silhouetted. There was noise, wrangling, shouting of odds. Delaguerra went towards the light.

Suddenly, as if at a signal, the noise stopped and out of the silence came the sharp click of balls, the dull thud of cue ball against cushion after cushion, the final click of a three-bank carom. Then the noise flared up again.

Delaguerra stopped beside a sheeted table and got a ten-dollar bill from his wallet, got a small gummed label from a pocket in the wallet. He wrote on it: "Where is Joe?" pasted it to the bill, folded the bill in four. He went on to the fringe of the crowd and inched his way through until he was close to the table.

A tall, pale man with an impassive face and neatly parted brown hair was chalking a cue, studying the set-up on the table. He leaned over, bridged with strong white fingers. The betting ring noise dropped like a stone. The tall man made a smooth, effortless three-cushion shot.

A chubby-faced man on a high stool intoned: "Forty for Chill. Eight's the break."

The tall man chalked his cue again, looked around idly. His eyes passed over Delaguerra without sign. Delaguerra stepped closer to him, said: "Back yourself, Max? Five-spot against the next shot."

The tall man nodded. "Take it."

Delaguerra put the folded bill on the edge of the table. A youth in a striped shirt reached for it. Max Chill blocked him off without seeming to, tucked the bill in a pocket of is vest, said tonelessly: "Five bet," and bent to make another shot.

It was a clean crisscross at the top of the table, a hairline shot. There was a lot of applause. The tall man handed his cue to his helper in the striped shirt, said: "Time out. I got to go a place."

He went back through the shadows, through a door marked MEN. Delaguerra lit a cigarette, looked around at the usual Newton Street riffraff. Max Chill's opponent, another tall, pale, impassive man, stood beside the marker and talked to him without looking at him. Near them, alone and supercilious, a very good-looking Filipino in a smart tan suit was puffing at a chocolate-colored cigarette.

Max Chill came back to the table, reached for his cue, chalked it. He reached a hand into his vest, said lazily: "Owe you five, buddy," passed a folded bill to Delaguerra.

He made three caroms in a row, almost without stopping. The marker said: "Forty-four for Chill. Twelve's the break."

Two men detached themselves from the edge of the crowd, started towards the entrance. Delaguerra fell in behind them, followed them among the sheeted tables to the foot of the steps. He stopped there, unfolded the bill in his hand, read the address scribbled on the label under his question. He crumpled the bill in his hand, started it towards his pocket.

Something hard poked into his back. A twangy voice like a plucked banjo string said: "Help a guy out, huh?"

Delaguerra's nostrils quivered, got sharp. He looked up the steps at the legs of the two men ahead, at the reflected glare of street lights.

"Okey," the twangy voice said grimly.

Delaguerra dropped sidewise, twisting in the air. He shot a snakelike arm back. His hand grabbed an ankle as he fell. A swept gun missed his head, cracked the point of his shoulder and sent a dart of pain down his left arm. There was hard, hot breathing. Something without force slammed his straw hat. There was a thin tearing snarl close to him. He rolled, twisted the ankle, tucked a knee under him and lunged up. He was on his feet, catlike, lithe. He threw the ankle away from him, hard.

The Filipino in the tan suit hit the floor with his back. A gun wobbled up. Delaguerra kicked it out of a small brown hand and it skidded under a table. The Filipino lay still on his back, his head straining up, his snap-brim hat still glued to his oily hair.

At the back of the poolroom the three-cushion match went on peacefully. If anyone noticed the scuffling sound, at least no one moved to investigate. Delaguerra jerked a thonged black-jack from his hip pocket, bent over. The Filipino's tight brown face cringed.

"Got lots to learn. On the feet, baby."

Delaguerra's voice was chilled but casual. The dark man scrambled up, lifted his arms, then his left hand snaked for his right shoulder. The blackjack knocked it down, with a careless flip of Delaguerra's wrist. The brown man screamed thinly, like a hungry kitten.

Delaguerra shrugged. His mouth moved in a sardonic grin.

"Stick-up, huh? Okey, yellowpuss, some other time. I'm busy now. Dust!"

The Filipino slid back among the tables, crouched down. Delaguerra shifted the blackjack to his left hand, shot his right to a gun butt. He stood for a moment like that, watching the Filipino's eyes. Then he turned and went quickly up the steps, out of sight.

The brown man darted forward along the wall, crept under the table for his gun.

NINE

Joey Chill, who jerked the door open, held a short, worn gun without a foresight. He was a small man, hardbitten, with a tight, worried face. He needed a shave and a clean shirt. A harsh animal smell came out of the room behind him.

He lowered the gun, grinned sourly, stepped back into the room.

"Okey, copper. Took your sweet time gettin' here."

Delaguerra went in and shut the door. He pushed his straw hat far back on his wiry hair, and looked at Joey Chill without any expression. He said: "Am I supposed to remember the address of every punk in town? I had to get it from Max."

The small man growled something and went and lay down on the bed, shoved his gun under the pillow. He clasped his hands behind his head and blinked at the ceiling.

"Got a C note on you, copper?"

Delaguerra jerked a straight chair in front of the bed and straddled it. He got his bulldog pipe out, filled it slowly, looking with distaste at the shut window, the chipped enamel of the bed frame, the dirty, tumbled bedclothes, the wash bowl in the corner with two smeared towels hung over it, the bare dresser with half a bottle of gin planked on top of the Gideon Bible.

"Holed up?" he inquired, without much interest.

"I'm hot, copper. I mean I'm hot. I got something see. It's worth a C note."

Delaguerra put his pouch away slowly, indifferently, held a lighted match to his pipe, puffed with exasperating leisure. The small man on the bed fidgeted, watching him with sidelong looks. Delaguerra said slowly: "You're a good stoolie, Joey. I'll always say that for you. But a hundred bucks is important money to a copper."

"Worth it, guy. If you like the Marr killing well enough to want to break it right."

Delaguerra's eyes got steady and very cold. His teeth clamped on the pipe stem. He spoke very quietly, very grimly.

"I'll listen, Joey. I'll pay if it's worth it. It better be right, though."

The small man rolled over on his elbow. "Know who the girl was with Imlay in those pajama-pajama snaps?"

"Know her name," Delaguerra said evenly. "I haven't seen the pictures."

"Stella La Motte's a hoofer name. Real name Stella Chill. My kid sister."

Delaguerra folded his arms on the back of the chair. "That's nice," he said. "Go on."

"She framed him, copper. Framed him for a few bindles of heroin from a slant-eyed Flip."

"Flip?" Delaguerra spoke the word swiftly, harshly. His face was tense now.

"Yeah, a little brown brother. A looker, a neat dresser, a snow peddler. A goddamn dodo. Name, Toribo. They call him the Caliente Kid. He had a place across the hall from Stella. He got to feedin' her the stuff. Then he works her into the frame. She puts heavy drops in Imlay's liquor and he passes out. She lets the Flip in to shoot pictures with a Minny camera. Cute, huh? . . . And then, just like a broad, she gets sorry and spills the whole thing to Max and me."

Delaguerra nodded, silent, almost rigid.

The little man grinned sharply, showed his small teeth.

"What do I do? I take a plant on the Flip. I live in his shadow, copper. And after a while I tail him bang into Dave Aage's skyline apartment in the Vendome . . . I guess that rates a yard."

Delaguerra nodded slowly, shook a little ash into the palm of his hand and blew it off. "Who else knows this?"

"Max. He'll back me up, if you handle him right. Only he don't want any part of it. He don't play those games. He gave Stella dough to leave town and signed off. Because those boys are tough."

"Max couldn't know where you followed the Filipino to, Joey."

The small man sat up sharply, swung his feet to the floor. His face got sullen.

"I'm not kidding you, copper. I never have."

Delaguerra said quietly, "I believe you, Joey. I'd like more proof, though. What do you make of it?"

The little man snorted. "Hell, it sticks up so hard it hurts. Either the Flip's working for Masters and Aage before or he makes a deal with them after he gets the snaps. Then Marr gets the pictures and it's a cinch he don't get them unless they say so and he don't know they had them. Imlay was running for judge, on their ticket. Okey, he's their punk, but he's still a punk. It happens he's a guy who drinks and has a nasty temper. That's known."

Delaguerra's eyes glistened a little. The rest of his face was like carved wood. The pipe in his mouth was as motionless as though set in cement.

Joey Chill went on, with his sharp little grin: "So they deal the big one. They get the pictures to Marr without Marr's knowing where they came from. Then Imlay gets tipped off who has them, what they are, that Marr is set to put the squeeze on him. What would a guy like Imlay do? He'd go hunting, copper—and Big John Masters and his sidekick would eat the ducks."

"Or the venison," Delaguerra said absently.

"Huh? Well, does it rate?"

Delaguerra reached for his wallet, shook the money out of it, counted some bills on his knee. He rolled them into a tight wad and flipped them on to the bed.

"I'd like a line to Stella pretty well, Joey. How about it?"

The small man stuffed the money in his shirt pocket, shook his head. "No can do. You might try Max again. I think she's left town, and me, I'm doin' that too, now I've got the scratch. Because those boys are tough like I said—and maybe I didn't tail so good . . . Because some mugg's been tailin' me." He stood up, yawned, added: "Snort of gin?"

Delaguerra shook his head, watched the little man go over to the dresser and lift the gin bottle, pour a big dose into a thick glass. He drained the glass, started to put it down.

Glass tinkled at the window. There was a sound like the loose slap of a glove. A small piece of the window glass dropped to the bare stained wood beyond the carpet, almost at Joey Chill's feet.

The little man stood quite motionless for two or three seconds. Then the glass fell from his hand, bounced and rolled against the wall. Then his legs gave. He went down on his side, slowly, rolled slowly over on his back.

Blood began to move sluggishly down his cheek from a hole over his left eye. It moved faster. The hole got large and red. Joey Chill's eyes looked blankly at the ceiling, as if those things no longer concerned him at all.

Delaguerra slipped quietly down out of the chair to his hands and knees. He crawled along the side of the bed, over to the wall by the window, reached out from there and groped inside Joey Chill's shirt. He held fingers against his heart for a little while, took them away, shook his head. He squatted down low, took his hat off, and pushed his head up very carefully until he could see over a lower corner of the window.

He looked at the high blank wall of a storage warehouse, across an alley. There were scattered windows in it, high up, none of them lighted. Delaguerra pulled his head down again, said quietly, under his breath: "Silenced rifle, maybe. And very sweet shooting."

His hand went forward again, diffidently, took the little roll of bills from Joey Chill's shirt. He went back along the wall to the door, still crouched, reached up and got the key from the door, opened it, straightened and stepped through quickly, locked the door from the outside.

He went along a dirty corridor and down four flights of steps to a narrow lobby. The lobby was empty. There was a desk and a bell on it, no one behind it. Delaguerra stood behind the plate-glass street door and looked across the street at a frame rooming house where a couple of old men rocked on the porch, smoking. They looked very peaceful. He watched them for a couple of minutes.

He went out, searched both sides of the block quickly with sharp glances, walked along beside parked cars to the next corner. Two blocks over he picked up a cab and rode back to Stoll's Billiard Parlors on Newton Street.

Lights were lit all over the poolroom now. Balls clicked and spun, players weaved in and out of a thick haze of cigarette smoke. Delaguerra looked around, then went to where a chubby-faced man sat on a high stool beside a cash register.

"You Stoll?"

The chubby-faced man nodded.

"Where did Max Chill get to?"

"Long gone, brother. They only played a hundred up. Home, I guess."

"Where's home?"

The chubby-faced man gave him a swift, flickering glance that passed like a finger of light.

"I wouldn't know."

Delaguerra lifted a hand to the pocket where he carried his badge. He dropped it again—tried not to drop it too quickly. The chubby-faced man grinned.

"Flattie, eh? Okey, he lives at the Mansfield, three blocks west on Grand."

TEN

Cefarino Toribo, the good-looking Filipino in the well-cut tan suit, gathered two dimes and three pennies off the counter in the telegraph office, smiled at the bored blonde who was waiting on him.

"That goes out right away, Sugar?"

She glanced at the message icily. "Hotel Mansfield? Be there in twenty minutes—and save the sugar."

"Okey, Sugar."

Toribo dawdled elegantly out of the office. The blonde spiked the message with a jab, said over her shoulder: "Guy must be nuts. Sending a wire to a hotel three blocks away."

Ceferino Toribo strolled along Spring Street, trailing smoke over his neat shoulder from a chocolate-colored cigarette. At Fourth he turned west, went three blocks more, turned into the side entrance of the Mansfield, by the barbershop. He went up some marble steps to a mezzanine, along the back of a writing room and up carpeted steps to the third floor. He passed the elevators and swaggered down a long corridor to the end, looking at the numbers on doors.

He came back halfway to the elevators, sat down in an open space where there was a pair of windows on the court, a glass-topped table and chairs. He lit a fresh cigarette from his stub, leaned back and listened to the elevators.

He leaned forward sharply whenever one stopped at that floor, listening for steps. The steps came in something over ten minutes. He stood up and went to the corner of the wall where the widened-out space began. He took a long thin gun out from under his right arm, transferred it to his right hand, held it down against the wall beside his leg.

A squat, pockmarked Filipino in bellhop's uniform came along the corridor, carrying a small tray. Toribo made a hissing noise, lifted the gun. The squat Filipino whirled. His mouth opened and his eyes bulged at the gun.

Toribo said, "What room, punk?"

The squat Filipino smiled very nervously, placatingly. He came close, showed Toribo a yellow envelope on his tray. The figures 338 were penciled on the window of the envelope.

"Put it down," Toribo said calmly.

The squat Filipino put the telegram on the table. He kept his eyes on the gun.

"Beat it," Toribo said. "You put it under the door, see?"

The squat Filipino ducked his round black head, smiled nervously again, and went away very quicky towards the elevators.

Toribo put the gun in his jacket pocket, took out a folded white paper. He opened it very carefully, shook glistening white powder from it on to the hollow place formed between his left thumb and forefinger when he spread his hand. He sniffed the powder sharply up his nose, took out a flame-colored silk handkerchief and wiped his nose.

He stood still for a little while. His eyes got the dullness of slate and the skin on his brown face seemed to tighten over his high cheekbones. He breathed audibly between his teeth.

He picked the yellow envelope up and went along the corridor to the end, stopped in front of the last door, knocked.

A voice called out. He put his lips close to the door, spoke in a high-pitched, very deferential voice.

"Mail for you, sar."

Bedsprings creaked. Steps came across the floor inside. A key turned and the door opened. Toribo had his thin gun out again by this time. As the door opened he stepped swiftly into the opening, sidewise, with a graceful sway of his hips. He put the muzzle of the thin gun against Max Chill's abdomen.

"Back up!" he snarled, and his voice now had the metallic twang of a plucked banjo string.

Max Chill backed away from the gun. He backed across the room to the bed, sat down on the bed when his legs struck the side of it. Springs creaked and a newspaper rustled. Max Chill's pale face under the neatly parted brown hair had no expression at all.

Toribo shut the door softly, snapped the lock. When the door latch snapped, Max Chill's face suddenly became a sick face. His lips began to shake, kept on shaking.

Toribo said mockingly, in his twangy voice: "You talk to the cops, huh? *Adios.*"

The thin gun jumped in his hand, kept on jumping. A little pale smoke lisped from the muzzle. The noise the gun made was no louder than a hammer striking a nail or knuckles rapping sharply on wood. It made that noise seven times.

Max Chill lay down on the bed very slowly. His feet stayed on the floor. His eyes went blank, and his lips parted and a pinkish froth seethed on them. Blood showed in several places on the front of his loose shirt. He lay quite still on his back and looked at the ceiling with his feet touching the floor and the pink froth bubbling on his blue lips.

Toribo moved the gun to his left hand and put it away under his arm. He sidled over to the bed and stood beside it, looking down at Max Chill. After a while the pink froth stopped bubbling and Max Chill's face became the quiet, empty face of a dead man.

Toribo went back to the door, opened it, started to back out, his eyes still on the bed. There was a stir of movement behind him.

He started to whirl, snatching a hand up. Something looped at his head. The floor tilted queerly before his eyes, rushed up at his face. He didn't know when it struck his face.

Delaguerra kicked the Filipino's legs into the room, out of the way of the door. He shut the door, locked it, walked stiffly over to the bed, swinging a thonged sap at his side. He stood beside the bed for quite a long time. At last he said under his breath: "They clean up. Yeah—they clean up."

He went back to the Filipino, rolled him over and went through his pockets. There was a well-lined wallet without any identification, a gold lighter set with garnets, a gold cigarette case, keys, a gold pencil and knife, the flame-colored handkerchief, loose money, two guns and spare clips for them, and five bindles of heroin powder in the ticket pocket of the tan jacket.

He left it thrown around on the floor, stood up. The Filipino breathed heavily, with his eyes shut, a muscle twitching in one cheek. Delaguerra took a coil of thin wire out of his pocket and wired the brown man's wrists behind him. He dragged him over to the bed, sat him up against the leg, looped a strand of the wire around his neck and around the bed post. He tied the flame-colored handkerchief to the looped wire.

He went into the bathroom and got a glass of water and threw it into the Filipino's face as hard as he could throw it.

Toribo jerked, gagged sharply as the wire caught his neck. His eyes jumped open. He opened his mouth to yell.

Delaguerra jerked the wire taut against the brown throat. The yell was cut off as though by a switch. There was a strained anguished gurgle. Toribo's mouth drooled.

Delaguerra let the wire go slack again and put his head down close to the Filipino's head. He spoke to him gently, with a dry, very deadly gentleness.

"You want to talk to me, spig. Maybe not right away, maybe not even soon. But after a while you want to talk to me."

The Filipino's eyes rolled yellowly. He spat. Then his lips came together, tight.

Delaguerra smiled a faint, grim smile. "Tough boy," he said softly. He jerked the handkerchief back, held it tight and hard, biting into the brown throat above the adam's apple.

The Filipino's legs began to jump on the floor. His body moved in sudden lunges. The brown of his face became a thick congested purple. His eyes bulged, shot with blood.

Delaguerra let the wire go loose again.

The Filipino gasped air into his lungs. His head sagged, then jerked back against the bedpost. He shook with a chill.

"Sí . . . I talk," he breathed.

ELEVEN

When the bell rang Ironhead Toomey very carefully put a black ten down on a red jack. Then he licked his lips and put all the cards down and looked around towards the front door of the bungalow, through the dining-room arch. He stood up slowly, a big brute of a man with loose gray hair and a big nose.

In the living room beyond the arch a thin blonde girl was lying on a davenport, reading a magazine under a lamp with a torn red shade. She was pretty, but too pale, and her thin, high-arched eyebrows gave her face a startled look. She put the magazine down and swung her feet to the floor and looked at Ironhead Toomey with sharp, sudden fear in her eyes.

Toomey jerked his thumb silently. The girl stood up and went very quickly through the arch and through a swing door into the kitchen. She shut the swing door slowly, so that it made no noise.

The bell rang again, longer. Toomey shoved his white-socked feet into carpet slippers, hung a pair of glasses on his big nose, took a revolver off a chair beside him. He picked a crumpled newspaper off the floor and arranged it loosely in front of the gun, which he held in his left hand. He strolled unhurriedly to the front door.

He was yawning as he opened it, peering with sleepy eyes through the glasses at the tall man who stood on the porch.

"Okey," he said wearily. "Talk it up."

Delaguerra said: "I'm a police officer. I want to see Stella La Motte."

Ironhead Toomey put an arm like a Yule log across the door frame and leaned solidly against it. His expression remained bored.

"Wrong dump, copper. No broads here."

Delaguerra said: "I'll come in and look."

Toomey said cheerfully: "You will—like hell."

54

▼

Delaguerra jerked a gun out of his pocket very smoothly and swiftly, smashed it at Toomey's left wrist. The newspaper and the big revolver fell down on the floor of the porch. Toomey's face got a less bored expression.

"Old gag," Delaguerra snapped. "Let's go in."

Toomey shook his left wrist, took his other arm off the door frame and swung hard at Delaguerra's jaw. Delaguerra moved his head about four inches. He frowned, made a disapproving noise with his tongue and lips.

Toomey dived at him. Delaguerra sidestepped and chopped the gun at a big gray head. Toomey landed on his stomach, half in the house and half out on the porch. He grunted, planted his hands firmly and started to get up again, as if nothing had hit him.

Delaguerra kicked Toomey's gun out of the way. A swing door inside the house made a light sound. Toomey was up on one knee and one hand as Delaguerra looked towards the noise. He took a swing at Delaguerra's stomach, hit him. Delaguerra grunted and hit Toomey on the head again, hard. Toomey shook his head, growled: "Sappin' me is a waste of time, bo."

He dived sidewise, got hold of Delaguerra's leg, jerked the leg off the floor. Delaguerra sat down on the boards of the porch, jammed in the doorway. His head hit the side of the doorway, dazed him.

The thin blonde rushed through the arch with a small automatic in her hand. She pointed it at Delaguerra, said furiously: "Reach, damn you!"

Delaguerra shook his head, started to say something, then caught his breath as Toomey twisted his foot. Toomey set his teeth hard and twisted the foot as if he was all alone in the world with it and it was his foot and he could do what he liked with it.

Delaguerra's head jerked back again and his face got white. His mouth twisted into a harsh grimace of pain. He heaved up, grabbed Toomey's hair with his left hand, dragged the big head up and over until his chin came up, straining. Delaguerra smashed the barrel of his Colt on the skin.

Toomey became limp, an inert mass, fell across his legs and pinned him to the floor. Delaguerra couldn't move. He was propped on the floor on his right hand, trying to keep from being pushed flat by Toomey's weight. He couldn't get his right hand with the gun in it off the floor. The blonde was closer to him now, wild-eyed, white-faced with rage.

Delaguerra said in a spent voice: "Don't be a fool, Stella. Joey—"

The blonde's face was unnatural. Her eyes were unnatural, with small pupils, a queer flat glitter in them.

"Cops!" she almost screamed. "Cops! God, how I hate cops!"

The gun in her hand crashed. The echoes of it filled the room, went out of the open front door, died against the high-board fence across the street.

A sharp blow like the blow of a club hit the left side of Delaguerra's head. Pain filled his head. Light flared—blinding white light that filled the world. Then it was dark. He fell soundlessly, into bottomless darkness.

TWELVE

Light came back as a red fog in front of his eyes. Hard, bitter pain racked the side of his head, his whole face, ground in his teeth. His tongue was hot and thick when he tried to move it. He tried to move his hands. They were far away from him, not his hands at all.

Then he opened his eyes and the red fog went away and he was looking at a face. It was a big face, very close to him, a huge face. It was fat and had sleek blue jowls and there was a cigar with a bright band in a grinning, thick-lipped mouth. The face chuckled. Delaguerra closed his eyes again and the pain washed over him, submerged him. He passed out.

Seconds, or years, passed. He was looking at the face again. He heard a thick voice.

"Well, he's with us again. A pretty tough lad at that."

The face came closer, the end of the cigar glowed cherry-red. Then he was coughing rackingly, gagging on smoke. The side of his head seemed to burst open. He felt fresh blood slide down his cheekbone, tickling the skin, then slide over stiff dried blood that had already caked on his face.

"That fixes him up swell," the thick voice said.

Another voice with a touch of brogue to it said something gentle and obscene. The big face whirled towards the sound, snarling.

Delaguerra came wide awake then. He saw the room clearly, saw the four people in it. The big face was the face of Big John Masters.

The thin blonde girl was hunched on one end of the davenport, staring at the floor with a doped expression, her arms stiff at her sides, her hands out of sight in the cushions.

Dave Aage had his long lank body propped against a wall beside a curtained window. His wedge-shaped face looked bored. Commissioner Drew was on the other end of the davenport, under the frayed lamp. The light made silver in his hair. His blue eyes were very bright, very intent.

There was a shiny gun in Big John Masters' hand. Delaguerra blinked at it, started to get up. A hard hand jerked at his chest, jarred him back. A wave of nausea went over him. The thick voice said harshly: "Hold it, pussyfoot. You've had your fun. This is our party."

Delaguerra licked his lips, said: "Give me a drink of water."

Dave Aage stood away from the wall and went through the dining-room arch. He came back with a glass, held it to Delaguerra's mouth. Delaguerra drank.

Masters said: "We like your guts, copper. But you don't use them right. It seems you're a guy that can't take a hint. That's too bad. That makes you through. Get me?"

The blonde turned her head and looked at Delaguerra with heavy eyes, looked away again. Aage went back to his wall. Drew began to stroke the side of his face with quick nervous fingers, as if Delaguerra's bloody head made his own face hurt.

Delaguerra said slowly: "Killing me will just hang you a little higher, Masters. A sucker on the big time is still a sucker. You've had two men killed already for no reason at all. You don't even know what you're trying to cover."

The big man swore harshly, jerked the shiny gun up, then lowered it slowly, with a heavy leer. Aage said indolently: "Take it easy, John. Let him speak his piece."

Delaguerra said in the same slow, careless voice: "The lady over there is the sister of the two men you've had killed. She told them her story, about framing Imlay, who got the pictures, how they got to Donegan Marr. Your little Filipino hood has done some singing. I get the general idea all right. You couldn't be sure Imlay would kill Marr. Maybe Marr would get Imlay. It would work out all right either way. Only, if Imlay did kill Marr, the case had to be broken fast. That's where you slipped. You started to cover up before you really knew what happened."

Masters said harshly: "Crummy, copper, crummy. You're wasting my time."

The blonde turned her head towards Delaguerra, towards Masters' back. There was hard green hate in her eyes now. Delaguerra shrugged very slightly, went on: "It was routine stuff for you to put killers on the Chill brothers. It was routine stuff to get me off the investigation, get me framed, and suspended because you figured I was on Marr's payroll. But it wasn't routine when you couldn't find Imlay—and that crowded you."

Masters' hard black eyes got wide and empty. His thick neck swelled. Aage came away from the wall a few feet and stood rigidly. After a moment Masters snapped his teeth, spoke very quietly: "That's a honey, copper. Tell us about that one."

Delaguerra touched his smeared face with the tips of two fingers, looked at the fingers. His eyes were depthless, ancient.

"Imlay is dead, Masters. He was dead before Marr was killed."

The room was very still. Nobody moved in it. The four people Delaguerra looked at were frozen with shock. After a long time Masters drew in a harsh breath and blew it out and almost whispered: "Tell it, copper. Tell it fast, or by God I'll——"

Delaguerra's voice cut in on him coldly, without any emotion at all: "Imlay went to see Marr all right. Why wouldn't he? He didn't know he was double-crossed. Only he went to see him last night, not today. He rode up to the cabin at Puma Lake with him, to talk things over in a friendly way. That was the gag, anyhow. Then, up there, they had their fight and Imlay got killed, got dumped off the end of the porch, got his head smashed open on some rocks. He's dead as last Christmas, in the woodshed of Marr's cabin . . . Okey, Marr hid him and came back to town. Then today he got a phone call, mentioning the name Imlay, making a date for twelve-fifteen. What would Marr do? Stall, of course, send his office girl off to lunch, put a gun where he could reach it in a hurry. He was all set for trouble then. Only the visitor fooled him and he didn't use the gun."

Masters said gruffly: "Hell, man, you're just cracking wise. You couldn't know all those things."

He looked back at Drew. Drew was gray-faced, taut. Aage came a little farther away from the wall and stood close to Drew. The blonde girl didn't move a muscle.

Delaguerra said wearily: "Sure, I'm guessing, but I'm guessing to fit the facts. It had to be like that. Marr was no slouch with a gun and he was on edge, all set. Why didn't he get a shot in? Because it was a woman that called on him."

He lifted an arm, pointed at the blonde. "There's your killer. She loved Imlay even though she framed him. She's a junkie and junkies are like that. She got sad and sorry and she went after Marr herself. Ask her!"

The blonde stood up in a smooth lunge. Her right hand jerked up from the cushions with a small automatic in it, the one she had shot Delaguerra with. Her green eyes were pale and empty and staring. Masters whirled around, flailed at her arm with the shiny revolver.

She shot him twice, point-blank, without a flicker of hesitation. Blood spurted from the side of his thick neck, down the front of his coat. He staggered, dropped the shiny revolver, almost at Delaguerra's feet. He fell outwards towards the wall behind Delaguerra's chair, one arm groping out for the wall. His hand hit the wall and trailed down it as he fell. He crashed heavily, didn't move again.

Delaguerra had the shiny revolver almost in his hand.

Drew was on his feet yelling. The girl turned slowly towards Aage, seemed to ignore Delaguerra. Aage jerked a Luger from under his arm and knocked Drew out of the way with his arm. The small automatic and the Luger roared at the same time. The small gun missed. The girl was flung down on the davenport, her left hand clutching at her breast. She rolled her eyes, tried to lift the gun again. Then she fell sidewise on the cushions and her left hand went lax, dropped away from her breast. The front of her dress was a sudden welter of blood. Her eyes opened and shut, opened and stayed open.

Aage swung the Luger towards Delaguerra. His eyebrows were twisted up into a sharp grin of intense strain. His smoothly combed, sand-colored hair flowed down his bony scalp as tightly as though it were painted on it.

Delaguerra shot him four times, so rapidly that the explosions were like the rattle of a machine gun.

In the instant of time before he fell Aage's face became the thin, empty face of an old man, his eyes the vacant eyes of an idiot. Then his long body jackknifed to the floor, the Luger still in his hand. One leg doubled under him as if there was no bone in it.

Powder smell was sharp in the air. The air was stunned by the sound of guns. Delaguerra got to his feet slowly, motioned to Drew with the shiny revolver.

"Your party, Commissioner. Is this anything like what you wanted?"

Drew nodded slowly, white-faced, quivering. He swallowed, moved slowly across the floor, past Aage's sprawled body. He looked down at the girl on the davenport, shook his head. He went over to Masters, went down on one knee, touched him. He stood up again.

"All dead, I think," he muttered.

Delaguerra said: "That's swell. What happened to the big boy? The bruiser?"

"They sent him away. I—I don't think they meant to kill you, Delaguerra."

Delaguerra nodded a little. His face began to soften, the rigid lines began to go out of it. The side that was not a bloodstained mask began to look human again. He sopped at his face with a handkerchief. It came away bright red with blood. He threw it away and lightly fingered his matted hair into place. Some of it was caught in the dried blood.

"The hell they didn't," he said.

The house was very still. There was no noise outside. Drew listened, sniffed, went to the front door and looked out. The street outside was dark, silent. He came back close to Delaguerra. Very slowly a smile worked itself on to his face.

"It's a hell of a note," he said, "when a commissioner of police has to be his own undercover man—and a square cop had to be framed off the force to help him."

Delaguerra looked at him without expression. "You want to play it that way?"

Drew spoke calmly now. The pink was back in his face. "For the good of the department, man, and the city—and ourselves, it's the only way to play it."

Delaguerra looked him straight in the eyes.

"I like it that way too," he said in a dead voice. "If it gets played—*exactly* that way."

THIRTEEN

Marcus braked the car to a stop and grinned admiringly at the big tree-shaded house.

"Pretty nice," he said. "I could go for a long rest there myself."

Delaguerra got out of the car slowly, as if he was stiff and very tired. He was hatless, carried his straw under his arm. Part of the left side of his head was shaved and the shaved part covered by a thick pad of gauze and tape, over the stitches. A wick of wiry black hair stuck up over one edge of the bandage, with a ludicrous effect.

He said: "Yeah—but I'm not staying here, sap. Wait for me."

He went along the path of stones that wound through the grass. Trees speared long shadows across the lawn, through the morning sunlight. The house was very still, with drawn blinds, a dark wreath on the brass knocker. Delaguerra didn't go up to the door. He turned off along another path under the windows and went along the side of the house past the gladioli beds.

There were more trees at the back, more lawn, more flowers, more sun and shadow. There was a pond with water lilies in it and a big stone bullfrog. Beyond was a half-circle of lawn chairs around an iron table with a tile top. In one of the chairs Belle Marr sat.

She wore a black-and-white dress, loose and casual, and there was a wide-brimmed garden hat on her chestnut hair. She sat very still, looking into the distance across the lawn. Her face was white. The make-up glared on it.

She turned her head slowly, smiled a dull smile, motioned to a chair beside her. Delaguerra didn't sit down. He took his straw from under his arm, snapped a finger at the brim, said: "The case is closed. There'll be inquests, investigations, threats, a lot of people shouting their mouths off to horn in on the publicity, that sort of thing. The papers will play it big for a while. But underneath, on the record, it's closed. You can begin to try to forget it."

The girl looked at him suddenly, widened her vivid blue eyes, looked away again, over the grass.

"Is your head very bad, Sam?" she asked softly.

Delaguerra said: "No. It's fine . . . What I mean is the La

Motte girl shot Masters—and she shot Donny. Aage shot her. I shot Aage. All dead, ring around the rosy. Just how Imlay got killed we'll not know ever, I guess. I can't see that it matters now."

Without looking up at him Belle Marr said quietly: "But how did you know it was Imlay up at the cabin? The paper said—" She broke off, shuddered suddenly.

He stared woodenly at the hat he was holding. "I didn't. I thought a woman shot Donny. It looked like a good hunch that was Imlay up at the lake. It fitted his description."

"How did you know it was a woman . . . that killed Donny?" Her voice had a lingering, half-whispered stillness.

"I just knew."

He walked away a few steps, stood looking at the trees. He turned slowly, came back, stood beside her chair again. His face was very weary.

"We had great times together—the three of us. You and Donny and I. Life seems to do nasty things to people. It's all gone now—all the good part."

Her voice was still a whisper saying: "Maybe not all gone, Sam. We must see a lot of each other, from now on."

A vague smile moved the corners of his lips, went away again. "It's my first frame-up," he said quietly. "I hope it will be my last."

Belle Marr's head jerked a little. Her hands took hold of the arms of the chair, looked white against the varnished wood. Her whole body seemed to get rigid.

After a moment Delaguerra reached in his pocket and something gold glittered in his hand. He looked down at it dully.

"Got the badge back," he said. "It's not quite as clean as it was. Clean as most, I suppose. I'll try to keep it that way." He put it back in his pocket.

Very slowly the girl stood up in front of him. She lifted her chin, stared at him with a long level stare. Her face was a mask of white plaster behind the rouge.

She said: "My God, Sam—I begin to understand."

Delaguerra didn't look at her face. He looked past her shoulder at some vague spot in the distance. He spoke vaguely, distantly.

"Sure . . . I thought it was a woman because it was a small gun such as a woman would use. But not only on that account. After I went up to the cabin I knew Donny was primed for trouble and it wouldn't be that easy for a man to get the drop on him. But it was a perfect set-up for Imlay to have done it. Masters and Aage assumed he'd done it and had a lawyer phone in admitting he did it and promising to surrender him in the morning. So it was natural for anyone who didn't know Imlay was dead to fall in line. Besides, no cop would expect a woman to pick up her shells.

"After I got Joey Chill's story I thought it might be the La Motte girl. But I didn't think so when I said it in front of her. That was dirty. It got her killed, in a way. Though I wouldn't give much for her chances anyway, with that bunch."

Belle Marr was still staring at him. The breeze blew a wisp of her hair and that was the only thing about her that moved.

He brought his eyes back from the distance, looked at her gravely for a brief moment, looked away again. He took a small bunch of keys out of his pocket, tossed them down on the table.

"Three things were tough to figure until I got completely wise. The writing on the pad, the gun in Donny's hand, the missing shells. Then I tumbled to it. He didn't die right away. He had guts and he used them to the last flicker—to protect somebody. The writing on the pad was a bit shaky. He wrote it afterwards, when he was alone, dying. He had been thinking of Imlay and writing the name helped mess the trail. Then he got the gun out of his desk to die with it in his hand. That left the shells. I got that too, after a while.

"The shots were fired close, across the desk, and there were books on one end of the desk. The shells fell there, stayed on the desk where he could get them. He couldn't have got them off the floor. There's a key to the office on your ring. I went there last night, late. I found the shells in a humidor with his cigars. Nobody looked for them there. You only find what you expect to find, after all."

He stopped talking and rubbed the side of his face. After a moment he added: "Donny did the best he could—and then he died. It was a swell job—and I'm letting him get away with it."

Belle Marr opened her mouth slowly. A kind of babble came out of it first, then words, clear words.

"It wasn't just women, Sam. It was the kind of women he had." She shivered. "I'll go downtown now and give myself up."

Delaguerra said: "No. I told you I was letting him get away with it. Downtown they like it the way it is. It's swell politics. It gets the city out from under the Masters-Aage mob. It puts Drew on top for a little while, but he's too weak to last. So that doesn't matter . . . You're not going to do anything about any of it. You're going to do what Donny used his last strength to show he wanted. You're staying out. Goodbye."

He looked at her white shattered face once more, very quickly. Then he swung around, walked away over the lawn, past the pool with the lily pads and the stone bullfrog along the side of the house and out to the car.

Pete Marcus swung the door open. Delaguerra got in and sat down and put his head far back against the seat, slumped down in the car and closed his eyes. He said flatly: "Take it easy, Pete. My head hurts like hell."

Marcus started the car and turned into the street, drove slowly back along De Neve Lane towards town. The tree-shaded house disappeared behind them. The tall trees finally hid it.

When they were a long way from it Delaguerra opened his eyes again.

I'LL BE
WAITING

At one o'clock in the morning, Carl, the night porter, turned down the last of three table lamps in the main lobby of the Windermere Hotel. The blue carpet darkened a shade or two and the walls drew back into remoteness. The chairs filled with shadowy loungers. In the corners were memories like cobwebs.

Tony Reseck yawned. He put his head on one side and listened to the frail, twittery music from the radio room beyond a dim arch at the far side of the lobby. He frowned. That should be his radio room after one A.M. Nobody should be in it. That red-haired girl was spoiling his nights.

The frown passed and a miniature of a smile quirked at the corners of his lips. He sat relaxed, a short, pale, paunchy, middle-aged man with long, delicate fingers clasped on the elk's tooth on his watch chain; the long delicate fingers of a sleight-of-hand artist, fingers with shiny, molded nails and tapering first joints, fingers a little spatulate at the ends. Handsome fingers. Tony Reseck rubbed them gently together and there was peace in his quiet sea-gray eyes.

The frown came back on his face. The music annoyed him. He got up with a curious litheness, all in one piece, without moving his clasped hands from the watch chain. At one moment he was leaning back relaxed, and the next he was standing balanced on his feet, perfectly still, so that the movement of rising seemed to be a thing perfectly perceived, an error of vision. . . .

He walked with small, polished shoes delicately across the blue carpet and under the arch. The music was louder. It contained the hot, acid blare, the frenetic, jittering runs of a jam session. It was too loud. The red-haired girl sat there and stared silently at the fretted part of the big radio cabinet as though she could see the band with its fixed professional grin and the sweat running down its back. She was curled up with her feet under her on a davenport which seemed to contain most of the cushions in the room. She was tucked among them carefully, like a corsage in the florist's tissue paper.

She didn't turn her head. She leaned there, one hand in a small fist on her peach-colored knee. She was wearing lounging pajamas of heavy ribbed silk embroidered with black lotus buds.

"You like Goodman, Miss Cressy?" Tony Reseck asked.

The girl moved her eyes slowly. The light in there was dim, but the violet of her eyes almost hurt. They were large, deep eyes without a trace of thought in them. Her face was classical and without expression.

She said nothing.

Tony smiled and moved his fingers at his sides, one by one, feeling them move. "You like Goodman, Miss Cressy?" he repeated gently.

"Not to cry over," the girl said tonelessly.

Tony rocked back on his heels and looked at her eyes. Large, deep, empty eyes. Or were they? He reached down and muted the radio.

"Don't get me wrong," the girl said. "Goodman makes money, and a lad that makes legitimate money these days is a lad you have to respect. But this jitterbug music gives me the backdrop of a beer flat. I like something with roses in it."

"Maybe you like Mozart," Tony said.

"Go on, kid me," the girl said.

"I wasn't kidding you, Miss Cressy. I think Mozart was the greatest man that ever lived—and Toscanini is his prophet."

"I thought you were the house dick." She put her head back on a pillow and stared at him through her lashes.

"Make me some of that Mozart," she added.

"It's too late," Tony sighed. "You can't get it now."

She gave him another long lucid glance. "Got the eye on me, haven't you, flatfoot?" She laughed a little, almost under her breath. "What did I do wrong?"

Tony smiled his toy smile. "Nothing, Miss Cressy. Nothing at all. But you need some fresh air. You've been five days in this hotel and you haven't been outdoors. And you have a tower room."

She laughed again. "Make me a story about it. I'm bored."

"There was a girl here once had your suite. She stayed in the hotel a whole week, like you. Without going out at all, I mean. She didn't speak to anybody hardly. What do you think she did then?"

The girl eyed him gravely. "She jumped her bill."

He put his long delicate hand out and turned it slowly, fluttering the fingers, with an effect almost like a lazy wave breaking. "Unh-uh. She sent down for her bill and paid it. Then she told the hop to be back in half an hour for her suitcases. Then she went out on her balcony."

The girl leaned forward a little, her eyes still grave, one hand capping her peach-colored knee. "What did you say your name was?"

"Tony Reseck."

"Sounds like a hunky."

"Yeah," Tony said. "Polish."

"Go on, Tony."

"All the tower suites have private balconies, Miss Cressy. The walls of them are too low for fourteen stories above the street. It was a dark night, that night, high clouds." He dropped his hand with a final gesture, a farewell gesture. "Nobody saw her jump. But when she hit, it was like a big gun going off."

"You're making it up, Tony." Her voice was a clean dry whisper of sound.

He smiled his toy smile. His quiet sea-gray eyes seemed

aimost to be smoothing the long waves of her hair. "Eve Cressy,"
he said musingly. "A name waiting for lights to be in."

"Waiting for a tall dark guy that's no good, Tony. You wouldn't
care why. I was married to him once. I might be married to
him again. You can make a lot of mistakes in just one lifetime."
The hand on her knee opened slowly until the fingers were
strained back as far as they would go. Then they closed quickly
and tightly, and even in that dim light the knuckles shone like
the little polished bones. "I played him a low trick once. I put
him in a bad place—without meaning to. You wouldn't care
about that either. It's just that I owe him something."

He leaned over softly and turned the knob on the radio. A
waltz formed itself dimly on the warm air. A tinsel waltz, but
a waltz. He turned the volume up. The music gushed from
the loudspeaker in a swirl of shadowed melody. Since Vienna
died, all waltzes are shadowed.

The girl put her hand on one side and hummed three or
four bars and stopped with a sudden tightening of her mouth.

"Eve Cressy," she said. "It was in lights once. At a bum
night club. A dive. They raided it and the lights went out."

He smiled at her almost mockingly. "It was no dive while
you were there, Miss Cressy . . . That's the waltz the orchestra
always played when the old porter walked up and down in front
of the hotel entrance, all swelled up with his medals on his
chest. *The Last Laugh*. Emil Jannings. You wouldn't remember
that one, Miss Cressy."

" 'Spring, Beautiful Spring,' " she said. "No, I never saw it."

He walked three steps away from her and turned. "I have
to go upstairs and palm doorknobs. I hope I didn't bother you.
You ought to go to bed now. It's pretty late."

The tinsel waltz stopped and a voice began to talk. The girl
spoke through the voice. "You really thought something like
that—about the balcony?"

He nodded. "I might have," he said softly. "I don't any more."

"No chance, Tony." Her smile was a dim lost leaf. "Come
and talk to me some more. Redheads don't jump, Tony. They
hang on—and wither."

He looked at her gravely for a moment and then moved away over the carpet. The porter was standing in the archway that led to the main lobby. Tony hadn't looked that way yet, but he knew somebody was there. He always knew if anybody was close to him. He could hear the grass grow, like the donkey in *The Blue Bird.*

The porter jerked his chin at him urgently. His broad face above the uniform collar looked sweaty and excited. Tony stepped up close to him and they went together through the arch and out to the middle of the dim lobby.

"Trouble?" Tony asked wearily.

"There's a guy outside to see you, Tony. He won't come in. I'm doing a wipe-off on the plate glass of the doors and he comes up beside me, a tall guy. 'Get Tony,' he says, out of the side of his mouth."

Tony said: "Uh-huh," and looked at the porter's pale blue eyes. "Who was it?"

"Al, he said to say he was."

Tony's face became as expressionless as dough. "Okey." He started to move off.

The porter caught his sleeve. "Listen, Tony. You got any enemies?"

Tony laughed politely, his face still like dough.

"Listen, Tony." The porter held his sleeve tightly. "There's a big black car down the block, the other way from the hacks. There's a guy standing beside it with his foot on the running board. This guy that spoke to me, he wears a dark-colored, wrap-around overcoat with a high collar turned up against his ears. His hat's way low. You can't hardly see his face. He says, 'Get Tony,' out of the side of his mouth. You ain't got any enemies, have you, Tony?"

"Only the finance company," Tony said. "Beat it."

He walked slowly and a little stiffly across the blue carpet, up the three shallow steps to the entrance lobby with the three elevators on one side and the desk on the other. Only one elevator was working. Beside the open doors, his arms folded, the night operator stood silent in a neat blue uniform with

70
▼

silver facings. A lean, dark Mexican named Gomez. A new boy, breaking in on the night shift.

The other side was the desk, rose marble, with the night clerk leaning on it delicately. A small neat man with a wispy reddish mustache and cheeks so rosy they looked roughed. He stared at Tony and poked a nail at his mustache.

Tony pointed a stiff index finger at him, folded the other three fingers tight to his palm, and flicked his thumb up and down on the stiff finger. The clerk touched the other side of his mustache and looked bored.

Tony went on past the closed and darkened newsstand and the side entrance to the drugstore, out to the brassbound plate-glass doors. He stopped just inside them and took a deep, hard breath. He squared his shoulders, pushed the doors open and stepped out into the cold damp night air.

The street was dark, silent. The rumble of traffic on Wilshire, two blocks away, had no body, no meaning. To the left were two taxis. Their drivers leaned against a fender, side by side, smoking. Tony walked the other way. The big dark car was a third of a block from the hotel entrance. Its lights were dimmed and it was only when he was almost up to it that he heard the gentle sound of its engine turning over.

A tall figure detached itself from the body of the car and strolled toward him, both hands in the pockets of the dark overcoat with the high collar. From the man's mouth a cigarette tip glowed faintly, a rusty pearl.

They stopped two feet from each other.

The tall man said, "Hi, Tony. Long time no see."

"Hello, Al. How's it going?"

"Can't complain." The tall man started to take his right hand out of his overcoat pocket, then stopped and laughed quietly. "I forgot. Guess you don't want to shake hands."

"That don't mean anything," Tony said. "Shaking hands. Monkeys can shake hands. What's on your mind, Al?"

"Still the funny little fat guy, eh, Tony?"

"I guess." Tony winked his eyes tight. His throat felt tight. "You like your job back there?"

71
▼

"It's a job."

Al laughed his quiet laugh again. "You take it slow, Tony. I'll take it fast. So it's a job and you want to hold it. Okey. There's a girl named Eve Cressy flopping in your quiet hotel. Get her out. Fast and right now."

"What's the trouble?"

The tall man looked up and down the street. A man behind in the car coughed lightly. "She's hooked with a wrong number. Nothing against her personal, but she'll lead trouble to you. Get her out, Tony. You got maybe an hour."

"Sure," Tony said aimlessly, without meaning.

Al took his hand out of his pocket and stretched it against Tony's chest. He gave him a light lazy push. "I wouldn't be telling you just for the hell of it, little fat brother. Get her out of there."

"Okey," Tony said, without any tone in his voice.

The tall man took back his hand and reached for the car door. He opened it and started to slip in like a lean black shadow.

Then he stopped and said something to the men in the car and got out again. He came back to where Tony stood silent, his pale eyes catching a little dim light from the street.

"Listen, Tony. You always kept your nose clean. You're a good brother, Tony."

Tony didn't speak.

Al leaned toward him, a long urgent shadow, the high collar almost touching his ears. "It's trouble business, Tony. The boys won't like it, but I'm telling you just the same. This Cressy was married to a lad named Johmy Ralls. Ralls is out of Quentin two, three days, or a week. He did a three-spot for manslaughter. The girl put him there. He ran down an old man one night when he was drunk, and she was with him. He wouldn't stop. She told him to go in and tell it, or else. He didn't go in. So the Johns come for him."

Tony said, "That's too bad."

"It's kosher, kid. It's my business to know. This Ralls flapped his mouth in stir about how the girl would be waiting for him when he got out, all set to forgive and forget, and he was going straight to her."

Tony said, "What's he to you?" His voice had a dry, stiff crackle, like thick paper.

Al laughed. "The trouble boys want to see him. He ran a table at a spot on the Strip and figured out a scheme. He and another guy took the house for fifty grand. The other lad coughed up, but we still need Johnny's twenty-five. The trouble boys don't get paid to forget."

Tony looked up and down the dark street. One of the taxi drivers flicked a cigarette stub in a long arc over the top of one of the cabs. Tony watched it fall and spark on the pavement. He listened to the quiet sound of the big car's motor.

"I don't want any part of it," he said. "I'll get her out."

Al backed away from him, nodding. "Wise kid. How's mom these days?"

"Okey," Tony said.

"Tell her I was asking for her."

"Asking for her isn't anything," Tony said.

Al turned quickly and got into the car. The car curved lazily in the middle of the block and drifted back toward the corner. Its lights went up and sprayed on a wall. It turned a corner and was gone. The lingering smell of its exhaust drifted past Tony's nose. He turned and walked back to the hotel and into it. He went along to the radio room.

The radio still muttered, but the girl was gone from the davenport in front of it. The pressed cushions were hollowed out by her body. Tony reached down and touched them. He thought they were still warm. He turned the radio off and stood there, turning a thumb slowly in front of his body, his hand flat against his stomach. Then he went back through the lobby toward the elevator bank and stood beside a majolica jar of white sand. The clerk fussed behind a pebbled-glass screen at one end of the desk. The air was dead.

The elevator bank was dark. Tony looked at the indicator of the middle car and saw that it was at 14.

"Gone to bed," he said under his breath.

The door of the porter's room beside the elevators opened and the little Mexican night operator came out in street clothes. He looked at Tony with a quiet sidewise look out of eyes the color of dried-out chestnuts.

"Good night, boss."

"Yeah," Tony said absently.

He took a thin dappled cigar out of his vest pocket and smelled it. He examined it slowly, turning it around in his neat fingers. There was a small tear along the side. He frowned at that and put the cigar away.

There was a distant sound and the hand on the indicator began to steal around the bronze dial. Light glittered up in the shaft and the straight line of the car floor dissolved the darkness below. The car stopped and the doors opened, and Carl came out of it.

His eyes caught Tony's with a kind of jump and he walked over to him, his head on one side, a thin shine along his pink upper lip.

"Listen, Tony."

Tony took his arm in a hard swift hand and turned him. He pushed him quickly, yet somehow casually, down the steps to the dim main lobby and steered him into a corner. He let go of the arm. His throat tightened again, for no reason he could think of.

"Well?" he said darkly. "Listen to what?"

The porter reached into a pocket and hauled out a dollar bill. "He gimme this," he said loosely. His glittering eyes looked past Tony's shoulder at nothing. They winked rapidly. "Ice and ginger ale."

"Don't stall," Tony growled.

"Guy in Fourteen-B," the porter said.

"Lemme smell your breath."

The porter leaned toward him obediently.

"Liquor," Tony said harshly.

"He gimme a drink."

Tony looked down at the dollar bill. "Nobody's in Fourteen-B. Not on my list," he said.

"Yeah. There is." The porter licked his lips and his eyes opened and shut several times. "Tall dark guy."

"All right," Tony said crossly. "All right. There's a tall dark guy in Fourteen-B and he gave you a buck and a drink. Then what?"

"Gat under his arm," Carl said, and blinked.

Tony smiled, but his eyes had taken on the lifeless glitter of thick ice. "You take Miss Cressy up to her room?"

Carl shook his head. "Gomez. I saw her go up."

"Get away from me," Tony said between his teeth. "And don't accept any more drinks from the guests."

He didn't move until Carl had gone back into his cubbyhole by the elevators and shut the door. Then he moved silently up the three steps and stood in front of the desk, looking at the veined rose marble, the onyx pen set, the fresh registration card in its leather frame. He lifted a hand and smacked it down hard on the marble. The clerk popped out from behind the glass screen like a chipmunk coming out of its hole.

Tony took a flimsy out of his breast pocket and spread it on the desk. "No Fourteen-B on this," he said in a bitter voice.

The clerk wisped politely at his mustache. "So sorry. You must have been out to supper when he checked in."

"Who?"

"Registered as James Watterson, San Diego." The clerk yawned.

"Ask for anybody?"

The clerk stopped in the middle of the yawn and looked at the top of Tony's head. "Why yes. He asked for a swing band. Why?"

"Smart, fast and funny," Tony said. "If you like 'em that way." He wrote on his flimsy and stuffed it back into his pocket. "I'm going upstairs and palm doorknobs. There's four tower rooms you ain't rented yet. Get up on your toes, son. You're slipping."

"I made out," the clerk drawled, and completed his yawn. "Hurry back, pop. I don't know how I'll get through the time."

"You could shave that pink fuzz off your lip," Tony said, and went across to the elevators.

He opened up a dark one and lit the dome light and shot the car up to fourteen. He darkened it again, stepped out and closed the doors. This lobby was smaller than any other, except the one immediately below it. It had a single blue-paneled door in each of the walls other than the elevator wall. On each door was a gold number and letter with a gold wreath around it. Tony walked over to 14A and put his ear to the panel. He heard nothing. Eve Cressy might be in bed asleep, or in the bathroom, or out on the balcony. Or she might be sitting there in the room, a few feet from the door, looking at the wall. Well, he wouldn't expect to be able to hear her sit and look at the wall. He went over to 14B and put his ear to that panel. This was different. There was a sound in there. A man coughed. It sounded somehow like a solitary cough. There were no voices. Tony pressed the small nacre button beside the door.

Steps came without hurry. A thickened voice spoke through the panel. Tony made no answer, no sound. The thickened voice repeated the question. Lightly, maliciously, Tony pressed the bell again.

Mr. James Watterson, or San Diego, should now open the door and give forth noise. He didn't. A silence fell beyond that door that was like the silence of a glacier. Once more Tony put his ear to the wood. Silence utterly.

He got out a master key on a chain and pushed it delicately into the lock of the door. He turned it, pushed the door inward three inches and withdrew the key. Then he waited.

"All right," the voice said harshly. "Come in and get it."

Tony pushed the door wide and stood there, framed against the light from the lobby. The man was tall, black-haired, angular and white-faced. He held a gun. He held it as though he knew about guns.

"Step right in," he drawled.

Tony went in through the door and pushed it shut with his shoulder. He kept his hands a little out from his sides, the clever fingers curled and slack. He smiled his quiet little smile.

"Mr. Watterson?"

"And after that what?"

"I'm the house detective here."

"It slays me."

The tall, white-faced, somehow handsome and somehow not handsome man backed slowly into the room. It was a large room with a low balcony around two sides of it. French doors opened out on the little private open-air balcony that each of the tower rooms had. There was a grate set for a log fire behind a paneled screen in front of a cheerful davenport. A tall misted glass stood on a hotel tray beside a deep, cozy chair. The man backed toward this and stood in front of it. The large, glistening gun drooped and pointed at the floor.

"It slays me," he said. "I'm in the dump an hour and the house copper gives me the bus. Okey, sweetheart, look in the closet and bathroom. But she just left."

"You didn't see her yet," Tony said.

The man's bleached face filled with unexpected lines. His thickened voice edged toward a snarl. "Yeah? Who didn't I see yet?"

"A girl named Eve Cressy."

The man swallowed. He put his gun down on the table beside the tray. He let himself down into the chair backwards, stiffly, like a man with a touch of lumbago. Then he leaned forward and put his hands on his kneecaps and smiled brightly between his teeth. "So she got here, huh? I didn't ask about her yet. I'm a careful guy. I didn't ask yet."

"She's been here five days," Tony said. "Waiting for you. She hasn't left the hotel a minute."

The man's mouth worked a little. His smile had a knowing tilt to it. "I got delayed a little up north," he said smoothly. "You know how it is. Visiting old friends. You seem to know a lot about my business, copper."

"That's right, Mr. Ralls."

The man lunged to his feet and his hand snapped at the gun. He stood leaning over, holding it on the table, staring. "Dames talk too much," he said with a muffled sound in his voice as though he held something soft between his teeth and talked through it.

"Not dames, Mr. Ralls."

"Huh?" The gun slithered on the hard wood of the table. "Talk it up, copper. My mind reader just quit."

"Not dames, guys. Guys with guns."

The glacier silence fell between them again. The man straightened his body out slowly. His face was washed clean of expression, but his eyes were haunted. Tony leaned in front of him, a shortish plump man with a quiet, pale, friendly face and eyes as simple as forest water.

"They never run out of gas—those boys," Johnny Ralls said, and licked at his lip. "Early and late, they work. The old firm never sleeps."

"You know who they are?" Tony said softly.

"I could maybe give nine guesses. And twelve of them would be right."

"The trouble boys," Tony said, and smiled a brittle smile.

"Where is she?" Johnny Ralls asked harshly.

"Right next door to you."

The man walked to the wall and left his gun lying on the table. He stood in front of the wall, studying it. He reached up and gripped the grillwork of the balcony railing. When he dropped his hand and turned, his face had lost some of its lines. His eyes had a quieter glint. He moved back to Tony and stood over him.

"I've got a stake," he said. "Eve sent me some dough and I built it up with a touch I made up north. Case dough, what I mean. The trouble boys talk about twenty-five grand." He smiled crookedly. "Five C's I can count. I'd have a lot of fun making them believe that, I would."

"What did you do with it?" Tony asked indifferently.

"I never had it, copper. Leave that lay. I'm the only guy in the world that believes it. It was a little deal that I got suckered on."

"I'll believe it," Tony said.

"They don't kill often. But they can be awful tough."

"Mugs," Tony said with a sudden bitter contempt. "Guys with guns. Just mugs."

Johnny Ralls reached for his glass and drained it empty. The ice cubes tinkled softly as he put it down. He picked his gun up, danced it on his palm, then tucked it, nose down, into an inner breast pocket. He stared at the carpet.

"How come you're telling me this, copper?"

"I thought maybe you'd give her a break."

"And if I wouldn't?"

"I kind of think you will," Tony said.

Johnny Ralls nodded quietly. "Can I get out of here?"

"You could take the service elevator to the garage. You could rent a car. I can give you a card to the garage man."

"You're a funny little guy," Johnny Ralls said.

Tony took out a worn ostrich-skin billfold and scribbled on a printed card. Johnny Ralls read it, and stood holding it, tapping it against a thumbnail.

"I could take her with me," he said, his eyes narrow.

"You could take a ride in a basket too," Tony said. "She's been here five days, I told you. She's been spotted. A guy I know called me up and told me to get her out of here. Told me what it was all about. So I'm getting you out instead."

"They'll love that," Johnny Ralls said. "They'll send you violets."

"I'll weep about it on my day off."

Johnny Ralls turned his hand over and stared at the palm. "I could see her, anyway. Before I blow. Next door to here, you said?"

Tony turned on his heel and started for the door. He said over his shoulder, "Don't waste a lot of time, handsome. I might change my mind."

The man said, almost gently: "You might be spotting me right now, for all I know."

Tony didn't turn his head. "That's a chance you have to take."

He went on to the door and passed out of the room. He shut it carefully, silently, looked once at the door of 14A and got into his dark elevator. He rode it down to the linen-room floor and got out to remove the basket that held the service elevator open at that floor. The door slid quietly shut. He held it so that it made no noise. Down the corridor, light came from the open door of the housekeeper's office. Tony got back into his elevator and went on down to the lobby.

The little clerk was out of sight behind his pebbled-glass screen, auditing accounts. Tony went through the main lobby and turned into the radio room. The radio was on again, soft. She was there, curled on the davenport again. The speaker hummed to her, a vague sound so low that what it said was as wordless as the murmur of trees. She turned her head slowly and smiled at him.

"Finished palming doorknobs? I couldn't sleep worth a nickel. So I came down again. Okey?"

He smiled and nodded. He sat down in a green chair and patted the plump brocade arms of it. "Sure, Miss Cressy."

"Waiting is the hardest kind of work, isn't it? I wish you'd talk to that radio. It sounds like a pretzel being bent."

Tony fiddled with it, got nothing he liked, set it back where it had been.

"Beer-parlor drunks are all the customers now."

She smiled at him again.

"I don't bother you being here, Miss Cressy?"

"I like it. You're a sweet little guy, Tony."

He looked stiffly at the floor and a ripple touched his spine. He waited for it to go away. It went slowly. Then he sat back, relaxed again, his neat fingers clasped on his elk's tooth. He listened. Not to the radio—to far-off, uncertain things, menacing things. And perhaps to just the safe whir of wheels going away into a strange night.

"Nobody's all bad," he said out loud.

The girl looked at him lazily. "I've met two or three I was wrong on, then."

He nodded. "Yeah," he admitted judiciously. "I guess there's some that are."

The girl yawned and her deep violet eyes half closed. She

80

▼

nestled back into the cushions. "Sit there for a while, Tony. Maybe I could nap."

"Sure. Not a thing for me to do. Don't know why they pay me."

She slept quickly and with complete stillness, like a child. Tony hardly breathed for ten minutes. He just watched her, his mouth a little open. There was a quiet fascination in his limpid eyes, as if he was looking at an altar.

Then he stood up with infinite care and padded away under the arch to the entrance lobby and the desk. He stood at the desk listening for a little while. He heard a pen rustling out of sight. He went around the corner to the row of house phones in little glass cubbyholes. He lifted one and asked the night operator for the garage.

It rang three or four times and then a boyish voice answered: "Windermere Hotel. Garage speaking."

"This is Tony Reseck. That guy Watterson I gave a card to. He leave?"

"Sure, Tony. Half an hour almost. Is it your charge?"

"Yeah," Tony said. "My party. Thanks. Be seein' you."

He hung up and scratched his neck. He went back to the desk and slapped a hand on it. The clerk wafted himself around the screen with his greeter's smile in place. It dropped when he saw Tony.

"Can't a guy catch up on his work?" he grumbled.

"What's the professional rate on Fourteen-B?"

The clerk stared morosely. "There's no professional rate in the tower."

"Make one. The fellow left already. Was there only an hour."

"Well, well," the clerk said airily. "So the personality didn't click tonight. We get a skip-out."

"Will five bucks satisfy you?

"Friend of yours?"

"No. Just a drunk with delusions of grandeur and no dough."

"Guess we'll have to let it ride, Tony. How did he get out?"

"I took him down the service elevator. You was asleep. Will five bucks satisfy you?"

"Why?"

The worn ostrich-skin wallet came out and a weedy five slipped across the marble. "All I could shake him for," Tony said loosely.

The clerk took the five and looked puzzled. "You're the boss," he said, and shrugged. The phone shrilled on the desk and he reached for it. He listened and then pushed it toward Tony. "For you."

Tony took the phone and cuddled it close to his chest. He put his mouth close to the transmitter. The voice was strange to him. It had a metallic sound. Its syllables were meticulously anonymous.

"Tony? Tony Reseck?"

"Talking."

"A message from Al. Shoot?"

Tony looked at the clerk. "Be a pal," he said over the mouthpiece. The clerk flicked a narrow smile at him and went away. "Shoot," Tony said into the phone.

"We had a little business with a guy in your place. Picked him up scramming. Al had a hunch you'd run him out. Tailed him and took him to the curb. Not so good. Backfire."

Tony held the phone very tight and his temples chilled with the evaporation of moisture. "Go on," he said. "I guess there's more."

"A little. The guy stopped the big one. Cold. Al—Al said to tell you goodbye."

Tony leaned hard against the desk. His mouth made a sound that was not speech.

"Get it?" The metallic voice sounded impatient, a little bored. "This guy had him a rod. He used it. Al won't be phoning anybody any more."

Tony lurched at the phone, and the base of it shook on the rose marble. His mouth was a hard dry knot.

The voice said: "That's as far as we go, bub. G'night." The phone clicked dryly, like a pebble hitting a wall.

Tony put the phone down in its cradle very carefully, so as not to make any sound. He looked at the clenched palm of his left hand. He took a handkerchief out and rubbed the palm softly and straightened the fingers out with his other hand. Then he wiped his forehead. The clerk came around the screen again and looked at him with glinting eyes.

"I'm off Friday. How about lending me that phone number?"

Tony nodded at the clerk and smiled a minute frail smile. He put his handkerchief away and patted the pocket he had put it in. He turned and walked away from the desk, across the entrance lobby, down the three shallow steps, along the shadowy reaches of the main lobby, and so in through the arch to the radio room once more. He walked softly, like man moving in a room where somebody is very sick. He reached the chair he had sat in before and lowered himself into it inch by inch. The girl slept on, motionless, in that curled-up looseness achieved by some women and all cats. Her breath made no slightest sound against the vague murmur of the radio.

Tony Reseck leaned back in the chair and clasped his hands on his elk's tooth and quietly closed his eyes.

THE KING
IN YELLOW

ONE

George Millar, night auditor at the Carlton Hotel, was a dapper wiry little man, with a soft deep voice like a torch singer's. He kept it low, but his eyes were sharp and angry, as he said into the PBX mouthpiece: "I'm very sorry. It won't happen again. I'll send up at once."

He tore off the headpiece, dropped it on the keys of the switchboard and marched swiftly from behind the pebbled screen and out into the entrance lobby. It was past one and the Carlton was two thirds residential. In the main lobby, down three shallow steps, lamps were dimmed and the night porter had finished tidying up. The place was deserted—a wide space of dim furniture, rich carpet. Faintly in the distance a radio sounded. Millar went down the steps and walked quickly towards the sound, turned through an archway and looked at a man stretched out on a pale green davenport and what looked like all the loose cushions in the hotel. He lay on his side dreamy-eyed and listened to the radio two yards away from him.

Millar barked: "Hey, you! Are you the house dick here or the house cat?"

Steve Grayce turned his head slowly and looked at Millar. He was a long black-haired man, about twenty-eight, with deep-set silent eyes and a rather gentle mouth. He jerked a thumb at the radio and smiled. "King Leopardi, George. Hear that trumpet tone. Smooth as an angel's wing, boy."

"Swell! Go on back upstairs and get him out of the corridor!"

Steve Grayce looked shocked. "What—again? I thought I had those birds put to bed long ago." He swung his feet to the floor and stood up. He was at least a foot taller than Millar.

"Well, Eight-sixteen says no. Eight-sixteen says he's out in the hall with two of his stooges. He's dressed in yellow satin shorts and a trombone and he and his pals are putting on a jam session. And one of those hustlers Quillan registered in Eight-eleven is out there truckin' for them. Now get on to it, Steve—and this time make it stick."

Steve Grayce smiled wryly. He said: "Leopardi doesn't belong here anyway. Can I use chloroform or just my blackjack?"

He stepped long legs over the pale-green carpet, through the arch and across the main lobby to the single elevator that was open and lighted. He slid the doors shut and ran it up to Eight, stopped it roughly and stepped out into the corridor.

The noise hit him like a sudden wind. The walls echoed with it. Half a dozen doors were open and angry guests in night robes stood in them peering.

"It's O.K. folks," Steve Grayce said rapidly. "This is absolutely the last act. Just relax."

He rounded a corner and the hot music almost took him off his feet. Three men were lined up against the wall, near an open door from which light streamed. The middle one, the one with the trombone, was six feet tall, powerful and graceful, with a hairline mustache. His face was flushed and his eyes had an alcoholic glitter. He wore yellow satin shorts with large initials embroidered in black on the left leg—nothing more. His torso was tanned and naked.

The two with him were in pajamas, the usual halfway-good-looking band boys, both drunk, but not staggering drunk. One jittered madly on a clarinet and the other on a tenor saxophone.

Back and forth in front of them, strutting, trucking, preening herself like a magpie, arching her arms and her eyebrows,

bending her fingers back until the carmine nails almost touched
her arms, a metallic blonde swayed and went to town on the
music. Her voice was a throaty screech, without melody, as
false as her eyebrows and as sharp as her nails. She wore high-
heeled slippers and black pajamas with a long purple sash.

Steve Grayce stopped dead and made a sharp downward motion with his hand. "Wrap it up!" he snapped. "Can it. Put it
on ice. Take it away and bury it. The show's out. Scram,
now—scram!"

King Leopardi took the trombone from his lips and bellowed:
"Fanfare to a house dick!"

The three drunks blew a stuttering note that shook the walls.
The girl laughed foolishly and kicked out. Her slipper caught
Steve Grayce in the chest. He picked it out of the air, jumped
towards the girl and took hold of her wrist.

"Tough, eh?" he grinned. "I'll take you first."

"Get him!" Leopardi yelled. "Sock him low! Dance the gum-
heel on his neck!"

Steve swept the girl off her feet, tucked her under his arm
and ran. He carried her as easily as a parcel. She tried to kick
his legs. He laughed and shot a glance through a lighted doorway. A man's brown brogues lay under a bureau. He went on
past that to a second lighted doorway, slammed through and
kicked the door shut, turned far enough to twist the tabbed
key in the lock. Almost at once a fist hit the door. He paid no
attention to it.

He pushed the girl along the short passage past the bathroom,
and let her go. She reeled away from him and put her back to
the bureau, panting, her eyes furious. A lock of damp gold-
dipped hair swung down over one eye. She shook her head
violently and bared her teeth.

"How would you like to get vagged, sister?"

"Go to hell!" she spit out. "The King's a friend of mine, see?
You better keep your paws off me, copper."

"You run the circuit with the boys?"

She spat at him again.

"How'd you know they'd be here?"

Another girl was sprawled across the bed, her head to the wall, tousled black hair over a white face. There was a tear in the leg of her pajamas. She lay limp and groaned.

Steve said harshly: "Oh, oh, the torn-pajama act. It flops here, sister, it flops hard. Now listen, you kids. You can go to bed and stay till morning or you can take the bounce. Make up your minds."

The black-haired girl groaned. The blonde said: "You get out of my room, you damned gum-heel!"

She reached behind her and threw a hand mirror. Steve ducked. The mirror slammed against the wall and fell without breaking. The black-haired girl rolled over on the bed and said wearily: "Oh lay off. I'm sick."

She lay with her eyes closed, the lids fluttering.

The blonde swiveled her hips across the room to a desk by the window, poured herself a full half-glass of Scotch in a water glass and gurgled it down before Steve could get to her. She choked violently, dropped the glass and went down on her hands and knees.

Steve said grimly: "That's the one that kicks you in the face, sister."

The girl crouched, shaking her head. She gagged once, lifted the carmine nails to paw at her mouth. She tried to get up, and her foot skidded out from under her and she fell down on her side and went fast asleep.

Steve sighed, went over and shut the window and fastened it. He rolled the black-haired girl over and straightened her on the bed and got the bedclothes from under her, tucked a pillow under her head. He picked the blonde bodily off the floor and dumped her on the bed and covered both girls to the chin. He opened the transom, switched off the ceiling light and unlocked the door. He relocked it from the outside, with a master key on a chain.

"Hotel business," he said under his breath. "Phooey."

The corridor was empty now. One lighted door still stood open. Its number was 815, two doors from the room the girls were in. Trombone music came from it softly—but not softly enough for 1:25 A.M.

Steve Grayce turned into the room, crowded the door shut with his shoulder and went along past the bathroom. King Leopardi was alone in the room.

The bandleader was sprawled out in an easy chair, with a tall misted glass at his elbow. He swung the trombone in a tight circle as he played it and the lights danced in the horn.

Steve lit a cigarette, blew a plume of smoke and stared through it at Leopardi with a queer, half-admiring, half-contemptuous expression.

He said softly: "Lights out, yellow-pants. You play a sweet trumpet and your trombone don't hurt either. But we can't use it here. I already told you that once. Lay off. Put that thing away."

Leopardi smiled nastily and blew a stuttering raspberry that sounded like a devil laughing.

"Says you," he sneered. "Leopardi does what he likes, where he likes, when he likes. Nobody's stopped him yet, gum-shoe. Take the air."

Steve hunched his shoulders and went close to the tall dark man. He said patiently: "Put that bazooka down, big-stuff. People are trying to sleep. They're funny that way. You're a great guy on a band shell. Everywhere else you're just a guy with a lot of jack and a personal reputation that stinks from here to Miami and back. I've got a job to do and I'm doing it. Blow that thing again and I'll wrap it around your neck."

Leopardi lowered the trombone and took a long drink from the glass at his elbow. His eyes glinted nastily. He lifted the trombone to his lips again, filled his lungs with air and blew a blast that rocked the walls. Then he stood up very suddenly and smoothly and smashed the instrument down on Steve's head.

"I never did like house peepers," he sneered. "They smell like public toilets."

Steve took a short step back and shook his head. He leered, slid forward on one foot and smacked Leopardi open-handed. The blow looked light, but Leopardi reeled all the way across the room and sprawled at the foot of the bed, sitting on the floor, his right arm draped in an open suitcase.

For a moment neither man moved. Then Steve kicked the trombone away from him and squashed his cigarette in a glass tray. His black eyes were empty but his mouth grinned whitely.

"If you want trouble," he said, "I come from where they make it."

Leopardi smiled, thinly, tautly, and his right hand came up out of the suitcase with a gun in it. His thumb snicked the safety catch. He held the gun steady, pointing.

"Make some with this," he said, and fired.

The bitter roar of the gun seemed a tremendous sound in the closed room. The bureau mirror splintered and glass flew. A sliver cut Steve's cheek like a razor blade. Blood oozed in a small narrow line on his skin.

He left his feet in a dive. His right shoulder crushed against Leopardi's bare chest and his left hand brushed the gun away from him, under the bed. He rolled swiftly to his right and came up on his knees spinning.

He said thickly, harshly: "You picked the wrong gee, brother."

He swarmed on Leopardi and dragged him to his feet by his hair, by main strength. Leopardi yelled and hit him twice on the jaw and Steve grinned and kept his left hand twisted in the bandleader's long sleek black hair. He turned his hand and the head twisted with it and Leopardi's third punch landed on Steve's shoulder. Steve took hold of the wrist behind the punch and twisted that and the bandleader went down on his knees yowling. Steve lifted him by the hair again, let go of his wrist and punched him three times in the stomach, short terrific jabs. He let go of the hair then as he sank the fourth punch almost to his wrist.

Leopardi sagged blindly to his knees and vomited.

Steve stepped away from him and went into the bathroom and got a towel off the rack. He threw it at Leopardi, jerked the open suitcase onto the bed and started throwing things into it.

Leopardi wiped his face and got to his feet still gagging. He swayed, braced himself on the end of the bureau. He was white as a sheet.

Steve Grayce said: "Get dressed, Leopardi. Or go out the way you are. It's all one to me.

Leopardi stumbled into the bathroom, pawing the wall like a blind man.

TWO

Millar stood very still behind the desk as the elevator opened. His face was white and scared and his cropped black mustache was a smudge across his upper lip. Leopardi came out of the elevator first, a muffler around his neck, a lightweight coat tossed over his arm, a hat tilted on his head. He walked stiffly, bent forward a little, his eyes vacant. His face had a greenish pallor.

Steve Grayce stepped out behind him carrying a suitcase, and Carl, the night porter, came last with two more suitcases and two instrument cases in black leather. Steve marched over to the desk and said harshly: "Mr. Leopardi's bill—if any. He's checking out."

Millar goggled at him across the marble desk. "I—I don't think, Steve—"

"O.K. I thought not."

Leopardi smiled very thinly and unpleasantly and walked out through the brass-edged swing doors the porter held open for him. There were two nighthawk cabs in the line. One of them came to life and pulled up to the canopy and the porter loaded Leopardi's stuff into it. Leopardi got into the cab and leaned forward to put his head to the open window. He said slowly and thickly: "I'm sorry for you, gum-heel. I mean sorry."

Steve Grayce stepped back and looked at him woodenly. The cab moved off down the street, rounded a corner and was gone. Steve turned on his heel, took a quarter from his pocket and tossed it up in the air. He slapped it into the night porter's hand.

"From the King," he said. "Keep it to show your grand-children."

He went back into the hotel, got into the elevator without looking at Millar, shot it up to Eight again and went along the corridor, master-keyed his way into Leopardi's room. He re-locked it from the inside, pulled the bed out from the wall and went in behind it. He got a .32 automatic off the carpet, put it in his pocket and prowled the floor with his eyes looking for the ejected shell. He found it against the wastebasket, reached to pick it up, and stayed bent over, staring into the basket. His mouth tightened. He picked up the shell and dropped it absently into his pocket, then reached a questing finger into the basket and lifted out a torn scrap of paper on which a piece of news-print had been pasted. Then he picked up the basket, pushed the bed back against the wall and dumped the contents of the basket out on it.

From the trash of torn papers and matches he separated a number of pieces with newsprint pasted to them. He went over to the desk with them and sat down. A few minutes later he had the torn scraps put together like a jigsaw puzzle and could read the message that had been made by cutting words and letters from magazines and pasting them on a sheet.

TEN GRand BY TH U RS DAY NI GHT,
LEO PAR DI. DAY AFTER YOU OPEN AT
T HE CL U B SHAL OTTE. OR EL SE—CUR-
TAINS. FROM HER BROTHER.

Steve Grayce said: "Huh." He scooped the torn pieces into a hotel envelope, put that in his inside breast pocket and lit a cigarette. "The guy had guts," he said. "I'll grant him that—and his trumpet."

He locked the room, listened a moment in the now silent corridor, then went along to the room occupied by the two girls. He knocked softly and put his ear to the panel. A chair squeaked and feet came towards the door.

"What is it?" The girl's voice was cool, wide awake. It was not the blonde's voice.

"The house man. Can I speak to you a minute?"

"You're speaking to me."

"Without the door between, lady."

"You've got the passkey. Help yourself." The steps went away. He unlocked the door with his master key, stepped quietly inside, and shut it. There was a dim light in a lamp with a shirred shade on the desk. On the bed the blonde snored heavily, one hand clutched in her briiliant metallic hair. The black-haired girl sat in the chair by the window, her legs crossed at right angles like a man's and stared at Steve emptily.

He went close to her and pointed to the long tear in her pajama leg. He said softly: "You're not sick. You were not drunk. That tear was done a long time ago. What's the racket? A shakedown on the King?"

The girl stared at him coolly, puffed at a cigarette and said nothing.

"He checked out," Steve said. "Nothing doing in that direction now, sister." He watched her like a hawk, his black eyes hard and steady on her face.

"Aw, you house dicks make me sick!" the girl said with sudden anger. She surged to her feet and went past him into the bathroom, shut and locked the door.

Steve shrugged and felt the pulse of the girl asleep in the bed—a thumpy, draggy pulse, a liquor pulse.

"Poor damn hustlers," he said under his breath.

He looked at a large purple bag that lay on the bureau, lifted it idly and let it fall. His face stiffened again. The bag made a heavy sound on the glass top, as if there were a lump of lead inside it. He snapped it open quickly and plunged a hand in. His fingers touched the cold metal of a gun. He opened the bag wide and stared down into it at a small .25 automatic. A scrap of white paper caught his eye. He fished it out and held it to the light—a rent receipt with a name and address. He stuffed it into his pocket, closed the bag and was standing by the window when the girl came out of the bathroom.

"Hell, are you stlll haunting me?" she snapped. "You know what happens to hotel dicks that master-key their way into ladies' bedrooms at night?"

Steve said loosely: "Yeah. They get in trouble. They might even get shot at."

The girl's face became set, but her eyes crawled sideways and looked at the purple bag. Steve looked at her. "Know Leopardi in Frisco?" he asked. "He hasn't played here in two years. Then he was just a trumpet player in Vane Utigore's band— a cheap outfit."

The girl curled her lip, went past him and sat down by the window again. Her face was white, stiff. She said dully: "Blossom did. That's Blossom on the bed."

"Know he was coming to this hotel tonight?"

"What makes it your business?"

"I can't figure him coming here at all," Steve said. "This is a quiet place. So I can't figure anybody coming here to put the bite on him."

"Go somewhere else and figure. I need sleep."

Steve said: "Good night, sweetheart—and keep your door locked."

▼

A thin man with thin blond hair and thin face was standing by the desk, tapping on the marble with thin fingers. Millar was still behind the desk and he still looked white and scared. The thin man wore a dark gray suit with a scarf inside the collar of the coat. He had a look of having just got up. He turned sea-green eyes slowly on Steve as he got out of the elevator, waited for him to come up to the desk and throw a tabbed key on it.

Steve said: "Leopardi's key, George. There's a busted mirror in his room and the carpet has his dinner on it—mostly Scotch." He turned to the thin man.

"You want to see me, Mr. Peters?"

"What happened, Grayce?" The thin man had a tight voice that expected to be lied to.

"Leopardi and two of his boys were on Eight, the rest of the gang on Five. The bunch on Five went to bed. A couple of obvious hustlers managed to get themselves registered just two rooms from Leopardi. They managed to contact him and everybody was having a lot of nice noisy fun out in the hall. I could only stop it by getting a little tough."

"There's blood on your cheek," Peters said coldly. "Wipe it off."

Steve scratched at his cheek with a handkerchief. The thin thread of blood had dried. "I got the girls tucked away in their room," he said. "The two stooges took the hint and holed up, but Leopardi still thought the guests wanted to hear trombone music. I threatened to wrap it around his neck and he beaned me with it. I slapped him open-handed and he pulled a gun and took a shot at me. Here's the gun."

He took the .32 automatic out of his pocket and laid it on the desk. He put the used shell beside it. "So I beat some sense into him and threw him out," he added.

Peters tapped on the marble. "Your usual tact seems to have been well in evidence."

Steve stared at him. "He shot at me," he repeated quietly. "With a gun. This gun. I'm tender to bullets. He missed, but suppose he hadn't? I like my stomach the way it is, with just one way in and one way out."

Peters narrowed his tawny eyebrows. He said very politely: "We have you down on the payroll here as a night clerk, because we don't like the name house detective. But neither night clerks nor house detectives put guests out of the hotel without consulting me. Not ever, Mr. Grayce."

Steve said: "The guy shot at me, pal. With a gun. Catch on? I don't have to take that without a kickback, do I?" His face was a little white.

Peters said: "Another point for your consideration. The controlling interest in this hotel is owned by Mr. Halsey G. Walters. Mr. Walters also owns the Club Shalotte, where King

Leopardi is opening on Wednesday night. And that, Mr. Grayce, is why Leopardi was good enough to give us his business. Can you think of anything else I should like to say to you?"

"Yeah. I'm canned," Steve said mirthlessly.

"Very correct, Mr. Grayce. Good-night, Mr. Grayce."

The thin blond man moved to the elevator and the night porter took him up.

Steve looked at Millar.

"Jumbo Walters, huh?" he said softly. "A tough, smart guy. Much too smart to think this dump and the Club Shalotte belong to the same sort of customers. Did Peters write Leopardi to come here?"

"I guess he did, Steve." Millar's voice was low and gloomy.

"Then why wasn't he put in a tower suite with a private balcony to dance on, at twenty-eight bucks a day? Why was he put on a medium-priced transient floor? And why did Quillan let those girls get so close to him?"

Millar pulled at his black mustache. "Tight with money—as well as with Scotch, I suppose. As to the girls, I don't know."

Steve slapped the counter open-handed. "Well, I'm canned, for not letting a drunken heel make a parlor house and a shooting gallery out of the eighth floor. Nuts! Well, I'll miss the joint at that."

"I'll miss you too, Steve," Millar said gently. "But not for a week. I take a week off starting tomorrow. My brother has a cabin at Crestline."

"Didn't know you had a brother," Steve said absently. He opened and closed his fist on the marble desk top.

"He doesn't come into town much. A big guy. Used to be a fighter."

Steve nodded and straightened from the counter. "Well, I might as well finish out the night," he said. "On my back. Put this gun away somewhere, George."

He grinned coldly and walked away, down the steps into the dim main lobby and across to the room where the radio was. He punched the pillows into shape on the pale green davenport, then suddenly reached into his pocket and took out the scrap of white paper he had lifted from the black-haired girl's purple handbag. It was a receipt for a week's rent, to a Miss Marilyn Delorme, Apt. 211, Ridgeland Apartments, 118 Court Street.

He tucked it into his wallet and stood staring at the silent radio. "Steve, I think you got another job," he said under his breath. "Something about this set-up smells."

He slipped into a closetlike phone both in the corner of the room, dropped a nickel and dialed an all-night radio station. He had to dial four times before he got a clear line to the Owl Program announcer.

"How's to play King Leopardi's record of 'Solitude' again?" he asked him.

"Got a lot of requests piled up. Played it twice already. Who's calling?"

"Steve Grayce, night man at the Carlton Hotel."

"Oh, a sober guy on his job. For you, pal, anything."

Steve went back to the davenport, snapped the radio on and lay down on his back, with his hands clasped behind his head.

Ten minutes later the high, piercingly sweet trumpet notes of King Leopardi came softly from the radio, muted almost to a whisper, and sustaining E above high C for an almost incredible period of time.

"Shucks," Steve grumbled, when the record ended. "A guy that can play like that—maybe I was too tough with him."

THREE

Court Street was old town, wop town, crook town, arty town. It lay across the top of Bunker Hill and you could find anything there from down-at-heels ex-Greenwich-villagers to crooks on the lam, from ladies of anybody's evening to County Relief clients brawling with haggard landladies in grand old houses with scrolled porches, parquetry floors, and immense sweeping banisters of white oak, mahogany and Circassian walnut.

It had been a nice place once, had Bunker Hill, and from the days of its niceness there still remained the funny little funicular railway, called the Angel's Flight, which crawled up and down a yellow clay bank from Hill Street. It was afternoon when Steve Grayce got off the car at the top, its only passenger. He walked along in the sun, a tall, wide-shouldered, rangy-looking man in a well-cut blue suit.

He turned west at Court and began to read the numbers. The one he wanted was two from the corner, across the street from a red brick funeral parlor with a sign in gold over it: Paolo Perrugini Funeral Home. A swarthy iron-gray Italian in a cut-away coat stood in front of the curtained door of the red brick building, smoking a cigar and waiting for somebody to die.

One-eighteen was a three-storied frame apartment house. It had a glass door, well masked by a dirty net curtain, a hall runner eighteen inches wide, dim doors with numbers painted on them with dim-paint, a staircase halfway back. Brass stair rods glittered in the dimness of the hallway.

Steve Grayce went up the stairs and prowled back to the front. Apartment 211, Miss Marilyn Delorme, was on the right, a front apartment. He tapped lightly on the wood, waited, tapped again. Nothing moved beyond the silent door, or in the hallway. Behind another door across the hall somebody coughed and kept on coughing.

Standing there in the half-light Steve Grayce wondered why he had come. Miss Delorme had carried a gun. Leopardi had received some kind of a threat letter and torn it up and thrown it away. Miss Delorme had checked out of the Carlton about an hour after Steve told her Leopardi was gone. Even at that—

He took out a leather keyholder and studied the lock of the door. It looked as if it would listen to reason. He tried a pick on it, snicked the bolt back and stepped softly into the room. He shut the door, but the pick wouldn't lock it.

The room was dim with drawn shades across two front windows. The air smelled of face powder. There was light-painted furniture, a pull-down double bed which was pulled down but had been made up. There was a magazine on it, a glass tray full of cigarette butts, a pint bottle half full of whiskey, and a glass on a chair beside the bed. Two pillows had been used for a back rest and were still crushed in the middle.

On the dresser there was a composition toilet set, neither cheap nor expensive, a comb with black hair in it, a tray of manicuring stuff, plenty of spilled powder—in the bathroom, nothing. In a closet behind the bed a lot of clothes and two suitcases. The shoes were all one size.

Steve stood beside the bed and pinched his chin. "Blossom, the spitting blonde, doesn't live here," he said under his breath. "Just Marilyn the torn-pants brunette."

He went back to the dresser and pulled drawers out. In the bottom drawer, under the piece of wall paper that lined it, he found a box of .25 copper-nickel automatic shells. He poked at the butts in the ash tray. All had lipstick on them. He pinched his chin again, then feathered the air with the palm of his hand, like an oarsman with a scull.

"Bunk," he said softly. "Wasting your time, Stevie."

He walked over to the door and reached for the knob, then turned back to the bed and lifted it by the footrail.

Miss Marllyn Delorme was in.

She lay on her side on the floor under the bed, long legs scissored out as if in running. One mule was on, one off. Garters and skin showed at the tops of her stockings, and a blue rose on something pink. She wore a square-necked, short-sleeved dress that was not too clean. Her neck above the dress was blotched with purple bruises.

Her face was a dark plum color, her eyes had the faint stale glitter of death, and her mouth was open so far that it foreshortened her face. She was colder than ice, and still quite limp. She had been dead two or three hours at least, six hours at most.

The purple bag was beside her, gaping like her mouth. Steve didn't touch any of the stuff that had been emptied out on the floor. There was no gun and there were no papers.

He let the bed down over her again, then made the rounds of the apartment, wiping everything he had touched and a lot of things he couldn't remember whether he had touched or not.

He listened at the door and stepped out. The hall was still empty. The man behind the opposite door still coughed. Steve went down the stairs, looked at the mailboxes and went back along the lower hall to a door.

Behind this door a chair creaked monotonously. He knocked and a woman's sharp voice called out. Steve opened the door with his handkerchief and stepped in.

In the middle of the room a woman rocked in an old Boston rocker, her body in the slack boneless attitude of exhaustion. She had a mud-colored face, stringy hair, gray cotton stockings—everything a Bunker Hill landlady should have. She looked at Steve with the interested eye of a dead goldfish.

"Are you the manager?"

The woman stopped rocking, screamed, "Hi, Jake! Company!" at the top of her voice, and started rocking again.

An icebox door thudded shut behind a partly open inner door and a very big man came into the room carrying a can of beer. He had a doughy mooncalf face, a tuft of fuzz on top of an otherwise bald head, a thick brutal neck and chin, and brown pig eyes about as expressionless as the woman's. He needed a shave—had needed one the day before—and his collarless shirt gaped over a big hard hairy chest. He wore scarlet suspenders with large gilt buckles on them.

He held the can of beer out to the woman. She clawed it out of his hand and said bitterly: "I'm so tired I ain't got no sense."

The man said: "Yah. You ain't done the halls so good at that."

The woman snarled: "I done 'em as good as I aim to." She sucked the beer thirstily.

Steve looked at the man and said: "Manager?"

"Yah. 'S me. Jake Stoyanoff. Two hun'erd eighty-six stripped, and still plenty tough."

Steve said: "Who lives in Two-eleven?"

The big man leaned forward a little from the waist and

snapped his suspenders. Nothing changed in his eyes. The skin along his big jaw may have tightened a little. "A dame," he said.

"Alone?"

"Go on—ask me," the big man said. He stuck his hand out and lifted a cigar off the edge of a stained-wood table. The cigar was burning unevenly and it smelled as if somebody had set fire to the doormat. He pushed it into his mouth with a hard, thrusting motion, as if he expected his mouth wouldn't want it to go in.

"I'm asking you," Steve said.

"Ask me out in the kitchen," the big man drawled.

He turned and held the door open. Steve went past him.

The big man kicked the door shut against the squeak of the rocking chair, opened up the icebox and got out two cans of beer. He opened them and handed one to Steve.

"Dick?"

Steve drank some of the beer, put the can down on the sink, got a brand-new card out of his wallet—a business card printed that morning. He handed it to the man.

The man read it, put it down on the sink, picked it up and read it again. "One of them guys," he growled over his beer. "What's she pulled this time?"

Steve shrugged and said: "I guess it's the usual. The torn-pajama act. Only there's a kickback this time."

"How come? You handling it, huh? Must be a nice cozy one."

Steve nodded. The big man blew smoke from his mouth. "Go ahead and handle it," he said.

"You don't mind a pinch here?"

The big man laughed heartily. "Nuts to you, brother," he said pleasantly enough. "You're a private dick. So it's a hush. O.K. Go out and hush it. And if it *was* a pinch—that bothers me like a quart of milk. Go into your act. Take all the room you want. Cops don't bother Jake Stoyanoff."

Steve stared at the man. He didn't say anything. The big man talked it up some more, seemed to get more interested.

"Besides," he went on, making motions with the cigar, "I'm softhearted. I never turn up a dame. I never put a frill in the middle." He finished his beer and threw the can in a basket under the sink, and pushed his hand out in front of him, revolving the large thumb slowly against the next two fingers. "Unless there's some of that," he added.

Steve said softly: "You've got big hands. You could have done it."

"Huh?" His small brown leathery eyes got silent and stared.

Steve said: "Yeah. You might be clean. But with those hands the cops'd go round and round with you just the same."

The big man moved a little to his left, away from the sink. He let his right hand hang down at his side, loosely. His mouth got so tight that the cigar almost touched his nose.

"What's the beef, huh?" he barked. "What you shovin' at me, guy? What—"

"Cut it," Steve drawled. "She's been croaked. Strangled. Upstairs, on the floor under her bed. About midmorning, I'd say. Big hands did it—hands like yours."

The big man did a nice job of getting the gun off his hip. It arrived so suddenly that it seemed to have grown in his hand and been there all the time.

Steve frowned at the gun and didn't move. The big man looked him over. "You're tough," he said. "I been in the ring long enough to size up a guy's meat. You're plenty hard, boy. But you ain't as hard as lead. Talk it up fast."

"I knocked at her door. No answer. The lock was a pushover. I went in. I almost missed her because the bed was pulled down and she had been sitting on it, reading a magazine. There was no sign of struggle. I lifted the bed just before I left—and there she was. Very dead, Mr. Stoyanoff. Put the gat away. Cops don't bother you, you said a minute ago."

The big man whispered: "Yes and no. They don't make me happy neither. I get a bump once'n a while. Mostly a Dutch. You said something about my hands, mister."

Steve shook his head. "That was a gag," he said. "Her neck has nail marks. You bite your nails down close. You're clean."

The big man didn't look at his fingers. He was very pale. There was sweat on his lower lips, in the black stubble of his beard. He was still leaning forward, still motionless, when there was a knocking beyond the kitchen door, the door from the living room to the hallway. The creaking chair stopped and the woman's sharp voice screamed: "Hi, Jake! Company!"

The big man cocked his head. "That old slut wouldn't climb off'n her fanny if the house caught fire," he said thickly.

He stepped to the door and slipped through it, locking it behind him.

Steve ranged the kitchen swiftly with his eyes. There was a small high window beyond the sink, a trap low down for a garbage pail and parcels, but no other door. He reached for his card Stoyanoff had left lying on the drainboard and slipped it back into his pocket. Then he took a short-barreled Detective Special out of his left breast pocket where he wore it nose down, as in a holster.

He had got that far when the shots roared beyond the wall —muffled a little, but still loud—four of them blended in a blast of sound.

Steve stepped back and hit the kitchen door with his leg out straight. It held and jarred him to the top of his head and in his hip joint. He swore, took the whole width of the kitchen and slammed into it with his left shoulder. It gave this time. He pitched into the living room. The mud-faced woman sat leaning forward in her rocker, her head to one side and a lock of mousy hair smeared down over her bony forehead.

"Backfire, huh?" she said stupidly. "Sounded kinda close. Musta been in the alley."

Steve jumped across the room, yanked the outer door open and plunged out into the hall.

The big man was still on his feet, a dozen feet down the hallway, in the direction of a screen door that opened flush on an alley. He was clawing at the wall. His gun lay at his feet. His left knee buckled and he went down on it.

A door was flung open and a hard-looking woman peered

out, and instantly slammed her door shut again. A radio suddenly gained in volume beyond her door.

The big man got up off his left knee and the leg shook violently inside his trousers. He went down on both knees and got the gun into his hand and began to crawl towards the screen door. Then, suddenly he went down flat on his face and tried to crawl that way, grinding his face into the narrow hall runner.

Then he stopped crawling and stopped moving altogether. His body went limp and the hand holding the gun opened and the gun rolled out of it.

Steve hit the screen door and was out in the alley. A gray sedan was speeding towards the far end of it. He stopped, steadied himself and brought his gun up level, and the sedan whisked out of sight around the corner.

A man boiled out of another apartment house across the alley. Steve ran on, gesticulating back at him and pointing ahead. As he ran he slipped the gun back into his pocket. When he reached the end of the alley, the gray sedan was out of sight. Steve skidded around the wall onto the sidewalk, slowed to a walk and then stopped.

Half a block down a man finished parking a car, got out and went across the sidewalk to a lunchroom. Steve watched him go in, then straightened his hat and walked along the wall to the lunchroom.

He went in, sat at the counter and ordered coffee. In a little while there were sirens.

Steve drank his coffee, asked for another cup and drank that. He lit a cigarette and walked down the long hill to Fifth, across to Hill, back to the foot of the Angel's Flight, and got his convertible out of a parking lot.

He drove out west, beyond Vermont, to the small hotel where he had taken a room that morning.

FOUR

Bill Dockery, floor manager of the Club Shalotte, teetered on his heels and yawned in the unlighted entrance to the dining room. It was a dead hour for business, late cocktail time, too early for dinner, and much too early for the real business of the club, which was high-class gambling.

Dockery was a handsome mug in a midnight-blue dinner jacket and a maroon carnation. He had a two-inch forehead under black lacquer hair, good features a little on the heavy side, alert brown eyes and very long curly eyelashes which he liked to let down over his eyes, to fool troublesome drunks into taking a swing at him.

The entrance door of the foyer was opened by the uniformed dooman and Steve Grayce came in.

Dockery said, "Ho, hum," tapped his teeth and leaned his weight forward. He walked across the lobby slowly to meet the guest. Steve stood just inside the doors and ranged his eyes over the high foyer walled with milky glass, lighted softly from behind. Molded in the glass were etchings of sailing ships, beasts of the jungle, Siamese pagodas, temples of Yucatan. The doors were square frames of chromium, like photo frames. The Club Shalotte had all the class there was, and the mutter of voices from the bar lounge on the left was not noisy. The faint Spanish music behind the voices was delicate as a carved fan.

Dockery came up and leaned his sleek head forward an inch. "May I help you?"

"King Leopardi around?"

Dockery leaned back again. He looked less interested. "The bandleader? He opens tomorrow night."

"I thought he might be around—rehearsing or something."

"Friend of his?"

"I know him. I'm not job-hunting, and I'm not a song plugger if that's what you mean."

Dockery teetered on his heels. He was tone-deaf and Leopardi meant no more to him than a bag of peanuts. He half smiled. "He was in the bar lounge a while ago." He pointed with his square rock-like chin. Steve Grayce went into the bar lounge.

It was about a third full, warm and comfortable and not too dark nor too light. The little Spanish orchestra was in an archway, playing with muted strings small seductive melodies that were more like memories than sounds. There was no dance floor. There was a long bar with comfortable seats, and there were small round composition-top tables, not too close together. A wall seat ran around three sides of the room. Waiters flitted among the tables like moths.

Steve Grayce saw Leopardi in the far corner, with a girl. There was an empty table on each side of him. The girl was a knockout.

She looked tall and her hair was the color of a brush fire seen through a dust cloud. On it, at the ultimate rakish angle, she wore a black velvet double-pointed beret with two artificial butterflies made of polka-dotted feathers and fastened on with tall silver pins. Her dress was burgundy-red wool and the blue fox draped over one shoulder was at least two feet wide. Her eyes were large, smoke-blue, and looked bored. She slowly turned a small glass on the table top with a gloved left hand.

Leopardi faced her, leaning forward, talking. His shoulders looked very big in a shaggy, cream-colored sports coat. Above the neck of it his hair made a point on his brown neck. He laughed across the table as Steve came up and his laugh had a confident, sneering sound.

Steve stopped, then moved behind the next table. The movement caught Leopardi's eye. His head turned, he looked annoyed, and then his eyes got very wide and brilliant and his whole body turned slowly, like a mechanical toy.

Leopardi put both his rather small well-shaped hands down on the table, on either side of a highball glass. He smiled. Then he pushed his chair back and stood up. He put one finger up and touched his hairline mustache, with theatrical delicacy. Then he said drawlingly, but distinctly: "You son of a bitch!"

A man at a nearby table turned his head and scowled. A waiter who had started to come over stopped in his tracks, then faded back among the tables. The girl looked at Steve Grayce and then leaned back against the cushions of the wall seat and moistened the end of one bare finger on her right hand and smoothed a chestnut eyebrow.

Steve stood quite still. There was a sudden high flush on his cheekbones. He said softly: "You left something at the hotel last night. I think you ought to do something about it. Here."

He reached a folded paper out of his pocket and held it out. Leopardi took it, still smiling, opened it and read it. It was a sheet of yellow paper with torn pieces of white paper pasted on it. Leopardi crumpled the sheet and let it drop at his feet.

He took a smooth step towards Steve and repeated more loudly: "You son of a bitch!"

The man who had first looked around stood up sharply and turned. He said clearly: "I don't like that sort of language in front of my wife."

Without even looking at the man Leopardi said: "To hell with you and your wife."

The man's face got a dusky red. The woman with him stood up and grabbed a bag and a coat and walked away. After a moment's indecision the man followed her. Everybody in the place was staring now. The waiter who had faded back among the tables went through the doorway into the entrance foyer, walking very quickly.

Leopardi took another, longer step and slammed Steve Grayce on the jaw. Steve rolled with the punch and stepped back and put his hand down on another table and upset a glass. He turned to apologize to the couple at the table. Leopardi jumped forward very fast and hit him behind the ear.

Dockery came through the doorway, split two waiters like a banana skin and started down the room showing all his teeth.

Steve gagged a little and ducked away. He turned and said

thickly: "Wait a minute, you fool—that isn't all of it—there's——"

Leopardi closed in fast and smashed him full on the mouth. Blood oozed from Steve's lip and crawled down the line at the corner of his mouth and glistened on his chin. The girl with the red hair reached for her bag, white-faced with anger, and started to get up from behind her table.

Leopardi turned abruptly on his heel and walked away. Dockery put out a hand to stop him. Leopardi brushed it aside and went on, went out of the lounge.

The tall red-haired girl put her bag down on the table again and dropped her handkerchief on the floor. She looked at Steve quietly, spoke quietly. "Wipe the blood off your chin before it drips on your shirt." She had a soft, husky voice with a trill in it.

Dockery came up harsh-faced, took Steve by the arm and put weight on the arm. "All right, you! Let's go!"

Steve stood quite still, his feet planted, staring at the girl. He dabbed at his mouth with a handkerchief. He half smiled. Dockery couldn't move him an inch. Dockery dropped his hand, signaled two waiters and they jumped behind Steve, but didn't touch him.

Steve felt his lip carefully and looked at the blood on his handkerchief. He turned to the people at the table behind him and said: "I'm terribly sorry. I lost my balance."

The girl whose drink he had spilled was mopping her dress with a small fringed napkin. She smiled up at him and said: "It wasn't your fault."

The two waiters suddenly grabbed Steve's arms from behind. Dockery shook his head and they let go again. Dockery said tightly: "You hit him?"

"No."

"You say anything to make him hit you?"

"No."

The girl at the corner table bent down to get her fallen handkerchief. It took her quite a time. She finally got it and slid into the corner behind the table again. She spoke coldly.

"Quite right, Bill. It was just some more of the King's sweet way with his public."

Dockery said "Huh?" and swiveled his head on his thick hard neck. Then he grinned and looked back at Steve.

Steve said grimly: "He gave me three good punches, one from behind, without a return. You look pretty hard. See can you do it."

Dockery measured him with his eyes. He said evenly: "You win. I couldn't . . . Beat it!" he added sharply to the waiters. They went away. Dockery sniffed his carnation, and said quietly: "We don't go for brawls in here." He smiled at the girl again and went away, saying a word here and there at the tables. He went out through the foyer doors.

Steve tapped his lip, put his handkerchief in his pocket and stood searching the floor with his eyes.

The red-haired girl said calmly: "I think I have what you want—in my handkerchief. Won't you sit down?"

Her voice had a remembered quality, as if he had heard it before.

He sat down opposite her, in the chair where Leopardi had been sitting.

The red-haired girl said: "The drink's on me. I was with him."

Steve said, "Coke with a dash of bitters," to the waiter.

The waiter said: "Madame?"

"Brandy and soda. Light on the brandy, please." The waiter bowed and drifted away. The girl said amusedly: "Coke with a dash of bitters. That's what I love about Hollywood. You meet so many neurotics."

Steve stared into her eyes and said softly: "I'm an occasional drinker, the kind of guy who goes out for a beer and wakes up in Singapore with a full beard."

"I don't believe a word of it. Have you known the King long?"

"I met him last night. I didn't get along with him."

"I sort of noticed that." She laughed. She had a rich low laugh, too.

"Give me that paper, lady."

"Oh, one of these impatient men. Plenty of time." The handkerchief with the crumpled yellow sheet inside it was clasped tightly in her gloved hand. Her middle right finger played with an eyebrow. "You're not in pictures, are you?"

"Hell, no."

"Same here. Me, I'm too tall. The beautiful men have to wear stilts in order to clasp me to their bosoms."

The waiter set the drinks down in front of them, made a grace note in the air with his napkin and went away.

Steve said quietly, stubbornly: "Give me that paper, lady."

"I don't like that 'lady' stuff. It sounds like cop to me."

"I don't know your name."

"I don't know yours. Where did you meet Leopardi?"

Steve sighed. The music from the little Spanish orchestra had a melancholy minor sound now and the muffled clicking of gourds dominated it.

Steve listened to it with his head on one side. He said: "The E string is a half-tone flat. Rather cute effect."

The girl stared at him with new interest. "I'd never have noticed that," she said. "And I'm supposed to be a pretty good singer. But you haven't answered my question."

He said slowly: "Last night I was house dick at the Carlton Hotel. They called me night clerk, but house dick was what I was. Leopardi stayed there and cut up too rough. I threw him out and got canned."

The girl said: "Ah. I begin to get the idea. He was being the King and you were being—if I might guess—a pretty tough order of house detective."

"Something like that. Now will you please—"

"You still haven't told me your name."

He reached for his wallet, took one of the brand-new cards out of it and passed it across the table. He sipped his drink while she read it.

"A nice name," she said slowly. "But not a very good address. And *Private investigator* is bad. It should have been *Investigations*, very small, in the lower left-hand corner."

"They'll be small enough," Steve grinned. "Now will you please—"

She reached suddenly across the table and dropped the crumpled ball of paper in his hand.

"Of course I haven't read it—and of course I'd like to. You do give me that much credit, I hope"—she looked at the card again, and added—"Steve. Yes, and your office should be in a Georgian or very modernistic building in the Sunset Eighties. Suite Something-or-other. And your clothes should be very jazzy. Very jazzy indeed, Steve. To be inconspicuous in this town is to be a busted flush."

He grinned at her. His deep-set black eyes had lights in them. She put the card away in her bag, gave her fur piece a yank, and drank about half of her drink. "I have to go." She signaled the waiter and paid the check. The waiter went away and she stood up.

Steve said sharply: "Sit down."

She stared at him wonderingly. Then she sat down again and leaned against the wall, still staring at him. Steve leaned across the table, asked "How well do *you* know Leopardi?"

"Off and on for years. If it's any of your business. Don't go masterful on me, for God's sake. I loathe masterful men. I once sang for him, but not for long. You can't just sing for Leopardi—if you get what I mean."

"You were having a drink with him."

She nodded slightly and shrugged. "He opens here tomorrow night. He was trying to talk me into singing for him again. I said no, but I may have to, for a week or two anyway. The man who owns the Club Shalotte also owns my contract—and the radio station where I work a good deal."

"Jumbo Walters," Steve said. "They say he's tough but square. I never met him, but I'd like to. After all I've got a living to get. Here."

He reached back across the table and dropped the crumpled paper. "The name was—"

"Dolores Chiozza."

Steve repeated it lingeringly. "I like it. I like your singing

110
▼

too. I've heard a lot of it. You don't oversell a song, like most of these high-money torchers." His eyes glistened.

The girl spread the paper on the table and read it slowly, without expression. Then she said quietly: "Who tore it up?"

"Leopardi, I guess. The pieces were in his wastebasket last night. I put them together, after he was gone. The guy has guts—or else he gets these things so often they don't register any more."

"Or else he thought it was a gag." She looked across the table levelly, then folded the paper and handed it back.

"Maybe. But if he's the kind of guy I hear he is—one of them is going to be on the level and the guy behind it is going to do more than just shake him down."

Dolores Chiozza said: "He's the kind of guy you hear he is."

"It wouldn't be hard for a woman to get to him then—would it—a woman with a gun?"

She went on staring at him. "No. And everybody would give her a big hand, if you ask me. If I were you, I'd just forget the whole thing. If he wants protection—Walters can throw more around him than the police. If he doesn't—who cares? I don't. I'm damn sure I don't."

"You're kind of tough yourself, Miss Chiozza—over some things."

She said nothing. Her face was a little white and more than a little hard.

Steve finished his drink, pushed his chair back and reached for his hat. He stood up. "Thank you very much for the drink, Miss Chiozza. Now that I've met you I'll look forward all the more to hearing you sing again."

"You're damn formal all of a sudden," she said.

He grinned. "So long, Dolores."

"So long, Steve. Good luck—in the sleuth racket. If I hear of anything—"

He turned and walked among the tables out of the bar lounge.

FIVE

In the crisp fall evening the lights of Hollywood and Los Angeles winked at him. Searchlight beams probed the cloudless sky as if searching for bombing-planes.

Steve got his convertible out of the parking lot and drove it east along Sunset. At Sunset and Fairfax he bought an evening paper and pulled over to the curb to look through it. There was nothing in the paper about 118 Court Street.

He drove on and ate dinner at the little coffee shop beside his hotel and went to a movie. When he came out he bought a Home Edition of the *Tribune*, a morning sheet. They were in that—both of them.

Police thought Jake Stoyanoff might have strangled the girl, but she had not been attacked. She was described as a stenographer, unemployed at the moment. There was no picture of her. There was a picture of Stoyanoff that looked like a touched-up police photo. Police were looking for a man who had been talking to Stoyanoff just before he was shot. Several people said he was a tall man in a dark suit. That was all the description the police got—or gave out.

Steve grinned sourly, stopped at the coffee shop for a good-night cup of coffee and then went up to his room. It was a few minutes to eleven o'clock. As he unlocked his door the telephone started to ring.

He shut the door and stood in the darkness remembering where the phone was. Then he walked straight to it, catlike in the dark room, sat in an easy chair and reached the phone up from the lower shelf of a small table. He held the one-piece to his ear and said: "Hello."

"Is this Steve?" It was a rich, husky voice, low, vibrant. It held a note of strain.

"Yeah, this is Steve. I can hear you. I know who you are."

There was a faint dry laugh. "You'll make a detective after

112
▼

all. And it seems I'm to give you your first case. Will you come over to my place at once? It's Twenty-four-twelve Renfrew—North, there isn't any South—just half a block below Fountain. It's a sort of bungalow court. My house is the last in line, at the back."

Steve said: "Yes. Sure. What's the matter?"

There was a pause. A horn blared in the street outside the hotel. A wave of white light went across the ceiling from some car rounding the corner uphill. The low voice said very slowly: "Leopardi. I can't get rid of him. He's—he's passed out in my bedroom." Then a tinny laugh that didn't go with the voice at all.

Steve held the phone so tight his hand ached. His teeth clicked in the darkness. He said flatly, in a dull, brittle voice: "Yeah. It'll cost you twenty bucks."

"Of course. Hurry, please."

He hung up, sat there in the dark room breathing hard. He pushed his hat back on his head, then yanked it forward again with a vicious jerk and laughed out loud. "Hell," he said, "*That* kind of a dame."

Twenty-four-twelve Renfrew was not strictly a bungalow court. It was a staggered row of six bungalows, all facing the same way, but so-arranged that no two of their front entrances overlooked each other. There was a brick wall at the back and beyond the brick wall a church. There was a long smooth lawn, moon-silvered.

The door was up two steps, with lanterns on each side and an iron-work grill over the peep hole. This opened to his knock and a girl's face looked out, a small oval face with a Cupid's-bow mouth, arched and plucked eyebrows, wavy brown hair. The eyes were like two fresh and shiny chestnuts.

Steve dropped a cigarette and put his foot on it. "Miss Chiozza. She's expecting me. Steve Grayce."

"Miss Chiozza has retired, sir," the girl said with a half-insolent twist to her lips.

"Break it up, kid. You heard me, I'm expected."

The wicket slammed shut. He waited, scowling back along

113
▼

the narrow moonlit lawn towards the street. O.K. So it was like that—well, twenty bucks was worth a ride in the moonlight anyway.

The lock clicked and the door opened wide. Steve went past the maid into a warm cheerful room, old-fashioned with chintz. The lamps were neither old nor new and there were enough of them—in the right places. There was a hearth behind a paneled copper screen, a davenport close to it, a bar-top radio in the corner.

The maid said stiffly: "I'm sorry, sir. Miss Chiozza forgot to tell me. Please have a chair." The voice was soft, and it might be cagey. The girl went off down the room—short skirts, sheer silk stockings, and four-inch spike heels.

Steve sat down and held his hat on his knee and scowled at the wall. A swing door creaked shut. He got a cigarette out and rolled it between his fingers and then deliberately squeezed it to a shapeless flatness of white paper and ragged tobacco. He threw it away from him, at the fire screen.

Dolores Chiozza came towards him. She wore green velvet lounging pajamas with a long gold-fringed sash. She spun the end of the sash as if she might be going to throw a loop with it. She smiled a slight artificial smile. Her face had a clean scrubbed look and her eyelids were bluish and they twitched.

Steve stood up and watched the green morocco slippers peep out under the pajamas as she walked. When she was close to him he lifted his eyes to her face and said dully: "Hello."

She looked at him very steadily, then spoke in a high, carrying voice. "I know it's late, but I knew you were used to being up all night. So I thought what we had to talk over—Won't you sit down?"

She turned her head very slightly, seemed to be listening for something.

Steve said: "I never go to bed before two. Quite all right."

She went over and pushed a bell beside the hearth. After a moment the maid came through the arch.

"Bring some ice cubes, Agatha. Then go along home. It's getting pretty late."

114

▼

"Yes'm." The girl disappeared.

There was a silence then that almost howled till the tall girl took a cigarette absently out of a box, put it between her lips and Steve struck a match clumsily on his shoe. She pushed the end of the cigarette into the flame and her smoke-blue eyes were very steady on his black ones. She shook her head very slightly.

The maid came back with a copper ice bucket. She pulled a low Indian-brass tray-table between them before the davenport, put the ice bucket on it, then a siphon, glasses and spoons, and a triangular bottle that looked like good Scotch had come in it except that it was covered with silver filigree work and fitted with a stopper.

Dolores Chiozza said, "Will you mix a drink?" in a formal voice.

He mixed two drinks, stirred them, handed her one. She sipped it, shook her head. "Too light," she said. He put more whiskey in it and handed it back. She said, "Better," and leaned back against the corner of the davenport.

The maid came into the room again. She had a small rakish red hat on her wavy brown hair and was wearing a gray coat trimmed with nice fur. She carried a black brocade bag that could have cleaned out a fair-sized icebox. She said: "Good night, Miss Dolores."

"Good night, Agatha."

The girl went out the front door, closed it softly. Her heels clicked down the walk. A car door opened and shut distantly and a motor started. Its sound soon dwindled away. It was a very quiet neighborhood.

Steve put his drink down on the brass tray and looked levelly at the tall girl, said harshly: "That means she's out of the way?"

"Yes. She goes home in her own car. She drives me home from the studio in mine—when I go to the studio, which I did tonight. I don't like to drive a car myself."

"Well, what are you waiting for?"

The red-haired girl looked steadily at the paneled fire screen and the unlit log fire behind it. A muscle twitched in her cheek.

After a moment she said: "Funny that I called you instead of Walters. He'd have protected me better than you can. Only he wouldn't have believed me. I thought perhaps you would. I didn't invite Leopardi here. So far as I know—we two are the only people in the world who know he's here."

Something in her voice jerked Steve upright.

She took a small crisp handkerchief from the breast pocket of the green velvet pajama-suit, dropped it on the floor, picked it up swiftly and pressed it against her mouth. Suddenly, without making a sound, she began to shake like a leaf.

Steve said swiftly: "What the hell—I can handle that heel in my hip pocket. I did last night—and last night he had a gun and took a shot at me."

Her head turned. Her eyes were very wide and staring. "But it couldn't have been my gun," she said in a dead voice.

"Huh? Of course not—what—?"

"It's my gun tonight," she said and stared at him. "You said a woman could get to him with a gun very easily."

He just stared at her. His face was white now and he made a vague sound in his throat.

"He's not drunk, Steve," she said gently. "He's dead. In yellow pajamas—in my bed. With my gun in his hand. You didn't think he was just drunk—did you, Steve?"

He stood up in a swift lunge, then became absolutely motionless, staring down at her. He moved his tongue on his lips and after a long time he formed words with it. "Let's go look at him," he said in a hushed voice.

SIX

The room was at the back of the house to the left. The girl took a key out of her pocket and unlocked the door. There was a low light on a table, and the venetian blinds were drawn. Steve went in past her silently, on cat feet.

Leopardi lay squarely in the middle of the bed, a large smooth silent man, waxy and artificial in death. Even his mustache looked phony. His half-open eyes, sightless as marbles, looked as if they had never seen. He lay on his back, on the sheet, and the bedclothes were thrown over the foot of the bed.

The King wore yellow silk pajamas, the slip-on kind, with a turned collar. They were loose and thin. Over his breast they were dark with blood that had seeped into the silk as if into blotting-paper. There was a little blood on his bare brown neck.

Steve stared at him and said tonelessly: "The King in Yellow. I read a book with that title once. He liked yellow, I guess. I packed some of his stuff last night. And he wasn't yellow either. Guys like him usually are—or are they?"

The girl went over to the corner and sat down in a slipper chair and looked at the floor. It was a nice room, as modernistic as the living room was casual. It had a chenille rug, café-au-lait color, severely angled furniture in inlaid wood, and a trick dresser with a mirror for a top, a kneehole and drawers like a desk. It had a box mirror above and a semi-cylindrical frosted wall light set above the mirror. In the corner there was a glass table with a crystal greyhound on top of it, and a lamp with the deepest drum shade Steve had ever seen.

He stopped looking at all this and looked at Leopardi again. He pulled the King's pajamas up gently and examined the wound. It was directly over the heart and the skin was scorched and mottled there. There was not so very much blood. He had died in a fraction of a second.

A small Mauser automatic lay cuddled in his right hand, on top of the bed's second pillow.

"That's artistic," Steve said and pointed. "Yeah, that's a nice touch. Typical contact wound, I guess. He even pulled his pajama shirt up. I've heard they do that. A Mauser seven-six-three about. Sure it's your gun?"

"Yes." She kept on looking at the floor. "It was in a desk in the living room—not loaded. But there were shells. I don't know why. Somebody gave it to me once. I didn't even know how to load it."

117
▼

Steve smiled. Her eyes lifted suddenly and she saw his smile and shuddered. "I don't expect anybody to believe that," she said. "We may as well call the police, I suppose."

Steve nodded absently, put a cigarette in his mouth and flipped it up and down with his lips that were still puffy from Leopardi's punch. He lit a match on his thumbnail, puffed a small plume of smoke and said quietly: "No cops. Not yet. Just tell it."

The red-haired girl said: "I sing at KFQC, you know. Three nights a week—on a quarter-hour automobile program. This was one of the nights. Agatha and I got home—oh, close to half-past ten. At the door I remembered there was no fizzwater in the house, so I sent her back to the liquor store three blocks away, and came in alone. There was a queer smell in the house. I don't know what it was. As if several men had been in here, somehow. When I came in the bedroom—he was exactly as he is now. I saw the gun and I went and looked and then I knew I was sunk. I didn't know what to do. Even if the police cleared me, everywhere I went from now on—"

Steve said sharply: "He got in here—how?"

"I don't know."

"Go on," he said.

"I locked the door. Then I undressed—with that on my bed. I went into the bathroom to shower and collect my brains, if any. I locked the door when I left the room and took the key. Agatha was back then, but I don't think she saw me. Well, I took the shower and it braced me up a bit. Then I had a drink and then I came in here and called you."

She stopped and moistened the end of a finger and smoothed the end of her left eyebrow with it. "That's all, Steve—absolutely all."

"Domestic help can be pretty nosy. This Agatha's nosier than most—or I miss my guess." He walked over to the door and looked at the lock. "I bet there are three or four keys in the house that knock this over." He went to the windows and felt the catches, looked down at the screens through the glass. He said over his shoulder, casually: "Was the King in love with you?"

Her voice was sharp, almost angry. "He never was in love with any woman. A couple of years back in San Francisco, when I was with his band for a while, there was some slap-silly publicity about us. Nothing to it. It's been revived here in the hand-outs to the press, to build up his opening. I was telling him this afternoon I wouldn't stand for it, that I wouldn't be linked with him in anybody's mind. His private life was filthy. It reeked. Everybody in the business knows that. And it's not a business where daisies grow very often."

Steve said: "Yours was the only bedroom he couldn't make?"

The girl flushed to the roots of her dusky red hair.

"That sounds lousy," he said. "But I have to figure the angles. That's about true, isn't it?"

"Yes—I suppose so. I wouldn't say the only one."

"Go on out in the other room and buy yourself a drink."

She stood up and looked at him squarely across the bed. "I didn't kill him, Steve. I didn't let him into this house tonight. I didn't know he was coming here, or had any reason to come here. Believe that or not. But something about this is wrong. Leopardi was the last man in the world to take his lovely life himself."

Steve said: "He didn't, angel. Go buy that drink. He was murdered. The whole thing is a frame—to get a cover-up from Jumbo Walters. Go on out."

He stood silent, motionless, until sounds he heard from the living room told him she was out there. Then he took out his handkerchief and loosened the gun from Leopardi's right hand and wiped it over carefully on the outside, broke out the magazine and wiped that off, spilled out all the shells and wiped every one, ejected the one in the breech and wiped that. He reloaded the gun and put it back in Leopardi's dead hand and closed his fingers around it and pushed his index finger against the trigger. Then he let the hand fall naturally back on the bed.

He pawed through the bedclothes and found an ejected shell and wiped that off, put it back where he had found it. He put the handkerchief to his nose, sniffed it wryly, went around the bed to a clothes closet and opened the door.

"Careless of your clothes, boy," he said softly.

The rough cream-colored coat hung in there, on a hook, over dark gray slacks with a lizard-skin belt. A yellow satin shirt and a wine-colored tie dangled alongside. A handkerchief to match the tie flowed loosely four inches from the breast pocket of the coat. On the floor lay a pair of gazelle-leather nutmeg-brown sports shoes, and socks without garters. And there were yellow satin shorts with heavy black initials on them lying close by.

Steve felt carefully in the gray slacks and got out a leather keyholder. He left the room, went along the cross-hall and into the kitchen. It had a solid door, a good spring lock with a key stuck in it. He took it out and tried keys from the bunch in the keyholder, found none that fitted, put the other key back and went into the living room. He opened the front door, went outside and shut it again without looking at the girl huddled in a corner of the davenport. He tried keys in the lock, finally found the right one. He let himself back into the house, returned to the bedroom and put the keyholder back in the pocket of the gray slacks again. Then he went to the living room.

The girl was still huddled motionless, staring at him.

He put his back to the mantel and puffed at cigarette. "Agatha with you all the time at the studio?"

She nodded. "I suppose so. So he had a key. That was what you were doing, wasn't it?"

"Yes. Had Agatha long?"

"About a year."

"She steal from you? Small stuff, I mean?"

Dolores Chiozza shrugged wearily. "What does it matter? Most of them do. A little face cream or powder, a handkerchief, a pair of stockings once in a while. Yes, I think she stole from me. They look on that sort of thing as more or less legitimate."

"Not the nice ones, angel."

"Well—the hours were a little trying. I work at night, often get home very late. She's a dresser as well as a maid."

"Anything else about her? She use cocaine or weed. Hit the bottle? Ever have laughing fits?"

"I don't think so. What has she got to do with it, Steve?"

"Lady, she sold somebody a key to your apartment. That's obvious. You didn't give him one, the landlord wouldn't give him one, but Agatha had one. Check?"

Her eyes had a stricken look. Her mouth trembled a little, not much. A drink was untasted at her elbow. Steve bent over and drank some of it.

She said slowly: "We're wasting time, Steve. We have to call the police. There's nothing anybody can do. I'm done for as a nice person, even if not as a lady at large. They'll think it was a lovers' quarrel and I shot him and that's that. If I could convince them I didn't, then he shot himself in my bed, and I'm still ruined. So I might as well make up my mind to face the music."

Steve said softly: "Watch this. My mother used to do it."

He put a finger to his mouth, bent down and touched her lips at the same spot with the same finger. He smiled, said: "We'll go to Walters—or you will. He'll pick his cops and the ones he picks won't go screaming through the night with reporters sitting in their laps. They'll sneak in quiet, like process servers. Walters can handle this. That was what was counted on. Me, I'm going to collect Agatha. Because I want a description of the guy she sold that key to—and I want it fast. And by the way, you owe me twenty bucks for coming over here. Don't let that slip your memory."

The tall girl stood up, smiling. "You're a kick, you are," she said. "What makes you so sure he was murdered?"

"He's not wearing his own pajamas. His have his initials on them. I packed his stuff last night—before I threw him out of the Carlton. Get dressed, angel—and get me Agatha's address."

He went into the bedroom and pulled a sheet over Leopardi's body, held it a moment above the still, waxen face before letting it fall.

"So long, guy," he said gently. "You were a louse—but you sure had music in you."

It was a small frame house on Brighton Avenue near Jefferson, in a block of small frame houses, all old-fashioned, with front porches. This one had a narrow concrete walk which the moon made whiter than it was.

Steve mounted the steps and looked at the light-edged shade of the wide front window. He knocked. There were shuffling steps and a woman opened the door and looked at him through the hooked screen—a dumpy elderly woman with frizzled gray hair. Her body was shapeless in a wrapper and her feet slithered in loose slippers. A man with a polished bald head and milky eyes sat in a wicker chair beside a table. He held his hands in his lap and twisted the knuckles aimlessly. He didn't look towards the door.

Steve said: "I'm from Miss Chiozza. Are you Agatha's mother?"

The woman said dully: "I reckon. But she ain't home, mister." The man in the chair got a handkerchief from somewhere and blew his nose. He snickered darkly.

Steve said: "Miss Chiozza's not feeling so well tonight. She was hoping Agatha would come back and stay the night with her."

The milky-eyed man snickered again, sharply. The woman said: "We dunno where she is. She don't come home. Pa'n me waits up for her to come home. She stays out till we're sick."

The old man snapped in a reedy voice: "She'll stay out till the cops get her one of these times."

"Pa's half blind," the woman said. "Makes him kinda mean. Won't you step in?"

Steve shook his head and turned his hat around in his hands like a bashful cowpuncher in a horse opera. "I've got to find her," he said. "Where would she go?"

"Out drinkin' liquor with cheap spenders," Pa cackled. "Pantywaists with silk handkerchiefs 'stead of neckties. If I had eyes, I'd strap her till she dropped." He grabbed the arms of his chair and the muscles knotted on the backs of his hands. Then he began to cry. Tears welled from his milky eyes and started through the white stubble on his cheeks. The woman went across and took the handkerchief out of his fist and wiped his face with it. Then she blew her nose on it and came back to the door.

"Might be anywhere," she said to Steve. "This is a big town, mister. I dunno where at to say."

Steve said dully: "I'll call back. If she comes in, will you hang onto her. What's your phone number?"

"What's the phone number, Pa?" the woman called back over her shoulder.

"I ain't sayin'," Pa snorted.

The woman said: "I remember now. South Two-four-five-four. Call any time. Pa'n me ain't got nothing to do."

Steve thanked her and went back down the white walk to the street and along the walk half a block to where he had left his car. He glanced idly across the way and started to get into his car, then stopped moving suddenly with his hand gripping the car door. He let go of that, took three steps sideways and stood looking across the street tight-mouthed.

All the houses in the block were much the same, but the one opposite had a FOR RENT placard stuck in the front window and a real-estate sign spiked into the small patch of front lawn. The house itself looked neglected, utterly empty, but in its little driveway stood a small neat black coupe.

Steve said under his breath: "Hunch. Play it up, Stevie."

He walked almost delicately across the wide dusty street, his hand touching the hard metal of the gun in his pocket, and came up behind the little car, stood and listened. He moved silently along its left side, glanced back across the street, then looked in the car's open left-front window.

The girl sat almost as if driving, except that her head was tipped a little too much into the corner. The little red hat was still on her head, the gray coat, trimmed with fur, still around her body. In the reflected moonlight her mouth was strained open. Her tongue stuck out. And her chestnut eyes stared at the roof of the car.

Steve didn't touch her. He didn't have to touch her to look any closer to know there would be heavy bruises on her neck.

"Tough on women, these guys," he muttered.

The girl's big black brocade bag lay on the seat beside her, gaping open like her mouth—like Miss Marilyn Delorme's mouth, and Miss Marilyn Delorme's purple bag.

"Yeah—tough on women."

He backed away till he stood under a small palm tree by the entrance to the driveway. The street was as empty and deserted as a closed theater. He crossed silently to his car, got into it and drove away.

Nothing to it. A girl coming home alone late at night, stuck up and strangled a few doors from her own home by some tough guy. Very simple. The first prowl car that cruised that block —if the boys were half awake—would take a look the minute they spotted the FOR RENT sign. Steve tramped hard on the throttle and went away from there.

At Washington and Figueroa he went into an all-night drugstore and pulled shut the door of the phone booth at the back. He dropped his nickel and dialed the number of police headquarters.

He asked for the desk and said: "Write this down, will you, sergeant? Brighton Avenue, thirty-two-hundred block, west side, in driveway of empty house. Got that much?"

"Yeah. So what?"

"Car with dead woman in it," Steve said, and hung up.

SEVEN

Quillan, head day clerk and assistant manager of the Carlton Hotel, was on night duty, because Millar, the night auditor, was off for a week. It was half-past one and things were dead and Quillan was bored. He had done everything there was to

do long ago, because he had been a hotel man for twenty years
and there was nothing to it.

The night porter had finished cleaning up and was in his
room beside the elevator bank. One elevator was lighted and
open, as usual. The main lobby had been tidied up and the
lights had been properly dimmed. Everything was exactly as
usual.

Quillan was a rather short, rather thickset man with clear
bright toadlike eyes that seemed to hold a friendly expression
without really having any expression at all. He had pale sandy
hair and not much of it. His pale hands were clasped in front
of him on the marble top of the desk. He was just the right
height to put his weight on the desk without looking as if he
were sprawling. He was looking at the wall across the entrance
lobby, but he wasn't seeing it. He was half asleep, even though
his eyes were wide open, and if the night porter struck a match
behind his door, Quillan would know it and bang on his bell.

The brass-trimmed swing doors at the street entrance pushed
open and Steve Grayce came in, a summer-weight coat turned
up around his neck, his hat yanked low and a cigarette wisping
smoke at the corner of his mouth. He looked very casual, very
alert, and very much at ease. He strolled over to the desk and
rapped on it.

"Wake up!" he snorted.

Quillan moved his eyes an inch and said: "All outside rooms
with bath. But positively no parties on the eighth floor. Hiyah,
Steve. So you finally got the axe. And for the wrong thing.
That's life."

Steve said: "O.K. Have you got a new night man here?"

"Don't need one, Steve. Never did, in my opinion."

"You'll need one as long as old hotel men like you register
floozies on the same corridor with people like Leopardi."

Quillan half closed his eyes and then opened them to where
they had been before. He said indifferently: "Not me, pal. But
anybody can make a mistake. Millar's really an accountant—
not a desk man."

Steve leaned back and his face became very still. The smoke almost hung at the tip of his cigarette. His eyes were like black glass now. He smiled a little dishonestly.

"And why was Leopardi put in an eight-dollar room on Eight instead of in a tower suite at twenty-eight per?"

Quillan smiled back at him. "I didn't register Leopardi, old sock. There were reservations in. I supposed they were what he wanted. Some guys don't spend. Any other questions, Mr. Grayce?"

"Yeah. Was Eight-fourteen empty last night?"

"It was on change, so it was empty. Something about the plumbing. Proceed."

"Who marked it on change?"

Quillan's bright fathomless eyes turned and became curiously fixed. He didn't answer.

Steve said: "Here's why. Leopardi was in Eight-fifteen and the two girls in Eight-eleven. Just Eight-thirteen between. A lad with a passkey could have gone into Eight-thirteen and turned both the bolt locks on the communicating doors. Then, if the folks in the two other rooms had done the same thing on their side, they'd have a suite set up."

"So what?" Quillan asked. "We got chiseled out of eight bucks, eh? Well, it happens, in better hotels than this." His eyes looked sleepy now.

Steve said: "Millar could have done that. But hell, it doesn't make sense. Miliar's not that kind of a guy. Risk a job for a buck tip—phooey. Millar's no dollar pimp."

Quillan said: "All right, policeman. Tell me what's really on your mind."

"One of the girls in Eight-eleven had a gun. Leopardi got a threat letter yesterday—I don't know where or how. It didn't faze him, though. He tore it up. That's how I know. I collected the pieces from his basket. I suppose Leopardi's boys all checked out of here."

"Of course. They went to the Normandy."

"Call the Normandy, and ask to speak to Leopardi. If he's there, he'll still be at the bottle. Probably with a gang."

"Why?" Quillan asked gently.

"Because you're a nice guy. If Leopardi answers—just hang up." Steve paused and pinched his chin hard. "If he went out, try to find out where."

Quillan straightened, gave Steve another long quiet look and went behind the pebbled-glass screen. Steve stood very still, listening, one hand clenched at his side, the other tapping noiselessly on the marble desk.

In about three minutes Quillan came back and leaned on the desk again and said: "Not there. Party going on in his suite—they sold him a big one—and sounds loud. I talked to a guy who was fairly sober. He said Leopardi got a call around ten—some girl. He went out preening himself, as the fellow says. Hinting about a very juicy date. The guy was just lit enough to hand me all this."

Steve said: "You're a real pal. I hate not to tell you the rest. Well, I liked working here. Not much work at that."

He started towards the entrance doors again. Quillan let him get his hand on the brass handle before he called out. Steve turned and came back slowly.

Quillan said: "I heard Leopardi took a shot at you. I don't think it was noticed. It wasn't reported down here. And I don't think Peters fully realized that until he saw the mirror in Eight-fifteen. If you care to come back, Steve—"

Steve shook his head. "Thanks for the thought."

"And hearing about that shot," Quillan added, "made me remember something. Two years ago a girl shot herself in Eight-fifteen."

Steve straightened his back so sharply that he almost jumped. "What girl?"

Quillan looked surprised. "I don't know. I don't remember her real name. Some girl who had been kicked around all she could stand and wanted to die in a clean bed—alone."

Steve reached across and took hold of Quillan's arm. "The hotel files," he rasped. "The clippings, whatever there was in the papers will be in them. I want to see those clippings."

Quillan stared at him for a long moment. Then he said:

"Whatever game you're playing, kid—you're playing it damn close to your vest. I will say that for you. And me bored stiff with a night to kill."

He reached along the desk and thumped the call bell. The door of the night porter's room opened and the porter came across the entrance lobby. He nodded and smiled at Steve.

Quillan said: "Take the board, Carl. I'll be in Mr. Peters' office for a little while."

He went to the safe and got keys out of it.

EIGHT

The cabin was high up on the side of the mountain, against a thick growth of digger pine, oak and incense cedar. It was solidly built, with a stone chimney, shingled all over and heavily braced against the slope of the hill. By daylight the roof was green and the sides dark reddish brown and the window frames and draw curtains red. In the uncanny brightness of an all-night mid-October moon in the mountains, it stood out sharply in every detail, except color.

It was at the end of a road, a quarter of a mile from any other cabin. Steve rounded the bend towards it without lights, at five in the morning. He stopped his car at once, when he was sure it was the right cabin, got out and walked soundlessly along the side of the gravel road, on a carpet of wild iris.

On the road level there was a rough pine board garage, and from this a path went up to the cabin porch. The garage was unlocked. Steve swung the door open carefully, groped in past the dark bulk of a car and felt the top of the radiator. It was still warmish. He got a small flash out of his pocket and played it over the car. A gray sedan, dusty, the gas gauge low. He snapped the flash off, shut the garage door carefully and slipped into place the piece of wood that served for a hasp. Then he climbed the path to the house.

There was light behind the drawn red curtains. The porch was high and juniper logs were piled on it, with the bark still on them. The front door had a thumb latch and a rustic door handle above.

He went up, neither too softly nor too noisily, lifted his hand, sighed deep in his throat, and knocked. His hand touched the butt of the gun in the inside pocket of his coat, once, then came away empty.

A chair creaked and steps padded across the floor and a voice called out softly: "What is it?" Millar's voice.

Steve put his lips close to the wood and said: "This is Steve, George. You up already?"

The key turned, and the door opened. George Millar, the dapper night auditor of the Carlton House, didn't look dapper now. He was dressed in old trousers and a thick blue sweater with a roll collar. His feet were in ribbed wool socks and fleece-lined slippers. His clipped black mustache was a curved smudge across his pale face. Two electric bulbs burned in their sockets in a low beam across the room, below the slope of the high roof. A table lamp was lit and its shade was tilted to throw light on a big Morris chair with a leather seat and back-cushion. A fire burned lazily in a heap of soft ash on the big open hearth.

Millar said in his low, husky voice: "Hell's sake, Steve. Glad to see you. How'd you find us anyway? Come on in, guy."

Steve stepped through the door and Millar locked it. "City habit," he said grinning. "Nobody locks anything in the mountains. Have a chair. Warm your toes. Cold out at this time of night."

Steve said: "Yeah. Plenty cold."

He sat down in the Morris chair and put his hat and coat on the end of the solid wood table behind it. He leaned forward and held his hands out to the fire.

Millar said: "How the hell did you find us, Steve?"

Steve didn't look at him. He said quietly: "Not so easy at that. You told me last night your brother had a cabin up here—remember? So I had nothing to do, so I thought I'd drive up and bum some breakfast. The guy in the inn at Crestline didn't know who had cabins where. His trade is with people passing through. I rang up a garage man and he didn't know any Millar cabin. Then I saw a light come on down the street in a coal-and-wood yard and a little guy who is forest ranger and deputy sheriff and wood-and-gas dealer and half a dozen other things was getting his car out to go down to San Bernardino for some tank gas. A very smart little guy. The minute I said your brother had been a fighter he wised up. So here I am."

Millar pawed at his mustache. Bedsprings creaked at the back of the cabin somewhere. "Sure, he still goes under his fighting name—Gaff Talley. I'll get him up and we'll have some coffee. I guess you and me are both in the same boat. Used to working at night and can't sleep. I haven't been to bed at all."

Steve looked at him slowly and looked away. A burly voice behind them said: "Gaff is up. Who's your pal, George?"

Steve stood up casually and turned. He looked at the man's hands first. He couldn't help himself. They were large hands, well kept as to cleanliness, but coarse and ugly. One knuckle had been broken badly. He was a big man with reddish hair. He wore a sloppy bathrobe over outing-flannel pajamas. He had a leathery expressionless face, scarred over the cheekbones. There were fine white scars over his eyebrows and at the corners of his mouth. His nose was spread and thick. His whole face looked as if it had caught a lot of gloves. His eyes alone looked vaguely like Millar's eyes.

Millar said: "Steve Grayce. Night man at the hotel—until last night." His grin was a little vague.

Gaff Talley came over and shook hands. "Glad to meet you," he said. "I'll get some duds on and we'll scrape a breakfast off the shelves. I slept enough. George ain't slept any, the poor sap."

He went back across the room towards the door through which he'd come. He stopped there and leaned on an old phonograph, put his big hand down behind a pile of records in paper envelopes. He stayed just like that, without moving.

Millar said: "Any luck on a job, Steve? Or did you try yet?"

"Yeah. In a way. I guess I'm a sap, but I'm going to have a shot at the private-agency racket. Not much in it unless I can land some publicity." He shrugged. Then he said very quietly: "King Leopardi's been bumped off."

Millar's mouth snapped wide open. He stayed like that for almost a minute—perfectly still, with his mouth open. Gaff Talley leaned against the wall and stared without showing anything in his face. Millar finally said: "Bumped off? Where? Don't tell me—"

"Not in the hotel, George. Too bad, wasn't it? In a girl's apartment. Nice girl too. She didn't entice him there. The old suicide gag—only it won't work. And the girl is my client."

Millar didn't move. Neither did the big man. Steve leaned his shoulders against the stone mantel. He said softly: "I went out to the Club Shalotte this afternoon to apologize to Leopardi. Silly idea, because I didn't owe him an apology. There was a girl there in the bar lounge with him. He took three socks at me and left. The girl didn't like that. We got rather clubby. Had a drink together. Then late tonight—last night—she called me up and said Leopardi was over at her place and—he was drunk and she couldn't get rid of him. I went there. Only he wasn't drunk. He was dead, in her bed, in yellow pajamas."

The big man lifted his left hand and roughed back his hair. Millar leaned slowly against the edge of the table, as if he were afraid the edge might be sharp enough to cut him. His mouth twitched under the clipped black mustache.

He said huskily: "That's lousy."

The big man said: "Well, for cryin' into a milk bottle."

Steve said: "Only they weren't Leopardi's pajamas. His had initials on them—big black initials. And his were satin, not silk. And although he had a gun in his hand—this girl's gun by the way—*he* didn't shoot himself in the heart. The cops will determine that. Maybe you birds never heard of the Lund test, with paraffin wax, to find out who did or didn't fire a gun recently. The kill ought to have been pulled in the hotel last night, in Room Eight-fifteen. I spoiled that by heaving him out on his neck before that black-haired girl in Eight-eleven could get to him. Didn't I, George?"

Millar said: "I guess you did—if I know what you're talking about."

Steve said slowly: "I think you know what I'm talking about, George. It would have been a kind of poetic justice if King Leopardi had been knocked off in Room Eight-fifteen. Because that was the room where a girl shot herself two years ago. A girl who registered as Mary Smith—but whose usual name was Eve Talley. And whose real name was Eve Millar."

The big man leaned heavily on the victrola and said thickly: "Maybe I ain't woke up yet. That sounds like it might grow up to be a dirty crack. We had a sister named Eve that shot herself in the Carlton. So what?"

Steve smiled a little crookedly. He said: "Listen, George. You told me Quillan registered those girls in Eight-eleven. *You* did. You told me Leopardi registered on Eight, instead of in a good suite, because he was tight. He wasn't tight. He just didn't care where he was put, as long as female company was handy. And you saw to that. You planned the whole thing, George. You even got Peters to write Leopardi at the Raleigh in Frisco and ask him to use the Carlton when he came down—because the same man owned it who owned the Club Shalotte. As if a guy like Jumbo Walters would care where a bandleader registered."

Millar's face was dead white, expressionless. His voice cracked. "Steve—for God's sake, Steve, what are you tallking about? How the hell could I—"

"Sorry, kid. I liked working with you. I liked you a lot. I guess I still like you. But I don't like people who strangle women—or people who smear women in order to cover up a revenge murder."

His hand shot up—and stopped. The big man said: "Take it easy—and look at this one."

Gaff's hand had come up from behind the pile of records. A Colt .45 was in it. He said between his teeth: "I always thought house dicks were just a bunch of cheap grafters. I guess I missed out on you. You got a few brains. Hell, I bet you even run out to One-eighteen Court Street. Right?"

Steve let his hand fall empty and looked straight at the big Colt. "Right. I saw the girl—dead—with your fingers marked into her neck. They can measure those, fella. Killing Dolores Chiozza's maid the same way was a mistake. They'll match up the two sets of marks, find out that your black-haired gun girl was at the Carlton last night, and piece the whole story together. With the information they get at the hotel they can't miss. I give you two weeks, if you beat it quick. And I mean quick."

Millar licked his dry lips and said softly: "There's no hurry, Steve. No hurry at all. Our job is done. Maybe not the best way, maybe not the nicest way, but it wasn't a nice job. And Leopardi was the worst kind of a louse. We loved our sister, and he made a tramp out of her. She was a wide-eyed kid that fell for a flashy greaseball, and the greaseball went up in the world and threw her out on her ear for a red-headed torcher who was more his kind. He threw her out and broke her heart and she killed herself."

Steve said harshly: "Yeah—and what were you doing all that time—manicuring your nails?"

"We weren't around when it happened. It took us a little time to find out the why of it."

Steve said: "So that was worth killing four people for, was it? And as for Dolores Chiozza, she wouldn't have wiped her feet on Leopardi—then, or any time since. But you had to put her in the middle too, with your rotten little revenge murder. You make me sick, George. Tell your big tough brother to get on with his murder party."

The big man grinned and said: "Nuff talk, George. See has he a gat—and don't get behind him or in front of him. This bean-shooter goes on through."

Steve stared at the big man's .45. His face was hard as white bone. There was a thin cold sneer on his lips and his eyes were cold and dark.

Millar moved softly in his fleece-lined slippers. He came

around the end of the table and went close to Steve's side and reached out a hand to tap his pockets. He stepped back and pointed: "In there."

Steve said softly: "I must be nuts. I could have taken you then, George."

Gaff Talley barked: "Stand away from him."

He walked solidly across the room and put the big Colt against Steve's stomach hard. He reached up with his left hand and worked the Detective Special from the inside breast pocket. His eyes were sharp on Steve's eyes. He held Steve's gun out behind him. "Take this, George."

Millar took the gun and went over beyond the big table again and stood at the far corner of it. Gaff Talley backed away from Steve.

"You're through, wise guy," he said. "You got to know that. There's only two ways outa these mountains and we gotta have time. And maybe you didn't tell nobody. See?"

Steve stood like a rock, his face white, a twisted half-smile working at the corners of his lips. He stared hard at the big man's gun and his stare was faintly puzzled.

Millar said: "Does it have to be that way, Gaff?" His voice was a croak now, without tone, without its usual pleasant huskiness.

Steve turned his head a little and looked at Millar. "Sure it has, George. You're just a couple of cheap hoodlums after all. A couple of nasty-minded sadists playing at being revengers of wronged girlhood. Hillbilly stuff. And right this minute you're practically cold meat—cold, rotten meat."

Gaff Talley laughed and cocked the big revolver with his thumb. "Say your prayers, guy," he jeered.

Steve said grimly: "What makes you think you're going to bump me off with that thing? No shells in it, strangler. Better try to take me the way you handle women—with your hands."

The big man's eyes flicked down, clouded. Then he roared with laughter. "Geez, the dust on that one must be a foot thick," he chuckled. "Watch."

134
▼

He pointed the big gun at the floor and squeezed the trigger. The firing pin clicked dryly—on an empty chamber. The big man's face convulsed.

For a short moment nobody moved. Then Gaff turned slowly on the balls of his feet and looked at his brother. He said almost gently: "You, George?"

Milar licked his lips and gulped. He had to move his mouth in and out before he could speak.

"Me. Gaff. I was standing by the window when Steve got out of his car down the road, I saw him go into the garage. I knew the car would still be warm. There's been enough killing, Gaff. Too much. So I took the shells out of your gun."

Millar's thumb moved back the hammer on the Detective Special. Gaff's eyes bulged. He stared fascinated at the snub-nosed gun. Then he lunged violently towards it, flailing with the empty Colt. Millar braced himself and stood very still and said dimly, like an old man: "Goodbye, Gaff."

The gun jumped three times in his small neat hand. Smoke curled lazily from its muzzle. A piece of burned log fell over in the fireplace.

Gaff Talley smiled queerly and stooped and stood perfectly still. The gun dropped at his feet. He put his big heavy hands against his stomach, said slowly, thickly: " 'S all right, kid. 'S all right, I guess . . . I guess I . . ."

His voice trailed off and his legs began to twist under him. Steve took three long quick silent steps, and slammed Millar hard on the angle of the jaw. The big man was still falling—as slowly as a tree falls.

Millar spun across the room and crashed against the end wall and a blue-and-white plate fell off the plate-molding and broke. The gun sailed from his fingers. Steve dived for it and came up with it. Millar crouched and watched his brother.

Gaff Talley bent his head to the floor and braced his hands and then lay down quietly, on his stomach, like a man who was very tired. He made no sound of any kind.

Daylight showed at the windows, around the red glass-curtains. The piece of broken log smoked against the side of the hearth and the rest of the fire was a heap of soft gray ash with a glow at its heart.

Steve said dully: "You saved my life, George—or at least you saved a lot of shooting. I took the chance because what I wanted was evidence. Step over there to the desk and write it all out and sign it."

Millar said: "Is he dead?"

"He's dead, George. You killed him. Write that too."

Millar said quietly: "It's funny. I wanted to finish Leopardi myself, with my own hands, when he was at the top, when he had the farthest to fall. Just finish him and then take what came. But Gaff was the guy who wanted it done cute. Gaff, the tough mug who never had any education and never dodged a punch in his life, wanted to do it smart and figure angles. Well, maybe that's why he owned property, like that apartment house on Court Street that Jake Stoyanoff managed for him. I don't know how he got to Dolores Chiozza's maid. It doesn't matter much, does it?"

Steve said: "Go and write it. You were the one called Leopardi up and pretended to be the girl, huh?"

Millar said: "Yes. I'll write it all down, Steve. I'll sign it and then you'll let me go—just for an hour. Won't you, Steve? Just an hour's start. That's not much to ask of an old friend, is it, Steve?"

Millar smiled. It was a small, frail, ghostly smile. Steve bent beside the big sprawled man and felt his neck artery. He looked up, said: "Quite dead . . . Yes, you get an hour's start, George —if you write it all out."

Millar walked softly over to a tall oak highboy desk, studded with tarnished brass nails. He opened the flap and sat down and reached for a pen. He unscrewed the top from a bottle of ink and began to write in his neat, clear accountant's hand-writing.

Steve Grayce sat down in front of the fire and lit a cigarette and stared at the ashes. He held the gun with his left hand on his knee. Outside the cabin, birds began to sing. Inside there was no sound but the scratching pen.

NINE

The sun was well up when Steve left the cabin, locked it up, walked down the steep path and along the narrow gravel road to his car. The garage was empty now. The gray sedan was gone. Smoke from another cabin floated lazily above the pines and oaks half a mile away. He started his car, drove it around a bend, past two old boxcars that had been converted into cabins, then on to a main road with a stripe down the middle and so up the hill to Crestline.

He parked on the main street before the Rim-of-the-World Inn, had a cup of coffee at the counter, then shut himself in a phone booth at the back of the empty lounge. He had the long distance operator get Jumbo Walters' number in Los Angeles, then called the owner of the Club Shalotte.

A voice said silkily: "This is Mr. Walters' residence."

"Steve Grayce. Put him on, if you please."

"One moment, please." A click, another voice, not so smooth and much harder. "Yeah?"

"Steve Grayce. I want to speak to Mr. Walters."

"Sorry. I don't seem to know you. It's a little early, amigo. What's your business?"

"Did he go to Miss Chiozza's place?"

"Oh." A pause. "The shamus. I get it. Hold the line, pal."

Another voice now—lazy, with the faintest color of Irish in it. "You can talk, son. This is Walters."

"I'm Steve Grayce. I'm the man—"

"I know all about that, son. The lady is O.K., by the way. I think she's asleep upstairs. Go on."

"I'm at Crestline—top of the Arrowhead grade. Two men

murdered Leopardi. One was George Millar, night auditor at the Carlton Hotel. The other his brother, an ex-fighter named Gaff Talley. Talley's dead—shot by his brother. Millar got away—but he left me a full confession signed, detailed, complete."

Walters said slowly: "You're a fast worker, son—unless you're just plain crazy. Better come in here fast. Why did they do it?"

"They had a sister."

Walters repeated quietly: "They had a sister . . . What about this fellow that got away? We don't want some hick sheriff or publicity-hungry county attorney to get ideas—"

Steve broke in quietly: "I don't think you'll have to worry about that, Mr. Walters. I think I know where he's gone."

He ate breakfast at the inn, not because he was hungry, but because he was weak. He got into his car again and started down the long smooth grade from Crestline to San Bernardino, a broad paved boulevard skirting the edge of a sheer drop into the deep valley. There were places where the road went close to the edge, white guard-fences alongside.

Two miles below Crestline was the place. The road made a sharp turn around a shoulder of the mountain. Cars were parked on the gravel off the pavement—several private cars, an official car, and a wrecking car. The white fence was broken through and men stood around the broken place looking down.

Eight hundred feet below, what was left of a gray sedan lay silent and crumpled in the morning sunshine.

PEARLS ARE
A NUISANCE

ONE

It is quite true that I wasn't doing anything that morning except looking at a blank sheet of paper in my typewriter and thinking about writing a letter. It is also quite true that I don't have a great deal to do any morning. But that is no reason why I should have to go out hunting for old Mrs. Penruddock's pearl necklace. I don't happen to be a policeman.

It was Ellen Macintosh who called me up, which made a difference, of course. "How are you, darling?" she asked. "Busy?"

"Yes and no," I said. "Mostly no. I am very well. What is it now?"

"I don't think you love me, Walter. And anyway you ought to get some work to do. You have too much money. Somebody has stolen Mrs. Penruddock's pearls and I want you to find them."

"Possibly you think you have the police department on the line," I said coldly. "This is the residence of Walter Gage. Mr. Gage talking."

"Well, you can tell Mr. Gage from Miss Ellen Macintosh," she said, "that if he is not out here in half an hour, he will receive a small parcel by registered mail containing one diamond engagement ring."

"And a lot of good it did me," I said. "That old crow will live for another fifty years."

But she had already hung up so I put my hat on and went down and drove off in the Packard. It was a nice late April morning, if you care for that sort of thing. Mrs. Penruddock lived on a wide quiet street in Carondelet Park. The house had probably looked exactly the same for the last fifty years, but that didn't make me any better pleased that Ellen Macintosh might live in it another fifty years, unless old Mrs. Penruddock died and didn't need a nurse any more. Mr. Penruddock had died a few years before, leaving no will, a thoroughly tangled-up estate, and a list of pensioners as long as a star boarder's arm.

I rang the front doorbell and the door was opened, not very soon, by a little old woman with a maid's apron and a strangled knot of gray hair on the top of her head. She looked at me as if she had never seen me before and didn't want to see me now.

"Miss Ellen Macintosh, please," I said. "Mr. Walter Gage calling."

She sniffed, turned without a word and we went back into the musty recesses of the house and came to a glassed-in porch full of wicker furniture and the smell of Egyptian tombs. She went away, with another sniff.

In a moment the door opened again and Ellen Macintosh came in. Maybe you don't like tall girls with honey-colored hair and skin like the first strawberry peach the grocer sneaks out of the box for himself. If you don't, I'm sorry for you.

"Darling, so you did come," she cried. "That was nice of you, Walter. Now sit down and I'll tell you all about it."

We sat down.

"Mrs. Penruddock's pearl necklace has been stolen, Walter."

"You told me that over the telephone. My temperature is still normal."

"If you will excuse a professional guess," she said, "it is probably subnormal—permanently. The pearls are a string of forty-nine matched pink ones which Mr. Penruddock gave to Mrs. Penruddock for her golden wedding present. She hardly ever wore them lately, except perhaps on Christmas or when she had a couple of very old friends in to dinner and was well enough to sit up. And every Thanksgiving she gives a dinner

140
▼

to all the pensioners and friends and old employees Mr. Penruddock left on her hands, and she wore them then."

"You are getting your verb tenses a little mixed," I said, "but
the general idea is clear. Go on."

"Well, Walter," Ellen said, with what some people call an
arch look, "the pearls have been stolen. Yes, I know that is
the third time I told you that, but there's a strange mystery
about it. They were kept in a leather case in an old safe which
was open half the time and which I should judge a strong man
could open with his fingers even when it was locked. I had to
go there for a paper this morning and I looked in at the pearls
just to say hello—"

"I hope your idea in hanging on to Mrs. Penruddock has not
been that she might leave you that necklace," I said stiffly.
"Pearls are all very well for old people and fat blondes, but for
tall willowy—"

"Oh shut up, darling," Ellen broke in. "I should certainly not
have been waiting for these pearls—because they were false."

I swallowed hard and stared at her. "Well," I said, with a
leer, "I have heard that old Penruddock pulled some cross-eyed
rabbits out of the hat occasionally, but giving his own wife a
string of phony pearls on her golden wedding gets my money."

"Oh, don't be such a fool, Walter! They were real enough
then. The fact is Mrs. Penruddock sold them and had imitations made. One of her old friends, Mr. Lansing Gallemore of
the Gallemore Jewelry Company, handled it all for her very
quietly, because of course she didn't want anyone to know.
And that is why the police have not been called in. You *will*
find them for her, won't you, Walter?"

"How? And what did she sell them for?"

"Because Mr. Penruddock died suddenly without making
any provision for all these people he had been supporting. Then
the depression came, and there was hardly any money at all.
Only just enough to carry on the household and pay the servants, all of whom have been with Mrs. Penruddock so long
that she would rather starve than let any of them go."

"That's different," I said. "I take my hat off to her. But how the dickens am I going to find them, and what does it matter anyway—if they were false?"

"Well, the pearls—imitations, I mean—cost two hundred dollars and were specially made in Bohemia and it took several months and the way things are over there now she might never be able to get another set of really good imitations. And she is terrified somebody will find out they were false, or that the thief will blackmail her, when he finds out they were false. You see, darling, I know who stole them."

I said, "Huh?" a word I very seldom use as I do not think it part of the vocabulary of a gentleman.

"The chauffeur we had here a few months, Walter—a horrid big brute named Henry Eichelberger. He left suddenly the day before yesterday, for no reason at all. Nobody ever leaves Mrs. Penruddock. Her last chauffeur was a very old man and he died. But Henry Eichelberger left without a word and I'm sure he had stolen the pearls. He tried to kiss me once, Walter."

"Oh, he did," I said in a different voice. "Tried to kiss you, eh? Where is this big slab of meat, darling? Have you any idea at all? It seems hardly likely he would be hanging around on the street corner for me to punch his nose for him."

Ellen lowered her long silky eyelashes at me—and when she does that I go limp as a scrubwoman's back hair.

"He didn't run away. He must have known the pearls were false and that he was safe enough to blackmail Mrs. Penruddock. I called up the agency he came from and he has been back there and registered again for employment. But they said it was against their rules to give his address."

"Why couldn't somebody else have taken the pearls? A burglar, for instance?"

"There is no one else. The servants are beyond suspicion and the house is locked up as tight as an icebox every night and there were no signs of anybody having broken in. Besides Henry Eichelberger knew where the pearls were kept, because he saw me putting them away after the last time she wore them—which was when she had two very dear friends in to dinner on the occasion of the anniversary of Mr. Penruddock's death."

"That must have been a pretty wild party," I said. "All right, I'll go down to the agency and make them give me his address. Where is it?"

"It is called the Ada Twomey Domestic Employment Agency, and it is in the two-hundred block on East Second, a very unpleasant neighborhood."

"Not half as unpleasant as my neighborhood will be to Henry Eichelberger," I said. "So he tried to kiss you, eh?"

"The pearls, Walter," Ellen said gently, "are the important thing. I do hope he hasn't already found out they are false and thrown them in the ocean."

"If he has, I'll make him dive for them."

"He is six feet three and very big and strong, Walter," Ellen said coyly. "But not handsome like you, of course."

"Just my size," I said. "It will be a pleasure. Good-bye, darling."

She took hold of my sleeve. "There is just one thing, Walter. I don't mind a little fighting because it is manly. But you mustn't cause a disturbance that would bring the police in, you know. And although you are very big and strong and played right tackle at college, you are a little weak about one thing. Will you promise me not to drink any whiskey?"

"This Eichelberger," I said, "is all the drink I want."

TWO

The Ada Twomey Domestic Employment Agency on East Second Street proved to be all that the name and location implied. The odor of the anteroom, in which I was compelled to wait for a short time, was not at all pleasant. The agency was presided over by a hard-faced middle-aged woman who said that Henry Eichelberger was registered with them for employment as a chauffeur, and that she could arrange to have him call upon me, or could bring him there to the office for an interview.

But when I placed a ten-dollar bill on her desk and indicated that it was merely an earnest of good faith, without prejudice to any commission which might become due to her agency, she relented and gave me his address, which was out west on Santa Monica Boulevard, near the part of the city which used to be called Sherman.

I drove out there without delay, for fear that Henry Eichelberger might telephone in and be informed that I was coming. The address proved to be a seedy hotel, conveniently close to the interurban car tracks and having its entrance adjoining a Chinese laundry. The hotel was upstairs, the steps being covered—in places—with strips of decayed rubber matting to which were screwed irregular fragments of unpolished brass. The smell of the Chinese laundry ceased about halfway up the stairs and was replaced by a smell of kerosene, cigar butts, slept-in air and greasy paper bags. There was a register at the head of the stairs on a wooden shelf. The last entry was in pencil, three weeks previous as to date, and had been written by someone with a very unsteady hand. I deduced from this that the management was not over-particular.

There was a bell beside the book and a sign reading: MAN-AGER. I rang the bell and waited. Presently a door opened down the hall and feet shuffled towards me without haste. A man appeared wearing frayed leather slippers and trousers of a nameless color, which had the two top buttons unlatched to permit more freedom to the suburbs of his extensive stomach. He also wore red suspenders, his shirt was darkened under the arms, and elsewhere, and his face badly needed a thorough laundering and trimming.

He said, "Full-up, bud," and sneered.

I said: "I am not looking for a room. I am looking for one Eichelberger, who, I am informed lives here, but who, I observe, has not registered in your book. And this, as of course you know, is contrary to the law."

"A wise guy," the fat man sneered again. "Down the hall, bud. Two-eighteen." He waved a thumb the color and almost the size of a burnt baked potato.

"Have the kindness to show me the way," I said.

"Geez, the lootenant-governor," he said, and began to shake his stomach. His small eyes disappeared in folds of yellow fat. "O.K., bud. Follow on."

We went into the gloomy depths of the back hall and came to a wooden door at the end with a closed wooden transom above it. The fat man smote the door with a fat hand. Nothing happened.

"Out," he said.

"Have the kindness to unlock the door," I said. "I wish to go in and wait for Eichelberger."

"In a pig's valise," the fat man said nastily. "Who the hell you think you are, bum?"

This angered me. He was a fair-sized man, about six feet tall, but too full of the memories of beer. I looked up and down the dark hall. The place seemed utterly deserted.

I hit the fat man in the stomach.

He sat down on the floor and belched and his right kneecap came into sharp contact with his jaw. He coughed and tears welled up in his eyes.

"Cripes, bud," he whined. "You got twenty years on me. That ain't fair."

"Open the door," I said. "I have no time to argue with you."

"A buck," he said, wiping his eyes on his shirt. "Two bucks and no tip-off."

I took two dollars out of my pocket and helped the man to his feet. He folded the two dollars and produced an ordinary passkey which I could have purchased for five cents.

"Brother, you sock," he said. "Where you learn it? Most big guys are muscle-bound." He unlocked the door.

"If you hear any noises later on," I said, "ignore them. If there is any damage, it will be paid for generously."

He nodded and I went into the room. He locked the door behind me and his steps receded. There was silence.

The room was small, mean and tawdry. It contained a brown chest of drawers with a small mirror hanging over it, a straight wooden chair, a wooden rocking chair, a single bed of chipped enamel, with a much mended cotton counterpane. The curtains at the single window had fly marks on them and the green shade was without a slat at the bottom. There was a wash bowl in the corner with two paper-thin towels hanging beside it. There was, of course, no bathroom, and there was no closet. A piece of dark figured material hanging from a shelf made a substitute for the latter. Behind this I found a gray business suit of the largest size made, which would be my size, if I wore ready-made clothes, which I do not. There was a pair of black brogues on the floor, size number twelve at least. There was also a cheap fiber suitcase, which of course I searched, as it was not locked.

I also searched the bureau and was surprised to find that everything in it was neat and clean and decent. But there was not much in it. Particularly there were no pearls in it. I searched in all other likely and unlikely places in the room but I found nothing of interest.

I sat on the side of the bed and lit a cigarette and waited. It was now apparent to me that Henry Eichelberger was either a very great fool or entirely innocent. The room and the open trail he had left behind him did not suggest a man dealing in operations like stealing pearl necklaces.

I had smoked four cigarettes, more than I usually smoke in an entire day, when approaching steps sounded. They were light quick steps but not at all clandestine. A key was thrust into the door and turned and the door swung carelessly open. A man stepped through it and looked at me.

I am six feet three inches in height and weigh over two hundred pounds. This man was tall, but he seemed lighter. He wore a blue serge suit of the kind which is called neat for lack of anything better to say about it. He had thick wiry blond hair, a neck like a Prussian corporal in a cartoon, very wide shoulders and large hard hands, and he had a face that had taken much battering in its time. His small greenish eyes glinted at me with what I then took to be evil humor. I saw at once that he was not a man to trifle with, but I was not afraid of him. I was his equal in size and strength, and, I had small doubt, his superior in intelligence.

I stood up off the bed calmly and said: "I am looking for one Eichelberger."

"How you get in here, bud?" It was a cheerful voice, rather heavy, but not unpleasant to the ear.

"The explanation of that can wait," I said stiffly. "I am looking for one Eichelberger. Are you he?"

"Haw," the man said. "A gut-buster. A comedian. Wait'll I loosen my belt." He took a couple of steps farther into the room and I took the same number towards him.

"My name is Walter Gage," I said. "Are you Eichelberger?"

"Gimme a nickel," he said, "and I'll tell you."

I ignored that. "I am the fiancé of Miss Ellen Macintosh," I told him coldly. "I am informed that you tried to kiss her."

He took another step towards me and I another towards him. "Whaddaya mean—tried?" he sneered.

I led sharply with my right and it landed flush on his chin. It seemed to me a good solid punch, but it scarcely moved him. I then put two hard left jabs into his neck and landed a second hard right at the side of his rather wide nose. He snorted and hit me in the solar plexus.

I bent over and took hold of the room with both hands and spun it. When I had it nicely spinning I gave it a full swing and hit myself on the back of the head with the floor. This made me lose my balance temporarily and while I was thinking about how to regain it a wet towel began to slap at my face and I opened my eyes. The face of Henry Eichelberger was close to mine and bore a certain appearance of solicitude.

"Bud," his voice said, "your stomach is as weak as a China-man's tea."

"Brandy!" I croaked. "What happened?"

"You tripped on a little tear in the carpet, bud. You really got to have liquor?"

"Brandy," I croaked again, and closed my eyes.

"I hope it don't get me started," his voice said.

A door opened and closed. I lay motionless and tried to avoid being sick at my stomach. The time passed slowly, in a long gray veil. Then the door of the room opened and closed once more and a moment later something hard was being pressed against my lips. I opened my mouth and liquor poured down my throat. I coughed, but the fiery liquid coursed through my veins and strengthened me at once. I sat up.

"Thank you, Henry," I said. "May I call you Henry?"

"No tax on it, bud."

I got to my feet and stood before him. He stared at me curiously. "You look O.K.," he said. "Why'n't you told me you was sick?"

"Damn you, Eichelberger!" I said and hit with all my strength on the side of his jaw. He shook his head and his eyes seemed annoyed. I delivered three more punches to his face and jaw while he was still shaking his head.

"So you wanta play for keeps!" he yelled and took hold of the bed and threw it at me.

I dodged the corner of the bed, but in doing so I moved a little too quickly and lost my balance and pushed my head about four inches into the baseboard under the window.

A wet towel began to slap at my face. I opened my eyes.

"Listen, kid. You got two strikes and no balls on you. Maybe you oughta try a lighter bat."

"Brandy," I croaked.

"You'll take rye." He pressed a glass against my lips and I drank thirstily. Then I climbed to my feet again.

The bed, to my astonishment, had not moved. I sat down on it and Henry Eichelberger sat down beside me and patted my shoulder.

"You and me could get along," he said. "I never kissed your girl, although I ain't saying I wouldn't like to. Is that all is worrying at you?"

He poured himself half a waterglassful of the whiskey out of the pint bottle which he had gone out to buy. He swallowed the liquor thoughtfully.

"No, there is another matter," I said.

"Shoot. But no more haymakers. Promise?"

I promised him rather reluctantly. "Why did you leave the employ of Mrs. Penruddock?" I asked him.

He looked at me from under his shaggy blond eyebrows. Then he looked at the bottle he was holding in his hand. "Would you call me a looker?" he asked.

"Well, Henry—"

"Don't pansy up on me," he snarled.

"No, Henry, I should not call you very handsome. But unquestionably you are virile."

He poured another half-waterglassful of whiskey and handed it to me. "Your turn," he said. I drank it down without fully realizing what I was doing. When I had stopped coughing Henry took the glass out of my hand and refilled it. He took his own drink moodily. The bottle was now nearly empty.

"Suppose you fell for a dame with all the looks this side of heaven. With a map like mine. A guy like me, a guy from the stockyards that played himself a lot of very tough left end at a cow college and left his looks and education on the scoreboard. A guy that has fought everything but whales and freight hogs —engines to you—and licked 'em all, but naturally had to take a sock now and then. Then I get a job where I see this lovely all the time and every day and know it's no dice. What would you do, pal? Me, I just quit the job."

"Henry, I'd like to shake your hand," I said.

He shook hands with me listlessly. "So I ask for my time," he said. "What else would I do?" He held the bottle up and looked at it against the light. "Bo, you made an error when you had me get this. When I start drinking it's a world cruise. You got plenty dough?"

"Certainly," I said. "If whiskey is what you want, Henry, whiskey is what you shall have. I have a very nice apartment on Franklin Avenue in Hollywood and while I cast no aspersions on your own humble and of course quite temporary abode, I now suggest we repair to my apartment, which is a good deal larger and gives one more room to extend one's elbow." I waved my hand airily.

"Say, you're drunk," Henry said, with admiration in his small green eyes.

"I am not yet drunk, Henry, although I do in fact feel the

149

effect of that whiskey and very pleasantly. You must not mind my way of talking which is a personal matter, like your own clipped and concise method of speech. But before we depart there is one other rather insignificant detail I wish to discuss with you. I am empowered to arrange for the return of Mrs. Penruddock's pearls. I understand there is some possibility that you may have stolen them."

"Son, you take some awful chances," Henry said softly.

"This is a business matter, Henry, and plain talk is the best way to settle it. The pearls are only false pearls, so we should very easily be able to come to an agreement. I mean you no ill will, Henry, and I am obliged to you for procuring the whiskey, but business is business. Will you take fifty dollars and return the pearls and no questions asked?"

Henry laughed shortly and mirthlessly, but he seemed to have no animosity in his voice when he said: "So you think I stole some marbles and am sitting around here waiting for a flock of dicks to swarm me?"

"No police have been told, Henry, and you may not have known the pearls were false. Pass the liquor, Henry."

He poured me most of what was left in the bottle, and I drank it down with the greatest good humor. I threw the glass at the mirror, but unfortunately missed. The glass, which was of heavy and cheap construction, fell on the floor and did not break. Henry Eichelberger laughed heartily.

"What are you laughing at, Henry?"

"Nothing," he said. "I was just thinking what a sucker some guy is finding out he is—about them marbles."

"You mean you did not steal the pearls, Henry?"

He laughed again, a little gloomily. "Yeah," he said, "meaning no. I oughta sock you, but what the hell? Any guy can get a bum idea. No, I didn't steal no pearls, bud. If they was ringers, I wouldn't be bothered, and if they was what they looked like the one time I saw them on the old lady's neck, I wouldn't decidedly be holed up in no cheap flot in L.A. waiting for a couple carloads of johns to put the sneeze on me."

I reached for his hand again and shook it.

"That is all I required to know," I said happily. "Now I am at peace. We shall now go to my apartment and consider ways and means to recover these pearls. You and I together should make a team that can conquer any opposition, Henry."

"You ain't kidding me, huh?"

I stood up and put my hat on—upside down. "No, Henry. I am making you an offer of employment which I understand you need, and all the whiskey you can drink. Let us go. Can you drive a car in your condition?"

"Hell, I ain't drunk," Henry said, looking surprised.

We left the room and walked down the dark hallway. The fat manager very suddenly appeared from some nebulous shade and stood in front of us rubbing his stomach and looking at me with small greedy expectant eyes. "Everything okey?" he inquired, chewing on a time-darkened toothpick.

"Give him a buck," Henry said.

"What for, Henry?"

"Oh, I dunno. Just give him a buck."

I withdrew a dollar bill from my pocket and gave it to the fat man.

"Thanks, pal," Henry said. He chucked the fat man under the Adam's apple, and removed the dollar bill deftly from between his fingers. "That pays for the hooch," he added. "I hate to have to bum dough."

We went down the stairs arm in arm, leaving the manager trying to cough the toothpick up from his esophagus.

THREE

At five o'clock that afternoon I awoke from slumber and found that I was lying on my bed in my apartment in the Chateau Moraine, on Franklin Avenue near Ivar Street, in Hollywood. I turned my head, which ached, and saw that Henry Eichelberger was lying beside me in his undershirt and trousers. I then perceived that I also was as lightly attired. On the table near by there stood an almost full bottle of Old Pantation rye whiskey, the full quart size, and on the floor lay an entirely empty bottle of the same excellent brand. There were garments lying here and there on the floor, and a cigarette had burned a hole in the brocaded arm of one of my easy chairs.

I felt myself over carefully. My stomach was stiff and sore and my jaw seemed a little swollen on one side. Otherwise I was none the worse for wear. A sharp pain darted through my temples as I stood up off the bed, but I ignored it and walked steadily to the bottle on the table and raised it to my lips. After a steady draught of the fiery liquid I suddenly felt much better. A hearty and cheerful mood came over me and I was ready for any adventure. I went back to the bed and shook Henry firmly by the shoulder.

"Wake up, Henry," I said. "The sunset hour is nigh. The robins are calling and the squirrels are scolding and the morning glories furl themselves in sleep."

Like all men of action Henry Eichelberger came awake with his fist doubled. "What was that crack?" he snarled. "Oh, yeah. Hi, Walter. How you feel?"

"I feel splendid. Are you rested?"

"Sure." He swung his shoeless feet to the floor and rumpled his thick blond hair with his fingers. "We was going swell until you passed out," he said. "So I had me a nap. I never drink solo. You O.K.?"

"Yes, Henry, I feel very well indeed. And we have work to do."

"Swell." He went to the whiskey bottle and quaffed from it freely. He rubbed his stomach with the flat of his hand. His green eyes shone peacefully. "I'm a sick man," he said, "and I got to take my medicine." He put the bottle down on the table and surveyed the apartment. "Geez," he said, "we thrown it into us so fast I ain't hardly looked at the dump. You got a nice little place here, Walter. Geez, a white typewriter and a white telephone. What's the matter, kid—you just been confirmed?"

"Just a foolish fancy, Henry," I said, waving an airy hand.

Henry went over and looked at the typewriter and the telephone side by side on my writing desk, and the silver-mounted desk set, each piece chased with my initials.

"Well fixed, huh?" Henry said, turning his green gaze on me.

"Tolerably so, Henry," I said modestly.

"Well, what next pal? You got any ideas or do we just drink some?"

"Yes, Henry, I do have an idea. With a man like you to help me I think it can be put into practice. I feel that we must, as they say, tap the grapevine. When a string of pearls is stolen, all the underworld knows it at once. Pearls are hard to sell, Henry, inasmuch as they cannot be cut and can be identified by experts, I have read. The underworld will be seething with activity. It should not be too difficult for us to find someone who would send a message to the proper quarter that we are willing to pay a reasonable sum for their return."

"You talk nice—for a drunk guy," Henry said, reaching for the bottle. "But ain't you forgot these marbles are phonies?"

"For sentimental reasons I am quite willing to pay for their return, just the same."

Henry drank some whiskey, appeared to enjoy the flavor of it and drank some more. He waved the bottle at me politely.

"That's O.K.—as far as it goes," he said. "But this underworld that's doing all this here seething you spoke of ain't going to seethe a hell of a lot over a string of glass beads. Or am I screwy?"

"I was thinking, Henry, that the underworld probably has a sense of humor and the laugh that would go around would be quite emphatic."

"There's an idea in that," Henry said. "Here's some mug finds out lady Penruddock has a string of oyster fruit worth oodles of kale, and he does hisself a neat little box job and trots down to the fence. And the fence gives him the belly laugh. I would say something like that could get around the poolrooms and start a little idle chatter. So far, so nutty. But this box man is going to dump them beads in a hurry, because he has a three-to-ten on him even if they are only worth a nickel plus sales tax. Breaking and entering is the rap, Walter."

"However, Henry," I said, "there is another element in the situation. If this thief is very stupid, it will not, of course, have much weight. But if he is even moderately intelligent, it will. Mrs. Penruddock is a very proud woman and lives in a very exclusive section of the city. If it should become known that she wore imitation pearls, and above all, if it should be even hinted in the public press that these were the very pearls her own husband had given her for her golden wedding present—well, I am sure you see the point, Henry."

"Box guys ain't too bright," he said and rubbed his stony chin. Then he lifted his right thumb and bit it thoughtfully. He looked at the windows, at the corner of the room, at the floor. He looked at me from the corners of his eyes.

"Blackmail, huh?" he said. "Maybe. But crooks don't mix their rackets much. Still, the guy might pass the word along. There's a chance, Walter. I wouldn't care to hock my gold fillings to buy me a piece of it, but there's a chance. How much you figure to put out?"

"A hundred dollars should be ample, but I am willing to go as high as two hundred, which is the actual cost of the imitations."

Henry shook his head and patronized the bottle. "Nope. The guy wouldn't uncover hisself for that kind of money. Wouldn't be worth the chance he takes. He'd dump the marbles and keep his nose clean."

"We can at least try, Henry."

"Yeah, but where? And we're getting low on liquor. Maybe I better put my shoes on and run out, huh?"

At that very moment, as if in answer to my unspoken prayer, a soft dull thump sounded on the door of my apartment. I opened it and picked up the final edition of the evening paper. I closed the door again and carried the paper back across the room, opening it up as I went. I touched it with my right forefinger and smiled confidently at Henry Eichelberger.

"Here. I will wager you a full quart of Old Plantation that the answer will be on the crime page of this paper."

"There ain't any crime page," Henry chortled. "This is Los Angeles. I'll fade you."

I opened the paper to page three with some trepidation, for, although I had already seen the item I was looking for in an early edition of the paper while waiting in Ada Twomey's Domestic Employment Agency, I was not certain it would appear intact in the later editions. But my faith was rewarded. It had not been removed, but appeared midway of column three exactly as before. The paragraph, which was quite short, was headed: LOU GANDESI QUESTIONED IN GEM THEFTS. "Listen to this, Henry," I said, and began to read.

Acting on an anonymous tip police late last night picked up Louis G. (Lou) Gandesi, proprietor of a well-known Spring Street tavern, and quizzed him intensively concerning the recent wave of dinner-party hold-ups in an exclusive western section of this city, hold-ups during which, it is alleged, more than two hundred thousand dollars' worth of valuable jewels have been torn at gun's point from women guests in fashionable homes. Gandesi was released at a late hour and refused to make any statement to reporters. "I never kibitz the cops," he said modestly. Captain William Norgaard, of the General Robbery Detail, announced himself as satisfied that Gandesi had no connection with the robberies, and that the tip was merely an act of personal spite.

I folded the paper and threw it on the bed.

"You win, bo," Henry said, and handed me the bottle. I took a long drink and returned it to him. "Now what? Brace this Gandesi and take him through the hoops?"

"He may be a dangerous man, Henry. Do you think we are equal to it?"

Henry snorted contemptuously. "Yah, a Spring Street punk. Some fat slob with a phony ruby on his mitt. Lead me to him. We'll turn the slob inside out and drain his liver. But we're just about fresh out of liquor. All we got is maybe a pint." He examined the bottle against the light.

"We have had enough for the moment, Henry."

"We ain't drunk, are we? I only had seven drinks since I got here, maybe nine."

"Certainly we are not drunk, Henry, but you take very large drinks, and we have a difficult evening before us. I think we should now get shaved and dressed, and I further think that we should wear dinner clothes. I have an extra suit which will fit you admirably, as we are almost exactly the same size. It is certainly a remarkable omen that two such large men should be associated in the same enterprise. Evening clothes impress these low characters, Henry."

"Swell," Henry said. "They'll think we're mugs workin' for some big shot. This Gandesi will be scared enough to swallow his necktie."

We decided to do as I had suggested and I laid out clothes for Henry, and while he was bathing and shaving I telephoned to Ellen Macintosh.

"Oh, Walter, I am so glad you called up," she cried. "Have you found anything?"

"Not yet, darling," I said. "But we have an idea. Henry and I are just about to put it into execution."

"Henry, Walter? Henry who?"

"Why, Henry Eichelberger, of course, darling. Have you forgotten him so soon? Henry and I are warm friends and we—"

She interrupted me coldly. "Are you drinking, Walter?" she demanded in a very distant voice.

"Certainly not, darling. Henry is a teetotaler."

She sniffed sharply. I could hear the sound distinctly over the telephone. "But didn't Henry take the pearls?" she asked, after quite a long pause.

"Henry, angel? Of course not. Henry left because he was in love with you."

"Oh, Walter. That ape? I'm sure you're drinking terribly. I don't ever want to speak to you again. Goodbye." And she hung the phone up very sharply so that a painful sensation made itself felt in my ear.

I sat down in a chair with a bottle of Old Plantation in my hand wondering what I had said that could be construed as offensive or indiscreet. As I was unable to think of anything, I consoled myself with the bottle until Henry came out of the bathroom looking extremely personable in one of my pleated shirts and a wing collar and black bow tie.

It was dark when we left the apartment and I, at least, was full of hope and confidence, although a little depressed by the way Ellen Macintosh had spoken to me over the telephone.

FOUR

Mr. Gandesi's establishment was not difficult to find, inasmuch as the first taxicab driver Henry yelled at on Spring Street directed us to it. It was called the Blue Lagoon and its interior was bathed in an unpleasant blue light. Henry and I entered it steadily, since we had consumed a partly solid meal at Mandy's Caribbean Grotto before starting out to find Mr. Gandesi. Henry looked almost handsome in my second-best dinner suit, with a fringed white scarf hanging over his shoulder, a lightweight black felt hat on the back of his head (which was only a little larger than mine), and a bottle of whiskey in each of the side pockets of the summer overcoat he was wearing.

The bar of the Blue Lagoon was crowded, but Henry and I went on back to the small dim dining room behind it. A man in a dirty dinner suit came up to us and Henry asked him for Gandesi, and he pointed out a fat man who sat alone at a small table in the far corner of the room. We went that way.

The man sat with a small glass of red wine in front of him and slowly twisted a large green stone on his finger. He did not look up. There were no other chairs at the table, so Henry leaned on it with both elbows.

"You Gandesi?" he said.

The man did not look up even then. He moved his thick black eyebrows together and said in an absent voice: "Si. Yes."

"We got to talk to you in private," Henry told him. "Where we won't be disturbed."

Gandesi looked up now and there was extreme boredom in his flat black almond-shaped eyes. "So?" he asked and shrugged. "Eet ees about what?"

"About some pearls," Henry said. "Forty-nine on the string, matched and pink."

"You sell—or you buy?" Gandesi inquired and his chin began to shake up and down as if with amusement.

"Buy," Henry said.

The man at the table crooked his finger quietly and a very large waiter appeared at his side. "Ees dronk," he said lifelessly. "Put dees men out."

The waiter took hold of Henry's shoulder. Henry reached up carelessly and took hold of the waiter's hand and twisted it. The waiter's face in that bluish light turned some color I could not describe, but which was not at all healthy. He let out a low moan. Henry dropped the hand and said to me: "Put a C-note on the table."

I took my wallet out and extracted from it one of the two hundred-dollar bills I had taken the precaution to obtain from the cashier at the Chateau Moraine. Gandesi stared at the bill and made a gesture to the large waiter, who went away rubbing his hand and holding it tight against his chest.

"What for?" Gandesi asked.

"Five minutes of your time alone."

"Ees very fonny. O.K., I bite." Gandesi took the bill and folded it neatly and put it in his vest pocket. Then he put both hands on the table and pushed himself heavily to his feet. He started to waddle away without looking at us.

Henry and I followed him among the crowded tables to the far side of the dining room and through a door in the wainscoting and then down a narrow dim hallway. At the end of this Gandesi opened a door into a lighted room and stood holding it for us, with a grave smile on his olive face. I went in first.

As Henry passed in front of Gandesi into the room the latter, with surprising agility, took a small shiny black leather club from his clothes and hit Henry on the head with it very hard. Henry sprawled forward on his hands and knees. Gandesi shut the door of the room very quickly for a man of his build and leaned against it with the small club in his left hand. Now, very suddenly, in his right hand appeared a short but heavy black revolver.

"Ees very fonny," he said politely, and chuckled to himself.

Exactly what happened then I did not see clearly. Henry was at one instant on his hands and knees with his back to Gandesi. In the next, or possibly even in the same instant, something swirled like a big fish in water and Gandesi grunted. I then saw that Henry's hard blond head was buried in Gandesi's stomach and that Henry's large hands held both of Gandesi's hairy wrists. Then Henry straightened his body to its full height and Gandesi was high up in the air balanced on top of Henry's head, his mouth strained wide open and his face a dark purple color. Then Henry shook himself, as it seemed, quite lightly, and Gandesi landed on his back on the floor with a terrible thud and lay gasping. Then a key turned in the door and Henry stood with his back to it, holding both the club and the revolver in his left hand, and solicitously feeling the pockets which contained our supply of whiskey. All this happened with such rapidity that I leaned against the side wall and felt a little sick at my stomach.

"A gut-buster," Henry drawled. "A comedian. Wait'll I loosen my belt."

Gandesi rolled over and got to his feet very slowly and painfully and stood swaying and passing his hand up and down his face. His clothes were covered with dust.

"This here's a sap," Henry said, showing me the small black club. "He hit me with it, didn't he?"

"Why, Henry, don't you know?" I inquired.

"I just wanted to be sure," Henry said. "You don't do that to the Eichelbergers."

"O.K., what you boys want?" Gandesi asked abruptly, with no trace whatever of his Italian accent.

"I told you what we wanted, dough-face."

"I don't think I know you boys," Gandesi said and lowered his body with care into a wooden chair beside a shabby office desk. He mopped his face and neck and felt himself in various places.

"You got the wrong idea, Gandesi. A lady living in Carondelet Park lost a forty-nine bead pearl necklace a couple of days back. A box job, but a pushover. Our outfit's carrying a little insurance on those marbles. And I'll take that C note."

He walked over to Gandesi and Gandesi quickly reached the folded bill from his pocket and handed it to him. Henry gave me the bill and I put it back in my wallet.

"I don't think I hear about it," Gandesi said carefully.

"You hit me with a sap," Henry said. "Listen kind of hard."

Gandesi shook his head and then winced. "I don't back no petermen," he said, "nor no heist guys. You got me wrong."

"Listen hard," Henry said in a low voice. "You might hear something." He swung the small black club lightly in front of his body with two fingers of his right hand. The slightly too-small hat was still on the back of his head, although a little crumpled.

"Henry," I said, "you seem to be doing all the work this evening. Do you think that is quite fair?"

"O.K., work him over," Henry said. "These fat guys bruise something lovely."

By this time Gandesi had become a more natural color and was gazing at us steadily. "Insurance guys, huh?" he inquired dubiously.

"You said it, dough-face."

"You try Melachrino?" Gandesi asked.

"Haw," Henry began raucously, "a gut-buster. A—" but I interrupted him sharply.

"One moment, Henry," I said. Then turning to Gandesi, "Is this Melachrino a person?" I asked him.

Gandesi's eyes rounded in surprise. "Sure—a guy. You don't know him, huh?" A look of dark suspicion was born in his sloe-black eyes, but vanished almost as soon as it appeared.

"Phone him," Henry said, pointing to the instrument which stood on the shabby office desk.

"Phone is bad," Gandesi objected thoughtfully.

"So is sap poison," Henry said.

Gandesi sighed and turned his thick body in the chair and drew the telephone towards him. He dialed a number with an inky nail and listened. After an interval he said: "Joe? . . . Lou. Couple insurance guys tryin' to deal on a Carondelet Park job . . . Yeah . . . No, marbles . . . You ain't heard a whisper, huh? . . . O.K., Joe."

Gandesi replaced the phone and swung around in the chair again. He studied us with sleepy eyes. "No soap. What insurance outfit you boys work for?"

"Give him a card," Henry said to me.

I took my wallet out once more and withdrew one of my cards from it. It was an engraved calling card and contained nothing but my name. So I used my pocket pencil to write, Chateau Moraine Apartments, Franklin near Ivar, below the name. I showed the card to Henry and then gave it to Gandesi.

Gandesi read the card and quietly bit his finger. His face brightened suddenly. "You boys better see Jack Lawler," he said.

Henry stared at him closely. Gandesi's eyes were now bright and unblinking and guileless.

"Who's he?" Henry asked.

"Runs the Penguin Club. Out on the Strip—Eighty-six Forty-four Sunset or some number like that. He can find out, if any guy can."

"Thanks," Henry said quietly. He glanced at me. "You believe him?"

"Well, Henry," I said, "I don't really think he would be above telling us an untruth."

"Haw!" Gandesi began suddenly. "A gut-buster! A—"

"Can it!" Henry snarled. "That's my line. Straight goods, is it, Gandesi? About this Jack Lawler?"

Gandesi nodded vigorously. "Straight goods, absolute. Jack Lawler got a finger in everything high class that's touched. But he ain't easy to see."

"Don't worry none about that. Thanks, Gandesi."

Henry tossed the black club into the corner of the room and broke open the breech of the revolver he had been holding all this time in his left hand. He ejected the shells and then bent down and slid the gun along the floor until it disappeared under the desk. He tossed the cartridges idly in his hand for a moment and then let them spill on the floor.

So long, Gandesi," he said coldly. "And keep that schnozzle of yours clean, if you don't want to be looking for it under the bed."

He opened the door then and we both went out quickly and left the Blue Lagoon without interference from any of the employees.

FIVE

My car was parked a short distance away down the block. We entered it and Henry leaned his arms on the wheel and stared moodily through the windshield.

"Well, what you think, Walter?" he inquired at length.

"If you ask my opinion, Henry, I think Mr. Gandesi told us a cock-and-bull story merely to get rid of us. Furthermore I do not believe he thought we were insurance agents."

"Me too, and an extra helping," Henry said. "I don't figure there's any such guy as this Melachrino or this Jack Lawler and this Gandesi called up some dead number and had himself a phony chin with it. I oughta go back there and pull his arms and legs off. The hell with the fat slob."

"We had the best idea we could think of, Henry, and we executed it to the best of our ability. I now suggest that we return to my apartment and try to think of something else."

"And get drunk," Henry said, starting the car and guiding it away from the curb.

"We could perhaps have a small allowance of liquor, Henry."

"Yah!" Henry snorted. "A stall. I oughta go back there and wreck the joint."

He stopped at the intersection, although no traffic signal was in operation at the time; and raised a bottle of whiskey to his lips. He was in the act of drinking when a car came up behind us and collided with our car, but not very severely. Henry choked and lowered his bottle, spilling some of the liquor on his garments.

"This town's getting too crowded," he snarled. "A guy can't take hisself a drink without some smart monkey bumps his elbow."

Whoever it was in the car behind us blew a horn with some insistence, inasmuch as our car had not yet moved forward. Henry wrenched the door open and got out and went back. I heard voices of considerable loudness, the louder being Henry's voice. He came back after a moment and got into the car and drove on.

"I oughta have pulled his mush off," he said, "but I went soft." He drove rapidly the rest of the way to Hollywood and the Chateau Moraine and we went up to my apartment and sat down with large glasses in our hands.

"We got better than a quart and a half of hooch," Henry said, looking at the two bottles which he had placed on the table beside others which had long since been emptied. "That oughta be good for an idea."

"If it isn't enough, Henry, there is an abundant further supply where it came from," I drained my glass cheerfully.

"You seem a right guy," Henry said. "What makes you always talk so funny?"

"I cannot seem to change my speech, Henry. My father and mother were both severe purists in the New England tradition, and the vernacular has never come naturally to my lips, even while I was in college."

Henry made an attempt to digest this remark, but I could see that it lay somewhat heavily on his stomach.

We talked for a time concerning Gandesi and the doubtful quality of his advice, and thus passed perhaps half an hour. Then rather suddenly the white telephone on my desk began to ring. I hurried over to it, hoping that it was Ellen Macintosh and that she had recovered from her ill humor. But it proved to be a male voice and a strange one to me. It spoke crisply, with an unpleasant metallic quality of tone.

"You Walter Gage?"

"This is Mister Gage speaking."

"Well, *Mister* Gage, I understand you're in the market for some jewelry."

I held the phone very tightly and turned my body and made grimaces to Henry over the top of the instrument. But he was moodily pouring himself another large portion of Old Plantation.

"That is so," I said into the telephone, trying to keep my voice steady, although my excitement was almost too much for me. "If by jewelry you mean pearls."

"Forty-nine in a rope, brother. And five grand is the price."

"Why that is entirely absurd," I gasped. "Five thousand dollars for those—"

The voice broke in on me rudely. "You heard me, brother. Five grand. Just hold up the hand and count the fingers. No more, no less. Think it over. I'll call you later."

The phone clicked dryly and I replaced the instrument shakily in its cradle. I was trembling. I walked back to my chair and sat down and wiped my face with my handkerchief.

"Henry," I said in a low tense voice, "it worked. But how strangely."

Henry put his empty glass down on the floor. It was the first time that I had ever seen him put an empty glass down and leave it empty. He stared at me closely with his tight unblinking green eyes.

"Yeah?" he said gently. "What worked, kid?" He licked his lips slowly with the tip of his tongue.

"What we accomplished down at Gandesi's place, Henry. A man just called me on the telephone and asked me if I was in the market for pearls."

"Geez." Henry pursed his lips and whistled gently. "That damn dago had something after all."

"But the price is five thousand dollars, Henry. That seems beyond reasonable explanation."

"Huh?" Henry's eyes seemed to bulge as if they were about to depart from their orbits. "Five grand for them ringers? The guy's nuts. They cost two C's, you said. Bugs completely is what the guy is. Five grand? Why, for five grand I could buy me enough phony pearls to cover an elephant's caboose."

I could see that Henry seemed puzzled. He refilled our glasses silently and we stared at each other over them. "Well, what the heck can you do with that, Walter?" he asked after a long silence.

"Henry," I said firmly, "there is only one thing to do. It is true that Ellen Macintosh spoke to me in confidence, and as she did not have Mrs. Penruddock's express permission to tell me about the pearls, I suppose I should respect that confidence. But Ellen is now angry with me and does not wish to speak to me, for the reason that I am drinking whiskey in considerable quantities, although my speech and brain are still reasonably clear. This last is a very strange development and I think, in spite of everything, some close friend of the family should be consulted. Preferably of course, a man, someone of large business experience, and in addition to that a man who understands about jewels. There *is* such a man, Henry, and tomorrow morning I shall call upon him."

"Geez," Henry said. "You coulda said all that in nine words, bo. Who is this guy?"

"His name is Mr. Lansing Gallemore, and he is president of the Gallemore Jewelry Company on Seventh Street. He is a very old friend of Mrs. Penruddock—Ellen has often mentioned him—and is, in fact, the very man who procured for her the imitation pearls."

"But this guy will tip the bulls," Henry objected.

"I do not think so, Henry. I do not think he will do anything to embarrass Mrs. Penruddock in any way."

Henry shrugged. "Phonies are phonies," he said. "You can't make nothing else outa them. Not even no president of no jewlery store can't."

"Nevertheless, there must be a reason why so large a sum is demanded, Henry. The only reason that occurs to me is blackmail and, frankly, that is a little too much for me to handle alone, because I do not know enough about the background of the Penruddock family."

"Okey," Henry said, sighing. "If that's your hunch, you better follow it, Walter. And I better breeze on home and flop so as to be in good shape for the rough work, if any."

"You would not care to pass the night here, Henry?"

"Thanks, pal, but I'm O.K. back at the hotel. I'll just take this spare bottle of the tiger sweat to put me to sleep. I might happen to get a call from the agency in the A.M. and would have to brush my teeth and go after it. And I guess I better change my duds back to where I can mix with the common people."

So saying he went into the bathroom and in a short time emerged wearing his own blue serge suite. I urged him to take my car, but he said it would not be safe in his neighborhood. He did, however, consent to use the topcoat he had been wearing and, placing in it carefully the unopened quart of whiskey, he shook me warmly by the hand.

"One moment, Henry," I said and took out my wallet. I extended a twenty-dollar bill to him.

"What's that in favor of?" he growled.

"You are temporarily out of employment, Henry, and you have done a noble piece of work this evening, puzzling as are the results. You should be rewarded and I can well afford this small token."

"Well, thanks, pal," Henry said. "But it's just a loan." His voice was gruff with emotion. "Should I give you a buzz in the A.M.?"

"By all means. And there is one thing more that has occurred to me. Would it not be advisable for you to change your hotel? Suppose, through no fault of mine, the police learn of this theft. Would they not at least suspect you?"

"Hell, they'd bounce me up and down for hours," Henry said. "But what'll it get them? I ain't no ripe peach."

"It is for you to decide, of course, Henry."

"Yeah. Good night, pal, and don't have no nightmares."

He left me then and I felt suddenly very depressed and lonely. Henry's company had been very stimulating to me, in spite of his rough way of talking. He was very much of a man. I poured myself a rather large drink of whiskey from the remaining bottle and drank it quickly but gloomily.

The effect was such that I had an overmastering desire to speak to Ellen Macintosh at all costs. I went to the telephone and called her number. After a long wait a sleepy maid answered. But Ellen, upon hearing my name, refused to come to the telephone. That depressed me still further and I finished the rest of the whiskey almost without noticing what I was doing. I then lay down on the bed and fell into fitful slumber.

SIX

The busy ringing of the telephone awoke me and I saw that the morning sunlight was streaming into the room. It was nine o'clock and all the lamps were still burning. I arose feeling a little stiff and dissipated, for I was still wearing my dinner suit. But I am a healthy man with very steady nerves and I did not feel as badly as I expected. I went to the telephone and answered it.

Henry's voice said: "How you feel, pal? I got a hangover like twelve Swedes."

"Not too badly, Henry."

"I got a call from the agency about a job. I better go down and take a gander at it. Should I drop around later?"

"Yes, Henry, by all means do that. By eleven o'clock I should be back from the errand about which I spoke to you last night."

"Any more calls from you know?"

"Not yet, Henry."

"Check. Abyssinia." He hung up and I took a cold shower and shaved and dressed. I donned a quiet brown business suit and had some coffee sent up from the coffee shop downstairs. I also had the waiter remove the empty bottles from my apartment and gave him a dollar for his trouble. After drinking two cups of black coffee I felt my own man once more and drove downtown to the Gallemore Jewelry Company's large and brilliant store on West Seventh Street.

It was another bright, golden morning and it seemed that somehow things should adjust themselves on so pleasant a day.

Mr. Lansing Gallemore proved to be a little difficult to see, so that I was compelled to tell his secretary that it was a matter concerning Mrs. Penruddock and of a confidential nature. Upon this message being carried in to him I was at once ushered into a long paneled office, at the far end of which Mr. Gallemore stood behind a massive desk. He extended a thin pink hand to me.

"Mr. Gage? I don't believe we have met, have we?"

"No, Mr. Gallemore, I do not believe we have. I am the fiancé—or was until last night—of Miss Ellen Macintosh, who, as you probably know, is Mrs. Penruddock's nurse. I am come to you upon a very delicate matter and it is necessary that I ask for your confidence before I speak."

He was a man of perhaps seventy-five years of age, and very thin and tall and correct and well preserved. He had cold blue eyes but a warming smile. He was attired youthfully enough in a gray flannel suit with a red carnation at his lapel.

"That is something I make it a rule never to promise, Mr. Gage," he said. "I think it is almost always a very unfair request. But if you assure me the matter concerns Mrs. Penruddock and is really of a delicate and confidential nature, I will make an exception."

"It is indeed, Mr. Gallemore," I said, and thereupon told him the entire story, concealing nothing, not even the fact that I had consumed far too much whiskey the day before.

He stared at me curiously at the end of my story. His finely shaped hand picked up an old-fashioned white quill pen and he slowly tickled his right ear with the feather of it.

"Mr. Gage," he said, "can't you guess why they ask five thousand dollars for that string of pearls?"

"If you permit me to guess, in a matter of so personal a nature, I could perhaps hazard an explanation, Mr. Gallemore."

He moved the white feather around to his left ear and nodded. "Go ahead, son."

"The pearls are in fact real, Mr. Gallemore. You are a very old friend of Mrs. Penruddock—perhaps even a childhood sweetheart. When she gave you her pearls, her golden wedding present, to sell because she was in sore need of money for a generous purpose, you did not sell them, Mr. Gallemore. You only pretended to sell them. You gave her twenty thousand dollars of your own money, and you returned the real pearls to her, pretending that they were an imitation made in Czechoslovakia."

"Son, you think a lot smarter than you talk," Mr. Gallemore said. He arose and walked to a window, pulled aside a fine net curtain and looked down on the bustle of Seventh Street. He came back to his desk and seated himself and smiled a little wistfully.

"You are almost embarrassingly correct, Mr. Gage," he said, and sighed. "Mrs. Penruddock is a very proud woman, or I should simply have offered her the twenty thousand dollars as an unsecured loan. I happened to be the coadministrator of Mr. Penruddock's estate and I knew that in the condition of the financial market at that time it would be out of the question to raise enough cash, without damaging the corpus of the estate beyond reason, to care for all those relatives and pensioners. So Mrs. Penruddock sold her pearls—as she thought—but she insisted that no one should know about it. And I did what you

have guessed. It was unimportant. I could afford the gesture.
I have never married, Gage, and I am rated a wealthy man.
As a matter of fact, at that time, the pearls would not have
fetched more than half of what I gave her, or of what they
should bring today."

I lowered my eyes for fear this kindly old gentleman might
be troubled by my direct gaze.

"So I think we had better raise that five thousand, son," Mr.
Gallemore at once added in a brisk voice. "The price is pretty
low, although stolen pearls are a great deal more difficult to
deal in than cut stones. If I should care to trust you that far
on your face, do you think you could handle the assignment?"

"Mr. Gallemore," I said firmly but quietly, "I am a total
stranger to you and I am only flesh and blood. But I promise
you by the memories of my dead and revered parents that there
will be no cowardice."

"Well, there is a good deal of the flesh and blood, son," Mr.
Gallemore said kindly. "And I am not afraid of your stealing
the money, because possibly I know a little more about Miss
Ellen Macintosh and her boy friend than you might suspect.
Furthermore, the pearls are insured, in my name, of course,
and the insurance company should really handle this affair.
But you and your funny friend seem to have got along very
nicely so far, and I believe in playing out a hand. This Henry
must be quite a man."

"I have grown very attached to him, in spite of his uncouth
ways," I said.

Mr. Gallemore played with his white quill pen a little longer
and then he brought out a large checkbook and wrote a check,
which he carefully blotted and passed across the desk.

"If you get the pearls, I'll see that the insurance people re-
fund this to me," he said. "If they like my business, there will
be no difficulty about that. The bank is down at the corner and
I will be waiting for their call. They won't cash the check without telephoning me, probably. Be careful, son, and don't get hurt."

He shook hands with me once more and I hesitated. "Mr.
Gallemore, you are placing a greater trust in me than any man

ever has," I said. "With the exception, of course, of my own father."

"I am acting like a damn fool," he said with a peculiar smile. "It is so long since I heard anyone talk the way Jane Austen writes that it is making a sucker out of me."

"Thank you, sir. I know my language is a bit stilted. Dare I ask you to do me a small favor, sir?"

"What is it, Gage?"

"To telephone Miss Ellen Macintosh, from whom I am now a little estranged, and tell her that I am not drinking today, and that you have entrusted me with a very delicate mission."

He laughed aloud. "I'll be glad to, Walter. And as I know she can be trusted, I'll give her an idea of what's going on."

I left him then and went down to the bank with the check, and the teller, after looking at me suspiciously, then absenting himself from his cage for a long time, finally counted out the money in hundred-dollar bills with the reluctance one might have expected, if it had been his own money.

I placed the flat packet of bills in my pocket and said: "Now give me a roll of quarters, please."

"A roll of quarters, sir?" His eyebrows lifted.

"Exactly. I use them for tips. And naturally I should prefer to carry them home in the wrappings."

"Oh, I see. Ten dollars, please."

I took the fat hard roll of coins and dropped it into my pocket and drove back to Hollywood.

Henry was waiting for me in the lobby of the Chateau Moraine, twirling his hat between his rough hard hands. His face looked a little more deeply lined than it had the day before and I noticed that his breath smelled of whiskey. We went up to my apartment and he turned to me eagerly.

"Any luck, pal?"

"Henry," I said, "before we proceed further into this day I wish it clearly understood that I am not drinking. I see that already you have been at the bottle."

"Just a pick-up, Walter," he said a little contritely. "That job I went out for was gone before I got there. What's the good word?"

I sat down and lit a cigarette and stared at him evenly. "Well, Henry, I don't really know whether I should tell you or not. But it seems a little petty not to do so after all you did last night to Gandesi." I hesitated a moment longer while Henry stared at me and pinched the muscles of his left arm. "The pearls are real, Henry. And I have instructions to proceed with the business and I have five thousand dollars in cash in my pocket at this moment."

I told him briefly what had happened.

He was more amazed than words could tell. "Cripes!" he exclaimed, his mouth hanging wide open. "You mean you got the five grand from this Gallemore—just like that?"

"Precisely that, Henry."

"Kid," he said earnestly, "You got something with that daisy pan and that fluff talk that a lot of guys would give important dough to cop. Five grand—out of a business guy—just like that. Why, I'll be a monkey's uncle. I'll be a snake's daddy. I'll be a mickey finn at a woman's-club lunch."

At that exact moment, as if my entrance to the building had been observed, the telephone rang again and I sprang to answer it.

It was one of the voices I was awaiting, but not the one I wanted to hear with the greater longing. "How's it looking to you this morning, Gage?"

"It is looking better," I said. "If I can have any assurance of honorable treatment, I am prepared to go through with it."

"You mean you got the dough?"

"In my pocket at this exact moment."

The voice seemed to exhale a slow breath. "You'll get your marbles O.K.—if we get the price, Gage. We're in this business for a long time and we don't welsh. If we did, it would soon get around and nobody would play with us any more."

"Yes, I can readily understand that," I said. "Proceed with your instructions," I added coldly.

"Listen close, Gage. Tonight at eight sharp you be in Pacific Palisades. Know where that is?"

"Certainly. It is a small residential section west of the polo fields on Sunset Boulevard."

"Right. Sunset goes slap through it. There's one drugstore there—open till nine. Be there waiting a call at eight sharp tonight. Alone. And I mean alone, Gage. No cops and no strong-arm guys. It's rough country down there and we got a way to get you to where we want you and know if you're alone. Get all this?"

"I am not entirely an idiot," I retorted.

"No dummy packages, Gage. The dough will be checked. No guns. You'll be searched and there's enough of us to cover you from all angles. We know your car. No funny business, no smart work, no slip-up and nobody hurt. That's the way we do business. How's the dough fixed?"

"One-hundred-dollar bills," I said. "And only a few of them are new."

"Attaboy. Eight o'clock then. Be smart, Gage."

The phone clicked in my ear and I hung up. It rang again almost instantly. This time it was the *one* voice.

"Oh, Walter," Ellen cried, "I was so mean to you! Please forgive me, Walter. Mr. Gallemore has told me everything and I'm so frightened."

"There is nothing of which to be frightened," I told her warmly. "Does Mrs. Penruddock know, darling?"

"No, darling. Mr. Gallemore told me not to tell her. I am phoning from a store down on Sixth Street. Oh, Walter, I really am frightened. Will Henry go with you?"

"I am afraid not, darling. The arrangements are all made and they will not permit it. I must go alone."

"Oh, Walter! I'm terrified. I can't bear the suspense."

"There is nothing to fear," I assured her. "It is a simple business transaction. And I am not exactly a midget."

"But, Walter—oh, I *will* try to be brave, Walter. Will you promise me just one teensy-weensy little thing?"

"Not a drop, darling," I said firmly. "Not a single solitary drop."

"Oh, Walter!"

There was a little more of that sort of thing, very pleasant to me in the circumstances, although possibly not of great interest to others. We finally parted with my promise to telephone as soon as the meeting between the crooks and myself had been consummated.

I turned from the telephone to find Henry drinking deeply from a bottle he had taken from his hip pocket.

"Henry!" I cried sharply.

He looked at me over the bottle with a shaggy determined look. "Listen, pal," he said in a low hard voice. "I got enough of your end of the talk to figure the set-up. Some place out in the tall weeds and you go alone and they feed you the old sap poison and take your dough and leave you lying—with the marbles still in their kitty. Nothing doing, pal. I said—nothing doing!" He almost shouted the last words.

"Henry, it is my duty and I must do it," I said quietly.

"Haw!" Henry snorted. "I say no. You're a nut, but you're a sweet guy on the side. I say no. Henry Eichelberger of the Wisconsin Eichelbergers—in fact, I might just as leave say of the Milwaukee Eichelbergers—says no. And he says it with both hands working." He drank again from his bottle.

"You certainly will not help matters by becoming intoxicated," I told him rather bitterly.

He lowered the bottle and looked at me with amazement written all over his rugged features. "Drunk, Walter?" he boomed. "Did I hear you say drunk? An Eichelberger drunk? Listen, son. We ain't got a lot of time now. It would take maybe three months. Some day when you got three months and maybe five thousand gallons of whiskey and a funnel, I would be glad to take my own time and show you what an Eichelberger looks like when drunk. You wouldn't believe it. Son, there wouldn't be nothing left of this town but a few sprung girders and a lot of busted bricks, in the middle of which—Geez, I'll get talking English myself if I hang around you much longer—in the middle of which, peaceful, with no human life nearer than maybe fifty miles, Henry Eichelberger will be on his back smiling at the sun. Drunk, Walter. Not stinking drunk, not even country-club drunk. But you could use the word drunk and I wouldn't take no offense."

He sat down and drank again. I stared moodily at the floor. There was nothing for me to say.

"But that," Henry said, "is some other time. Right now I am just taking my medicine. I ain't myself without a slight touch of delirium tremens, as the guy says. I was brought up on it. And I'm going with you, Walter. Where is this place at?"

"It's down near the beach, Henry, and you are not going with me. If you must get drunk—get drunk, but you are not going with me."

"You got a big car, Walter. I'll hide in back on the floor under a rug. It's a cinch."

"No, Henry."

"Walter, you are a sweet guy," Henry said, "and I am going with you into this frame. Have a smell from the barrel, Walter. You look to me kind of frail."

We argued for an hour and my head ached and I began to feel very nervous and tired. It was then that I made what might have been a fatal mistake. I succumbed to Henry's blandishments and took a small portion of whiskey, purely for medicinal purposes. This made me feel so much more relaxed that I took another and larger portion. I had had no food except coffee that morning and only a very light dinner the evening before. At the end of another hour Henry had been out for two more bottles of whiskey and I was as bright as a bird. All difficulties had now disappeared and I had agreed heartily that Henry should lie in the back of my car hidden by a rug and accompany me to the rendezvous.

We had passed the time very pleasantly until two o'clock, at which hour I began to feel sleepy and lay down on the bed, and fell into a deep slumber.

SEVEN

When I awoke again it was almost dark. I rose from the bed with panic in my heart, and also a sharp shoot of pain through my temples. It was only six-thirty, however. I was alone in the apartment and lengthening shadows were stealing across the floor. The display of empty whiskey bottles on the table was very disgusting. Henry Eichelberger was nowhere to be seen. With an instinctive pang, of which I was almost immediately ashamed, I hurried to my jacket hanging on the back of a chair and plunged my hand into the inner breast pocket. The packet of bills was there intact. After a brief hesitation, and with a feeling of secret guilt, I drew them out and slowly counted them over. Not a bill was missing. I replaced the money and tried to smile at myself for this lack of trust, and then switched on a light and went into the bathroom to take alternate hot and cold showers until my brain was once more comparatively clear.

I had done this and was dressing in fresh linen when a key turned in the lock and Henry Eichelberger entered with two wrapped bottles under his arm. He looked at me with what I thought was genuine affection.

"A guy that can sleep it off like you is a real champ, Walter," he said admiringly. "I snuck your keys so as not to wake you. I had to get some eats and some more hooch. I done a little solo drinking, which as I told you is against my principles, but this is a big day. However, we take it easy from now on as to the hooch. We can't afford no jitters till it's all over."

He had unwrapped a bottle wlile he was speaking and poured me a small drink. I drank it gratefully and immediately felt a warm glow in my veins.

"I bet you looked in your poke for that deck of mazuma," Henry said, grinning at me.

I felt myself reddening, but I said nothing. "O.K., pal, you done right. What the heck do you know about Henry Eichelberger anyways? I done something else." He reached behind him and drew a short automatic from his hip pocket. "If these boys wanta play rough," he said, "I got me five bucks worth of iron that don't mind playin' rough a little itself. And the Eichelbergers ain't missed a whole lot of the guys they shot at."

"I don't like that, Henry," I said severely. "That is contrary to the agreement."

"Nuts to the agreement," Henry said. "The boys get their dough and no cops. I'm out to see that they hand over them marbles and don't pull any fast footwork."

I saw there was no use arguing with him, so I completed my dressing and prepared to leave the apartment. We each took one more drink and then Henry put a full bottle in his pocket and we left.

On the way down the hall to the elevator he explained in a low voice: "I got a hack out front to tail you, just in case these boys got the same idea. You might circle a few quiet blocks so as I can find out. More like they don't pick you up till down close to the beach."

"All this must be costing you a great deal of money, Henry," I told him, and while we were waiting for the elevator to come up I took another twenty-dollar bill from my wallet and offered it to him. He took the money reluctantly, but finally folded it and placed it in his pocket.

I did as Henry had suggested, driving up and down a number of the hilly streets north of Hollywood Boulevard, and presently I heard the unmistakable hoot of a taxicab horn behind me. I pulled over to the side of the road. Henry got out of the cab and paid off the driver and got into my car beside me.

"All clear," he said. "No tail. I'll just keep kind of slumped down and you better stop somewhere for some groceries on account of if we have to get rough with these mugs, a full head of steam will help."

So I drove westward and dropped down to Sunset Boulevard and presently stopped at a crowded drive-in restaurant where we sat at the counter and ate a light meal of omelette and black coffee. We then proceeded on our way. When we reached Beverly Hills, Henry again made me wind in and out through a number of residential streets where he observed very carefully through the rear window of the car.

Fully satisfied at last we drove back to Sunset, and without incident onwards through Bel-Air and the fringes of Westwood, almost as far as the Riviera Polo field. At this point, down in the hollow, there is a canyon called Mandeville Canyon, a very quiet place. Henry had me drive up this for a short distance. We then stopped and had a little whiskey from his bottle and he climbed into the back of the car and curled his big body up on the floor, with the rug over him and his automatic pistol and his bottle down on the floor conveniently to his hand. That done I once more resumed my journey.

Pacific Palisades is a district whose inhabitants seem to retire rather early. When I reached what might be called the business center nothing was open but the drugstore beside the bank. I parked the car, with Henry remaining silent under the rug in the back, except for a slight gurgling noise I noticed as I stood on the dark sidewalk. Then I went into the drugstore and saw by its clock that it was now fifteen minutes to eight. I bought a package of cigarettes and lit one and took up my position near the open telephone booth.

The druggist, a heavy-set red-faced man of uncertain age, had a small radio up very loud and was listening to some foolish serial. I asked him to turn it down, as I was expecting an important telephone call. This he did, but not with any good grace, and immediately retired to the back part of his store whence I saw him looking out at me malignantly through a small glass window.

At precisely one minute to eight by the drugstore clock the phone rang sharply in the booth. I hastened into it and pulled the door tight shut. I lifted the receiver, trembling a little in spite of myself.

It was the same cool metallic voice. "Gage?"

"This is Mr. Gage."

"You done just what I told you?"

"Yes," I said. "I have the money in my pocket and I am entirely alone." I did not like the feeling of lying so brazenly, even to a thief, but I steeled myself to it.

"Listen, then. Go back about three hundred feet the way you come. Beside the firehouse there's a service station, closed up, painted green and red and white. Beside that, going south, is a dirt road. Follow it three quarters of a mile and you come to a white fence of four-by-four built almost across the road. You can just squeeze your car by at the left side. Dim your lights and get through there and keep going down the little hill into a hollow with sage all around. Park there, cut your lights, and wait. Get it?"

"Perfectly," I said coldly, "and it shall be done exactly that way."

"And listen, pal. There ain't a house in half a mile, and there ain't any folks around at all. You got ten minutes to get there. You're watched right this minute. You get there fast and you get there alone—or you got a trip for biscuits. And don't light no matches or pills nor use no flashlights. On your way."

The phone went dead and I left the booth. I was scarcely outside the drugstore before the druggist rushed at his radio and turned it up to a booming blare. I got into my car and turned it and drove back along Sunset Boulevard, as directed. Henry was as still as the grave on the floor behind me.

I was now very nervous and Henry had all the liquor which we had brought with us. I reached the firehouse in no time at all and through its front window I could see four firemen playing cards. I turned to the right down the dirt road past the red-and-green-and-white service station and almost at once the night was so still, in spite of the quiet sound of my car, that I could hear the crickets and treefrogs chirping and trilling in all directions, and from some nearby watery spot came the hoarse croak of a solitary bullfrog.

The road dipped and rose again and far off there was a yellow window. Then ahead of me, ghostly in the blackness of the moonless night, appeared the dim white barrier across the road.

179
▼

I noted the gap at the side and then dimmed my headlamps and steered carefully through it and so on down a rough short hill into an oval-shaped hollow space surrounded by low brush and plentifully littered with empty bottles and cans and pieces of paper. It was entirely deserted, however, at this dark hour. I stopped my car and shut off the ignition, and the lights, and sat there motionless, hands on the wheel.

Behind me I heard no murmur of sound from Henry. I waited possibly five minutes, although it seemed much longer, but nothing happened. It was very still, very lonely, and I did not feel happy.

Finally there was a faint sound of movement behind me and I looked back to see the pale blur of Henry's face peering at me from under the rug.

His voice whispered huskily. "Anything stirring, Walter?"

I shook my head at him vigorously and he once more pulled the rug over his face. I heard a faint sound of gurgling.

Fully fifteen minutes passed before I dared to move again. By this time the tensity of waiting had made me stiff. I therefore boldly unlatched the door of the car and stepped out upon the rough ground. Nothing happened. I walked slowly back and forth with my hands in my pockets. More and more time dragged by. More than half an hour had now elapsed and I became impatient. I went to the rear window of the car and spoke softly into the interior.

"Henry, I fear we have been victimized in a very cheap way. I fear very much that this is nothing but a low practical joke on the part of Mr. Gandesi in retaliation for the way you handled him last night. There is no one here and only one possible way of arriving. It looks to me like a very unlikely place for the sort of meeting we have been expecting."

"The son of a bitch!" Henry whispered back, and the gurgling sound was repeated in the darkness of the car. Then there was movement and he appeared free of the rug. The door opened against my body. Henry's head emerged. He looked in all directions his eyes could command. "Sit down on the running board," he whispered. "I'm getting out. If they got a bead on us from them bushes, they'll only see one head."

I did what Henry suggested and turned my collar up high and pulled my hat down over my eyes. As noiselessly as a shadow Henry stepped out of the car and shut the door without sound and stood before me ranging the limited horizon with his eyes. I could see the dim reflection of light on the gun in his hand. We remained thus for ten more minutes.

Henry then got angry and threw discretion to the winds. "Suckered!" he snarled. "You know what happened, Walter?"

"No, Henry. I do not."

"It was just a tryout, that's what it was. Somewhere along the line these dirty-so-and-so's checked on you to see did you play ball, and then again they checked on you at that drugstore back there. I bet you a pair of solid platinum bicycle wheels that was a long-distance call you caught back there."

"Yes, Henry, now that you mention it, I am sure it was," I said sadly.

"There you are, kid. The bums ain't even left town. They are sitting back there beside their plush-lined spittoons giving you the big razzoo. And tomorrow this guy calls you again on the phone and says O.K. so far, but they had to be careful and they will try again tonight maybe out in San Fernando Valley and the price will be upped to ten grand, on account of their extra trouble. I oughta go back there and twist that Gandesi so he would be lookin' up his left pants leg."

"Well, Henry," I said, "after all, I did not do exactly what they told me to, because you insisted on coming with me. And perhaps they are more clever than you think. So I think the best thing now is to go back to town and hope there will be a chance tomorrow to try again. And you must promise me faithfully not to interfere."

"Nuts!" Henry said angrily. "Without me along they would take you the way the cat took the canary. You are a sweet guy, Walter, but you don't know as many answers as Baby Leroy. These guys are thieves and they have a string of marbles that might probably bring them twenty grand with careful handling. They are out for a quick touch, but they will squeeze all they can just the same. I oughta go back to that fat wop Gandesi right now. I could do things to that slob that ain't been invented yet."

"Now, Henry, don't get violent," I said.

"Haw," Henry snarled. "Them guys give me an ache in the back of my lap." He raised his bottle to his lips with his left hand and drank thirstily. His voice came down a few tones and sounded more peaceful. "Better dip the bill, Walter. The party's a flop."

"Perhaps you are right, Henry," I sighed. "I will admit that my stomach has been trembling like an autumn leaf for all of half an hour."

So I stood up boldly beside him and poured a liberal portion of the fiery liquid down my throat. At once my courage revived. I handed the bottle back to Henry and he placed it carefully down on the running board. He stood beside me dancing the short automatic pistol up and down on the broad palm of his hand.

"I don't need no tools to handle that bunch. The hell with it." And with a sweep of his arm he hurled the pistol off among the bushes, where it fell to the ground with a muffled thud. He walked away from the car and stood with his arms akimbo, looking up at the sky.

I moved over beside him and watched his averted face, insofar as I was able to see it in that dim light. A strange melancholy came over me. In the brief time I had known Henry I had grown very fond of him.

"Well, Henry," I said at last, "what is the next move?"

"Beat it on home, I guess," he said slowly and mournfully. "And get good and drunk." He doubled his hands into fists and shook them slowly. Then he turned to face me. "Yeah," he said. "Nothing else to do. Beat it on home, kid, is all that is left to us."

"Not quite yet, Henry," I said softly.

I took my right hand out of my pocket. I have large hands.

In my right hand nestled the roll of wrapped quarters which I had obtained at the bank that morning. My hand made a large fist around them.

"Good night, Henry," I said quietly, and swung my fist with all the weight of my arm and body. "You had two strikes on me, Henry," I said. "The big one is still left."

But Henry was not listening to me. My fist with the wrapped weight of metal inside it had caught him fairly and squarely on the point of his jaw. His legs became boneless and he pitched straight forward, brushing my sleeve as he fell. I stepped quickly out of his way.

Henry Eichelberger lay motionless on the ground, as limp as a rubber glove.

I looked down at him a little sadly, waiting for him to stir, but he did not move a muscle. He lay inert, completely unconscious. I dropped the roll of quarters back into my pocket, bent over him, searched him thoroughly, moving him around like a sack of meal, but it was a long time before I found the pearls. They were twined around his ankle inside his left sock.

"Well, Henry," I said, speaking to him for the last time, although he could not hear me, "you are a gentleman, even if you are a thief. You could have taken the money a dozen times this afternoon and given me nothing. You could have taken it a little while ago when you had the gun in your hand, but even that repelled you. You threw the gun away and we were man to man, far from help, far from interference. And even then you hesitated, Henry. In fact, Henry, I think for a successful thief you hesitated just a little too long. But as a man of sporting feelings I can only think the more highly of you. Goodbye, Henry, and good luck."

I took my wallet out and withdrew a one-hundred-dollar bill and placed it carefully in the pocket where I had seen Henry put his money. Then I went back to the car and took a drink out of the whiskey bottle and corked it firmly and laid it beside him, convenient to his right hand.

I felt sure that when he awakened he would need it.

EIGHT

It was past ten o'clock when I returned home to my apartment, but I at once went to the telephone and called Ellen Macintosh. "Darling!" I cried. "I have the pearls."

I caught the sound of her indrawn breath over the wire. "Oh darling," she said tensely and excitedly, "and you are not hurt? They did not hurt you, darling? They just took the money and let you go?"

"There were no 'they,' darling," I said proudly. "I still have Mr. Gallemore's money intact. There was only Henry."

"Henry!" she cried in a very strange voice. "But I thought —Come over here at once, Walter Gage, and tell me—"

"I have whiskey on my breath, Ellen."

"Darling! I'm sure you needed it. Come at once."

So once more I went down to the street and hurried to Carondelet Park and in no time at all was at the Penruddock residence. Ellen came out on the porch to meet me and we talked there quietly in the dark, holding hands, for the household had gone to bed. As simple as I could I told her my story.

"But darling," she said at last, "how did you know it was Henry? I thought Henry was your friend. And this other voice on the telephone—"

"Henry *was* my friend," I said a little sadly, "and that is what destroyed him. As to the voice on the telephone, that was a small matter and easily arranged. Henry was away from me a number of times to arrange it. There was just one small point that gave me thought. After I gave Gandesi my private card with the name of my apartment house scribbled upon it, it was necessary for Henry to communicate to his confederate that we had seen Gandesi and given him my name and address. For of course when I had this foolish, or perhaps not so very foolish idea of visiting some well-known underworld character in order to send a message that we would buy back the pearls, this was Henry's opportunity to make me think the telephone message came as a result of our talking to Gandesi, and telling him our difficulty. But since the first call came to me at my apartment before Henry had had a chance to inform his confederate of our meeting with Gandesi, it was obvious that a trick had been employed.

"Then I recalled that a car had bumped into us from behind and Henry had gone back to abuse the driver. And of course the bumping was deliberate, and Henry had made the opportunity for it on purpose, and his confederate was in the car. So Henry, while pretending to shout at him, was able to convey the necessary information."

"But, Walter," Ellen said, having listened to this explanation a little impatiently, "that is a very small matter. What I really want to know is how you decided that Henry had the pearls at all."

"But you told me he had them," I said. "You were quite sure of it. Henry is a very durable character. It would be just like him to hide the pearls somewhere, having no fear of what the police might do to him, and get another position and then after perhaps quite a long time, retrieve the pearls and quietly leave this part of the country."

Ellen shook her head impatiently in the darkness of the porch. "Walter," she said sharply, "you are hiding something. You could not have been sure and you would not have hit Henry in that brutal way, unless you had been sure. I know you well enough to know that."

"Well, darling," I said modestly, "there was indeed another small indication, one of those foolish trifles which the cleverest men overlook. As you know, I do not use the regular apartment-house telephone, not wishing to be annoyed by solicitors and such people. The phone which I use is a private line and its number is unlisted. But the calls I received from Henry's confederate came over that phone, and Henry had been in my apartment a great deal, and I had been careful not to give Mr. Gandesi that number, because of course I did not expect anything from Mr. Gandesi, as I was perfectly sure from the beginning that Henry had the pearls, if only I could get him to bring them out of hiding."

"Oh, darling," Ellen cried, and threw her arms around me. "How brave you are, and I really think that you are actually clever in your own peculiar way. Do you believe that Henry was in love with me?"

But that was a subject in which I had no interest whatever. I left the pearls in Ellen's keeping and late as the hour now was I drove at once to the residence of Mr. Lansing Gallemore and told him my story and gave him back his money.

A few months later I was happy to receive a letter postmarked in Honolulu and written on a very inferior brand of paper.

Well, pal, that Sunday punch of yours was the money and I did not think you had it in you, altho of course I was not set for it. But it was a pip and made me think of you for a week every time I brushed my teeth. It was too bad I had to scram because you are a sweet guy altho a little on the goofy side and I'd like to be getting plastered with you right now instead of wiping oil valves where I am at which is not where this letter is mailed by several thousand miles. There is just two things I would like you to know and they are both kosher. I did fall hard for that tall blonde and this was the main reason I took my time from the old lady. Glomming the pearls was just one of those screwy ideas a guy can get when he is dizzy with a dame. It was a crime the way they left them marbles lying around in that bread box and I worked for a Frenchy once in Djibouty and got to know pearls enough to tell them from snowballs. But when it came to the clinch down there in that brush with us two alone and no holds barred I just was too soft to go through with the deal. Tell that blonde you got a loop on I was asking for her.

Yrs. as ever,

HENRY EICHELBERGER (*Alias*)

P.S. What do you know, that punk that did the phone work on you tried to take me for a fifty cut on that C note you tucked in my vest. I had to twist the sucker plenty.

Yrs. H. E. (*Alias*)

PICKUP ON
NOON STREET

ONE

The man and the girl walked slowly, close together, past a dim stencil sign that said: Surprise Hotel. The man wore a purple suit, a Panama hat over his shiny, slicked-down hair. He walked splay-footed, soundlessly.

The girl wore a green hat and a short skirt and sheer stockings, four-and-a-half inch French heels. She smelled of Midnight Narcissus.

At the corner the man leaned close, said something in the girl's ear. She jerked away from him, giggled.

"You gotta buy liquor if you take *me* home, Smiler."

"Next time, baby. I'm fresh outa dough."

The girl's voice got hard. "Then I tells you goodbye in the next block, handsome."

"Like hell, baby," the man answered.

The arc at the intersection threw light on them. They walked across the street far apart. At the other side the man caught the girl's arm. She twisted away from him.

"Listen, you cheap grifter!" she shrilled. "Keep your paws down, see! Tinhorns are dust to me. Dangle!"

"How much liquor you gotta have, baby?"

"Plenty."

"Me bein' on the nut, where do I collect it?"

"You got hands, ain't you?" the girl sneered. Her voice dropped the shrillness. She leaned close to him again. "Maybe you got a gun, big boy. Got a gun?"

"Yeah. And no shells for it."

"The goldbricks over on Central don't know that."

"Don't be that way," the man in the purple suit snarled. Then he snapped his fingers and stiffened. "Wait a minute. I got me a idea."

He stopped and looked back along the street toward the dim stencil hotel sign. The girl slapped a glove across his chin caressingly. The glove smelled to him of the perfume, Midnight Narcissus.

The man snapped his fingers again, grinned widely in the dim light. "If that drunk is still holed up in Doc's place—I collect. Wait for me, huh?"

"Maybe, at home. If you ain't gone too long."

"Where's home, baby?"

The girl stared at him. A half-smile moved along her full lips, died at the corners of them. The breeze picked a sheet of newspaper out of the gutter and tossed it against the man's leg. He kicked at it savagely.

"Calliope Apartments. Four-B, Two-Forty-Six East Forty-Eight. How soon you be there?"

The man stepped very close to her, reached back and tapped his hip. His voice was low, chilling.

"You wait for me, baby."

She caught her breath, nodded. "Okey, handsome. I'll wait."

The man went back along the cracked sidewalk, across the intersection, along to where the stencil sign hung out over the street. He went through a glass door into a narrow lobby with a row of brown wooden chairs pushed against the plaster wall. There was just space to walk past them to the desk. A bald-headed colored man lounged behind the desk, fingering a large green pin in his tie.

The Negro in the purple suit leaned across the counter and

his teeth flashed in a quick, hard smile. He was very young, with a thin, sharp jaw, a narrow bony forehead, the flat brilliant eyes of the gangster. He said softly: "That pug with the husky voice still here? The guy that banked the crap game last night."

The bald-headed clerk looked at the flies on the ceiling fixture. "Didn't see him go out, Smiler."

"Ain't what I asked you, Doc."

"Yeah. He still here."

"Still drunk?"

"Guess so. Hasn't been out."

"Three-forty-nine, ain't it?"

"You been there, ain't you? What you wanta know for?"

"He cleaned me down to my lucky piece. I gotta make a touch."

The bald-headed man looked nervous. The Smiler stared softly at the green stone in the man's tie pin.

"Get rolling, Smiler. Nobody gets bent around here. We ain't no Central Avenue flop."

The Smiler said very softly: "He's my pal, Doc. He'll lend me twenty. You touch half."

He put his hand out palm up. The clerk stared at the hand for a long moment. Then he nodded sourly, went behind a ground-glass screen, came back slowly, looking toward the street door.

His hand went out and hovered over the palm. The palm closed over a passkey, dropped inside the cheap purple suit.

The sudden flashing grin on the Smiler's face had an icy edge to it.

"Careful, Doc—while I'm up above."

The clerk said: "Step on it. Some of the customers get home early." He glanced at the green electric clock on the wall. It was seven-fifteen. "And the walls ain't any too thick," he added.

The thin youth gave him another flashing grin, nodded, went delicately back along the lobby to the shadowy staircase. There was no elevator in the Surprise Hotel.

At one minute past seven Pete Anglich, narcotic squad under-cover man, rolled over on the hard bed and looked at the cheap strap watch on his left wrist. There were heavy shadows under his eyes, a thick dark stubble on his broad chin. He swung his bare feet to the floor and stood up in cheap cotton pajamas, flexed his muscles, stretched, bent over stiff-kneed and touched the floor in front of his toes with a grunt.

He walked across to a chipped bureau, drank from a quart bottle of cheap rye whiskey, grimaced, pushed the cork into the neck of the bottle, and rammed it down hard with the heel of his hand.

"Boy, have I got a hangover," he grumbled huskily.

He stared at his face in the bureau mirror, at the stubble on his chin, the thick white scar on his throat close to the windpipe. His voice was husky because the bullet that had made the scar had done something to his vocal chords. It was a smooth huskiness, like the voice of a blues singer.

He stripped his pajamas off and stood naked in the middle of the room, his toes fumbling the rough edge of a big rip in the carpet. His body was very broad, and that made him look a little shorter than he was. His shoulders sloped, his nose was a little thick, the skin over his cheekbones looked like leather. He had short, curly, black hair, utterly steady eyes, the small set mouth of a quick thinker.

He went into a dim, dirty bathroom, stepped into the tub and turned the shower on. The water was warmish, but not hot. He stood under it and soaped himself, rubbed his whole body over, kneaded his muscles, rinsed off.

He jerked a dirty towel off the rack and started to rub a glow into his skin.

A faint noise behind the loosely closed bathroom door stopped him. He held his breath, listened, heard the noise again, a creak of boarding, a click, a rustle of cloth. Pete Anglich reached for the door and pulled it open slowly.

The Negro in the purple suit and Panama hat stood beside the bureau, with Pete Anglich's coat in his hand. On the bureau in front of him were two guns. One of them was Pete Anglich's old worn Colt. The room door was shut and a key with a tag lay on the carpet near it, as though it had fallen out of the door, or been pushed out from the other side.

The Smiler let the coat fall to the floor and held a wallet in his left hand. His right hand lifted the Colt. He grinned.

"Okey, white boy. Just go on dryin' yourself off after your shower," he said.

Pete Anglich toweled himself. He rubbed himself dry, stood naked with the wet towel in his left hand.

The Smiler had the billfold empty on the bureau, was counting the money with his left hand. His right still clutched the Colt.

"Eighty-seven bucks. Nice money. Some of it's mine from the crap game, but I'm lifting it all, pal. Take it easy. I'm friends with the management here."

"Gimme a break, Smiler," Pete Anglich said hoarsely. "That's every dollar I got in the world. Leave a few bucks, huh?" He made his voice thick, coarse, heavy as though with liquor.

The Smiler gleamed his teeth, shook his narrow head. "Can't do it, pal. Got me a date and I need the kale."

Pete Anglich took a loose step forward and stopped, grinning sheepishly. The muzzle of his own gun had jerked at him.

The Smiler sidled over to the bottle of rye and lifted it.

"I can use this, too. My baby's got a throat for liquor. Sure has. What's in your pants is yours, pal. Fair enough?"

Pete Anglich jumped sideways, about four feet. The Smiler's face convulsed. The gun jerked around and the bottle of rye slid out of his left hand, slammed down on his foot. He yelped, kicked out savagely, and his toe caught in the torn place in the carpet.

Pete Anglich flipped the wet end of the bathtowel straight at the Smiler's eyes.

The Smiler reeled and yelled with pain. Then Pete Anglich held the Smiler's gun wrist in his hard left hand. He twisted up, around. His hand started to slide down over the Smiler's hand, over the gun. The gun turned inward and touched the Smiler's side.

A hard knee kicked viciously at Pete Anglich's abdomen. He gagged, and his finger tightened convulsively on the Smiler's trigger finger.

The shot was dull, muffled against the purple cloth of the suit. The Smiler's eyes rolled whitely and his narrow jaw fell slack.

Pete Anglich let him down on the floor and stood panting, bent over, his face greenish. He groped for the fallen bottle of rye, got the cork out, got some of the fiery liquid down his throat.

The greenish look went away from his face. His breathing slowed. He wiped sweat off his forehead with the back of his hand.

He felt the Smiler's pulse. The Smiler didn't have any pulse. He was dead. Pete Anglich loosened the gun from his hand, went over to the door and glanced out into the hallway. Empty. There was a passkey in the outside of the lock. He removed it, locked the door from the inside.

He put his underclothes and socks and shoes on, his worn blue serge suit, knotted a black tie around the crumpled shirt collar, went back to the dead man and took a roll of bills from his pocket. He packed a few odds and ends of clothes and toilet articles in a cheap fiber suitcase, stood it by the door.

He pushed a torn scrap of sheet through his revolver barrel with a pencil, replaced the used cartridge, crushed the empty shell with his heel on the bathroom floor and then flushed it down the toilet.

He locked the door from the outside and walked down the stairs to the lobby.

The bald-headed clerk's eyes jumped at him, then dropped. The skin of his face turned gray. Pete Anglich leaned on the counter and opened his hand to let two keys tinkle on the scarred wood. The clerk stared at the keys, shuddered.

Pete Anglich said in his slow, husky voice: "Hear any funny noises?"

The clerk shook his head, gulped.

"Creep joint, eh?" Pete Anglich said.

The clerk moved his head painfully, twisted his neck in his collar. His bald head winked darkly under the ceiling light.

"Too bad," Pete Anglich said. "What name did I register under last night?"

"You ain't registered," the clerk whispered.

"Maybe I wasn't here even," Pete Anglich said softly.

"Never saw you before, mister."

"You're not seeing me now. You never will see me—to know me—will you, Doc?"

The clerk moved his neck and tried to smile.

Pete Anglich drew his wallet out and shook three dollar bills from it.

"I'm a guy that likes to pay his way," he said slowly. "This pays for Room 349—till way in the morning, kind of late. The lad you gave the passkey to looks like a heavy sleeper." He paused, steadied his cool eyes on the clerk's face, added thoughtfully: "Unless, of course, he's got friends who would like to move him out."

Bubbles showed on the clerk's lips. He stuttered: "He ain't—ain't—"

"Yeah," Pete Anglich said. "What would you expect?"

He went across to the street door, carrying his suitcase, stepped out under the stencil sign, stood a moment looking toward the hard white glare of Central Avenue.

Then he walked the other way. The street was very dark, very quiet. There were four blocks of frame houses before he came to Noon Street. It was all a Negro quarter.

He met only one person on the way, a brown girl in a green hat, very sheer stockings, and four-and-a-half-inch heels, who smoked a cigarette under a dusty palm tree and stared back toward the Surprise Hotel.

TWO

The lunch wagon was an old buffet car without wheels, set end to the street in a space between a machine shop and a rooming house. The name Bella Donna was lettered in faded gold on the sides. Pete Anglich went up the two iron steps at the end, into a smell of fry grease.

The Negro cook's fat white back was to him. At the far end of the low counter a white girl in a cheap brown felt hat and a shabby polo coat with a high turned-up collar was sipping coffee, her cheek propped in her left hand. There was nobody else in the car.

Pete Anglich put his suitcase down and sat on a stool near the door, saying: "Hi, Mopsy!"

The fat cook turned a shiny black face over his white shoulder. The face split in a grin. A thick bluish tongue came out and wiggled between the cook's thick lips.

"How's a boy? W'at you eat?"

"Scramble two light, coffee, toast, no spuds."

"Dat ain't no food for a he-guy," Mopsy complained.

"I been drunk," Pete Anglich said.

The girl at the end of the counter looked at him sharply, looked at the cheap alarm clock on the shelf, at the watch on her gloved wrist. She drooped, stared into her coffee cup again.

The fat cook broke eggs into a pan, added milk, stirred them around. "You want a shot, boy?"

Pete Anglich shook his head.

"I'm driving the wagon, Mopsy."

The cook grinned. He reached a brown bottle from under the counter, and poured a big drink into a water glass, set the glass down beside Pete Anglich.

Pete Anglich reached suddenly for the glass, jerked it to his lips, drank the liquor down.

194
▼

"Guess I'll drive the wagon some other time." He put the glass down empty.

The girl stood up, came along the stools, put a dime on the counter. The fat cook punched his cash register, put down a nickel change. Pete Anglich stared casually at the girl. A shabby, innocent-eyed girl, brown hair curling on her neck, eyebrows plucked clean as a bone and startled arches painted above the place where they had been.

"Not lost, are you, lady?" he asked in his softly husky voice.

The girl had fumbled her bag open to put the nickel away. She started violently, stepped back and dropped the bag. It spilled its contents on the floor. She stared down at it, wide-eyed.

Pete Anglich went down on one knee and pushed things into the bag. A cheap nickel compact, cigarettes, a purple match-folder lettered in gold: The Juggernaut Club. Two colored handkerchiefs, a crumpled dollar bill and some silver and pennies.

He stood up with the closed bag in his hand, held it out to the girl.

"Sorry," he said softly. "I guess I startled you."

Her breath made a rushing sound. She caught the bag out of his hand, ran out of the car, and was gone.

The fat cook looked after her. "That doll don't belong in Tough Town," he said slowly.

He dished up the eggs and toast, poured coffee in a thick cup, put them down in front of Pete Anglich.

Pete Anglich touched the food, said absently: "Alone, and matches from the Juggernaut. Trimmer Waltz's spot. You know what happens to girls like that when he gets hold of them."

The cook licked his lips, reached under the counter for the whiskey bottle. He poured himself a drink, added about the same amount of water to the bottle, put it back under the counter.

"I ain't never been a tough guy, and don' want to start," he said slowly. "But I'se all tired of white boys like dat guy. Some day he gonna get cut."

Pete Angliich kicked his suitcase.

"Yeah. Keep the keister for me, Mopsy."

He went out.

Two or three cars flicked by in the crisp fall night, but the sidewalks were dark and empty. A colored night watchman moved slowly along the street, trying the doors of a small row of dingy stores. There were frame houses across the street, and a couple of them were noisy.

Pete Anglich went on past the intersection. Three blocks from the lunch wagon he saw the girl again.

She was pressed against a wall, motionless. A little beyond her, dim yellow light came from the stairway of a walk-up apartment house. Beyond that a small parking lot with billboards across most of its front. Faint light from somewhere touched her hat, her shabby polo coat with the turned-up collar, one side of her face. He knew it was the same girl.

He stepped into a doorway, watched her. Light flashed on her upraised arm, on something bright, a wrist watch. Somewhere not far off a clock struck eight, low, pealing notes.

Lights stabbed into the street from the corner behind. A big car swung slowly into view and as it swung its headlights dimmed. It crept along the block, a dark shininess of glass and polished paint.

Pete Anglich grinned sharply in his doorway. A custom-built Duesenberg, six blocks from Central Avenue! He stiffened at the sharp sound of running steps, clicking high heels.

The girl was running toward him along the sidewalk. The car was not near enough for its dimmed lights to pick her up. Pete Anglich stepped out of the doorway, grabbed her arm, dragged her back into the doorway. A gun snaked from under his coat.

The girl panted at his side.

The Duesenberg passed the doorway slowly. No shots came from it. The uniformed driver didn't slow down.

"I can't do it. I'm scared," the girl gasped in Pete Anglich's ear. Then she broke away from him and ran farther along the sidewalk, away from the car.

Pete Anglich looked after the Duesenberg. It was opposite the row of billboards that screened the parking lot. It was barely crawling now. Something sailed from its left front window, fell with a dry slap on the sidewalk. The car picked up speed soundlessly, purred off into the darkness. A block away its head lights flashed up full again.

Nothing moved. The thing that had been thrown out of the car lay on the inner edge of the sidewalk, almost under one of the billboards.

Then the girl was coming back again, a step at a time, haltingly. Pete Anglich watched her come, without moving. When she was level with him he said softly: "What's the racket? Could a fellow help?"

She spun around with a choked sound, as though she had forgotten all about him. Her head moved in the darkness at his side. There was a swift shine as her eyes moved. There was a pale flicker across her chin. Her voice was low, hurried, scared.

"You're the man from the lunch wagon. I saw you."

"Open up. What is it—a pay-off?"

Her head moved again in the darkness at his side, up and down.

"What's in the package?" Pete Anglich growled. "Money?"

Her words came in a rush. "Would you get it for me? Oh, would you please? I'd be so grateful. I'd—"

He laughed. His laugh had a low growling sound. "Get it for *you*, baby? I use money in my business, too. Come on, what's the racket? Spill."

She jerked away from him, but he didn't let go of her arm. He slid the gun out of sight under his coat, held her with both hands. Her voice sobbed as she whispered: "He'll kill me, if I don't get it."

Very sharply, coldly, Pete Anglich said, "Who will? Trimmer Waltz?"

She started violently, almost tore out of his grasp. Not quite. Steps shuffled on the sidewalk. Two dark forms showed in

197

front of the billboards, didn't pause to pick anything up. The steps came near, cigarette tips glowed.

A voice said softly: " 'Lo there, sweets. Yo' want to change yo'r boy frien', honey?"

The girl shrank behind Pete Anglich. One of the Negroes laughed gently, waved the red end of his cigarette.

"Hell, it's a white gal," the other one said quickly. "Le's dust."

They went on, chuckling. At the corner they turned, were gone.

"There you are," Pete Anglich growled. "Shows you where you are." His voice was hard, angry. "Oh, hell, stay here and I'll get your damn pay-off for you."

He left the girl and went lightly along close to the front of the apartment house. At the edge of the billboards he stopped, probed the darkness with his eyes, saw the package. It was wrapped in dark material, not large but large enough to see. He bent down and looked under the billboards. He didn't see anything behind them.

He went on four steps, leaned down and picked up the package, felt cloth and two thick rubber bands. He stood quite still, listening.

Distant traffic hummed on a main street. A light burned across the street in a rooming house, behind a glass-paneled door. A window was open and dark above it.

A woman's voice screamed shrilly behind him.

He stiffened, whirled, and the light hit him between the eyes. It came from the dark window across the street, a blinding white shaft that impaled him against the billboard.

His face leered in it, his eyes blinked. He didn't move any more.

Shoes dropped on cement and a smaller spot stabbed at him sideways from the end of the billboards. Behind the spot a casual voice spoke: "Don't shift an eyelash, bud. You're all wrapped up in law."

Men with revolvers out closed in on him from both ends of the line of billboards. Heels clicked far off on concrete. Then it was silent for a moment. Then a car with a red spotlight swung around the corner and bore down on the group of men with Pete Anglich in their midst.

The man with the casual voice said: "I'm Angus, detective-lieutenant. I'll take the packet, if you don't mind. And if you'll just keep your hands together a minute—"

The handcuffs clicked dryly on Pete Anglich's wrists.

He listened hard for the sound of the heels far off, running away. But there was too much noise around him now.

Doors opened and dark people began to boil out of the houses.

THREE

John Vidaury was six feet two inches in height and had the most perfect profile in Hollywood. He was dark, winsome, romantic, with an interesting touch of gray at his temples. His shoulders were wide, his hips narrow. He had the waist of an English guards officer, and his dinner clothes fit him so beautifully that it hurt.

So he looked at Pete Anglich as if he was about to apologize for not knowing him. Pete Anglich looked at his handcuffs, at his worn shoes on the thick rug, at the tall chiming clock against the wall. There was a flush on his face and his eyes were bright.

In a smooth, clear, modulated voice Vidaury said, "No, I've never seen him before." He smiled at Pete Anglich.

Angus, the plainclothes lieutenant, leaned against one end of a carved library table and snapped a finger against the brim of his hat. Two other detectives stood near a side wall. A fourth sat at a small desk with a stenographer's notebook in front of him.

Angus said, "Oh, we just thought you might know him. We can't get much of anything out of him."

Vidaury raised his eyebrows, smiled very faintly. "Really I'm surprised at that." He went around collecting glasses, and took them over to a tray, started to mix more drinks.

"It happens," Angus said.

"I thought you had ways," Vidaury said delicately, pouring Scotch into the glasses.

Angus looked at a fingernail. "When I say he won't tell us anything, Mr. Vidaury, I mean anything that counts. He says his name is Pete Anglich, that he used to be a fighter, but hasn't fought for several years. Up to about a year ago he was a private detective, but has no work now. He won some money in a crap game and got drunk, and was just wandering about. That's how he happened to be on Noon Street. He saw the package tossed out of your car and picked it up. We can vag him, but that's about all."

"It could happen that way," Vidaury said softly. He carried the glasses two at a time to the four detectives, lifted his own, and nodded slightly before he drank. He drank gracefully, with a superb elegance of movement. "No, I don't know him," he said again. "Frankly, he doesn't look like an acid-thrower to me." He waved a hand. "So I'm afraid bringing him here—"

Pete Anglich lifted his head suddenly, stared at Vidaury. His voice sneered.

"It's a great compliment, Vidaury. They don't often use up the time of four coppers taking prisoners around to call on people."

Vidaury smiled amiably. "That's Hollywood," he smiled. "After all, one had a reputation."

"Had," Pete Anglich said. "Your last picture was a pain where you don't tell the ladies."

Angus stiffened. Vidaury's face went white. He put his glass down slowly, let his hand fall to his side. He walked springily across the rug and stood in front of Pete Anglich.

"That's your opinion," he said harshly, "but I warn you——"

Pete Anglich scowled at him. "Listen, big shot. You put a grand on the line because some punk promised to throw acid at you if you didn't. I picked up the grand, but I didn't get any of your nice, new money. So you got it back. You get ten grand worth of publicity and it won't cost you a nickel. I call that pretty swell."

Angus said sharply, "That's enough from you, mug."

"Yeah?" Pete Anglich sneered. "I thought you wanted me to talk. Well, I'm talking, and I hate pikers, see?"

Vidaury breathed hard. Very suddenly he balled his fist and swung at Pete Anglich's jaw. Pete Anglich's head rolled under the blow, and his eyes blinked shut, then wide open. He shook himself and said coolly: "Elbow up and thumb down, Vidaury. You break a hand hitting a guy that way."

Vidaury stepped back and shook his head, looked at his thumb. His face lost its whiteness. His smile stole back.

"I'm sorry," he said contritely. "I am very sorry. I'm not used to being insulted. As I don't know this man, perhaps you'd better take him away, Lieutenant. Handcuffed, too. Not very sporting, was it?"

"Tell that to your polo ponies," Pete Anglich said. "I don't bruise so easy."

Angus walked over to him, tapped his shoulder. "Up on the dogs, bo. Let's drift. You're not used to nice people, are you?"

"No. I like bums," Pete Anglich said.

He stood up slowly, scuffed at the pile of the carpet.

The two dicks against the wall fell in beside him, and they walked away down the huge room, under an arch. Angus and the other man came behind. They waited in the small private lobby for the elevator to come up.

"What was the idea?" Angus snapped. "Getting gashouse with him?"

Pete Anglich laughed. "Jumpy," he said. "Just jumpy."

The elevator came up and they rode down to the huge, silent lobby of the Chester Towers. Two house detectives lounged at the end of the marble desk, two clerks stood alert behind it.

Pete Anglich lifted his manacled hands in the fighter's salute. "What, no newshawks yet?" he jeered. "Vidaury won't like hush-hush on this."

"Keep goin', smartie," one of the dicks snapped, jerking his arm.

They went down a corridor and out of a side entrance to a narrow street that dropped almost sheer to treetops. Beyond the treetops the lights of the city were a vast golden carpet, stitched with brilliant splashes of red and green and blue and purple.

Two starters whirred. Pete Anglich was pushed into the back seat of the first car. Angus and another man got in on either side of him. The cars drifted down the hill, turned east on Fountain, slid quietly through the evening for mile after mile. Fountain met Sunset, and the cars dropped downtown toward the tall, white tower of the City Hall. At the plaza the first car swung over to Los Angeles Street and went south. The other car went on.

After a while Pete Anglich dropped the corners of his mouth and looked sideways at Angus.

"Where you taking me? This isn't the way to headquarters."

Angus' dark, austere face turned toward him slowly. After a moment the big detective leaned back and yawned at the night. He didn't answer.

The car slid along Los Angeles to Fifth, east to San Pedro, south again for block after block, quiet blocks and loud blocks, blocks where silent men sat on shaky front porches and blocks where noisy young toughs of both colors snarled and wise-cracked at one another in front of cheap restaurants and drug-stores and beer parlors full of slot machines.

At Santa Barbara the police car turned east again, drifted slowly along the curb to Noon Street. It stopped at the corner above the lunch wagon. Pete Anglich's face tightened again, but he didn't say anything.

"Okey," Angus drawled. "Take the nippers off."

The dick on Pete Anglich's other side dug a key out of his vest, unlocked the handcuffs, jangled them pleasantly before he put them away on his hip. Angus swung the door open and stepped out of the car.

"Out," he said over his shoulder.

Pete Anglich got out. Angus walked a little way from the street light, stopped, beckoned. His hand moved under his coat, came out with a gun. He said softly: "Had to play it this way. Otherwise we'd tip the town. Pearson's the only one that knows you. Any ideas?"

Pete Anglich took his gun, shook his head slowly, slid the gun under his own coat, keeping his body between it and the car at the curb behind.

"The stake-out was spotted, I guess," he said slowly. "There was a girl hanging around there, but maybe that just happened, too."

Angus stared at him silently for a moment, then nodded and went back to the car. The door slammed shut, and the car drifted off down the street and picked up speed.

Pete Anglich walked along Santa Barbara to Central, south on Central. After a while a bright sign glared at him in violet letters—Juggernaut Club. He went up broad carpeted stairs toward noise and dance music.

FOUR

The girl had to go sideways to get between the close-set tables around the small dance floor. Her hips touched the back of a man's shoulder and he reached out and grabbed her hand, grinning. She smiled mechanically, pulled her hand away and came on.

She looked better in the bronze metal-cloth dress with bare arms and the brown hair curling low on her neck; better than in the shabby polo coat and cheap felt hat, better even than in skyscraper heels, bare legs and thighs, the irreducible minimum above the waistline, and a dull gold opera hat tipped rakishly over one ear.

Her face looked haggard, small, pretty, shallow. Her eyes had a wide stare. The dance band made a sharp racket over the clatter of dishes, the thick hum of talk, the shuffling feet on the dance floor. The girl came slowly up to Pete Anglich's table, pulled the other chair out and sat down.

She propped her chin on the backs of her hands, put her elbows on the tablecloth, stared at him.

"Hello there," she said in a voice that shook a little.

Pete Anglich pushed a pack of cigarettes across the table, watched her shake one loose and get it between her lips. He struck a match. She had to take it out of his hand to light her cigarette.

"Drink?"

"I'll say."

He signaled the fuzzy-haired, almond-eyed waiter, ordered a couple of sidecars. The waiter went away. Pete Anglich leaned back on his chair and looked at one of his blunt finger-tips.

The girl said very softly: "I got your note, mister."

"Like it?" His voice was stiffly casual. He didn't look at her.

She laughed off key. "We've got to please the customers."

Pete Anglich looked past her shoulder at the corner of the band shell. A man stood there smoking, beside a small microphone. He was heavily built, old for an m.c., with slick gray hair and a big nose and the thickened complexion of a steady drinker. He was smiling at everything and everybody. Pete Anglich looked at him a little while, watching the direction of his glances. He said stiffly, in the same casual voice, "But you'd be here anyway."

The girl stiffened, then slumped. "You don't have to insult me, mister."

He looked at her slowly, with an empty up-from-under look. "You're down and out, knee-deep in nothing, baby. I've been that way often enough to know the symptoms. Besides, you got me in plenty jam tonight. I owe you a couple insults.

The fuzzy-haired waiter came back and slid a tray on the cloth, wiped the bottoms of two glasses with a dirty towel, set them out. He went away again.

The girl put her hand around a glass, lifted it quickly and took a long drink. She shivered a little as she put the glass down. Her face was white.

"Wisecrack or something," she said rapidly. "Don't just sit there. I'm watched."

Pete Anglich touched his fresh drink, smiled very deliberately toward the corner of the band shell.

"Yeah, I can imagine. Tell me about that pick-up on Noon Street."

She reached out quickly and touched his arm. Her sharp nails dug into it. "Not here," she breathed. "I don't know how you found me and I don't care. You looked like the kind of Joe that would help a girl out. I was scared stiff. But don't talk about it here. I'll do anything you want, go anywhere you want. Only not here."

Pete Anglich took his arm from under her hand, leaned back again. His eyes were cold, but his mouth was kind.

"I get it. Trimmer's wishes. Was he tailing the job?"

She nodded quickly. "I hadn't gone three blocks before he picked me up. He thought it was a swell gag, what I did, but he won't think so when he sees you here. That makes you wise."

Pete Anglich sipped his drink. "He is coming this way," he said, coolly.

The gray-haired m.c. was moving among the tables, bowing and talking, but edging toward the one where Pete Anglich sat with the girl. The girl was staring into a big gilt mirror behind Pete Anglich's head. Her face was suddenly distorted, shattered with terror. Her lips were shaking uncontrollably.

Trimmer Waltz idled casually up to the table, leaned a hand down on it. He poked his big-veined nose at Pete Anglich. There was a soft, flat grin on his face.

"Hi, Pete. Haven't seen you around since they buried McKinley. How's tricks?"

"Not bad, not good," Pete Anglich said huskily. "I been on a drunk."

Trimmer Waltz broadened his smile, turned it on the girl. She looked at him quickly, looked away, picking at the table-cloth.

Waltz's voice was soft, cooing. "Know the little lady before—or just pick her out of the line-up?"

Pete Anglich shrugged, looked bored. "Just wanted somebody to share a drink with, Trimmer. Sent her a note. Okey?"

"Sure. Perfect." Waltz picked one of the glasses up, sniffed at it. He shook his head sadly. "Wish we could serve better stuff. At four bits a throw it can't be done. How about tipping a few out of a right bottle, back in my den?"

"Both of us?" Pete Anglich asked gently.

"Both of you is right. In about five minutes. I got to circulate a little first."

He pinched the girl's cheek, went on, with a loose swing of his tailored shoulders.

The girl said slowly, thickly, hopelessly, "So Pete's your name. You must want to die young, Pete. Mine's Token Ware. Silly name, isn't it?"

"I like it," Pete Anglich said softly.

The girl stared at a point below the white scar on Pete Anglich's throat. Her eyes slowly filled with tears.

Trimmer Waltz drifted among the tables, speaking to a customer here and there. He edged over to the far wall, came along it to the band shell, stood there ranging the house with his eyes until he was looking directly at Pete Anglich. He jerked his head, stepped back through a pair of thick curtains.

Pete Anglich pushed his chair back and stood up. "Let's go," he said.

Token Ware crushed a cigarette out in a glass tray with jerky fingers, finished the drink in her glass, stood up. They went back between the tables, along the edge of the dance floor, over to the side of the band shell.

The curtains opened on to a dim hallway with doors on both sides. A shabby red carpet masked the floor. The walls were chipped, the doors cracked.

"The one at the end on the left," Token Ware whispered.

They came to it. Pete Anglich knocked. Trimmer Waltz's voice called out to come in. Pete Anglich stood a moment looking at the door, then turned his head and looked at the girl with his eyes hard and narrow. He pushed the door open, gestured at her. They went in.

The room was not very light. A small oblong reading lamp on the desk shed glow on polished wood, but less on the shabby red carpet, and the long heavy red drapes across the outer wall. The air was close, with a thick, sweetish smell of liquor.

Trimmer Waltz sat behind the desk with his hands touching a tray that contained a cut-glass decanter, some gold-veined glasses, an ice bucket and a siphon of charged water.

He smiled, rubbed one side of his big nose.

"Park yourselves, folks. Liqueur Scotch at six-ninety a fifth. That's what it costs me—wholesale."

Pete Anglich shut the door, looked slowly around the room, at the floor-length window drapes, at the unlighted ceiling light. He unbuttoned the top button of his coat with a slow, easy movement.

"Hot in here," he said softly. "Any windows behind those drapes?"

The girl sat in a round chair on the opposite side of the desk from Waltz. He smiled at her very gently.

"Good idea," Waltz said. "Open one up, will you?"

Pete Anglich went past the end of the desk, toward the curtains. As he got beyond Waltz, his hand went up under his coat and touched the butt of his gun. He moved softly toward the red drapes. The tips of wide, square-toed black shoes just barely showed under the curtains, in the shadow between the curtains and the wall.

Pete Anglich reached the curtains, put his left hand out and jerked them open.

The shoes on the floor against the wall were empty. Waltz laughed dryly behind Pete Anglich. Then a thick, cold voice said: "Put 'em high, boy."

The girl made a strangled sound, not quite a scream. Pete Anglich dropped his hands and turned slowly and looked. The

Negro was enormous in stature, gorillalike, and wore a baggy checked suit that made him even more enormous. He had come soundlessly on shoeless feet out of a closet door, and his right hand almost covered a huge black gun.

Trimmer Waltz held a gun too, a Savage. The two men stared quietly at Pete Anglich. Pete Anglich put his hands up in the air, his eyes blank, his small mouth set hard.

The Negro in the checked suit came toward him in long, loose strides, pressed the gun against his chest, then reached under his coat. His hand came out with Pete Anglich's gun. He dropped it behind him on the floor. He shifted his own gun casually and hit Pete Anglich on the side of the jaw with the flat of it.

Pete Anglich staggered and the salt taste of blood came under his tongue. He blinked, said thickly: "I'll remember you a long time, big boy."

The Negro grinned. "Not so long, pal. Not so long."

He hit Pete Anglich again with the gun, then suddenly he jammed it into a side pocket and his two big hands shot out, clamped themselves on Pete Anglich's throat.

"When they's tough I likes to squeeze 'em," he said almost softly.

Thumbs that felt as big and hard as doorknobs pressed into the arteries on Pete Anglich's neck. The face before him and above him grew enormous, an enormous shadowy face with a wide grin in the middle of it. It waved in lessening light, an unreal, a fantastic face.

Pete Anglich hit the face, with puny blows, the blows of a toy balloon. His fists didn't feel anything as they hit the face. The big man twisted him around and put a knee into his back, and bent him down over the knee.

There was no sound for a while except the thunder of blood threshing in Pete Anglich's head. Then, far away, he seemed to hear a girl scream thinly. From still farther away the voice of Trimmer Waltz muttered: "Easy now, Rufe. Easy."

A vast blackness shot with hot red filled Pete Anglich's world.

The darkness grew silent. Nothing moved in it now, not even blood.

The Negro lowered Pete Anglich's limp body to the floor, stepped back and rubbed his hands together.

"Yeah, I likes to squeeze 'em," he said.

FIVE

The Negro in the checked suit sat on the side of the daybed and picked languidly at a five-stringed banjo. His large face was solemn and peaceful, a little sad. He plucked the banjo strings slowly, with his bare fingers, his head on one side, a crumpled cigarette-end sticking barely past his lips at one corner of his mouth.

Low down in his throat he was making a kind of droning sound. He was singing.

A cheap electric clock on the mantel said 11:35. It was a small living room with bright, overstuffed furniture, a red floor lamp with a cluster of French dolls at its base, a gay carpet with large diamond shapes in it, two curtained windows with a mirror between them.

A door at the back was ajar. A door near it opening into the hall was shut.

Pete Anglich lay on his back on the floor, with his mouth open and his arms outflung. His breath was a thick snore. His eyes were shut, and his face in the reddish glow of the lamp looked flushed and feverish.

The Negro put the banjo down out of his immense hands, stood up and yawned and stretched. He walked across the room and looked at a calendar over the mantel.

"This ain't August," he said disgustedly.

He tore a leaf from the calendar, rolled it into a ball and threw it at Pete Anglich's face. It hit the unconscious man's cheek. He didn't stir. The Negro spit the cigarette-end into his palm, held his palm out flat, and flicked a fingernail at it, sent it sailing in the same direction as the paper ball.

He loafed a few steps and leaned down, fingering a bruise on Pete Anglich's temple. He pressed the bruise, grinning softly. Pete Anglich didn't move.

The Negro straightened and kicked the unconscious man in the ribs thoughtfully, over and over again, not very hard. Pete Anglich moved a little, gurgled, and rolled his head to one side. The Negro looked pleased, left him, went back to the daybed. He carried his banjo over to the hall door and leaned it against the wall. There was a gun lying on a newspaper on a small table. He went through a partly open inner door and came back with a pint bottle of gin, half full. He rubbed the bottle over carefully with a handkerchief, set it on the mantel.

"About time now, pal," he mused out loud. "When you wake up, maybe you don't feel so good. Maybe need a shot . . . Hey, I gotta better hunch."

He reached for the bottle again, went down on one big knee, poured gin over Pete Anglich's mouth and chin, slopped it loosely on the front of his shirt. He stood the bottle on the floor, after wiping it off again, and flicked the glass stopper under the daybed.

"Grab it, white boy," he said softly. "Prints don't never hurt."

He got the newspaper with the gun on it, slid the gun off on the carpet, and moved it with his foot until it lay just out of reach of Pete Anglich's outflung hand.

He studied the layout carefully from the door, nodded, picked his banjo up. He opened the door, peeped out, then looked back.

"So long, pal," he said softly. "Time for me to breeze. You ain't got a lot of future comin', but what you got you get sudden."

He shut the door, went along the hallway to stairs and down the stairs. Radios made faint sound behind shut doors. The entrance lobby of the apartment house was empty. The Negro in the checked suit slipped into a pay booth in the dark corner of the lobby, dropped his nickel and dialed.

A heavy voice said: "Police department."

The Negro put his lips close to the transmitter and got a whine into his voice.

"This the cops? Say, there's been a shootin' scrape in the Calliope Apartments, Two-Forty-Six East Forty-Eight, Apartment Four-B. Got it? . . . Well, do somethin' about it, flatfoot!"

He hung up quickly, giggling, ran down the front steps of the apartment house and jumped into a small, dirty sedan. He kicked it to life and drove toward Central Avenue. He was a block from Central Avenue when the red eye of a prowl car swung around from Central on to East Forty-Eight Street.

The Negro in the sedan chuckled and went on his way. He was singing down in his throat when the prowl car whirred past him.

▼

The instant the door latch clicked Pete Anglich opened his eyes halfway. He turned his head slowly, and a grin of pain came on his face and stayed on it, but he kept on turning his head until he could see the emptiness of one end of the room and the middle. He tipped his head far back on the floor, saw the rest of the room.

He rolled toward the gun and took hold of it. It was his own gun. He sat up and snapped the gate open mechanically. His face stiffened out of the grin. One shell in the gun had been fired. The barrel smelled of powder fumes.

He came to his feet and crept toward the slightly open inner door, keeping his head low. When he reached the door he bent still lower, and slowly pushed the door wide open. Nothing happened. He looked into a bedroom with twin beds, made up and covered with rose damask with a gold design in it.

Somebody lay on one of the beds. A woman. She didn't move. The hard, tight grin came back on Pete Anglich's face. He rose straight up and walked softly on the balls of his feet over to the side of the bed. A door beyond was open on a bathroom, but no sound came from it. Pete Anglich looked down at the colored girl on the bed.

He caught his breath and let it out slowly. The girl was dead. Her eyes were half open, uninterested, her hands lazy at her sides. Her legs were twisted a little and bare skin showed above one sheer stocking, below the short skirt. A green hat lay on the floor. She had four-and-a-half-inch French heels. There was a scent of Midnight Narcissus in the room. He remembered the girl outside the Surprise Hotel.

She was quite dead, dead long enough for the blood to have clotted over the powder-scorched hole below her left breast.

Pete Anglich went back to the living room, grabbed up the gin bottle, and emptied it without stopping or choking. He stood a moment, breathing hard, thinking. The gun hung slack in his left hand. His small, tight mouth hardly showed at all.

He worked his fingers on the glass of the gin bottle, tossed it empty on top of the daybed, slid his gun into the underarm holster, went to the door and stepped quietly into the hall.

The hall was long and dim and yawning with chill air. A single bracket light loomed yellowly at the top of the stairs. A screen door led to a balcony over the front porch of the building. There was a gray splash of cold moonlight on one corner of the screen.

Pete Anglich went softly down the stairs to the front hall, put his hand out to the knob of the glass door.

A red spot hit the front of the door. It sifted a hard red glare through the glass and the sleazy curtain that masked it.

Pete Anglich slid down the door, below the panel, hunched along the wall to the side. His eyes ranged the place swiftly, held on the dark telephone booth.

"Man trap," he said softly, and dodged over to the booth, into it. He crouched and almost shut the door.

Steps slammed on the porch and the front door squeaked open. The steps hammered into the hallway, stopped.

A heavy voice said: "All quiet, huh? Maybe a phony."

Another voice said: "Four-B. Let's give it the dust, anyway."

The steps went along the lower hall, came back. They sounded on the stairs going up. They drummed in the upper hall.

Pete Anglich pushed the door of the booth back, slid over to the front door, crouched and squinted against the red glare.

The prowl car at the curb was a dark bulk. Its headlights burned along the cracked sidewalk. He couldn't see into it. He sighed, opened the door and walked quickly, but not too quickly, down the wooden steps from the porch.

The prowl car was empty, with both front doors hanging open. Shadowy forms were converging cautiously from across the street. Pete Anglich marched straight to the prowl car and got into it. He shut the doors quietly, stepped on the starter, threw the car in gear.

He drove off past the gathering crowd of neighbors. At the first corner he turned and switched off the red spot. Then he drove fast, wound in and out of blocks, away from Central, after a while turned back toward it.

When he was near its lights and chatter and traffic he pulled over to the side of the dusty tree-lined street, left the prowl car standing.

He walked towards Central.

SIX

Trimmer Waltz cradled the phone with his left hand. He put his right index finger along the edge of his upper lip, pushed the lip out of the way, and rubbed his finger slowly along his teeth and gums. His shallow, colorless eyes looked across the desk at the big Negro in the checked suit.

"Lovely," he said in a dead voice. "Lovely. He got away before the law jumped him. A very swell job, Rufe."

The Negro took a cigar stub out of his mouth and crushed it between a huge flat thumb and a huge flat forefinger.

"Hell, he was out cold," he snarled. "The prowlies passed me before I got to Central. Hell, he *can't* get away."

"That was him talking," Waltz said lifelessly. He opened the top drawer of his desk and laid his heavy Savage in front of him.

The Negro looked at the Savage. His eyes got dull and lightless, like obsidian. His lips puckered and gouged at each other.

"That gal's been cuttin' corners on me with three, four other guys," he grumbled. "I owed her the slug. Oky-doke. That's jake. Now, I go out and collect me the smart monkey."

He started to get up. Waltz barely touched the butt of his gun with two fingers. He shook his head, and the Negro sat down again. Waltz spoke.

"He got away, Rufe. And you called the buttons to find a dead woman. Unless they get him with the gun on him—one chance in a thousand—there's no way to tie it to him. That makes you the fall guy. You live there."

The Negro grinned and kept his dull eyes on the Savage.

He said: "That makes me get cold feet. And my feet are big enough to get plenty cold. Guess I take me a powder, huh?"

Waltz sighed. He said thoughtfully: "Yeah, I guess you leave town for a while. From Glendale. The 'Frisco late train will be about right."

The Negro looked sulky. "Nix on 'Frisco, boss. I put my thumbs on a frail there. She croaked. Nix on 'Frisco, boss."

"You've got ideas, Rufe," Waltz said calmly. He rubbed the side of his veined nose with one finger, then slicked his gray hair back with his palm. "I see them in your big brown eyes. Forget it. I'll take care of you. Get the car in the alley. We'll figure the angles on the way to Glendale."

The Negro blinked and wiped cigar ash off his chin with his huge hand.

"And better leave your big shiny gun here," Waltz added. "It needs a rest."

Rufe reached back and slowly drew his gun from a hip pocket. He pushed it across the polished wood of the desk with one finger. There was a faint, sleepy smile at the back of his eyes.

"Okey, boss," he said, almost dreamily.

He went across to the door, opened it, and went out. Waltz stood up and stepped over to the closet, put on a dark felt hat and a light-weight overcoat, a pair of dark gloves. He dropped the Savage into his left-hand pocket, Rufe's gun into the right. He went out of the room down the hall toward the sound of the dance band.

At the end he parted the curtains just enough to peer through. The orchestra was playing a waltz. There was a good crowd, a quiet crowd for Central Avenue. Waltz sighed, watched the dancers for a moment, let the curtains fall together again.

He went back along the hall past his office to a door at the end that gave on stairs. Another door at the bottom of the stairs opened on a dark alley behind the building.

Waltz closed the door gently, stood in the darkness against the wall. The sound of an idling motor came to him, the light clatter of loose tappets. The alley was blind at one end, at the other turned at right angles toward the front of the building. Some of the light from Central Avenue splashed on a brick wall at the end of the cross alley, beyond the waiting car, a small sedan that looked battered and dirty even in the darkness.

Waltz reached his right hand into his overcoat pocket, took out Rufe's gun and held it down in the cloth of his overcoat. He walked to the sedan soundlessly, went around to the right-hand door, opened it to get in.

Two huge hands came out of the car and took hold of his throat. Hard hands, hands with enormous strength in them. Waltz made a faint gurgling sound before his head was bent back and his almost blind eyes were groping at the sky.

Then his right hand moved, moved like a hand that had nothing to do with his stiff, straining body, his tortured neck, his bulging blind eyes. It moved forward cautiously, delicately, until the muzzle of the gun it held pressed against something soft. It explored the something soft carefully, without haste, seemed to be making sure just what it was.

Trimmer Waltz didn't see, he hardly felt. He didn't breathe. But his hand obeyed his brain like a detached force beyond the reach of Rufe's terrible hands. Waltz's finger squeezed the trigger.

The hands fell slack on his throat, dropped away. He staggered back, almost fell across the alley, hit the far wall with his shoulder. He straightened slowly, gasping deep down in his tortured lungs. He began to shake.

He hardly noticed the big gorilla's body fall out of the car and slam the concrete at his feet. It lay at his feet, limp, enormous, but no longer menacing. No longer important.

Waltz dropped the gun on the sprawled body. He rubbed his throat gently for a little while. His breathing was deep, racking, noisy. He searched the inside of his mouth with his tongue, tasted blood. His eyes looked up wearily at the indigo slit of the night sky above the alley.

After a while he said husklly, "I thought of that, Rufe . . . You see, I thought of that."

He laughed, shuddered, adjusted his coat collar, went around the sprawled body to the car and reached in to switch the motor off. He started back along the alley to the rear door of the Juggernaut Club.

A man stepped out of the shadows at the back of the car. Waltz's left hand flashed to his overcoat pocket. Shiny metal blinked at him. He let his hand fall loosely at his side.

Pete Anglich said, "Thought that call would bring you out, Trimmer. Thought you might come this way. Nice going."

After a moment Waltz said thickly: "He choked me. It was self-defense."

"Sure. There's two of us with sore necks. Mine's a pip."

"What do you want, Pete?"

"You tried to frame me for bumping off a girl."

Waltz laughed suddenly, almost crazily. He said quietly: "When I'm crowded I get nasty, Pete. You should know that. Better lay off little Token Ware."

Pete Anglich moved his gun so that the light flickered on the barrel. He came up to Waltz, pushed the gun against his stomach.

"Rufe's dead," he said softly. "Very convenient. Where's the girl?"

"What's it to you?"

"Don't be a bunny. I'm wise. You tried to pick some jack off John Vidaury. I stepped in front of Token. I want to know the rest of it."

Waltz stood very still with the gun pressing his stomach. His fingers twisted in the gloves.

"Okay," he said dully. "How much to button your lip—and keep it buttoned?"

"Couple of centuries. Rufe lifted my poke."

"What does it buy me?" Waltz asked slowly.

"Not a damn thing. I want the girl, too."

Waltz said very gently: "Five C's. But not the girl. Five C's is heavy dough for a Central Avenue punk. Be smart and take it, and forget the rest."

The gun went away from his stomach. Pete Anglich circled him deftly, patted pockets, took the Savage, made a gesture with his left hand, holding it.

"Sold," he said grudgingly. "What's a girl between pals? Feed it to me."

"Have to go up to the office," Waltz said.

Pete Anglich laughed shortly. "Better play ball, Trimmer. Lead on."

They went back along the upstairs hall. The dance band beyond the distant curtains was wailing a Duke Ellington lament, a forlorn monotone of stifled brasses, bitter violins, softly clicking gourds. Waltz opened his office door, snapped the light on, went across to his desk and sat down. He tilted his hat back, smiled, opened a drawer with a key.

Pete Anglich watched him, reached back to turn the key in the door, went along the wall to the closet and looked into it, went behind Waltz to the curtains that masked the windows. He still had his gun out.

He came back to the end of the desk. Waltz was pushing a loose sheaf of bills away from him.

Pete Anglich ignored the money, leaned down over the end of the desk.

"Keep that and give me the girl, Trimmer."

Waltz shook his head, kept on smiling.

"The Vidaury squeeze was a grand, Trimmer—or started with a grand. Noon Street is almost in your alley. Do you have to scare women into doing your dirty work? I think you wanted something on the girl, so you could make her say uncle."

Waltz narrowed his eyes a little, pointed to the sheaf of bills.

Pete Anglich said slowly: "A shabby, lonesome, scared kid. Probably lives in a cheap furnished room. No friends, or she wouldn't be working in your joint. Nobody would wonder about her, except me. You wouldn't have put her in a house, would you, Trimmer?"

"Take your money and beat it," Waltz said thinly. "You know what happens to rats in this district."

"Sure, they run night clubs," Pete Anglich said gently.

He put his gun down, started to reach for the money. His fist doubled, swept upward casually. His elbow went up with the punch, the fist turned, landed almost delicately on the angle of Waltz's jaw.

Waltz became a loose bag of clothes. His mouth fell open. His hat fell off the back of his head. Pete Anglich stared at him, grumbled: "Lot of good that does me."

The room was very still. The dance band sounded faintly, like a turned-down radio. Pete Anglich moved behind Waltz and reached down under his coat into his breast pocket. He took a wallet out, shook out money, a driver's license, a police pistol permit, several insurance cards.

He put the stuff back, stared morosely at the desk, rubbed a thumbnail on his jaw. There was a shiny buff memo pad in front of him. Impressions of writing showed on the top blank sheet. He held it sideways against the light, then picked up a pencil and began to make light loose strokes across the paper. Writing came out dimly. When the sheet was shaded all over Pete Anglich read: 4623 Noon Street. Ask for Reno.

He tore the sheet off, folded it into a pocket, picked his gun up and crossed to the door. He reversed the key, locked the room from the outside, went back to the stairs and down them to the alley.

The body of the Negro lay as it had fallen, between the small sedan and the dark wall. The alley was empty. Pete Anglich stooped, searched the dead man's pockets, came up with a roll of money. He counted the money in the dim light of a match, separated eighty-seven dollars from what there was, and started to put the few remaining bills back. A piece of torn paper fluttered to the pavement. One side only was torn, jaggedly.

Pete Anglich crouched beside the car, struck another match, looked at a half-sheet from a buff memo pad on which was written, beginning with the tear:————t. Ask for Reno.

He clicked his teeth and let the match fall. "Better," he said softly.

He got into the car, started it and drove out of the alley.

SEVEN

The number was on a front-door transom, faintly lit from behind, the only light the house showed. It was a big frame house, in the block above where the stakeout had been. The windows in front were closely curtained. Noise came from behind them, voices and laughter, the high-pitched whine of a colored girl's singing. Cars were parked along the curb, on both sides of the street.

A tall thin Negro in dark clothes and gold nose-glasses opened the door. There was another door behind him, shut. He stood in a dark box between the two doors.

Pete Anglich said: "Reno?"

The tall Negro nodded, said nothing.

"I've come for the girl Rufe left, the white girl."

The tall Negro stood a moment quite motionless, looking over Pete Anglich's head. When he spoke, his voice was a lazy rustle of sound that seemed to come from somewhere else.

"Come in and shut the do'."

Pete Anglich stepped into the house, shut the outer door behind him. The tall Negro opened the inner door. It was thick, heavy. When he opened it sound and light jumped at them. A purplish light. He went through the inner door, into a hallway.

The purplish light came through a broad arch from a long living room. It had heavy velour drapes, davenports and deep chairs, a glass bar in the corner, and a white-coated Negro behind the bar. Four couples lounged about the room drinking; slim, slick-haired Negro sheiks and girls with bare arms, sheer silk legs, plucked eyebrows. The soft, purplish light made the scene unreal.

Reno stared vaguely past Pete Anglich's shoulder, dropped his heavy-lidded eyes, said wearily: "You says which?"

The Negroes beyond the arch were quiet, staring. The barman stooped and put his hands down under the bar.

Pete Anglich put his hand into his pocket slowly, brought out a crumpled piece of paper.

"This any help?"

Reno took the paper, studied it. He reached languidly into his vest and brought out another piece of the same color. He fitted the pieces together. His head went back and he looked at the ceiling.

"Who send you?"

"Trimmer."

"I don' like it," the tall Negro said. "He done write my name. I don' like that. That ain't sma't. Apa't from that I guess I check you."

He turned and started up a long, straight flight of stairs. Pete Anglich followed him. One of the Negro youths in the living room snickered loudly.

Reno stopped suddenly, turned and went back down the steps, through the arch. He went up to the snickerer.

"This is business," he said exhaustedly. "Ain't no white folks comin' heah. Git me?"

The boy who had laughed said, "Okey, Reno," and lifted a tall, misted glass.

Reno came up the stairs again, talking to himself. Along the upper hall were many closed doors. There was faint pink light from flame-colored wall lamps. At the end Reno took a key out and unlocked the door.

He stood aside. "Git her out," he said tersely. "I don' handle no white cargo heah."

Pete Anglich stepped past him into a bedroom. An orange floor lamp glowed in the far corner near a flounced, gaudy bed. The windows were shut, the air heavy, sickish.

Token Ware lay on her side on the bed, with her face to the wall, sobbing quietly.

Pete Anglich stepped to the side of the bed, touched her. She whirled, cringed. Her head jerked around at him, her eyes dilated, her mouth half open as if to yell.

"Hello, there," he said quietly, very gently. "I've been looking all over for you."

The girl stared back at him. Slowly all the fear went out of her face.

EIGHT

The *News* photographer held the flashbulb holder high up in his left hand, leaned down over his camera.

"Now, the smile, Mr. Vidaury," he said. "The sad one—that one that makes 'em pant."

Vidaury turned in the chair and set his profile. He smiled at the girl in the red hat, then turned his face to the camera with the smile still on.

The bulb flared and the shutter clicked.

"Not bad, Mr. Vidaury. I've seen you do better."

"I've been under a great strain," Vidaury said gently.

"I'll say. Acid in the face is no fun," the photographer said.

The girl in the red hat tittered, then coughed, behind a gauntleted glove with red stitching on the back.

The photographer packed his stuff together. He was an oldish man in shiny blue serge, with sad eyes. He shook his gray head and straightened his hat.

"No, acid in the puss is no fun," he said. "Well, I hope our boys can see you in the morning, Mr. Vidaury."

"Delighted," Vidaury said wearily. "Just tell them to ring me from the lobby before they come up. And have a drink on your way out."

"I'm crazy," the photographer said. "I don't drink."

He hoisted his camera bag over his shoulder and trudged down the room. A small Jap in a white coat appeared from nowhere and let him out, then went away.

"Acid in the puss," the girl in the red hat said. "Ha, ha, ha! That's positively excruciating, if a nice girl may say so. Can I have a drink?"

"Nobody's stopping you," Vidaury growled.

"Nobody ever did, sweets."

She walked sinuously over to a table with a square Chinese tray on it. She mixed a stiff one. Vidaury said half absently: "That should be all till morning. The *Bulletin*, the *Press-Tribune*, the three wire services, the *News*. Not bad."

"I'd call it a perfect score," the girl in the red hat said.

Vidaury scowled at her. "But nobody caught," he said softly, "except an innocent passer-by. *You* wouldn't know anything about this squeeze, would you, Irma?"

Her smile was lazy, but cold. "Me take you for a measly grand? Be your forty years plus, Johnny. I'm a home-run hitter, always."

Vidaury stood up and crossed the room to a carved wood cabinet, unlocked a small drawer and took a large ball of crystal out of it. He went back to his chair, sat down, and leaned forward, holding the ball in his palms and staring into it, almost vacantly.

The girl in the red hat watched him over the rim of her glass. Her eyes widened, got a little glassy.

"Hell! He's gone psychic on the folks," she breathed. She put her glass down with a sharp slap on the tray, drifted over to his side and leaned down. Her voice was cooing, edged. "Ever hear of senile decay, Johnny? It happens to exceptionally wicked men in their forties. They get ga-ga over flowers and toys, cut out paper dolls and play with glass balls . . . Can it, for God's sake, Johnny! You're not a punk yet."

Vidaury stared fixedly into the crystal ball. He breathed slowly, deeply.

The girl in the red hat leaned still closer to him. "Let's go riding, Johnny," she cooed. "I like the night air. It makes me remember my tonsils."

"I don't want to go riding," Vidaury said vaguely. "I—I feel something. Something imminent."

The girl bent suddenly and knocked the ball out of his hands. It thudded heavily on the floor, rolled sluggishly in the deep nap of the rug.

Vidaury shot to his feet, his face convulsed.

"I want to go riding, handsome," the girl said coolly. "It's a nice night, and you've got a nice car. So I want to go riding."

Vidaury stared at her with hate in his eyes. Slowly he smiled. The hate went away. He reached out and touched her lips with two fingers.

"Of course we'll go riding, baby," he said softly.

He got the ball, locked it up in the cabinet, went through an inner door. The girl in the red hat opened a bag and touched her lips with rouge, pursed them, made a face at herself in the mirror of her compact, found a rough wool coat in beige braided with red, and shrugged into it carefully, tossed a scarflike collar end over her shoulder.

Vidaury came back with a hat and coat on, a fringed muffler hanging down his coat.

They went down the room.

"Let's sneak out the back way," he said at the door. "In case any more newshawks are hanging around."

"Why, Johnny!" the girl in the red hat raised mocking eyebrows. "People saw me come in, saw me here. Surely you wouldn't want them to think your girl friend stayed the night?"

"Hell!" Vidaury said violently and wrenched the door open.

The telephone bell jangled back in the room. Vidaury swore again, took his hand from the door and stood waiting while the little Jap in the white jacket came in and answered the phone.

The boy put the phone down, smiled deprecatingly and gestured with his hands.

"You take, prease? I not understand."

Vidaury walked back and lifted the instrument. He said, "Yes? This is John Vidaury." He listened.

Slowly his fingers tightened on the phone. His whole face tightened, got white. He said slowly, thickly: "Hold the line a minute."

He put the phone down on its side, put his hand down on the table and leaned on it. The girl in the red hat came up behind him.

"Bad news, handsome? You look like a washed egg."

Vidaury turned his head slowly and stared at her. "Get the hell out of here," he said tonelessly.

She laughed. He straightened, took a single long step and slapped her across the mouth, hard.

"I said, get the hell out of here," he repeated in an utterly dead voice.

She stopped laughing and touched her lips with fingers in the gauntleted glove. Her eyes were round, but not shocked.

"Why, Johnny. You sweep me right off my feet," she said wonderingly. "You're simply terrific. Of course I'll go.

She turned quickly, with a light toss of her head, went back along the room to the door, waved her hand, and went out.

Vidaury was not looking at her when she waved. He lifted the phone as soon as the door clicked shut after her, said into it grimly: "Get over here, Waltz—and get over here quick!"

He dropped the phone on its cradle, stood a moment blank-eyed. He went back through the inner door, reappeared in a moment without his hat and overcoat. He held a thick, short automatic in his hand. He slipped it nose-down into the inside breast pocket of his dinner jacket, lifted the phone again slowly, said into it coldly and firmly: "If a Mr. Anglich calls to see me, send him up. Anglich." He spelled the name out, put the phone down carefully, and sat down in the easy chair beside it.

He folded his arms and waited.

NINE

The white-jacketed Japanese boy opened the door, bobbed his head, smiled, hissed politely: "Ah, you come inside, prease. Quite so, prease."

Pete Anglich patted Token Ware's shoulder, pushed her through the door into the long, vivid room. She looked shabby and forlorn against the background of handsome furnishings. Her eyes were reddened from crying, her mouth was smeared.

The door shut behind them and the little Japanese stole away.

They went down the stretch of thick, noiseless carpet, past quiet brooding lamps, bookcases sunk into the wall, shelves of alabaster and ivory, and porcelain and jade knickknacks, a huge mirror framed in blue glass, and surrounded by a frieze of lovingly autographed photos, low tables with lounging chairs, high tables with flowers, more books, more chairs, more rugs —and Vidaury sitting remotely with a glass in his hand, staring at them coldly.

He moved his hand carelessly, looked the girl up and down.

"Ah, yes, the man the police had here. Of course. Something I can do for you? I heard they made a mistake."

Pete Anglich turned a chair a little, pushed Token Ware into it. She sat down slowly, stiffly, licked her lips and stared at Vidaury with a frozen fascination.

A touch of polite distaste curled Vidaury's lips. His eyes were watchful.

Pete Anglich sat down. He drew a stick of gum out of his

pocket, unwrapped it, slid it between his teeth. He looked worn, battered, tired. There were dark bruises on the side of his face and on his neck. He still needed a shave.

He said slowly, "This is Miss Ware. The girl that was supposed to get your dough."

Vidaury stiffened. A hand holding a cigarette began to tap restlessly on the arm of his chair. He stared at the girl, but didn't say anything. She half smiled at him, then flushed.

Pete Anglich said: "I hang around Noon Street. I know the sharpshooters, know what kind of folks belong there and what kind don't. I saw this little girl in a lunchwagon on Noon Street this evening. She looked uneasy and she was watching the clock. She didn't belong. When she left I followed her."

Vidaury nodded slightly. A gray tip of ash fell off the end of his cigarette. He looked down at it vaguely, nodded again.

"She went up Noon Street," Pete Anglich said. "A bad street for a white girl. I found her hiding in a doorway. Then a big Duesenberg slid around the corner and doused lights, and your money was thrown out on the sidewalk. She was scared. She asked me to get it. I got it."

Vidaury said smoothly, not looking at the girl: "She doesn't look like a crook. Have you told the police about her? I suppose not, or you wouldn't be here."

Pete Anglich shook his head, ground the gum around in his jaws. "Tell the law? A couple of times nix. This is velvet for us. We want our cut."

Vidaury started violently, then he was very still. His hand stopped beating the chair arm. His face got cold and white and grim. Then he reached up inside his dinner jacket and quietly took the short automatic out, held it on his knees. He leaned forward a little and smiled.

"Blackmailers," he said gravely, "are always rather interesting. How much would your cut be—and what have you got to sell?"

Pete Anglich looked thoughtfully at the gun. His jaws moved easily, crunching the gum. His eyes were unworried.

"Silence," he said gravely. "Just silence."

Vidaury made a sharp sudden gesture with the gun. "Talk," he said. "And talk fast. I don't like silence."

Pete Anglich nodded, said: "The acid-throwing threats were just a dream. You didn't get any. The extortion attempt was a phony. A publicity stunt. That's all." He leaned back in his chair.

Vidaury looked down the room past Pete Anglich's shoulder. He started to smile, then his face got wooden.

Trimmer Waltz had slid into the room through an open side door. He had his big Savage in his hand. He came slowly along the carpet without sound. Pete Anglich and the girl didn't see him.

Pete Anglich said, "Phony all the way through. Just a build-up. Guessing? Sure I am, but look a minute, see how soft it was played first—and how tough it was played afterward, after I showed in it. The girl works for Trimmer Waltz at the Juggernaut. She's down and out, and she scares easily. So Waltz sends her on a caper like that. Why? Because she's supposed to be nabbed. The stake-out's all arranged. If she squawks about Waltz, he laughs it off, points to the fact that the plant was almost in his alley, that it was a small stake at best, and his joint's doing all right. He points to the fact that a dumb girl goes to get it, and would he, a smart guy, pull anything like that? Certainly not.

"The cops will half believe him, and you'll make a big gesture and refuse to prosecute the girl. If she doesn't spill, you'll refuse to prosecute anyway, and you'll get your publicity just the same, either way. You need it bad, because you're slipping, and you'll get it, and all it will cost you is what you pay Waltz—or that's what you think. Is that crazy? Is that too far for a Hollywood heel to stretch? Then tell me why no Feds were on the case. Because those lads would keep on digging until they found the mouse, and then you'd be up for obstructing justice. That's why. The local law don't give a damn. They're so used to movie build-ups they just yawn and turn over and go to sleep again."

Waltz was halfway down the room now. Vidaury didn't look at him. He looked at the girl, smiled at her faintly.

"Now, see how tough it was played after I got into it," Pete Anglich said. "I went to the Juggernaut and talked to the girl. Waltz got us into his office and a big ape that works for him damn near strangled me. When I came to I was in an apartment and a dead girl was there, and she was shot, and a bullet was gone from my gun. The gun was on the floor beside me, and I stank of gin, and a prowl car was booming around the corner. And Miss Ware here was locked up in a whore house on Noon Street.

"Why all that hard stuff? Because Waltz had a perfectly swell blackmail racket lined up for you, and he'd have bled you whiter than an angel's wing. As long as you had a dollar, half of it would have been his. And you'd have paid it and liked it, Vidaury. You'd have had publicity, and you'd have had protection, but how you'd have paid for it!"

Waltz was close now, almost too close. Vidaury stood up suddenly. The short gun jerked at Pete Anglich's chest. Vidaury's voice was thin, an old man's voice. He said dreamily: "Take him, Waltz. I'm too jittery for this sort of thing."

Pete Anglich didn't even turn. His face became the face of a wooden Indian.

Waltz put his gun into Pete Anglich's back. He stood there half smiling, with the gun against Pete Anglich's back, looking across his shoulder at Vidaury.

"Dumb, Pete," he said dryly. "You had enough evening already. You ought to have stayed away from here—but I figured you couldn't pass it up."

Vidaury moved a little to one side, spread his legs, flattened his feet to the floor. There was a queer, greenish tint to his handsome face, a sick glitter in his deep eyes.

Token Ware stared at Waltz. Her eyes glittered with panic, the lids straining away from the eyeballs, showing the whites all around the iris.

Waltz said, "I can't do anything here, Vidaury. I'd rather not walk him out alone, either. Get your hat and coat."

Vidaury nodded very slightly. His head just barely moved. His eyes were still sick.

"What about the girl?" he asked whisperingly.

Waltz grinned, shook his head, pressed the gun hard into Pete Anglich's back.

Vidaury moved a little more to the side, spread his feet again. The thick gun was very steady in his hand, but not pointed at anything in particular.

He closed his eyes, held them shut a brief instant, then opened them wide. He said slowly, carefully: "It looked all right as it was planned. Things just as far-fetched, just as unscrupulous, have been done before in Hollywood, often. I just didn't expect it to lead to hurting people, to killing. I'm —I'm just not enough of a heel to go on with it, Waltz. Not any further. You'd better put your gun up and leave."

Waltz shook his head; smiled a peculiar strained smile. He stepped back from Pete Anglich and held the Savage a little to one side.

"The cards are dealt," he said coldly. "You'll play'em. Get going."

Vidaury sighed, sagged a little. Suddenly he was a lonely, forlorn man, no longer young.

"No," he said softly. "I'm through. The last flicker of a not-so-good reputation. It's my show, after all. Always the ham, but still my show. Put the gun up, Waltz. Take the air."

Waltz's face got cold and hard and expressionless. His eyes became the expressionless eyes of the killer. He moved the Savage a little more.

"Get—your—hat, Vidaury," he said very clearly.

"Sorry," Vidaury said, and fired.

Waltz's gun flamed at the same instant, the two explosions blended. Vidaury staggered to his left and half turned, then straightened his body again.

He looked steadily at Waltz. "Beginner's luck," he said, and waited.

Pete Anglich had his Colt out now, but he didn't need it. Waltz fell slowly on his side. His cheek and the side of his big-veined nose pressed the nap of the rug. He moved his left arm a little, tried to throw it over his back. He gurgled, then was still.

Pete Anglich kicked the Savage away from Waltz's sprawled body.

Vidaury asked draggingly: "Is he dead?"

Pete Anglich grunted, didn't answer. He looked at the girl. She was standing up with her back against the telephone table, the back of her hand to her mouth in the conventional attitude of startled horror. So conventional it looked silly.

Pete Anglich looked at Vidaury. He said sourly: "Beginner's luck—yeah. But suppose you'd missed him? He was bluffing. Just wanted you in a little deeper, so you wouldn't squawk. As a matter of fact, I'm his alibi on a kill."

Vidaury said: "Sorry . . . I'm sorry." He sat down suddenly, leaned his head back and closed his eyes.

"God, but he's handsome!" Token Ware said reverently. "And brave."

Vidaury put his hand to his left shoulder, pressed it hard against his body. Blood oozed slowly between his fingers. Token Ware let out a stifled screech.

Pete Anglich looked down the room. The little Jap in the white coat had crept into the end of it, stood silently, a small huddled figure against the wall. Pete Anglich looked at Vidaury again. Very slowly, as though unwillingly, he said: "Miss Ware has folks in 'Frisco. You can send her home, with a little present. That's natural—and open. She turned Waltz up to me. That's how I came into it. I told him you were wise and he came here to shut you up. Tough-guy stuff. The coppers will laugh at it, but they'll laugh in their cuffs. After all, they're getting publicity too. The phony angle is out. Check?"

Vidaury opened his eyes, said faintly, "You're—you're very decent about it. I won't forget." His head lolled.

"He's fainted," the girl cried.

"So he has," Pete Anglich said. "Give him a nice big kiss and he'll snap out of it . . . And you'll have something to remember all your life."

He ground his teeth, went to the phone, and lifted it.

SMART-ALECK
KILL

ONE

The doorman of the Kilmarnock was six foot two. He wore a pale blue uniform, and white gloves made his hands look enormous. He opened the door of the Yellow taxi as gently as an old maid stroking a cat.

Johnny Dalmas got out and turned to the red-haired driver. He said: "Better wait for me around the corner, Joey."

The driver nodded, tucked a toothpick a little farther back in the corner of his mouth, and swung his cab expertly away from the white-marked loading zone. Dalmas crossed the sunny sidewalk and went into the enormous cool lobby of the Kilmarnock. The carpets were thick, soundless. Bellboys stood with folded arms and the two clerks behind the marble desk looked austere.

Dalmas went across to the elevator lobby. He got into a paneled car and said: "End of the line, please."

The penthouse floor had a small quiet lobby with three doors opening off it, one to each wall. Dalmas crossed to one of them and rang the bell.

Derek Walden opened the door. He was about forty-five, possibly a little more, and had a lot of powdery gray hair and a handsome, dissipated face that was beginning to go pouchy.

He had on a monogrammed lounging robe and a glass full of whiskey in his hand. He was a little drunk.

He said thickly, morosely: "Oh, it's you. C'mon in, Dalmas."

He went back into the apartment, leaving the door open. Dalmas shut it and followed him into a long, high-ceilinged room with a balcony at one end and a line of french windows along the left side. There was a terrace outside.

Derek Walden sat down in a brown and gold chair against the wall and stretched his legs across a foot stool. He swirled the whiskey around in his glass, looking down at it.

"What's on your mind?" he asked.

Dalmas stared at him a little grimly. After a moment he said: "I dropped in to tell you I'm giving you back your job."

Walden drank the whiskey out of his glass and put it down on the corner of a table. He fumbled around for a cigarette, stuck it in his mouth and forgot to light it.

"Tha' so?" His voice was blurred but indifferent.

Dalmas turned away from him and walked over to one of the windows. It was open and an awning flapped outside. The traffic noise from the boulevard was faint.

He spoke over his shoulder:

"The investigation isn't getting anywhere—because you don't want it to get anywhere. *You* know why you're being black-mailed. *I* don't. Eclipse Fllms is interested because they have a lot of sugar tied up in film you have made."

"To hell with Eclipse Films," Walden said, almost quitely.

Dalmas shook his head and turned around. "Not from my angle. They stand to lose if you get in a jam the publicity hounds can't handle. You took me on because you were asked to. It was a waste of time. You haven't cooperated worth a cent."

Walden said in an unpleasant tone: "I'm handling this my own way and I'm not gettin' into any jam. I'll make my own deal—when I can buy something that'll stay bought . . . And all you have to do is make the Eclipse people think the situation's bein' taken care of. That clear?"

Dalmas came partway back across the room. He stood with

one hand on top of a table, beside an ash tray littered with cigarette stubs that had very dark lip rouge on them. He looked down at these absently.

"That wasn't explained to me, Walden," he said coldly.

"I thought you were smart enough to figure it out," Walden sneered. He leaned sidewise and slopped some more whiskey into his glass. "Have a drink?"

Dalmas said: "No, thanks."

Walden found the cigarette in his mouth and threw it on the floor. He drank. "What the hell!" he snorted. "You're a private detective and you're being paid to make a few motions that don't mean anything. It's a clean job—as your racket goes."

Dalmas said: "That's another crack I could do without hearing."

Walden made an abrupt, angry motion. His eyes glittered. The corners of his mouth drew down and his face got sulky. He avoided Dalmas' stare.

Dalmas said: "I'm not against you, but I never was for you. You're not the kind of guy I could go for, ever. If you had played with me, I'd have done what I could. I still will—but not for your sake. I don't want your money—and you can pull your shadows off my tail any time you like."

Walden put his feet on the floor. He laid his glass down very carefully on the table at his elbow. The whole expression of his face changed.

"Shadows? . . . I don't get you." He swallowed. "I'm not having you shadowed."

Dalmas stared at him. After a moment he nodded. "Okey, then. I'll backtrack on the next one and see if I can make him tell who he's working for . . . I'll find out."

Walden said very quietly: "I wouldn't do that, if I were you. You're—you're monkeying with people that might get nasty . . . I know what I'm talking about."

"That's something I'm not going to let worry me," Dalmas said evenly. "If it's the people that want *your* money, they were nasty a long time ago."

He held his hat out in front of him and looked at it. Walden's face glistened with sweat. His eyes looked sick. He opened his mouth to say something.

The door buzzer sounded.

Walden scowled quickly, swore. He stared down the room but did not move.

"Too damn many people come here without bein' announced," he growled. "My Jap boy is off for the day."

The buzzer sounded again, and Walden started to get up. Dalmas said: "I'll see what it is. I'm on my way anyhow."

He nodded to Walden, went down the room and opened the door.

Two men came in with guns in their hands. One of the guns dug sharply into Dalmas' ribs, and the man who was holding it said urgently: "Back up, and make it snappy. This is one of those stick-ups you read about."

He was dark and good-looking and cheerful. His face was as clear as a cameo, almost without hardness. He smiled.

The one behind him was short and sandy-haired. He scowled. The dark one said: "This is Walden's dick, Noddy. Take him over and go through him for a gun."

The sandy-haired man, Noddy, put a short-barreled revolver against Dalmas' stomach and his partner kicked the door shut, then strolled carelessly down the room toward Walden.

Noddy took a .38 Colt from under Dalmas' arm, walked around him and tapped his pockets. He put his own gun away and transferred Dalmas' Colt to his business hand.

"Okey, Ricchio. This one's clean," he said in a grumbling voice. Dalmas let his arms fall, turned and went back into the room. He looked thoughtfully at Walden. Walden was leaning forward with his mouth open and an expression of intense concentration on his face. Dalmas looked at the dark stick-up and said softly: "Ricchio?"

The dark boy glanced at him. "Over there by the table, sweetheart. I'll do all the talkin'."

Walden made a hoarse sound in his throat. Ricchio stood in front of him, looking down at him pleasantly, his gun dangling from one finger by the trigger guard.

"You're too slow on the pay-off, Walden. Too damn slow! So we came to tell you about it. Tailed your dick here too. Wasn't that cute?"

Dalmas said gravely, quietly: "This punk used to be your bodyguard, Walden—if his name is Ricchio."

Walden nodded silently and licked his lips. Ricchio snarled at Dalmas: "Don't crack wise, dick. I'm tellin' you again." He stared with hot eyes, then looked back at Walden, looked at a watch on his wrist.

"It's eight minutes past three, Walden. I figure a guy with your drag can still get dough out of the bank. We're giving you an hour to raise ten grand. Just an hour. And we're takin' your shamus along to arrange about delivery."

Walden nodded again, still silent. He put his hands down on his knees and clutched them until his knuckles whitened.

Ricchio went on: "We'll play clean. Our racket wouldn't be worth a squashed bug if we didn't. You'll play clean too. If you don't your shamus will wake up on a pile of dirt. Only he won't wake up. Get it?"

Dalmas said contemptuously: "And if he pays up—I suppose you turn me loose to put the finger on you."

Smoothly, without looking at him, Ricchio said: "There's an answer to that one, too . . . Ten grand today, Walden. The other ten the first of the week. Unless we have trouble. . . . If we do, we'll get paid for our trouble."

Walden made an aimless, defeated gesture with both hands outspread. "I guess I can arrange it," he said hurriedly.

"Swell. We'll be on our way then."

Ricchio nodded shortly and put his gun away. He took a brown kid glove out of his pocket, put it on his right hand, moved across then took Dalmas' Colt away from the sandy-haired man. He looked it over, slipped it into his side pocket and held it there with the gloved hand.

"Let's drift," he said with a jerk of his head.

They went out. Derek Walden stared after them bleakly.

The elevator car was empty except for the operator. They got off at the mezzanine and went across a silent writing room past a stained-glass window with lights behind it to give the effect of sunshine. Ricchio walked half a step behind on Dalmas' left. The sandy-haired man was on his right, crowding him.

They went down carpeted steps to an arcade of luxury shops, along that, out of the hotel through the side entrance. A small brown sedan was parked across the street. The sandy-haired man slid behind the wheel, stuck his gun under his leg and stepped on the starter. Ricchio and Dalmas got in the back. Ricchio drawled: "East on the boulevard, Noddy. I've got to figure."

Noddy grunted. "That's a kick," he growled over his shoulder. "Ridin' a guy down Wilshire in daylight."

"Drive the heap, bozo."

The sandy-haired man grunted again and drove the small sedan away from the curb, slowed a moment later for the boulevard stop. An empty Yellow pulled away from the west curb, swung around in the middle of the block and fell in behind. Noddy made his stop, turned right and went on. The taxi did the same. Ricchio glanced back at it without interest. There was a lot of traffic on Wilshire.

Dalmas leaned back against the upholstery and said thoughtfully: "Why wouldn't Walden use his telephone while we were coming down?"

Ricchio smiled at him. He took his hat off and dropped it in his lap, then took his right hand out of his pocket and held it under the hat with the gun in it.

"He wouldn't want us to get mad at him, dick."

"So he lets a couple of punks take me for the ride."

Ricchio said coldly: "It's not that kind of a ride. We need you in our business . . . And we ain't punks, see?"

Dalmas rubbed his jaw with a couple of fingers. He smiled quickly and snapped: "Straight ahead at Robertson?"

"Yeah. I'm still figuring," Ricchio said.

"What a brain!" the sandy-haired man sneered.

Ricchio grinned tightly and showed even white teeth. The

light changed to red half a block ahead. Noddy slid the sedan forward and was first in the line at the intersection. The empty Yellow drifted up on his left. Not quite level. The driver of it had red hair. His cap was balanced on one side of his head and he whistled cheerfully past a toothpick.

Dalmas drew his feet back against the seat and put his weight on them. He pressed his back hard against the upholstery. The tall traffic light went green and the sedan started forward, then hung a moment for a car that crowded into a fast left turn. The Yellow slipped forward on the left and the red-haired driver leaned over his wheel, yanked it suddenly to the right. There was a grinding, tearing noise. The riveted fender of the taxi plowed over the low-swung fender of the brown sedan, locked over its left front wheel. The two cars jolted to a stop.

Horn blasts behind the two cars sounded angrily, impatiently.

Dalmas' right fist crashed against Ricchio's jaw. His left hand closed over the gun in Ricchio's lap. He jerked it loose as Ricchio sagged in the corner. Ricchio's head wobbled. His eyes opened and shut flickeringly. Dalmas slid away from him along the seat and slipped the Colt under his arm.

Noddy was sitting quite still in the front seat. His right hand moved slowly towards the gun under his thigh. Dalmas opened the door of the sedan and got out, shut the door, took two steps and opened the door of the taxi. He stood beside the taxi and watched the sandy-haired man.

Horns of the stalled cars blared furiously. The driver of the Yellow was out in front tugging at the two cars with a great show of energy and with no result at all. His toothpick waggled up and down in his mouth. A motorcycle officer in amber glasses threaded the traffic, looked the situation over wearily, jerked his head at the driver.

"Get in and back up," he advised. "Argue it out somewhere else—we use this intersection."

The driver grinned and scuttled around the front end of his Yellow. He climbed into it, threw it in gear and worried it backwards with a lot of tooting and arm-waving. It came clear. The sandy-haired man peered woodenly from the sedan. Dalmas got into the taxi and pulled the door shut.

The motorcycle officer drew a whistle out and blew two sharp blasts on it, spread his arms from east to west. The brown sedan went through the intersection like a cat chased by a police dog.

The Yellow went after it. Half a block on, Dalmas leaned forward and tapped on the glass.

"Let 'em go, Joey. You can't catch them and I don't want them . . . That was a swell routine back there."

The redhead leaned his chin towards the opening in the panel. "Cinch, chief," he said, grinning. "Try me on on a hard one some time.

TWO

The telephone rang at twenty minutes to five. Dalmas was lying on his back on the bed. He was in his room at the Merrivale. He reached for the phone without looking at it, said: "Hello."

The girl's voice was pleasant and a little strained. "This is Mianne Crayle. Remember?"

Dalmas took a cigarette from between his lips. "Yes, Miss Crayle."

"Listen. You must please go over and see Derek Walden. He's worried stiff about something and he's drinking himself blind. Something's got to be done."

Dalmas stared past the phone at the ceiling. The hand holding his cigarette beat a tattoo on the side of the bed. He said slowly: "He doesn't answer his phone, Miss Crayle. I've tried to call him a time or two."

There was a short silence at the other end of the line. Then the voice said: "I left my key under the door. You'd better just go on in."

Dalmas' eyes narrowed. The fingers of his right hand became still. He said slowly: "I'll get over there right away, Miss Crayle. Where can I reach you?"

"I'm not sure . . . At John Sutro's, perhaps. We were supposed to go there."

Dalmas said: "That's fine." He waited for the click, then hung up and put the phone away on the night table. He sat up on the side of the bed and stared at a patch of sunlight on the wall for a minute or two. Then he shrugged, stood up. He finished a drink that stood beside the telephone, put on his hat, went down in the elevator and got into the second taxi in the line outside the hotel.

"Kilmarnock again, Joey. Step on it."

It took fifteen minutes to get to Kilmarnock.

The tea dance had let out and the streets around the big hotel were a mess of cars bucking their way out from the three entrances. Dalmas got out of the taxi half a block away and walked past groups of flushed débutantes and their escorts to the arcade entrance. He went in, walked up the stairs to the mezzanine, crossed the writing room and got into an elevator full of people. They all got out before the penthouse floor.

Dalmas rang Walden's bell twice. Then he bent over and looked under the door. There was a fine thread of light broken by an obstruction. He looked back at the elevator indicators, then stooped and teased something out from under the door with the blade of a penknife. It was a flat key. He went in with it . . . stopped . . . stared . . .

There was death in the big room. Dalmas went towards it slowly, walking softly, listening. There was a hard light in his gray eyes and the bone of his jaw made a sharp line that was pale against the tan of his cheek.

Derek Walden was slumped almost casually in the brown and gold chair. His mouth was slightly open. There was a blackened hole in his right temple, and a lacy pattern of blood spread down the side of his face and across the hollow of his neck as far as the soft collar of his shirt. His right hand trailed in the thick nap of the rug. The fingers held a small, black automatic.

The daylight was beginning to fade in the room. Dalmas stood perfectly still and stared at Derek Walden for a long time. There was no sound anywhere. The breeze had gone down and the awnings outside the french windows were still.

Dalmas took a pair of thin suede gloves from his left hip pocket and drew them on. He kneeled on the rug beside Walden and gently eased the gun from the clasp of his stiffening fingers. It was a .32, with a walnut grip, a black finish. He turned it over and looked at the stock. His mouth tightened. The number had been filed off and the patch of file marks glistened faintly against the dull black of the finish. He put the gun down on the rug and stood up, walked slowly towards the telephone that was on the end of a library table, beside a flat bowl of cut flowers.

He put his hand towards the phone but didn't touch it. He let the hand fall to his side. He stood there a moment, then turned and went quickly back and picked up the gun again. He slipped the magazine out and ejected the shell that was in the breech, picked that up and pressed it into the magazine. He forked two fingers of his left hand over the barrel, held the cocking piece back, twisted the breech block and broke the gun apart. He took the butt piece over to the window.

The number that was duplicated on the inside of the stock had not been filed off.

He reassembled the gun quickly, put the empty shell into the chamber, pushed the magazine home, cocked the gun and fitted it back into Derek Walden's dead hand. He pulled the suede gloves off his hands and wrote the number down in a small notebook.

He left the apartment, went down in the elevator, left the hotel. It was half-past five and some of the cars on the boulevard had switched on their lights.

THREE

The blond man who opened the door at Sutro's did it very thoroughly. The door crashed back against the wall and the blond man sat down on the floor—still holding on to the knob. He said indignantly: "Earthquake, by gad!"

Dalmas looked down at him without amusement.

"Is Miss Mianne Crayle here—or wouldn't you know?" he asked.

The blond man got off the floor and hurled the door away from him. It went shut with another crash. He said in a loud voice: "Everybody's here but the Pope's tomcat—and he's expected."

Dalmas nodded. "You ought to have a swell party."

He went past the blond man down the hall and turned under an arch into a big old-fashioned room with built-in china closets and a lot of shabby furniture. There were seven or eight people in the room and they were all flushed with liquor.

A girl in shorts and a green polo shirt was shooting craps on the floor with a man in dinner clothes. A fat man with nose-glasses was talking sternly into a toy telephone. He was saying: "Long Distance—Sioux City—and put some snap into it, sister!"

The radio blared "Sweet Madness."

Two couples were dancing around carelessly bumping into each other and the furniture. A man who looked like Al Smith was dancing all alone, with a drink in his hand and an absent expression on his face. A tall, white-faced blonde weaved towards Dalmas, slopping liquor out of her glass. She shrieked: "Darling! Fancy meeting you here!"

Dalmas went around her, went towards a saffron-colored woman who had just come into the room with a bottle of gin in each hand. She put the bottles on the piano and leaned against it, looking bored. Dalmas went up to her and asked for Miss Crayle.

The saffron-colored woman reached a cigarette out of an open box on the piano. "Outside—in the yard," she said tonelessly.

Dalmas said: "Thank you, Mrs. Sutro."

She stared at him blankly. He went under another arch, into a darkened room with wicker furniture in it. A door led to a glassed-in porch and a door out of that led down steps to a path that wound off through dim trees. Dalmas followed the path to the edge of a bluff that looked out over the lighted part of Hollywood. There was a stone seat at the edge of the bluff. A girl sat on it with her back to the house. A cigarette tip glowed in the darkness. She turned her head slowly and stood up.

She was small and dark and delicately made. Her mouth showed dark with rouge, but there was not enough light to see her face clearly. Her eyes were shadowed.

Dalmas said: "I have a cab outside, Miss Crayle. Or did you bring a car?"

"No car. Let's go. It's rotten here, and I don't drink gin."

They went back along the path and passed around the side of the house. A trellis-topped gate let them out on the sidewalk, and they went along by the fence to where the taxi was waiting. The driver was leaning against it with one heel hooked on the edge of the running board. He opened the cab door. They got in.

Dalmas said: "Stop at a drugstore for some butts, Joey."

"Okey."

Joey slid behind his wheel and started up. The cab went down a steep, winding hill. There was a little moisture on the surface of the asphalt pavement and the store fronts echoed back the swishing sound of the tires.

After a while Dalmas said: "What time did you leave Walden?"

The girl spoke without turning her head towards him. "About three o'clock."

"Put it a little later, Miss Crayle. He was alive at three o'clock—and there was somebody else with him."

The girl made a small, miserable sound like a strangled sob. Then, she said very softly: "I know . . . he's dead." She lifted her gloved hands and pressed them against her temples.

Dalmas said: "Sure. Let's not get any more tricky than we have to . . . Maybe we'll have to—enough."

She said very slowly, in a low voice: "I was there after he was dead."

Dalmas nodded. He did not look at her. The cab went on and after a while it stopped in front of a corner drugstore. The driver turned in his seat and looked back. Dalmas stared at him, but spoke to the girl.

"You ought to have told me more over the phone. I might have got in a hell of a jam. I may be in a hell of a jam now."

The girl swayed forward and started to fall. Dalmas put his arm out quickly and caught her, pushed her back against the cushions. Her head wobbled on her shoulders and her mouth was a dark gash in her stone-white face. Dalmas held her shoulder and felt her pulse with his free hand. He said sharply, grimly: "Let's go on to Carli's, Joey. Never mind the butts . . . This party has to have a drink—in a hurry."

Joey slammed the cab in gear and stepped on the accelerator.

FOUR

Carli's was a small club at the end of a passage between a sporting-goods store and a circulating library. There was a grilled door and a man behind it who had given up trying to look as if it mattered who came in.

Dalmas and the girl sat in a small booth with hard seats and looped-back green curtains. There were high partitions between the booths. There was a long bar down the other side of the room and a big juke box at the end of it. Now and then, when there wasn't enough noise, the bartender put a nickel in the juke box.

The waiter put two small glasses of brandy on the table and Mianne Crayle downed hers at a gulp. A little light came into her shadowed eyes. She peeled a black and white gauntlet off her right hand and sat playing with the empty fingers of it, staring down at the table. After a little while the waiter came back with a couple of brandy highballs.

When he had gone away again Mianne Crayle began to speak in a low, clear voice, without raising her head: "I wasn't the first of his women by several dozen. I wouldn't have been the last—by that many more. But he had his decent side. And believe it or not he didn't pay my room rent."

Dalmas nodded, didn't say anything. The girl went on without looking at him: "He was a heel in a lot of ways. When he was sober he had the dark blue sulks. When he was lit up he was vile. When he was nicely edged he was a pretty good sort of guy besides being the best smut director in Hollywood. He could get more smooth sexy tripe past the Hays office than any other three men."

Dalmas said without expression: "He was on his way out. Smut is on its way out, and that was all he knew."

The girl looked at him briefly, lowered her eyes again and drank a little of her highball. She took a tiny handkerchief out of the pocket of her sports jacket and patted her lips.

The people on the other side of the partition were making a great deal of noise.

Mianne Crayle said: "We had lunch on the balcony. Derek was drunk and on the way to get drunker. He had something on his mind. Something that worried him a lot."

Dalmas smiled faintly. "Maybe it was the twenty grand somebody was trying to pry loose from him—or didn't you know about that?"

"It might have been that. Derek was a bit tight about money."

"His liquor cost him a lot," Dalmas said dryly. "And that motor cruiser he liked to play about in—down below the border."

The girl lifted her head with a quick jerk. There were sharp lights of pain in her dark eyes. She said very slowly: "He bought all his liquor at Ensenada. Brought it in himself. He had to be careful—with the quantity he put away."

Dalmas nodded. A cold smile played about the corners of his mouth. He finished his drink and put a cigarette in his mouth, felt in his pocket for a match. The holder on the table was empty.

"Finish your story, Miss Crayle," he said.

"We went up to the apartment. He got two fresh bottles out and said he was going to get good and drunk . . . Then we quarreled . . . I couldn't stand any more of it. I went away. When I got home I began to worry about him. I called up but he wouldn't answer the phone. I went back finally . . . and let myself in with the key I had . . . and he was dead in the chair."

After a moment Dalmas said: "Why didn't you tell me some of that over the phone?"

She pressed the heels of her hands together, said very softly: "I was terribly afraid . . . And there was something . . . wrong."

Dalmas put his head back against the partition, stared at her with his eyes half closed.

"It's an old gag," she said. "I'm almost ashamed to spring it. But Derek Walden was left-handed . . . I'd know about that, wouldn't I?"

Dalmas said very softly: "A lot of people must have known that—but one of them might have got careless."

Dalmas stared at Mianne Crayle's empty glove. She was twisting it between her fingers.

"Walden was left-handed," he said slowly. "That means he didn't suicide. The gun was in his other hand. There was no sign of a struggle and the hole in his temple was powder-burned, looked as if the shot came from about the right angle. That means whoever shot him was someone who could get in there and get close to him. Or else he was paralyzed drunk, and in that case whoever did it had to have a key."

Mianne Crayle pushed the glove away from her. She clenched her hands. "Don't make it any plainer," she said sharply. "I know the police will think I did it. Well—I didn't. I loved the poor damn fool. What do you think of that?"

Dalmas said without emotion: "You *could* have done it, Miss Crayle. They'll think of that, won't they? And you might be smart enough to act the way you have afterwards. They'll think of that, too."

"That wouldn't be smart," she said bitterly. "Just smart-aleck."

"Smart-aleck kill!" Dalmas laughed grimly. "Not bad." He ran his fingers through his crisp hair. "No, I don't think we can pin it on you—and maybe the cops won't know he was left-handed . . . until somebody else gets a chance to find things out."

He leaned over the table a little, put his hands on the edge as if to get up. His eyes narrowed thoughtfully on her face.

"There's one man downtown that might give me a break. He's all cop, but he's an old guy and don't give a damn about his publicity. Maybe if you went down with me, let him size you up and hear the story, he'd stall the case a few hours and hold out on the papers."

He looked at her questioningly. She drew her glove on and said quietly: "Let's go."

FIVE

When the elevator doors at the Merrivale closed, the big man put his newspaper down from in front of his face and yawned. He got up slowly from the settee in the corner and loafed across the small but sedate lobby. He squeezed himself into a booth at the end of a row of house phones. He dropped a coin in the slot and dialed with a thick forefinger, forming the number with his lips.

After a pause he leaned close to the mouthpiece and said:

"This is Denny. I'm at the Merrivale. Our man just came in. I lost him outside and came here to wait for him to get back."

He had a heavy voice with a burr in it. He listened to the voice at the other end, nodded and hung up without saying anything more. He went out of the booth, crossed to the elevators. On the way he dropped a cigar butt into a glazed jar full of white sand.

In the elevator he said: "Ten," and took his hat off. He had straight black hair that was damp with perspiration, a wide, flat face and small eyes. His clothes were unpressed, but not shabby. He was a studio dick and he worked for Eclipse Films.

He got out at the tenth floor and went along a dim corridor, turned a corner and knocked at a door. There was a sound of steps inside. The door opened. Dalmas opened it.

The big man went in, dropped his hat casually on the bed, sat down in an easy chair by the window without being asked.

He said: "Hi, boy. I hear you need some help."

Dalmas looked at him for a moment without answering. Then he said slowly, frowningly: "Maybe—for a tail. I asked for Collins. I thought you'd be too easy to spot."

He turned away and went into the bathroom, came out with two glasses. He mixed the drinks on the bureau, handed one. The big man drank, smacked his lips and put his glass down on the sill of the open window. He took a short, chubby cigar out of his vest pocket.

"Collins wasn't around," he said. "And I was just countin' my thumbs. So the big cheese give me the job. Is it footwork?"

"I don't know. Probably not," Dalmas said indifferently.

"If it's a tail in a car, I'm okey. I brought my little coupe."

Dalmas took his glass and sat down on the side of the bed. He stared at the big man with a faint smile. The big man bit the end off his cigar and spit it out.

Then he bent over and picked up the piece, looked at it, tossed it out of the window.

"It's a swell night. A bit warm for so late in the year," he said.

Dalmas said slowly: "How well do you know Derek Walden, Denny?"

Denny looked out of the window. There was a sort of haze in the sky and the reflection of a red neon sign behind a nearby building looked like a fire.

He said: "I don't what you call know him. I've seen him around. I know he's one of the big money guys on the lot."

"Then you won't fall over if I tell you he's dead," Dalmas said evenly.

Denny turned around slowly. The cigar, still unlighted, moved up and down in his wide mouth. He looked mildly interested.

Dalmas went on: "It's a funny one. A blackmail gang has been working on him, Denny. Looks like it got his goat. He's dead—with a hole in his head and a gun in his hand. It happened this afternoon."

Denny opened his small eyes a little wider. Dalmas sipped his drink and rested the glass on his thigh.

"His girl friend found him. She had a key to the apartment in the Kilmarnock. The Jap boy was away and that's all the help he kept. The gal didn't tell anyone. She beat it and called me up. I went over . . . I didn't tell anybody either."

The big man said very slowly: "For Pete's sake! The cops'll stick it into you and break it off, brother. You can't get away with that stuff."

Dalmas stared at him, then turned his head away and stared at a picture on the wall. He said coldly: "I'm doing it—and you're helping me. We've got a job, and a damn powerful organization behind us. There's a lot of sugar at stake."

"How do you figure?" Denny asked grimly. He didn't look pleased.

"The girl friend doesn't think Walden suicided, Denny. I don't either, and I've got a sort of lead. But it has to be worked fast, because it's as good a lead for the law as us. I didn't expect to be able to check it right away, but I got a break."

Denny said: "Uh-huh. Don't make it too clever. I'm a slow thinker."

He struck a match and lit his cigar. His hand shook just a little.

Dalmas said: "It's not clever. It's kind of dumb. The gun that killed Walden is a filed gun. But I broke it and the inside number wasn't filed. And Headquarters has the number, in the special permits."

"And you just went in and asked for it and they gave it to you," Denny said grimly. "And when they pick Walden up and trace the gun themselves, they'll just think it was swell of you to beat them to it." He made a harsh noise in his throat.

Dalmas said: "Take it easy, boy. The guy that did the checking rates. I don't have to worry about that."

"Like hell you don't! And what would a guy like Walden be doin' with a filed gun? That's a felony rap."

Dalmas finished his drink and carried his empty glass over to the bureau. He held the whiskey bottle out. Denny shook his head. He looked very disgusted.

"If he had the gun, he might not have known about that, Denny. And it could be that it wasn't his gun at all. If it was a killer's gun, then the killer was an amateur. A professional wouldn't have that kind of artillery."

The big man said slowly: "Okey, what you get on the rod?"

Dalmas sat down on the bed again. He dug a package of cigarettes out of his pocket, lit one, and leaned forward to toss the match through the open window. He said: "The permit was issued about a year ago to a newshawk on the Press-Chronicle, name of Dart Burwand. This Burwand was bumped off last April on the ramp of the Arcade Depot. He was all set to leave town, but he didn't make it. They never cracked the case, but the hunch is that this Burwand was tied to some racket—like the Lingle killing in Chi—and that he tried to shake one of the big boys. The big boy backfired on the idea. Exit Burwand."

The big man was breathing deeply. He had let his cigar go out. Dalmas watched him gravely while he talked.

"I got that from Westfalls, on the Press-Chronicle," Dalmas

said. "He's a friend of mine. There's more of it. This gun was given back to Burwand's wife—probably. She still lives here —out on North Kenmore. She might tell me what she did with the gun . . . and she might be tied to some racket herself, Denny. In that case she wouldn't tell me, but after I talk to her she might make some contacts we ought to know about. Get the idea?"

Denny struck another match and held it on the end of his cigar. His voice said thickly: "What do I do—tail the broad after you put the idea to her, about the gun?"

"Right."

The big man stood up, pretended to yawn. "Can do," he grunted. "But why all the hush-hush about Walden? Why not let the cops work it out? We're just goin' to get ourselves a lot of bad marks at Headquarters."

Dalmas said slowly: "It's got to be risked. We don't know what the blackmail crowd had on Walden, and the studio stands to lose too much money if it comes out in the investigation and gets a front-page spread all over the country."

Denny said: "You talk like Walden was spelled Valentino. Hell, the guy's only a director. All they got to do is take his name off a couple of unreleased pictures."

"They figure different," Dalmas said. "But maybe that's because they haven't talked to you."

Denny said roughly: "Okey. But me, I'd let the girl friend take the damn rap! All the law ever wants is a fall guy."

He went around the bed to get his hat, crammed it on his head.

"Swell," he said sourly. "We gotta find out all about it before the cops even know Walden is dead." He gestured with one hand and laughed mirthlessly. "Like they do in the movies."

Dalmas put the whiskey bottle away in the bureau drawer and put his hat on. He opened the door and stood aside for Denny to go out. He switched off the lights.

It was ten minutes to nine.

SIX

The tall blonde looked at Dalmas out of greenish eyes with very small pupils. He went in past her quickly, without seeming to move quickly. He pushed the door shut with his elbow.

He said: "I'm a dick—private—Mrs. Burwand. Trying to dig up a little dope you might know about."

The blonde said: "The name is Dalton, Helen Dalton. Forget the Burwand stuff."

Dalmas smiled and said: "I'm sorry. I should have known."

The blonde shrugged her shoulders and drifted away from the door. She sat down on the edge of a chair that had a cigarette burn on the arm. The room was a furnished-apartment living room with a lot of department store bric-à-brac spread around. Two floor lamps burned. There were flounced pillows on the floor, a French doll sprawled against the base of one lamp, and a row of gaudy novels went across the mantel, above the gas fire.

Dalmas said politely, swinging his hat: "It's about a gun Dart Burwand used to own. It's showed up on a case I'm working. I'm trying to trace it—from the time you had it."

Helen Dalton scratched the upper part of her arm. She had half-inch-long fingernails. She said curtly: "I don't have an idea what you're talking about."

Dalmas stared at her and leaned against the wall. His voice got on edge.

"Maybe you remember that you used to be married to Dart Burwand and that he got bumped off last April . . . Or is that too far back?"

The blonde bit one of her knuckles and said: "Smart guy, huh?"

"Not unless I have to be. But don't fall asleep from that last shot in the arm."

Helen Dalton sat up very straight, suddenly. All the vagueness went out of her expression. She spoke between tight lips.

"What's the howl about the gun?"

"It killed a guy, that's all," Dalmas said carelessly.

She stared at him. After a moment she said: "I was broke. I hocked it. I never got it out. I had a husband that made sixty bucks a week but didn't spend any of it on me. I never had a dime."

Dalmas nodded. "Remember the pawnshop where you left it?" he asked. "Or maybe you still have the ticket."

"No. It was on Main. The street's lined with them. And I don't have the ticket."

Dalmas said: "I was afraid of that."

He walked slowly across the room, looked at the titles of some of the books on the mantel. He went on and stood in front of a small, folding desk. There was a photo in a silver frame on the desk. Dalmas stared at it for some time. He turned slowly.

"It's too bad about the gun, Helen. A pretty important name was rubbed out with it this afternoon. The number was filed off the outside. If you hocked it, I'd figure some hood bought it from the hockshop guy, except that a hood wouldn't file a gun that way. He'd know there was another number inside. So it wasn't a hood—and the man it was found with wouldn't be likely to get a gun in a hock shop."

The blonde stood up slowly. Red spots burned in her cheeks. Her arms were rigid at her sides and her breath whispered. She said slowly, strainedly: "You can't maul me around, dick. I don't want any part of any police business—and I've got some good friends to take care of me. Better scram."

Dalmas looked back towards the frame on the desk. He said: "Johnny Sutro oughtn't to leave his mug around in a broad's apartment that way. Somebody might think he was cheating."

The blonde walked stiff-legged across the room and slammed the photo into the drawer of the desk. She slammed the drawer shut, and leaned her hips against the desk.

"You're all wet, shamus. That's not anybody called Sutro. Get on out, will you, for gawd's sake?"

Dalmas laughed unpleasantly. "I saw you at Sutro's house this afternoon. You were so drunk you don't remember."

The blonde made a movement as though she were going to jump at him. Then she stopped, rigid. A key turned in the room door. It opened and a man came in. He stood just inside the door and pushed it shut very slowly. His right hand was in the pocket of a light tweed overcoat. He was dark-skinned, high-shouldered, angular, with a sharp nose and chin.

Dalmas looked at him quietly and said: "Good evening, Councilman Sutro."

The man looked past Dalmas at the girl. He took no notice of Dalmas. The girl said shakily: "This guy says he's a dick. He's giving me a third about some gun he says I had. Throw him out, will you?"

Sutro said: "A dick, eh?"

He walked past Dalmas without looking at him. The blonde backed away from him and fell into a chair. Her face got a pasty look and her eyes were scared. Sutro looked down at her for a moment, then turned around and took a small automatic out of his pocket. He held it loosely, pointed down at the floor.

He said: "I haven't a lot of time."

Dalmas said: "I was just going." He moved near the door. Sutro said sharply: "Let's have the story first."

Dalmas said: "Sure."

He moved lithely, without haste, and threw the door wide open. The gun jerked up in Sutro's hand. Dalmas said: "Don't be a sap. You're not starting anything here and you know it."

The two men stared at each other. After a moment or two Sutro put the gun back into his pocket and licked his thin lips. Dalmas said: "Miss Dalton had a gun once that killed a man —recently. But she hasn't had it for a long time. That's all I wanted to know."

Sutro nodded slowly. There was a peculiar expression in his eyes.

"Miss Dalton is a friend of my wife's. I wouldn't want her to be bothered," he said coldly.

"That's right. You wouldn't," Dalmas said "But a legitimate dick has a right to ask legitimate questions. I didn't break in here."

Sutro eyed him slowly: "Okey, but take it easy on my friends. I draw water in this town and I could hang a sign on you."

Dalmas nodded. He went quietly out of the door and shut it. He listened a moment. There was no sound inside that he could hear. He shrugged and went on down the hall, down three steps and across a small lobby that had no switchboard. Outside the apartment house he looked along the street. It was an apartment-house district and there were cars parked up and down the street. He went towards the lights of the taxi that was waiting for him.

Joey, the red-haired driver, was standing on the edge of the curb in front of his hack. He was smoking a cigarette, staring across the street, apparently at a big, dark coupe that was parked with its left side to the curb. As Dalmas came up to him he threw his cigarette away and came to meet him.

He spoke quickly: "Listen, boss. I got a look at the guy in that Cad—"

Pale flame broke in bitter streaks from above the door of the coupe. A gun racketed between the buildings that faced each other across the street. Joey fell against Dalmas. The coupe jerked into sudden motion. Dalmas went down sidewise, on to one knee, with the driver clinging to him. He tried to reach his gun, couldn't make it. The coupe went around the corner with a squeal of rubber, and Joey fell down Dalmas' side and rolled over on his back on the sidewalk. He beat his hands up and down on the cement and a hoarse, anguished sound came from deep inside him.

Tires screeched again and Dalmas flung up to his feet, swept his hand to his left armpit. He relaxed as a small car skidded to a stop and Denny fell out of it, charged across the intervening space towards him.

Dalmas bent over the driver. Light from the lanterns beside

the entrance to the apartment house showed blood on the front of Joey's whipcord jacket, blood that was seeping out through the material. Joey's eyes opened and shut like the eyes of a dying bird.

Denny said: "No use to follow that bus. Too fast."

"Get on a phone and call an ambulance," Dalmas said quickly. "The kid's got a bellyful . . . Then take a plant on the blonde."

The big man hurried back to his car, jumped into it and tore off around the corner. A window went open somewhere and a man yelled down. Some cars stopped.

Dalmas bent down over Joey and muttered: "Take it easy, oldtimer . . . Easy, boy . . . easy."

SEVEN

The homicide lieutenant's name was Weinkassel. He had thin, blond hair, icy blue eyes and a lot of pockmarks. He sat in a swivel chair with his feet on the edge of a pulled-out drawer and a telephone scooped close to his elbow. The room smelled of dust and cigar butts.

A man named Lonergan, a bulky dick with gray hair and a gray mustache, stood near an open window, looking out of it morosely.

Weinkassel chewed on a match, stared at Dalmas, who was across the desk from him. He said: "Better talk a bit. The hack driver can't. You've had luck in this town and you wouldn't want to run it into the ground."

Lonergan said: "He's hard. He won't talk." He didn't turn around when he said it.

"A little less of your crap would go farther, Lonnie," Weinkassel said in a dead voice.

Dalmas smiled faintly and rubbed the palm of his hand against the side of the desk. It made a squeaking sound.

"What would I talk about?" he asked. "It was dark and I

didn't get a flash of the man behind the gun. The car was a Cadillac coupe, without lights. I've told you this already, Lieutenant."

"It don't listen," Weinkassel grumbled. "There's something screwy about it. You gotta have some kind of a hunch who it could be. It's a cinch the gun was for you."

Dalmas said: "Why? The hack driver was hit and I wasn't. Those lads get around a lot. One of them might be in wrong with some tough boys."

"Like you," Lonergan said. He went on staring out of the window.

Weinkassel frowned at Lonergan's back and said patiently: "The car was outside while you was still inside. The hack driver was outside. If the guy with the gun had wanted him, he didn't have to wait for you to come out."

Dalmas spread his hands and shrugged. "You boys think I know who it was?"

"Not exactly. We think you could give us some names to check on, though. Who'd you go to see in them apartments?"

Dalmas didn't say anything for a moment. Lonergan turned away from the window, sat on the end of the desk and swung his legs. There was a cynical grin on his flat face.

"Come through, baby," he said cheerfully.

Dalmas tilted his chair back and put his hands into his pockets. He stared at Weinkassel speculatively, ignored the gray-haired dick as though he didn't exist.

He said slowly: "I was there on business for a client. You can't make me talk about that."

Weinkassel shrugged and stared at him coldly. Then he took the chewed match out of his mouth, looked at the flattened end of it, tossed it away.

"I might have a hunch your business had something to do with the shootin'," he said grimly. "That way the hush-hush would be out. Wouldn't it?"

"Maybe," Dalmas said. "If that's the way it's going to work out. But I ought to have a chance to talk to my client."

Weinkassel said: "Okey. You can have till the morning. Then you put your papers on the desk, see."

Dalmas nodded and stood up. "Fair enough, Lieutenant."

"Hush-hush is all a shamus knows," Lonergan said roughly.

Dalmas nodded to Weinkassel and went out of the office. He walked down a bleak corridor and up steps to the lobby floor. Outside the City Hall he went down a long flight of concrete steps and across Spring Street to where a blue Packard roadster, not very new, was parked. He got into it and drove around the corner, then though the Second Street tunnel, dropped over a block and drove out west. He watched in the mirror as he drove.

At Alvarado he went into a drugstore and called his hotel. The clerk gave him a number to call. He called it and heard Denny's heavy voice at the other end of the line. Denny said urgently: "Where you been? I've got that broad out here at my place. She's drunk. Come on out and we'll get her to tell us what you want to know."

Dalmas stared out through the glass of the phone booth without seeing anything. After a pause he said slowly: "The blonde? How come?"

"It's a story, boy. Come on out and I'll give it to you. Fourteen-fifty-four South Livesay. Know where that is?"

"I've got a map. I'll find it," Dalmas said in the same tone.

Denny told him just how to find it, at some length. At the end of the explanation he said: "Make it fast. She's asleep now, but she might wake up and start yellin' murder."

Dalmas said: "Where you live it probably wouldn't matter much . . . I'll be right out, Denny."

He hung up and went out to his car. He got a pint bottle of bourbon out of the car pocket and took a long drink. Then he started up and drove towards Fox Hills. Twice on the way he stopped and sat still in the car, thinking. But each time he went on again.

EIGHT

The road turned off Pico into a scattered subdivision that spread itself out over rolling hills between two golf courses. It followed the edge of one of the golf courses, separated from it by a high wire fence. There were bungalows here and there dotted about the slopes. After a while the road dipped into a hollow and there was a single bungalow in the hollow, right across the street from the golf course.

Dalmas drove past it and parked under a giant eucalyptus that etched deep shadow on the moonlit surface of the road. He got out and walked back, turned up a cement path to the bungalow. It was wide and low and had cottage windows across the front. Bushes grew halfway up the screens. There was faint light inside and the sound of a radio, turned low, came through the open windows.

A shadow moved across the screens and the front door came open. Dalmas went into a living room built across the front of the house. One small bulb burned in a lamp and the luminous dial of the radio glowed. A little moonlight came into the room.

Denny had his coat off and his sleeves rolled up on his big arms.

He said: "The broad's still asleep. I'll wake her up when I've told you how I got her here."

Dalmas said: "Sure you weren't tailed?"

"Not a chance." Denny spread a big hand.

Dalmas sat down in a wicker chair in the corner, between the radio and the end of the line of windows. He put his hat on the floor, pulled out the bottle of bourbon and regarded it with a dissatisfied air.

"Buy us a real drink, Denny. I'm tired as hell. Didn't get any dinner."

Denny said: "I've got some Three-Star Martel. Be right up."

He went out of the room and light went on in the back part

of the house. Dalmas put the bottle on the floor beside his hat and rubbed two fingers across his forehead. His head ached. After a little while the light went out in the back and Denny came back with two tall glasses.

The brandy tasted clean and hard. Denny sat down in another wicker chair. He looked very big and dark in the half-lit room. He began to talk slowly, in his gruff voice.

"It sounds goofy, but it worked. After the cops stopped milling around I parked in the alley and went in the back way. I knew which apartment the broad had but I hadn't seen her. I thought I'd make some kind of a stall and see how she was makin' out. I knocked on her door, but she wouldn't answer. I could hear her movin' around inside, and in a minute I could hear a telephone bein' dialed. I went back along the hall and tried the service door. It opened and I went in. It fastened with one of them screw bolts that get out of line and don't fasten when you think they do."

Dalmas nodded, said: "I get the idea, Denny."

The big man drank out of his glass and rubbed the edge of it up and down on his lower lip. He went on.

"She was phoning a guy named Gayn Donner. Know him?"

"I've heard of him," Dalmas said. "So she has that kind of connections."

"She was callin' him by name and she sounded mad," Denny said. "That's how I knew. Donner has that place on Mariposa Canyon Drive—the Mariposa Club. You hear his band over the air—Hank Munn and his boys."

Dalmas said: "I've heard it, Denny."

"Okey. When she hung up I went in on her. She looked snowed, weaved around funny, didn't seem to know much what was going on. I looked around and there was a photo of John Sutro, the Councilman, in a desk there. I used that for a stall. I said that Sutro wanted her to duck out for a while and that I was one of his boys and she was to come along. She fell for it. Screwy. She wanted some liquor. I said I had some in the car. She got her little hat and coat."

Dalmas said softly: "It was that easy, huh?"

"Yeah," Denny said. He finished his drink and put the glass somewhere. "I bottle-fed her in the car to keep her quiet and we came out here. She went to sleep and that's that. What do you figure? Tough downtown?"

"Tough enough," Dalmas said. "I didn't fool the boys much."

"Anything on the Walden kill?"

Dalmas shook his head slowly.

"I guess the Jap didn't get home yet, Denny."

"Want to talk to the broad?"

The radio was playing a waltz. Dalmas listened to it for a moment before he answered. Then he said in a tired voice: "I guess that's what I came out here for."

Denny got up and went out of the room. There was the sound of a door opening and muffled voices.

Dalmas took his gun out from under his arm and put it down in the chair beside his leg.

The blonde staggered a little too much as she came in. She stared around, giggled, made vague motions with her long hands. She blinked at Dalmas, stood swaying a moment, then slid down into the chair Denny had been sitting in. The big man kept near her and leaned against a library table that stood by the inside wall.

She said drunkenly: "My old pal the dick. Hey, hey, stranger! How about buyin' a lady a drink?"

Dalmas stared at her without expression. He said slowly: "Got any new ideas about that gun? You know, the one we were talking about when Johnny Sutro crashed in . . . The filed gun . . . The gun that killed Derek Walden."

Denny stiffened, then made a sudden motion towards his hip. Dalmas brought his Colt up and came to his feet with it. Denny looked at it and became still, relaxed. The girl had not moved at all, but the drunkenness dropped away from her like a dead leaf. Her face was suddenly tense and bitter.

Dalmas said evenly: "Keep the hands in sight, Denny, and everything'll be jake . . . Now suppose you two cheap crossers tell me what I'm here for."

The big man said thickly: "For gawd's sake! What's eatin' you? You scared me when you said 'Walden' to the girl."

Dalmas grinned. "That's all right, Denny. Maybe she never heard of him. Let's get this ironed out in a hurry. I have an idea I'm here for trouble."

"You're crazy as hell!" the big man snarled.

Dalmas moved the gun slightly. He put his back against the end wall of the room, leaned over and turned the radio off with his left hand. Then he spoke bitterly: "You sold out, Denny. That's easy. You're too big for a tail and I've spotted you following me around half a dozen times lately. When you horned in on the deal tonight I was pretty sure . . . And when you told me that funny story about how you got baby out here I was *damn* sure . . . Hell's sake, do you think a guy that's stayed alive as long as I have would believe that one? Come on, Denny, be a sport and tell me who you're working for . . . I might let you take a powder . . . Who you working for? Donner? Sutro? Or somebody I don't know? And why the plant out here in the woods?"

The girl shot to her feet suddenly and sprang at him. He threw her off with his free hand and she sprawled on the floor. She yelled: "Get him, you big punk? Get him!"

Denny didn't move. "Shut up, snow-bird!" Dalmas snapped. "Nobody's getting anybody. This is just a talk between friends. Get up on your feet and stop throwing curves!"

The blonde stood up slowly.

Denny's face had a stony, immovable look in the dimness. His voice came with a dull rasp. He said: "I sold out. It was lousy. Okey, that's that. I got fed up with watchin' a bunch of extra girls trying to pinch each other's lipstick . . . You can take a plug at me, if you feel like it."

He still didn't move. Dalmas nodded slowly and said again: "Who is it, Denny? Who you working for?"

Denny said: "I don't know. I call a number, get orders, and report that way. I get dough in the mail. I tried to break the twist here, but no luck . . . I don't think you're on the spot and I don't know a damn thing about that shootin' in the street."

261
▼

Dalmas stared at him. He said slowly: "You wouldn't be stalling—to keep me here—would you, Denny?"

The big man raised his head slowly. The room suddenly seemed to get very still. A car had stopped outside. The faint throbbing of its motor died.

A red spotlight hit the top of the screens.

It was blinding. Dalmas slid down on one knee, shifted his position sidewise very quickly, silently. Denny's harsh voice in the silence said: "Cops, for gawd's sake!"

The red light dissolved the wire mesh of the screens into a rosy glow, threw a great splash of vivid color on the oiled finish of the inside wall. The girl made a choked sound and her face was a red mask for an instant before she sank down out of the fan of light. Dalmas looked into the light, his head low behind the sill of the end window. The leaves of the bushes were black spearpoints in the red glare.

Steps sounded on the walk.

A harsh voice rasped: "Everybody out! Mitts in the air!"

There was a sound of movement inside the house. Dalmas swung his gun—uselessly. A switch clicked and a porch light went on. For a moment, before they dodged back, two men in blue police uniforms showed up in the cone of the porch light. One of them held a sub-machine gun and the other had a long Luger with a special magazine fitted to it.

There was a grating sound. Denny was at the door, opening the peep panel. A gun came up in his hand and crashed.

Something heavy clattered on the cement and a man swayed forward into the light, swayed back again. His hands were against his middle. A stiff-vizored cap fell down and rolled on the walk.

Dalmas hit the floor low down against the baseboard as the machine gun cut loose. He ground his face into the wood of the floor. The girl screamed behind him.

The chopper raked the room swiftly from end to end and the air filled with plaster and splinters. A wall mirror crashed down. A sharp stench of powder fought with the sour smell of the plaster dust. This seemed to go on for a very long time. Something fell across Dalmas' legs. He kept his eyes shut and his face pressed against the floor.

The stuttering and crashing stopped. The rain of plaster inside the walls kept on. A voice yelled: "How d'you like it, pals?"

Another voice far back snapped angrily: "Come on—let's go!"

Steps sounded again, and a dragging sound. More steps. The motor of the car roared into life. A door slammed heavily. Tires screeched on the gravel of the road and the song of the motor swelled and died swiftly.

Dalmas got up on his feet. His ears boomed and his nostrils were dry. He got his gun off the floor, unclipped a thin flash from an inside pocket, snapped it on. It probed weakly through the dusty air. The blonde lay on her back with her eyes wide open and her mouth twisted into a sort of grin. She was sobbing. Dalmas bent over her. There didn't seem to be a mark on her.

He went on down the room. He found his hat untouched beside the chair that had half the top shot off. The bottle of bourbon lay beside the hat. He picked them both up. The man with the chopper had raked the room waist-high, back and forth, without lowering it far enough. Dalmas went on farther, came to the door.

Denny was on his knees in front of the door. He was swaying backwards and forwards and holding one of his hands in the other. Blood dribbled between his thick fingers.

Dalmas got the door open and went out. There was a smear of blood and a litter of shells on the walk. There was nobody in sight. He stood there with the blood beating in his face, like little hammers. The skin around his nose prickled.

He drank some whiskey out of the bottle and turned and went back into the house. Denny was up on his feet now. He had a handkerchief out and was tying it around his bloody hand. He looked dazed, drunk. He swayed on his feet. Dalmas put the beam of the flash on his face.

He said: "Hurt much?"

"No. Clipped on the hand," the big man said thickly. His fingers were clumsy on the handkerchief.

"The blonde's scared blind," Dalmas said. "It's your party, boy. Nice pals you have. They meant to get all three of us. You rattled them when you took a pot out of the peephole. I guess I owe you something for that, Denny . . . The gunner wasn't so good."

Denny said: "Where you goin'?"

"Where d'you think?"

Denny looked at him. "Sutro's your man," he said slowly. "I'm through—washed up. They can all go to hell."

Dalmas went through the door again, down the path to the street. He got into his car and drove away without lights. When he had turned corners and gone some distance he switched the lights on and got out and dusted himself off.

NINE

Black and silver curtains opened in an inverted V against a haze of cigarette and cigar smoke. The brasses of the dance band shot brief flashes of color through the haze. There was a smell of food and liquor and perfume and face powder. The dance floor was an empty splash of amber light and looked slightly larger than a screen star's bath mat.

Then the band started up and the lights went down, and a headwaiter came up the carpeted steps tapping a gold pencil against the satin stripe of his trousers. He had narrow, lifeless eyes and blond-white hair sleeked back off a bony forehead.

Dalmas said: "I'd like to see Mister Donner."

The headwaiter tapped his teeth with his gold pencil. "I'm afraid he's busy. What name?"

"Dalmas. Tell him I'm a special friend of Johnny Sutro's."

The headwaiter said: "I'll try."

He went across to a panel that had a row of buttons on it and a small one-piece phone. He took it off the hook and put it to his ear, staring at Dalmas across the cup with the impersonal stare of a stuffed animal.

Dalmas said: "I'll be in the lobby."

He went back through the curtains and prowled over to the Men's Room. Inside he got out the bottle of bourbon and drank what was left of it, tilting his head back and standing splay-legged in the middle of the tiled floor. A wizened Negro in a white jacket fluttered at him, said anxiously: "No drinkin' in here, boss."

Dalmas threw the empty bottle into a receptacle for towels. He took a clean towel off the glass shelf, wiped his lips with it, put a dime down on the edge of the basin and went out.

There was a space between an inner and outer door. He leaned against the outer door and took a small automatic about four inches long out of his vest pocket. He held it with three fingers against the inside of his hat and went on out, swinging the hat gently beside his body.

After a while a tall Filipino with silky black hair came into the lobby and looked around. Dalmas went towards him. The headwaiter looked out through the curtains and nodded at the Filipino.

The Filipino spoke to Dalmas: "This way, boss."

They went down a long, quiet corridor. The sound of the dance band died away behind them. Some deserted green-topped tables showed through an open door. The corridor turned into another that was at right angles, and at the end of this one some light came out through a doorway.

The Filipino paused in midstride and made a graceful, complicated movement, at the end of which he had a big, black automatic in his hand. He prodded it politely into Dalmas' ribs.

"Got to frisk you, boss. House rules."

Dalmas stood still and held his arms out from his sides. The Filipino took Dalmas' Colt away from him and dropped it into his pocket. He patted the rest of Dalmas' pockets, stepped back and holstered his own cannon.

Dalmas lowered his arms and let his hat fall on the floor and the little automatic that had been inside the hat peered neatly at the Filipino's belly. The Filipino looked down at it with a shocked grin.

Dalmas said: "That was fun, spig. Let me do it."

He put his Colt back where it belonged, took the big automatic from under the Filipino's arm, slipped the magazine out of it and ejected the shell that was in the chamber. He gave the empty gun back to the Filipino.

"You can still use it for a sap. If you stay in front of me, your boss don't have to know that's all it's good for."

The Filipino licked his lips. Dalmas felt him for another gun, and they went on along the corridor, went in at the door that was partly open. The Filipino went first.

It was a big room with walls paneled in diagonal strips of wood. A yellow Chinese rug on the floor, plenty of good furniture, countersunk doors that told of soundproofing, and no windows. There were several gilt gratings high up and a built-in ventilator fan made a faint, soothing murmur. Four men were in the room. Nobody said anything.

Dalmas sat down on a leather divan and stared at Ricchio, the smooth boy who had walked him out of Walden's apartment. Ricchio was tied to a high-backed chair. His arms were pulled around behind it and fastened together at the wrists. His eyes were mad and his face was a welter of blood and bruises. He had been pistol whipped. The sandy-haired man, Noddy, who had been with him at the Kilmarnock sat on a sort of stool in the corner, smoking.

John Sutro was rocking slowly in a red leather rocker, staring down at the floor. He did not look up when Dalmas came into the room.

The fourth man sat behind a desk that looked as if it had cost a lot of money. He had soft brown hair parted in the middle and brushed back and down; thin lips and reddish-brown eyes that had hot lights in them. He watched Mallory while he sat down and looked around. Then he spoke, glancing at Ricchio.

"The punk got a little out of hand. We've been telling him about it. I guess you're not sorry."

Dalmas laughed shortly, without mirth. "All right as far as it goes, Donner. How about the other one? I don't see any marks on him."

"Noddy's all right. He worked under orders," Donner said evenly. He picked up a long-handled file and began to file one of his nails. "You and I have things to talk about. That's why you got in here. You look all right to me—if you don't try to cover too much ground with your private-dick racket."

Dalmas' eyes widened a little. He said: "I'm listening, Donner."

Sutro lifted his eyes and stared at the back of Donner's head. Donner went on talking in a smooth indifferent voice.

"I know all about the play at Derek Walden's place and I know about the shooting on Kenmore. If I'd thought Ricchio would go that crazy, I'd have stopped him before. As it is, I figure it's up to me to straighten things out . . . And when we get through here Mister Ricchio will go downtown and speak his piece.

"Here's how it happened. Ricchio used to work for Walden when the Hollywood crowd went in for bodyguards. Walden bought his liquor in Ensenada—still does, for all I know—and brought it in himself. Nobody bothered him. Ricchio saw a chance to bring in some white goods under good cover. Walden caught him at it. He didn't want a scandal, so he just showed Ricchio the gate. Ricchio took advantage of that by trying to shake Walden down, on the theory that he wasn't clean enough to stand the working-over the Feds would give him. Walden didn't shake fast enough to suit Ricchio, so he went hog-wild and decided on a strong-arm play. You and your driver messed it up and Ricchio went gunning for you."

Donner put down his file and smiled. Dalmas shrugged and glanced at the Filipino, who was standing by the wall, at the end of the divan.

Dalmas said: "I don't have your organization, Donner, but

I get around. I think that's a smooth story and it would have got by—with a little co-operation downtown. But it won't fit the facts as they are now."

Donner raised his eyebrows. Sutro began to swing the tip of his polished shoe up and down in front of his knee.

Dalmas said: "How does Mister Sutro fit into all this?"

Sutro stared at him and stopped rocking. He made a swift, impatient movement. Donner smiled "He's a friend of Walden's. Walden talked to him a little and Sutro knows Ricchio worked for me. But being a councilman he didn't want to tell Walden everything he knew."

Dalmas said grimly: "I'll tell you what's wrong with your story, Donner. There's not enough fear in it. Walden was too scared to help me even when I was working for him . . . And this afternoon somebody was so scared of him that he got shot."

Donner leaned forward and his eyes got small and tight. His hands balled into fists on the desk before him.

"Walden is—dead?" he almost whispered.

Dalmas nodded. "Shot in the right temple . . . with a thirty-two. It looks like suicide. It isn't."

Sutro put his hand up quickly and covered his face. The sandy-haired man got rigid on his stool in the corner.

Dalmas said: "Want to hear a good honest guess, Donner? . . . We'll call it a guess . . . Walden was in the dope-smuggling racket himself—and not all by his lonesome. But after Repeal he wanted to quit. The coast guards wouldn't have to spend so much time watching liquor ships, and dope-smuggling up the coast wasn't going to be gravy any more. And Walden got sweet on a gal that had good eyes and could add up to ten. So he wanted to walk out on the dope racket."

Donner moistened his lips and said: "What dope racket?"

Dalmas eyed him. "You wouldn't know about anything like that, would you, Donner? Hell, no, that's something for the bad boys to play with. And the bad boys didn't like the idea of Walden quitting that way. He was drinking too much—and he might start to broadcast to his girl friend. They wanted him to quit the way he did—on the receiving end of a gun."

Donner turned his head slowly and stared at the bound man on the high-backed chair. He said very softly: "Ricchio."

Then he got up and walked around his desk. Sutro took his hand down from his face and watched with his lips shaking.

Donner stood in front of Ricchio. He put his hand out against Ricchio's head and jarred it back against the chair. Ricchio moaned. Donner smiled down at him.

"I must be slowing up. *You* killed Walden, you bastard! You went back and croaked him. You forgot to tell us about that part, baby."

Ricchio opened his mouth and spit a stream of blood against Donner's hand and wrist. Donner's face twitched and he stepped back and away, holding the hand straight out in front of him. He took out a handkerchief and wiped it off carefully, dropped the handkerchief on the floor.

"Lend me your gun, Noddy," he said quietly, going towards the sandy-haired man.

Sutro jerked and his mouth fell open. His eyes looked sick. The tall Filipino flicked his empty automatic into his hand as if he had forgotten it was empty. Noddy took a blunt revolver from under his right arm, held it out to Donner.

Donner took it from him and went back to Ricchio. He raised the gun.

Dalmas said: Ricchio didn't kill Walden."

The Filipino took a quick step forward and slashed at him with his big automatic. The gun hit Dalmas on the point of the shoulder, and a wave of pain billowed down his arm. He rolled away and snapped his Colt into his hand. The Filipino swung at him again, missed.

Dalmas slid to his feet, side-stepped and laid the barrel of the Colt along the side of the Filipino's head, with all his strength. The Filipino grunted, sat down on the floor, and the whites showed all around his eyes. He fell over slowly, clawing at the divan.

There was no expression on Donner's face and he held his blunt revolver perfectly still. His long upper lip was beaded with sweat.

Dalmas said: "Ricchio didn't kill Walden. Walden was kllled with a filed gun and the gun was planted in his hand. Ricchio wouldn't go within a block of a filed gun."

Sutro's face was ghastly. The sandy-haired man had got down off his stool and stood with his right hand swinging at his side.

"Tell me more," Donner said evenly.

"The filed gun traces to a broad named Helen Dalton or Burwand," Dalmas said. "It was her gun. She told me that she hocked it long ago. I didn't believe her. She's a good friend of Sutro's and Sutro was so bothered by my going to see her that he pulled a gat on me himself. Why do you suppose Sutro was bothered, Donner, and how do you suppose he knew I was likely to go see the broad?"

Donner said: "Go ahead and tell me." He looked at Sutro very quietly.

Dalmas took a step closer to Donner and held his Colt down at his side, not threateningly.

"I'll tell you how and why. I've been tailed ever since I started to work for Walden—talled by a clumsy ox of a studio dick I could spot a mile off. He was bought, Donner. The guy that killed Walden bought him. He figured the studio dick had a chance to get next to me, and I let him do just that—to give him rope and spot his game. His boss was Sutro. Sutro killed Walden—with his own hand. It was that kind of a job. An amateur job—a smart-aleck kill. The thing that made it smart was the thing that gave it away—the suicide plant, with a filed gun that the killer thought couldn't be traced because he didn't know most guns have numbers inside."

Donner swung the blunt revolver until it pointed midway between the sandy-haired man and Sutro. He didn't say anything. His eyes were thoughtful and interested.

Dalmas shifted his weight a little, on to the balls of his feet. The Filipino on the floor put a hand along the divan and his nails scratched on the leather.

"There's more of it, Donner, but what the hell! Sutro was Walden's pal, and he could get close to him, close enough to

▼

stick a gun to his head and let go. A shot wouldn't be heard on the penthouse floor of the Kilmarnock, one little shot from a thirty-two. So Sutro put the gun in Walden's hand and went on his way. But he forgot that Walden was left-handed and he didn't know the gun could be traced. When it was—and his bought man wised him up—and I tapped the girl—he hired himself a chopper squad and angled all three of us out to a house in Palms to button our mouths for good . . . Only the chopper squad, like everything else in this play, didn't do its stuff so good."

Donner nodded slowly. He looked at a spot in the middle of Sutro's stomach and lined his gun on it.

"Tell us about it, Johnny," he said softly. "Tell us how you got clever in your old age—"

The sandy-haired man moved suddenly. He dodged down behind the desk and as he went down his right hand swept for his other gun. It roared from behind the desk. The bullet came through the kneehole and pinged into the wall with a sound of striking metal behind the paneling.

Dalmas jerked his Colt and fired twice into the desk. A few splinters flew. The sandy-haired man yelled behind the desk and came up fast with his gun flaming in his hand. Donner staggered. His gun spoke twice, very quickly. The sandy-haired man yelled again, and blood jumped straight out from one of his cheeks. He went down behind the desk and stayed quiet.

Donner backed until he touched the wall. Sutro stood up and put his hands in front of his stomach and tried to scream.

Donner said: "Okey, Johnny. Your turn."

Then Donner coughed suddenly and slid down the wall with a dry rustle of cloth. He bent forward and dropped his gun and put his hands on the floor and went on coughing. His face got gray.

Sutro stood rigid, his hands in front of his stomach, and bent back at the wrists, the fingers curved clawlike. There was no light behind his eyes. They were dead eyes. After a moment his knees buckled and he fell down on the floor on his back.

Donner went on coughing quietly.

Dalmas crossed swiftly to the door of the room, listened at it, opened it and looked out. He shut it again quickly.

"Soundproof—and how!" he muttered.

He went back to the desk and lifted the telephone off its prongs. He put his Colt down and dialed, waited, said into the phone: "Captain Cathcart . . . Got to talk to him . . . Sure, it's important . . . very important."

He waited, drumming on the desk, staring hard-eyed around the room. He jerked a little as a sleepy voice came over the wire.

"Dalmas, Chief. I'm at the Casa Mariposa, in Gayn Donner's private office. There's been a little trouble, but nobody hurt bad . . . I've got Derek Walden's killer for you . . . Johnny Sutro did it . . . Yeah, the councilman . . . Make it fast, Chief . . . I wouldn't want to get in a fight with the help, you know. . . ."

He hung up and picked his Colt off the top of the desk, held it on the flat of his hand and stared across at Sutro.

"Get off the floor, Johnny," he said wearily. "Get up and tell a poor dumb dick how to cover this one up—smart guy!"

TEN

The light above the big oak table at Headquarters was too bright. Dalmas ran a finger along the wood, looked at it, wiped it off on his sleeve. He cupped his chin in his lean hands and stared at the wall above the roll-top desk that was beyond the table. He was alone in the room.

The loudspeaker on the wall droned: "Calling Car 71W in 72's district . . . at Third and Berendo . . . at the drugstore . . . meet a man . . ."

The door opened and Captain Cathcart came in, shut the

door carefully behind him. He was a big, battered man with a wide, moist face, a strained mustache, gnarled hands.

He sat down between the oak table and the roll-top desk and fingered a cold pipe that lay in the ashtray.

Dalmas raised his head from between his hands. Cathcart said: "Sutro's dead."

Dalmas stared, said nothing.

"His wife did it. He wanted to stop by his house a minute. The boys watched him good but they didn't watch her. She slipped him the dose before they could move."

Cathcart opened and shut his mouth twice. He had strong, dirty teeth.

"She never said a damn word. Brought a little gun around from behind her and fed him three slugs. One, two, three. Win, place, show. Just like that. Then she turned the gun around in her hand as nice as you could think of and handed it to the boys . . . What in hell she do that for?"

Dalmas said: "Get a confession?"

Cathcart stared at him and put the cold pipe in his mouth. He sucked on it noisily. "From him? Yeah—not on paper, though . . . What you suppose she done that for?"

"She knew about the blonde," Dalmas said. "She thought it was her last chance. Maybe she knew about his rackets."

The captain nodded slowly. "Sure," he said. "That's it. She figured it was her last chance. And why shouldn't she bop the bastard? If the D.A.'s smart, he'll let her take a manslaughter plea. That'd be about fifteen months at Tehachapi. A rest cure."

Dalmas moved in his chair. He frowned.

Cathcart went on: "It's a break for all of us. No dirt your way, no dirt on the administration. If she hadn't done it, it would have been a kick in the pants all around. She ought to get a pension."

"She ought to get a contract from Eclipse Films," Dalmas said. "When I got to Sutro I figured I was licked on the publicity angle. I might have gunned Sutro myself—if he hadn't been so yellow—and if he hadn't been a councilman."

"Nix on that, baby. Leave that stuff to the law," Cathcart growled. "Here's how it looks. I don't figure we can get Walden on the book as a suicide. The filed gun is against it and we got to wait for the autopsy and the gun-shark's report. And a paraffin test of the hand ought to show he didn't fire the gun at all. On the other hand, the case is closed on Sutro and what has to come out ought not to hurt too bad. Am I right?"

Dalmas took out a cigarette and rolled it between his fingers. He lit it slowly and waved the match until it went out.

"Walden was no lily," he said. "It's the dope angle that would raise hell—but that's cold. I guess we're jake, except for a few loose ends."

"Hell with the loose ends," Cathcart grinned. "Nobody's getting away with any fix that I can see. That sidekick of yours, Denny, will fade in a hurry and if I ever get my paws on the Dalton frail, I'll send her to Mendocino for the cure. We might get something on Donner—after the hospital gets through with him. We've got to put the rap on those hoods, for the stick-up and the taxi driver, whichever of 'em did that, but they won't talk. They still got a future to think about, and the taxi driver ain't so bad hurt. That leaves the chopper squad." Cathcart yawned. "Those boys must be from Frisco. We don't run to choppers around here much."

Dalmas sagged in his chair. "You wouldn't have a drink, would you, Chief?" he said dully.

Cathcart stared at him. "There's just one thing," he said grimly. "I want you to stay told about that. It was okey for you to break that gun—if you didn't spoil the prints. And I guess it was okey for you not to tell me, seein' the jam you were in. But I'll be damned if it's okey for you to beat our time by chiselin' on our own records."

Dalmas smiled thoughtfully at him. "You're right all the way, Chief," he said humbly. "It was the job—and that's all a guy can say."

Cathcart rubbed his cheeks vigorously. His frown went away and he grinned. Then he bent over and pulled out a drawer and brought up a quart bottle of rye. He put it on the desk and pressed a buzzer. A very large uniformed torso came part way into the room.

"Hey, Tiny!" Cathcart boomed. "Loan me that corkscrew you swiped out of my desk." The torso disappeared and came back.

"What'll we drink to?" the captain asked a couple of minutes later.

Dalmas said: "Let's just drink."

GUNS AT CYRANO'S

ONE

Ted Carmady liked the rain; liked the feel of it, the sound of it, the smell of it. He got out of his LaSalle coupe and stood for a while by the side entrance to the Carondelet, the high collar of his blue suede ulster tickling his ears, his hands in his pockets and a limp cigarette sputtering between his lips. Then he went in past the barbershop and the drugstore and the perfume shop with its rows of delicately lighted bottles, ranged like the ensemble in the finale of a Broadway musical.

He rounded a gold-veined pillar and got into an elevator with a cushioned floor.

" 'Lo Albert. A swell rain. Nine."

The slim tired-looking kid in pale blue and silver held a white-gloved hand against the closing doors, said: "Jeeze, you think I don't know your floor, Mister Carmady?"

He shot the car up to nine without looking at his signal light, whooshed the doors open, then leaned suddenly against the cage and closed his eyes.

Carmady stopped on his way out, flicked a sharp glance from bright brown eyes. "What's the matter, Albert? Sick?"

The boy worked a pale smile on his face. "I'm workin' double shift. Corky's sick. He's got boils. I guess maybe I didn't eat enough."

The tall, brown-eyed man fished a crumpled five-spot out of his pocket, snapped it under the boy's nose. The boy's eyes bulged. He heaved upright.

"Jeeze, Mister Carmady. I didn't mean—"

"Skip it, Albert. What's a fin between pals? Eat some extra meals on me."

He got out of the car and started along the corridor. Softly, under his breath, he said: "Sucker . . ."

The running man almost knocked him off his feet. He rounded the turn fast, lurched past Carmady's shoulder, ran for the elevator.

"Down!" He slammed through the closing doors.

Carmady saw a white set face under a pulled-down hat that was wet with rain; two empty black eyes set very close. Eyes in which there was a peculiar stare he had seen before. A load of dope.

The car dropped like lead. Carmady looked at the place where it had been for a long moment, then he went on down the corridor and around the turn.

He saw the girl lying half in and half out of the open door of 914.

She lay on her side, in a sheen of steel-gray lounging pajamas, her cheek pressed into the nap of the hall carpet, her head a mass of thick corn-blond hair, waved with glassy precision. Not a hair looked out of place. She was young, very pretty, and she didn't look dead.

Carmady slid down beside her, touched her cheek. It was warm. He lifted the hair softly away from her head and saw the bruise.

"Sapped." His lips pressed back against his teeth.

He picked her up in his arms, carried her through a short hallway to the living room of a suite, put her down on a big velour davenport in front of some gas logs.

She lay motionless, her eyes shut, her face bluish behind

the make-up. He shut the outer door and looked through the apartment, then went back to the hallway and picked up something that gleamed white against the baseboard. It was a bone-handled .22 automatic, sevenshot. He sniffed it, dropped it into his pocket and went back to the girl.

He took a big hammered-silver flask out of his inside breast pocket and unscrewed the top, opened her mouth with his fingers and poured whiskey against her small white teeth. She gagged and her head jerked out of his hand. Her eyes opened. They were deep blue, with a tint of purple. Light came into them and the light was brittle.

He lit a cigarette and stood looking down at her. She moved a little more. After a while she whispered: "I like your whiskey. Could I have a little more?"

He got a glass from the bathroom, poured whiskey into it. She sat up very slowly, touched her head, groaned. Then she took the glass out of his hand and put the liquor down with a practised flip of the wrist.

"I still like it," she said. "Who are you?"

She had a deep soft voice. He liked the sound of it. He said: "Ted Carmady. I live down the hall in 937."

"I got a dizzy spell, I guess."

"Uh-huh. You got sapped, angel." His bright eyes looked at her probingly. There was a smile tucked to the corners of his lips.

Her eyes got wider. A glaze came over them, the glaze of a protective enamel.

He said: "I saw the guy. He was snowed to the hairline. And here's your gun."

He took it out of his pocket, held it on the flat of his hand.

"I suppose that makes me think up a bedtime story," the girl said slowly.

"Not for me. If you're in a jam, I might help you. It all depends."

"Depends on what?" Her voice was colder, sharper.

"On what the racket is," he said softly. He broke the magazine from the small gun, glanced at the top cartridge. "Copper-nickel, eh? You know your ammunition, angel."

"Do you have to call me angel?"

"I don't know your name."

He grinned at her, then walked over to a desk in front of the windows, put the gun down on it. There was a leather photo frame on the desk, with two photos side by side. He looked at them casually at first, then his gaze tightened. A handsome dark woman and a thin blondish cold-eyed man whose high stiff collar, large knotted tie and narrow lapels dated the photo back many years. He stared at the man.

The girl was talking behind him. "I'm Jean Adrian. I do a number at Cyrano's, in the floor show."

Carmady still stared at the photo. "I know Benny Cyrano pretty well," he said absently. "These your parents?"

He turned and looked at her. She lifted her head slowly. Something that might have been fear showed in her deep blue eyes.

"Yes. They've been dead for years," she said dully. "Next question?"

He went quickly back to the davenport and stood in front of her. "Okey," he said thinly. "I'm nosey. So what? This is my town. My dad used to run it. Old Marcus Carmady, the People's Friend; this is my hotel. I own a piece of it. That snowed-up hoodlum looked like a life-taker to me. Why wouldn't I want to help out?"

The blond girl stared at him lazily. "I still like your whiskey," she said. "Could I—"

"Take it from the neck, angel. You get it down faster," he grunted.

She stood up suddenly and her face got a little white. "You talk to me as if I was a crook," she snapped. "Here it is, if you have to know. A boy friend of mine has been getting threats. He's a fighter, and they want him to drop a fight. Now they're trying to get at him through me. Does that satisfy you a little?"

Carmady picked his hat off a chair, took the cigarette end

out of his mouth and rubbed it out in a tray. He nodded quietly, said in a changed voice: "I beg your pardon." He started towards the door.

The giggle came when he was halfway there. The girl said behind him softly: "You have a nasty temper. And you've forgotten your flask."

He went back and picked the flask up. Then he bent suddenly, put a hand under the girl's chin and kissed her on the lips.

"To hell with you, angel. I like you," he said softly.

He went back to the hallway and out. The girl touched her lips with one finger, rubbed it slowly back and forth. There was a shy smile on her face.

TWO

Tony Acosta, the bell captain, was slim and dark and slight as a girl, with small delicate hands and velvety eyes and a hard little mouth. He stood in the doorway and said: "Seventh row was the best I could get, Mister Carmady. This Deacon Werra ain't bad and Duke Targo's the next light heavy champ."

Carmady said: "Come in and have a drink, Tony." He went over to the window, stood looking out at the rain. "If they buy it for him," he added over his shoulder.

"Well—just a short one, Mister Carmady."

The dark boy mixed a highball carefully at a tray on an imitation Sheraton desk. He held the bottle against the light and gauged his drink carefully, tinkled ice gently with a long spoon, sipped, smiled, showing small white teeth.

"Targo's a lu, Mister Carmady. He's fast, clever, got a sock in both mitts, plenty guts, don't ever take a step back."

"He has to hold up the bums they feed him," Carmady drawled.

"Well, they ain't fed him no lion meat yet," Tony said.

The rain beat against the glass. The thick drops flattened out and washed down the pane in tiny waves.

Carmady said: "He's a bum. A bum with color and looks, but still a bum."

Tony sighed deeply. "I wisht I was goin'. It's my night off, too."

Carmady turned slowly and went over to the desk, mixed a drink. Two dusky spots showed in his cheeks and his voice was tired, drawling.

"So that's it. What's stopping you?"

"I got a headache."

"You're broke again," Carmady almost snarled.

The dark boy looked sidewise under his long lashes, said nothing.

Carmady clenched his left hand, unclenched it slowly. His eyes were sullen.

"Just ask Carmady," he sighed. "Good old Carmady. He leaks dough. He's soft. Just ask Carmady. Okey, Tony, take the ducat back and get a pair together."

He reached into his pocket, held a bill out. The dark boy looked hurt.

"Jeeze, Mister Carmady, I wouldn't have you think—"

"Skip it! What's a fight ticket between pals? Get a couple and take your girl. To hell with this Targo."

Tony Acosta took the bill. He watched the older man carefully for a moment. Then his voice was very softly, saying: "I'd rather go with you, Mister Carmady. Targo knocks them over, and not only in the ring. He's got a peachy blonde right on this floor, Miss Adrian, in 914."

Carmady stiffened. He put his glass down slowly, turned it on the top of the desk. His voice got a little hoarse.

"He's still a bum, Tony. Okey, I'll meet you for dinner, in front of your hotel at seven."

"Jeeze, that's swell, Mister Carmady."

Tony Acosta went out softly, closed the outer door without a sound.

Carmady stood by the desk, his fingertips stroking the

top of it, his eyes on the floor. He stood like that for a long time.

"Carmady, the All-American sucker," he said grimly, out loud. "A guy that plays with the help and carries the torch for stray broads. Yeah."

He finished his drink, looked at his wrist watch, put on his hat and the blue suede raincoat, went out. Down the corridor in front of 914 he stopped, lifted his hand to knock, then dropped it without touching the door.

He went slowly on to the elevators and rode down to the street and his car.

▼

The *Tribune* office was at Fourth and Spring. Carmady parked around the corner, went in at the employees' entrance and rode to the fourth floor in a rickety elevator operated by an old man with a dead cigar in his mouth and a rolled magazine which he held six inches from his nose while he ran the elevator.

On the fourth floor big double doors were lettered City Room. Another old man sat outside them at a small desk with a call box.

Carmady tapped on the desk, said: "Adams. Carmady calling."

The old man made noises into the box, released a key, pointed with his chin.

Carmady went through the doors, past a horseshoe copy desk, then past a row of small desks at which typewriters were being banged. At the far end a lanky red-haired man was doing nothing with his feet on a pulled-out drawer, the back of his neck on the back of a dangerously tilted swivel chair and a big pipe in his mouth pointed straight at the ceiling.

When Carmady stood beside him he moved his eyes down without moving any other part of his body and said around the pipe: "Greetings, Carmady. How's the idle rich?"

Carmady said: "How's a glance at your clips on a guy named Courtway? State Senator John Myerson Courtway, to be precise."

Adams put his feet on the floor. He raised himself erect by pulling on the edge of his desk. He brought his pipe down level, took it out of his mouth and spit into a wastebasket. He said: "That old icicle? When was he ever news? Sure." He stood up wearily, added: "Come along, Uncle," and started along the end of the room.

They went along another row of desks, past a fat girl in smudged make-up who was typing and laughing at what she was writing.

They went through a door into a big room that was mostly six-foot tiers of filing cases with an occasional alcove in which there was a small table and a chair.

Adams prowled the filing cases, jerked one out and set a folder on a table.

"Park yourself. What's the graft?"

Carmady leaned on the table on an elbow, scuffed through a thick wad of cuttings. They were monotonous, political in nature, not front page. Senator Courtway said this and that on this and that matter of public interest, addressed this and that meeting, went or returned from this and that place. It all seemed very dull.

He looked at a few halftone cuts of a thin, white-haired man with a blank, composed face, deep set dark eyes in which there was no light or warmth. After a while he said: "Got a print I could sneeze? A real one, I mean."

Adams sighed, stretched himself, disappeared down the line of file walls. He came back with a shiny black and white photograph, tossed it down on the table.

"You can keep it," he said. "We got dozens. The guy lives forever. Shall I have it autographed for you?"

Carmady looked at the photo with narrow eyes, for a long time. "It's right," he said slowly. "Was Courtway ever married?"

"Not since I left off my diapers," Adams growled. "Probably not ever. Say, what'n hell's the mystery?"

Carmady smiled slowly at him. He reached his flask out, set

it on the table beside the folder. Adams' face brightened swiftly and his long arm reached.

"Then he never had a kid," Carmady said.

Adams leered over the flask. "Well—not for publication, I guess. If I'm any judge of a mug, not at all." He drank deeply, wiped his lips, drank again.

"And that," Carmady said, "is very funny indeed. Have three more drinks—and forget you ever saw me."

THREE

The fat man put his face close to Carmady's face. He said with a wheeze: "You think it's fixed, neighbor?"

"Yeah. For Werra."

"How much says so?"

"Count your poke."

"I got five yards that want to grow."

"Take it," Carmady said tonelessly, and kept on looking at the back of a corn-blond head in a ringside seat. A white wrap with white fur was below the glassily waved hair. He couldn't see the face. He didn't have to.

The fat man blinked his eyes and got a thick wallet carefully out of a pocket inside his vest. He held it on the edge of his knee, counted out ten fifty-dollar bills, rolled them up, edged the wallet back against his ribs.

"You're on, sucker," he wheezed. "Let's see your dough."

Carmady brought his eyes back, reached out a flat pack of new hundreds, riffled them. He slipped five from under the printed band, held them out.

"Boy, this is from home," the fat man said. He put his face close to Carmady's face again. "I'm Skeets O'Neal. No little powders, huh?"

Carmady smiled very slowly and pushed his money into the fat man's hand. "You hold it, Skeets. I'm Carmady. Old Marcus

Carmady's son. I can shoot faster than you can run—and fix it afterwards."

The fat man took a long hard breath and leaned back in his seat. Tony Acosta stared soft-eyed at the money in the fat man's pudgy tight hand. He licked his lips and turned a small embarrassed smile on Carmady.

"Gee, that's lost dough, Mister Carmady," he whispered. "Unless—unless you got something inside."

"Enough to be worth a five-yard plunge," Carmady growled.

The buzzer sounded for the sixth.

The first five had been anybody's fight. The big blond boy, Duke Targo, wasn't trying. The dark one, Deacon Werra, a powerful, loose-limbed Polack with bad teeth and only two cauliflower ears, had the physique but didn't know anything but rough clinching and a giant swing that started in the basement and never connected. He had been good enough to hold Targo off so far. The fans razzed Targo a good deal.

When the stool swung back out of the ring Targo hitched at his black and silver trunks, smiled with a small tight smile at the girl in the white wrap. He was very good-looking, without a mark on him. There was blood on his left shoulder from Werra's nose.

The bell rang and Werra charged across the ring, slid off Targo's shoulder, got a left hook in. Targo got more of the hook than was in it. He piled back into the ropes, bounced out, clinched.

Carmady smiled quietly in the darkness.

The referee broke them easily. Targo broke clean, Werra tried for an uppercut and missed. They sparred for a minute. There was waltz music from the gallery. Then Werra started a swing from his shoetops. Targo seemed to wait for it, to wait for it to hit him. There was a queer strained smile on his face. The girl in the white wrap stood up suddenly.

Werra's swing grazed Targo's jaw. It barely staggered him. Targo lashed a long right that caught Werra over the eye. A left hook smashed Werra's jaw, then a right cross almost to the same spot.

The dark boy went down on his hands and knees, slipped slowly all the way to the floor, lay with both his gloves under him. There were catcalls as he was counted out.

The fat man struggled to his feet, grinning hugely. He said: "How you like it, pal? Still think it was a set piece?"

"It came unstuck," Carmady said in a voice as toneless as a police radio.

The fat man said: "So long, pal. Come around lots." He kicked Carmady's ankle climbing over him.

Carmady sat motionless, watched the auditorium empty. The fighters and their handlers had gone down the stairs under the ring. The girl in the white wrap had disappeared in the crowd. The lights went out and the barnlike structure looked cheap, sordid.

Tony Acosta fidgeted, watching a man in striped overalls picking up papers between the seats.

Carmady stood up suddenly, said: "I'm going to talk to that bum, Tony. Wait outside in the car for me."

He went swiftly up the slope to the lobby, through the remnants of the gallery crowd to a gray door marked "No Admittance." He went through that and down a ramp to another door marked the same way. A special cop in faded and unbuttoned khaki stood in front of it, with a bottle of beer in one hand and a hamburger in the other.

Carmady flashed a police card and the cop lurched out of the way without looking at the card. He hiccoughed peacefully as Carmady went through the door, then along a narrow passage with numbered doors lining it. There was noise behind the doors. The fourth door on the left had a scribbled card with the name "Duke Targo" fastened to the panel by a thumbtack.

Carmady opened it into the heavy sound of a shower going, out of sight.

In a narrow and utterly bare room a man in a white sweater was sitting on the end of a rubbing table that had clothes scattered on it. Carmady recognized him as Targo's chief second.

He said: "Where's the Duke?"

The sweatered man jerked a thumb towards the shower noise. Then a man came around the door and lurched very close to Carmady. He was tall and had curly brown hair with hard gray color in it. He had a big drink in his hand. His face had the flat glitter of extreme drunkenness. His hair was damp, his eyes bloodshot. His lips curled and uncurled in rapid smiles without meaning. He said thickly: "Scramola, umpchay."

Carmady shut the door calmly and leaned against it and started to get his cigarette case from his vest pocket, inside his open blue raincoat. He didn't look at the curly-haired man at all.

The curly-haired man lunged his free right hand up suddenly, snapped it under his coat, out again. A blue steel gun shone dully against his light suit. The glass in his left hand slopped liquor.

"None of that!" he snarled.

Carmady brought the cigarette case out very slowly, showed it in his hand, opened it and put a cigarette between his lips. The blue gun was very close to him, not very steady. The hand holding the glass shook in a sort of jerky rhythm.

Carmady said loosely: "You *ought* to be looking for trouble."

The sweatered man got off the rubbing table. Then he stood very still and looked at the gun. The curly-haired man said: "We like trouble. Frisk him, Mike."

The sweatered man said: "I don't want any part of it, Shenvair. For Pete's sake, take it easy. You're lit like a ferry boat."

Carmady said: "It's okey to frisk me. I'm not rodded."

"Nix," the sweatered man said. "This guy is the Duke's bodyguard. Deal me out."

The curly-haired man said: "Sure, I'm drunk," and giggled.

"You're a friend of the Duke?" the sweatered man asked.

"I've got some information for him," Carmady said.

"About what?"

Carmady didn't say anything. "Okey," the sweatered man said. He shrugged bitterly.

"Know what, Mike?" the curly-haired man said suddenly

and violently. "I think this Sonofabitch wants my job. Hell, yes." He punched Carmady with the muzzle of the gun. "You ain't a shamus, are you, mister?"

"Maybe," Carmady said: "And keep your iron next to your own belly."

The curly-haired man turned his head a little and grinned back over his shoulder.

"What d'you know about that, Mike? He's a shamus. Sure he wants my job. Sure he does."

"Put the heater up, you fool," the sweatered man said disgustedly.

The curly-haired man turned a little more. "I'm his protection, ain't I?" he complained.

Carmady knocked the gun aside almost casually, with the hand that held his cigarette case. The curly-haired man snapped his head around again. Carmady slid close to him, sank a stiff punch in his stomach, holding the gun away with his forearm. The curly-haired man gagged, sprayed liquor down the front of Carmady's raincoat. His glass shattered on the floor. The blue gun left his hand and went over in a corner. The sweatered man went after it.

The noise of the shower had stopped unnoticed and the blond fighter came out toweling himself vigorously. He stared open-mouthed at the tableau.

Carmady said: "I don't need this any more."

He heaved the curly-haired man away from him and laced his jaw with a hard right as he went back. The curly-haired man staggered across the room, hit the wall, slid down it and sat on the floor.

The sweatered man snatched the gun up and stood rigid, watching Carmady.

Carmady got out a handkerchief and wiped the front of his coat, while Targo shut his large well-shaped mouth slowly and began to move the towel back and forth across his chest. After a moment he said: "Just who the hell may you be?"

Carmady said: "I used to be a private dick. Carmady's the name. I think you need help."

Targo's face got a little redder than the shower had left it. "Why?"

"I heard you were supposed to throw it, and I think you tried to. But Werra was too lousy. You couldn't help yourself. That means you're in a jam."

Targo said very slowly: "People get their teeth kicked in for saying things like that."

The room was very still for a moment. The drunk sat up on the floor and blinked, tried to get his feet under him, and gave it up.

Carmady added quietly: "Benny Cyrano is a friend of mine. He's your backer, isn't he?"

The sweatered man laughed harshly. Then he broke the gun and slid the shells out of it, dropped the gun on the floor. He went to the door, went out, slammed the door shut.

Targo looked at the shut door, looked back at Carmady. He said very slowly: "What did you hear?"

"Your friend Jean Adrian lives in my hotel, on my floor. She got sapped by a hood this afternoon. I happened by and saw the hood running away, picked her up. She told me a little of what it was all about."

Targo had put on his underwear and socks and shoes. He reached into a locker for a black satin shirt, put that on. He said: "She didn't tell me."

"She wouldn't—before the fight."

Targo nodded slightly. Then he said: "If you know Benny, you may be all right. I've been getting threats. Maybe it's a lot of birdseed and maybe it's some Spring Street punter's idea of how to make himself a little easy dough. I fought my fight the way I wanted to. Now you can take the air, mister."

He put on high-waisted black trousers and knotted a white tie on his black shirt. He got a white serge coat trimmed with black braid out of the locker, put that on. A black and white handkerchief flared from the pocket in three points.

Carmady stared at the clothes, moved a little towards the door and looked down at the drunk.

"Okey," he said. "I see you've got a bodyguard. It was just an idea I had. Excuse it, please."

He went out, closed the door gently, and went back up the ramp to the lobby, out to the street. He walked through the rain around the corner of the building to a big graveled parking lot.

The lights of a car blinked at him and his coupe slid along the wet gravel and pulled up. Tony Acosta was at the wheel.

Carmady got in at the right side and said: "Let's go out to Cyrano's and have a drink, Tony."

"Jeeze, that's swell. Miss Adrian's in the floor show there. You know, the blonde I told you about."

Carmady said: "I saw Targo. I kind of liked him—but I didn't like his clothes."

FOUR

Gus Neishacker was a two-hundred-pound fashion plate with very red cheeks and thin, exquisitely penciled eyebrows—eyebrows from a Chinese vase. There was a red carnation in the lapel of his wide-shouldered dinner jacket and he kept sniffing at it while he watched the headwaiter seat a party of guests. When Carmady and Tony Acosta came through the foyer arch he flashed a sudden smile and went to them with his hand out.

"How's a boy, Ted? Party?"

Carmady said: "Just the two of us. Meet Mister Acosta. Gus Neishacker, Cyrano's floor manager."

Gus Neishacker shook hands with Tony without looking at him. He said: "Let's see, the last time you dropped in—"

"She left town," Carmady said. "We'll sit near the ring but not too near. We don't dance together."

Gus Neishacker jerked a menu from under the headwaiter's arm and led the way down five crimson steps, along the tables that skirted the oval dance floor.

They sat down. Carmady ordered rye highballs and Denver sandwiches. Neishacker gave the order to a waiter, pulled a chair out and sat down at the table. He took a pencil out and made triangles on the inside of a match cover.

"See the fights?" he asked carelessly.

"Was that what they were?"

Gus Neishacker smiled indulgently. "Benny talked to the Duke. He says you're wise." He looked suddenly at Tony Acosta.

"Tony's all right," Carmady said.

"Yeah. Well do us a favor, will you? See it stops right here. Benny likes this boy. He wouldn't let him get hurt. He'd put protection all around him—real protection—if he thought that threat stuff was anything but some pool-hall bum's idea of a very funny joke. Benny never backs but one boxfighter at a time, and he picks them damn careful."

Carmady lit a cigarette, blew smoke from a corner of his mouth, said quietly: "It's none of my business, but I'm telling you it's screwy. I have a nose for that sort of thing."

Gus Neishacker stared at him a minute, then shrugged. He said: "I hope you're wrong," stood up quickly and walked away among the tables. He bent to smile here and there, and speak to a customer.

Tony Acosta's velvet eyes shone. He said: "Jeeze, Mister Carmady, you think it's rough stuff?"

Carmady nodded, didn't say anything. The waiter put their drinks and sandwiches on the table, went away. The band on the stage at the end of the oval floor blared out a long chord and a slick, grinning m.c. slid out on the stage and put his lips to a small open mike.

The floor show began. A line of half-naked girls ran out under a rain of colored lights. They coiled and uncoiled in a long sinuous line, their bare legs flashing, their navels little dimples of darkness in soft white, very nude flesh.

A hard-boiled redhead sang a hard-boiled song in a voice that could have been used to split firewood. The girls came back in black tights and silk hats, did the same dance with a slightly different exposure.

RAYMOND CHANDLER

The music softened and a tall high-yaller torch singer drooped under an amber light and sang of something very far away and unhappy, in a voice like old ivory.

Carmady sipped his drink, poked at his sandwich in the dim light. Tony Acosta's hard young face was a small tense blur beside him.

The torch singer went away and there was a little pause and then suddenly all the lights in the place went out except the lights over the music racks of the band and little pale amber lights at the entrances to the radiating aisles of booths beyond the tables.

There were squeals in the thick darkness. A single white spot winked on, high up under the roof, settled on a runway beside the stage. Faces were chalk-white in the reflected glare. There was the red glow of a cigarette tip here and there. Four tall black men moved in the light, carrying a white mummy case on their shoulders. They came slowly, in rhythm, down the runway. They wore white Egyptian headdresses and loin-cloths of white leather and white sandals laced to the knee. The black smoothness of their limbs was like black marble in the moonlight.

They reached the middle of the dance floor and slowly up-ended the mummy case until the cover tipped forward and fell and was caught. Then slowly, very slowly, a swathed white figure tipped forward and fell—slowly, like the last leaf from a dead tree. It tipped in the air, seemed to hover, then plunged towards the floor under a shattering roll of drums.

The light went off, went on. The swathed figure was upright on the floor, spinning, and one of the blacks was spinning the opposite way, winding the white shroud around his body. Then the shroud fell away and a girl was all tinsel and smooth white limbs under the hard light and her body shot through the air glittering and was caught and passed around swiftly among the four black men, like a baseball handled by a fast infield.

Then the music changed to a waltz and she danced among the black men slowly and gracefully, as though among four ebony pillars, very close to them but never touching them.

The act ended. The applause rose and fell in thick waves. The light went out and it was dark again, and then all the lights went up and the girl and the four black men were gone.

"Keeno," Tony Acosta breathed. "Oh, keeno. That was Miss Adrian, wasn't it?"

Carmady said slowly: "A little daring." He lit another cigarette, looked around. "There's another black and white number, Tony. The Duke himself, in person."

Duke Targo stood applauding violently at the entrance to one of the radiating booth aisles. There was a loose grin on his face. He looked as if he might have had a few drinks.

An arm came down over Carmady's shoulder. A hand planted itself in the ash tray at his elbow. He smelled Scotch in heavy gusts. He turned his head slowly, looked up at the liquor-shiny face of Shenvair, Duke Targo's drunken bodyguard.

"Smokes and a white gal," Shenvair said thickly. "Lousy. Crummy. Godawful crummy."

Carmady smiled slowly, moved his chair a little. Tony Acosta stared at Shenvair round-eyed, his little mouth a thin line.

"Blackface, Mister Shenvair. Not real smokes. I liked it."

"And who the hell cares what you like?" Shenvair wanted to know.

Carmady smiled delicately, laid his cigarette down on the edge of a plate. He turned his chair a little more.

"Still think I want your job, Shenvair?"

"Yeah. I owe you a smack in the puss too." He took his hand out of the ash tray, wiped it off on the tablecloth. He doubled it into a fist. "Like it now?"

A waiter caught him by the arm, spun him around.

"You lost your table, sir? This way."

Shenvair patted the waiter on the shoulder, tried to put an arm around his neck. "Swell, let's go nibble a drink. I don't like these people."

They went away, disappeared among the tables.

Carmady said: "To hell with this place, Tony," and stared moodily towards the band stage. Then his eyes became intent.

A girl with corn-blond hair, in a white wrap with a white

fur collar, appeared at the edge of the shell, went behind it, reappeared nearer. She came along the edge of the booths to the place where Targo had been standing. She slipped in between the booths there, disappeared.

Carmady said: "To hell with this place. Let's go Tony," in a low angry voice. Then very softly, in a tensed tone: "No—wait a minute. I see another guy I don't like."

The man was on the far side of the dance floor, which was empty at the moment. He was following its curve around, past the tables that fringed it. He looked a little different without his hat. But he had the same flat white expressionless face, the same close-set eyes. He was youngish, not more than thirty, but already having trouble with his bald spot. The slight bulge of a gun under his left arm was barely noticeable. He was the man who had run away from Jean Adrian's apartment in the Carondelet.

He reached the aisle into which Targo had gone, into which a moment before Jean Adrian had gone. He went into it.

Carmady said sharply: "Wait here, Tony." He kicked his chair back and stood up.

Somebody rabbit-punched him from behind. He swiveled, close to Shenvair's grinning sweaty face.

"Back again, pal," the curly-haired man chortled, and hit him on the jaw.

It was a short jab, well placed for a drunk. It caught Carmady off balance, staggered him. Tony Acosta came to his feet snarling, catlike. Carmady was still rocking when Shenvair let go with the other fist. That was too slow, too wide. Carmady slid inside it, uppercut the curly-haired man's nose savagely, got a handful of blood before he could get his hand away. He put most of it back on Shenvair's face.

Shenvair wobbled, staggered back a step and sat down on the floor, hard. He clapped a hand to his nose.

"Keep an eye on this bird, Tony," Carmady said swiftly.

Shenvair took hold of the nearest tablecloth and yanked it. It came off the table. Silver and glasses and china followed it to the floor. A man swore and a woman squealed. A waiter ran towards them with a livid, furious face.

Carmady almost didn't hear the two shots.

They were small and flat, close together, a small-caliber gun. The rushing waiter stopped dead, and a deeply etched white line appeared around his mouth as instantly as though the lash of a whip had cut it there.

A dark woman with a sharp nose opened her mouth to yell and no sound came from her. There was the instant when nobody makes a sound, when it almost seems as if there will never again be any sound—after the sound of a gun. Then Carmady was running.

He bumped into people who stood up and craned their necks. He reached the entrance to the aisle into which the white-faced man had gone. The booths had high walls and swing doors not so high. Heads stuck out over the doors, but no one was in the aisle yet. Carmady charged up a shallow carpeted slope, at the far end of which booth doors stood wide open.

Legs in dark cloth showed past the doors, slack on the floor, the knees sagged. The toes of black shoes were pointed into the booth.

Carmady shook an arm off, reached the place.

The man lay across the end of a table, his stomach and one side of his face on the white cloth, his left hand dropped between the table and the padded seat. His right hand on top of the table didn't quite hold a big black gun, a .45 with a cut barrel. The bald spot on his head glistened under the light, and the oily metal of the gun glistened beside it.

Blood leaked from under his chest, vivid scarlet on the white cloth, seeping into it as into blotting paper.

Duke Targo was standing up, deep in the booth. His left arm in the white serge coat was braced on the end of the table. Jean Adrian was sitting down at his side. Targo looked at Carmady blankly, as if he had never seen him before. He pushed his big right hand forward.

A small white-handled automatic lay on his palm.

"I shot him," Targo said. He pulled a gun on us and I shot him."

Jean Adrian was scrubbing her hands together on a scrap of handkerchief. Her face was strained, cold, not scared. Her eyes were dark.

"I shot him," Targo said. He threw the small gun down on the cloth. It bounced, almost hit the fallen man's head. "Let's—let's get out of here."

Carmady put a hand against the side of the sprawled man's neck, held it there a second or two, took it away.

"He's dead," he said. "When a citizen drops a redhot—that's news."

Jean Adrian was staring at him stiff-eyed. He flashed a smile at her, put a hand against Targo's chest, pushed him back.

"Sit down, Targo. You're not going any place."

Targo said: "Well—okey. I shot him, see."

"That's all right," Carmady said. "Just relax."

People were close behind him now, crowding him. He leaned back against the press of bodies and kept on smiling at the girl's white face.

FIVE

Benny Cyrano was shaped like two eggs, a little one that was his head on top of a big one that was his body. His small dapper legs and feet in patent-leather shoes were pushed into the kneehole of a dark sheenless desk. He held a corner of a handkerchief tightly between his teeth and pulled against it with his left hand and held his right hand out pudgily in front of him, pushing against the air. He was saying in a voice muffled by the handkerchief: "Now wait a minute, boys. Now wait a minute."

There was a striped built-in sofa in one corner of the office, and Duke Targo sat in the middle of it, between two Headquarters dicks. He had a dark bruise over one cheekbone, his thick blond hair was tousled and his black satin shirt looked as if somebody had tried to swing him by it.

One of the dicks, the gray-haired one, had a split lip. The young one with hair as blond as Targo's had a black eye. They both looked mad, but the blond one looked madder.

Carmady straddled a chair against the wall and looked sleepily at Jean Adrian, near him in a leather rocker. She was twisting a handkerchief in her hands, rubbing her palms with it. She had been doing this for a long time, as if she had forgotten she was doing it. Her small firm mouth was angry.

Gus Neishacker leaned against the closed door smoking.

"Now wait a minute, boys," Cyrano said. "If you didn't get tough with him, he wouldn't fight back. He's a good boy—the best I ever had. Give him a break."

Blood dribbled from one corner of Targo's mouth, in a fine thread down to his jutting chin. It gathered there and glistened. His face was empty, expressionless.

Carmady said coldly: "You wouldn't want the boys to stop playing blackjack pinochle, would you, Benny?"

The blond dick snarled: "You still got that private-dick license, Carmady?"

"It's lying around somewhere, I guess," Carmady said.

"Maybe we could take it away from you," the blond dick snarled.

"Maybe you could do a fan dance, copper. You might be all kinds of a smart guy for all I'd know."

The blond dick started to get up. The older one said: "Leave him be. Give him six feet. If he steps over that, we'll take the screws out of him."

Carmady and Gus Neishacker grinned at each other. Cyrano made helpless gestures in the air. The girl looked at Carmady under her lashes. Targo opened his mouth and spat blood straight before him on the blue carpet.

Something pushed against the door and Neishacker stepped to one side, opened it a crack, then opened it wide. McChesney came in.

McChesney was a lieutenant of detectives, tall, sandy-haired, fortyish, with pale eyes and a narrow suspicious face. He shut the door and turned the key in it, went slowly over and stood in front of Targo.

"Plenty dead," he said. "One under the heart, one in it. Nice snap shooting. In any league."

"When you've got to deliver you've got to deliver," Targo said dully.

"Make him?" the gray-haired dick asked his partner, moving away along the sofa.

McChesney nodded. "Torchy Plant. A gun for hire. I haven't seen him round for all of two years. Tough as an ingrowing toenail with his right load. A bindle punk."

"He'd have to be that to throw his party in here," the gray-haired dick said.

McChesney's long face was serious, not hard. "Got a permit for the gun, Targo?"

Targo said: "Yes. Benny got me one two weeks ago. I been getting a lot of threats."

"Listen, Lieutenant," Cyrano chirped, "some gamblers try to scare him into a dive, see? He wins nine straight fights by knockouts so they get a swell price. I told him he should take one at that maybe."

"I almost did," Targo said sullenly.

"So they sent the redhot to him," Cyrano said.

McChesney said: "I wouldn't say no. How'd you beat his draw, Targo? Where was your gun?"

"On my hip."

"Show me."

Targo put his hand back into his right hip pocket and jerked a handkerchief out quickly, stuck his finger through it like a gun barrel.

"That handkerchief in the pocket?" McChesney asked. "With the gun?"

Targo's big reddish face clouded a little. He nodded.

McChesney leaned forward casually and twitched the handkerchief from his hand. He sniffed at it, unwrapped it, sniffed at it again, folded it and put it away in his own pocket. His face said nothing.

"What did he say, Targo?"

"He said: 'I got a message for you, punk, and this is it.' Then he went for the gat and it stuck a little in the clip. I got mine out first."

McChesney smiled faintly and leaned far back, teetering on his heels. His faint smile seemed to slide off the end of his long nose. He looked Targo up and down.

"Yeah," he said softly. "I'd call it damn nice shooting with a twenty-two. But you're fast for a big guy . . . Who got these threats?"

"I did," Targo said. "Over the phone."

"Know the voice?"

"It might have been this same guy. I'm not just positive."

McChesney walked stiff-legged to the other end of the office, stood a moment looking at a hand-tinted sporting print. He came back slowly, drifted over to the door.

"A guy like that don't mean a lot," he said quietly, "but we got to do our job. The two of you will have to come downtown and make statements. Let's go."

He went out. The two dicks stood up, with Duke Targo between them. The gray-haired one snapped: "You goin' to act nice, bo?"

Targo sneered: "If I get to wash my face."

They went out. The blond dick waited for Jean Adrian to pass in front of him. He swung the door, snarled back at Carmady: "As for you—nuts!"

Carmady said softly: "I like them. It's the squirrel in me, copper."

Gus Neishacker laughed, then shut the door and went to the desk.

"I'm shaking like Benny's third chin," he said. "Let's all have a shot of cognac."

He poured three glasses a third full, took one over to the striped sofa and spread his long legs out on it, leaned his head back and sipped the brandy.

Carmady stood up and downed his drink. He got a cigarette out and rolled it around in his fingers, staring at Cyrano's smooth white face with an up-from-under look.

"How much would you say changed hands on that fight tonight?" he asked softly. "Bets."

Cyrano blinked, massaged his lips with a fat hand. "A few grand. It was just a regular weekly show. It don't listen, does it?"

Carmady put the cigarette in his mouth and leaned over the desk to strike a match. He said: "If it does, murder's getting awfully cheap in this town."

Cyrano didn't say anything. Gus Neishacker sipped the last of his brandy and carefully put the empty glass down on a round cork table beside the sofa. He stared at the ceiling, silently.

After a moment Carmady nodded at the two men, crossed the room and went out, closed the door behind him. He went along a corridor off which dressing rooms opened, dark now. A curtained archway let him out at the back of the stage.

In the foyer the headwaiter was standing at the glass doors, looking out at the rain and the back of a uniformed policeman. Carmady went into the empty cloakroom, found his hat and coat, put them on, came out to stand beside the headwaiter.

He said: "I guess you didn't notice what happened to the kid I was with?"

The headwaiter shook his head and reached forward to unlock the door.

"There was four hundred people here—and three hundred scrammed before the law checked in. I'm sorry."

Carmady nodded and went out into the rain. The uniformed man glanced at him casually. He went along the street to where the car had been left. It wasn't there. He looked up and down the street, stood for a few moments in the rain, then walked towards Melrose.

After a little while he found a taxi.

SIX

The ramp of the Carondelet garage curved down into semi-darkness and chilled air. The dark bulks of stalled cars looked ominous against the whitewashed walls, and the single drop-light in the small office had the relentless glitter of the death house.

A big Negro in stained overalls came out rubbing his eyes, then his face split in an enormous grin.

"Hello, there, Mistuh Carmady. You kinda restless tonight?"

Carmady said: "I get a little wild when it rains. I bet my heap isn't here."

"No, it ain't, Mistuh Carmady. I been all around wipin' off and yours ain't here aytall."

Carmady said woodenly: "I lent it to a pal. He probably wrecked it . . ."

He flicked a half-dollar through the air and went back up the ramp to the side street. He turned towards the back of the hotel, came to an alleylike street one side of which was the rear wall of the Carondelet. The other side had two frame houses and a four-story brick building. Hotel Blaine was lettered on a round milky globe over the door.

Carmady went up three cement steps and tried the door. It was locked. He looked through the glass panel into a small dim empty lobby. He got out two passkeys; the second one moved the lock a little. He pulled the door hard towards him, tried the first one again. That snicked the bolt far enough for the loosely fitted door to open.

He went in and looked at an empty counter with a sign "Manager" beside a plunger bell. There was an oblong of empty numbered pigeonholes on the wall. Carmady went around behind the counter and fished a leather register out of a space under the top. He read names back three pages, found the boyish scrawl: "Tony Acosta," and a room number in another writing.

He put the register away and went past the automatic elevator and upstairs to the fourth floor.

The hallway was very silent. There was weak light from a ceiling fixture. The last door but one on the left-hand side had a crack of light showing around its transom. That was the door—411. He put his hand out to knock, then withdrew it without touching the door.

The doorknob was heavily smeared with something that looked like blood.

Carmady's eyes looked down and saw what was almost a pool of blood on the stained wood before the door, beyond the edge of the runner.

His hand suddenly felt clammy inside his glove. He took the glove off, held the hand stiff, clawlike for a moment, then shook it slowly. His eyes had a sharp strained light in them.

He got a handkerchief out, grasped the doorknob inside it, turned it slowly. The door was unlocked. He went in.

He looked across the room and said very softly: "Tony . . . oh, Tony."

Then he shut the door behind him and turned a key in it, still with the handkerchief.

There was light from the bowl that hung on three brass chains from the middle of the ceiling. It shone on a made-up bed, some painted, light-colored furniture, a dull green carpet, a square writing desk of eucalyptus wood.

Tony Acosta sat at the desk. His head was slumped forward on his left arm. Under the chair on which he sat, between the legs of the chair and his feet, there was a glistening brownish pool.

Carmady walked across the room so rigidly that his ankles ached after the second step. He reached the desk, touched Tony Acosta's shoulder.

"Tony," he said thickly, in a low, meaningless voice. "My God, Tony!"

Tony didn't move. Carmady went around to his side. A blood-soaked bath towel glared against the boy's stomach, across his pressed-together thighs. His right hand was crouched against the front edge of the desk, as if he was trying to push himself up. Almost under his face there was a scrawled envelope.

Carmady pulled the envelope towards him slowly, lifted it like a thing of weight, read the wandering scrawl of words.

"Tailed him . . . woptown . . . 28 Court Street . . . over garage . . . shot me . . . think I got . . . him . . . your car . . ."

The line trailed over the edge of the paper, became a blot there. The pen was on the floor. There was a bloody thumbprint on the envelope.

Carmady folded it meticulously to protect the print, put the envelope in his wallet. He lifted Tony's head, turned it a little towards him. The neck was still warm; it was beginning to stiffen. Tony's soft dark eyes were open and they held the quiet brightness of a cat's eyes. They had that effect the eyes of the new-dead have of almost, but not quite, looking at you.

Carmady lowered the head gently on the outstretched left arm. He stood laxly, his head on one side, his eyes almost sleepy. Then his head jerked back and his eyes hardened.

He stripped off his raincoat and the suitcoat underneath, rolled his sleeves up, wet a face towel in the basin in the corner of the room and went to the door. He wiped the knobs off, bent down and wiped up the smeared blood from the floor outside.

He rinsed the towel and hung it up to dry, wiped his hands carefully, put his coat on again. He used his handkerchief to open the transom, to reverse the key and lock the door from the outside. He threw the key in over the top of the transom, heard it tinkle inside.

He went downstairs and out of the Hotel Blaine. It still rained. He walked to the corner, looked along a tree-shaded block. His car was a dozen yards from the intersection, parked carefully, the lights off, the keys in the ignition. He drew them out, felt the seat under the wheel. It was wet, sticky. Carmady wiped his hand off, ran the windows up and locked the car. He left it where it was.

Going back to the Carondelet he didn't meet anybody. The hard slanting rain still pounded down into the empty streets.

SEVEN

There was a thin thread of light under the door of 914. Carmady knocked lightly, looking up and down the hall, moved his gloved fingers softly on the panel while he waited. He waited a long time. Then a voice spoke wearily behind the wood of the door.

"Yes? What is it?"

"Carmady, angel. I have to see you. It's strictly business."

The door clicked, opened. He looked at a tired white face, dark eyes that were slatelike, not violet-blue. There were smudges under them as though mascara had been rubbed into the skin. The girl's strong little hand twitched on the edge of the door.

"You," she said wearily. "It would be you. Yes . . . Well, I've simply got to have a shower. I smell of policemen."

"Fifteen minutes?" Carmady asked casually, but his eyes were very sharp on her face.

She shrugged slowly, then nodded. The closing door seemed to jump at him. He went along to his own rooms, threw off his hat and coat, poured whiskey into a glass and went into the bathroom to get ice water from the small tap over the basin.

He drank slowly, looking out of the windows at the dark breadth of the boulevard. A car slid by now and then, two beams of white light attached to nothing, emanating from nowhere.

He finished the drink, stripped to the skin, went under a shower. He dressed in fresh clothes, refilled his big flask and put it in his inner pocket, took a snub-nosed automatic out of a suitcase and held it in his hand for a minute staring at it. Then he put it back in the suitcase, lit a cigarette and smoked it through.

He got a dry hat and a tweed coat and went back to 914.

The door was almost insidiously ajar. He slipped in with a light knock, shut the door, went on into the living room and looked at Jean Adrian.

She was sitting on the davenport with a freshly scrubbed look, in loose plum-colored pajamas and a Chinese coat. A tendril of damp hair drooped over one temple. Her small even features had the cameo-like clearness that tiredness gives to the very young.

Carmady said: "Drink?"

She gestured emptily. "I suppose so."

He got glasses, mixed whiskey and ice water, went to the davenport with them.

"Are they keeping Targo on ice?"

She moved her chin an eighth of an inch, staring into her glass.

"He cut loose again, knocked two cops halfway through the wall. They love that boy."

Carmady said: "He has a lot to learn about cops. In the morning the cameras will be all set for him. I can think of some nice headlines, such as: "Well-known Fighter Too Fast for Gunman." "Duke Targo Puts Crimp in Underworld Hot Rod.""

The girl sipped her drink. "I'm tired," she said. "And my foot itches. Let's talk about what makes this your business."

"Sure." He flipped his cigarette case open, held it under her chin. Her hand fumbled at it and while it still fumbled he said: "When you light that tell me why you shot him."

Jean Adrian put the cigarette between her lips, bent her head to the match, inhaled and threw her head back. Color awakened slowly in her eyes and a small smile curved the line of her pressed lips. She didn't answer.

Carmady watched her for a minute, turning his glass in his hands. Then he stared at the floor, said: "It was your gun— the gun I picked up here in the afternoon. Targo said he drew it from his hip pocket, the slowest draw in the world. Yet he's supposed to have shot twice, accurately enough to kill a man, while the man wasn't even getting his gun loose from a shoulder holster. That's hooey. But you, with the gun in a bag in your lap, and knowing the hood, might just have managed it. He would have been watching Targo."

The girl said emptily: "You're a private dick, I hear. You're the son of a boss politician. They talked about you downtown. They act a little afraid of you, of people you might know. Who sicked you on me?"

Carmady said: "They're not afraid of me, angel. They just talked like that to see how you'd react, if I was involved, so on. They don't know what it's all about."

"They were told plainly enough what it was all about."

Carmady shook his head. "A cop never believes what he gets without a struggle. He's too used to cooked-up stories. I think McChesney's wise you did the shooting. He knows by now if that handkerchief of Targo's had been in a pocket with a gun."

Her limp fingers discarded her cigarette half-smoked. A curtain eddied at the window and loose flakes of ash crawled around in the ash tray. She said slowly: "All right. I shot him. Do you think I'd hesitate after this afternoon?"

Carmady rubbed the lobe of his ear. "I'm playing this too light," he said softly. "You don't know what's in my heart. Something has happened, something nasty. Do you think the hood meant to kill Targo?"

"I thought so—or I wouldn't have shot a man."

"I think maybe it was just a scare, angel. Like the other one. After all a night club is a poor place for a getaway."

She said sharply: "They don't do many low tackles on forty-fives. He'd have got away all right. Of course he meant to kill somebody. And of course I didn't mean Duke to front for me. He just grabbed the gun out of my hand and slammed into his act. What did it matter? I knew it would all come out in the end."

She poked absently at the still burning cigarette in the tray, kept her eyes down. After a moment she said, almost in a whisper: "Is that all you wanted to know?"

Carmady let his eyes crawl sidewise, without moving his head, until he could just see the firm curve of her cheek, the strong line of her throat. He said thickly: "Shenvair was in on it. The fellow I was with at Cyrano's followed Shenvair to a hideout. Shenvair shot him. He's dead. He's dead, angel—just a young kid that worked here in the hotel. Tony, the bell captain. The cops don't know that yet."

The muffled clang of elevator doors was heavy through the silence. A horn tooted dismally out in the rain on the boulevard. The girl sagged forward suddenly, then sidewise, fell across Carmady's knees. Her body was half turned and she lay almost on her back across his thighs, her eyelids flickering. The small blue veins in them stood out rigid in the soft skin.

He put his arms around her slowly, loosely, then they tightened, lifted her. He brought her face close to his own face. He kissed her on the side of the mouth.

Her eyes opened, stared blankly, unfocused. He kissed her again, tightly, then pushed her upright on the davenport.

He said quietly: "That wasn't just an act, was it?"

She leaped to her feet, spun around. Her voice was low, tense and angry.

"There's something horrible about you! Something—satanic. You come here and tell me another man has been killed—and then you kiss me. It isn't real."

Carmady said dully: "There's something horrible about any man that goes suddenly gaga over another man's woman."

"I'm not his woman!" she snapped. "I don't even like him —and I don't like you."

Carmady shrugged. They stared at each other with bleak hostile eyes. The girl clicked her teeth shut, then said almost violently: "Get out! I can't talk to you any more. I can't stand you around. Will you get out?"

Carmady said: "Why not?" He stood up, went over and got his hat and coat.

The girl sobbed once sharply, then she went in light quick strides across the room to the windows, became motionless with her back to him.

Carmady looked at her back, went over near her and stood looking at the soft hair low down on her neck. He said: "Why the hell don't you let me help? I know there's something wrong. I wouldn't hurt you."

The girl spoke to the curtain in front of her face, savagely: "Get out! I don't want your help. Go away and stay away. I won't be seeing you—ever."

Carmady said slowly: "I think you've got to have help. Whether you like it or not. That man in the photo frame on the desk there—I think I know who he is. And I don't think he's dead."

The girl turned. Her face now was as white as paper. Her eyes strained at his eyes. She breathed thickly, harshly. After what seemed a long time she said: "I'm caught. Caught. There's nothing you can do about it."

Carmady lifted a hand and drew his fingers slowly down her cheek, down the angle of her tight jaw. His eyes held a hard brown glitter, his lips a smile. It was cunning, almost a dishonest smile.

He said: "I'm wrong, angel. I don't know him at all. Good night."

He went back across the room, through the little hallway, opened the door. When the door opened the girl clutched at the curtain and rubbed her face against it slowly.

Carmady didn't shut the door. He stood quite still halfway through it, looking at two men who stood there with guns.

They stood close to the door, as if they had been about to knock. One was thick, dark, saturnine. The other one was an albino with sharp red eyes, a narrow head that showed shining snow-white hair under a rain-spattered dark hat. He had the thin sharp teeth and the drawn-back grin of a rat.

Carmady started to close the door behind him. The albino said: "Hold it, rube. The door, I mean. We're goin' in."

The other man slid forward and pressed his left hand up and down Carmady's body carefully. He stepped away, said: "No gat, but a swell flask under his arm."

The albino gestured with his gun. "Back up, rube. We want the broad, too."

Carmady said tonelessly: "It doesn't take a gun, Critz. I

know you and I know your boss. If he wants to see me, I'll be glad to talk to him."

He turned and went back into the room with the two gunmen behind him.

Jean Adrian hadn't moved. She stood by the window still, the curtain against her cheek, her eyes closed, as if she hadn't heard the voices at the door at all.

Then she heard them come in and her eyes snapped open. She turned slowly, stared past Carmady at the two gunmen. The albino walked to the middle of the room, looked around it without speaking, went on into the bedroom and bathroom. Doors opened and shut. He came back in quiet catlike feet, pulled his overcoat open and pushed his hat back on his head.

"Get dressed, sister. We have to go for a ride in the rain. Okey?"

The girl stared at Carmady now. He shrugged, smiled a little, spread his hands.

"That's how it is, angel. Might as well fall in line."

The lines of her face got thin and contemptuous. She said slowly: "You—You——." Her voice trailed off into a sibilant, meaningless mutter. She went across the room stiffly and out of it into the bedroom.

The albino slipped a cigarette between his sharp lips, chuckled with a wet, gurgling sound, as if his mouth was full of saliva.

"She don't seem to like you, rube."

Carmady frowned. He walked slowly to the writing desk, leaned his hips against it, stared at the floor.

"She thinks I sold her out," he said dully.

"Maybe you did, rube," the albino drawled.

Carmady said: "Better watch her. She's neat with a gun."

His hands, reaching casually behind him on the desk, tapped the top of it lightly, then without apparent change of movement folded the leather photo frame down on its side and edged it under the blotter.

EIGHT

There was a padded arm rest in the middle of the rear seat of the car, and Carmady leaned an elbow on it, cupped his chin in his hand, stared through the half-misted windows at the rain. It was thick white spray in the headlights, and the noise of it on the top of the car was like drum fire very far off.

Jean Adrian sat on the other side of the arm rest, in the corner. She wore a black hat and a gray coat with tufts of silky hair on it, longer than caracul and not so curly. She didn't look at Carmady or speak to him.

The albino sat on the right of the thick dark man, who drove. They went through silent streets, past blurred houses, blurred trees, the blurred shine of street lights. There were neon signs behind the thick curtains of mist. There was no sky.

Then they climbed and a feeble arc light strung over an intersection threw light on a signpost, and Carmady read the name "Court Street."

He said softly: "This is woptown, Critz. The big guy can't be so dough-heavy as he used to be."

Lights flickered from the albino's eyes as he glanced back. "You should know, rube."

The car slowed in front of a big frame house with a trellised porch, walls finished in round shingles, blind, lightless windows. Across the street, a stencil sign on a brick building built sheer to the sidewalk said: "Paolo Perrugini Funeral Parlors."

The car swung out to make a wide turn into a gravel driveway. Lights splashed into an open garage. They went in, slid to a stop beside a big shiny undertaker's ambulance.

The albino snapped: "All out!"

Carmady said: "I see our next trip is all arranged for."

"Funny guy," the albino snarled. "A wise monkey."

"Uh-uh. I just have nice scaffold manners," Carmady drawled.

The dark man cut the motor and snapped on a big flash,

then cut the lights, got out of the car. He shot the beam of the flash up a narrow flight of wooden steps in the corner. The albino said: "Up you go, rube. Push the girl ahead of you. I'm behind with my rod."

Jean Adrian got out of the car past Carmady, without looking at him. She went up the steps stiffly, and the three men made a procession behind her.

There was a door at the top. The girl opened it and hard white light came out at them. They went into a bare attic with exposed studding, a square window in front and rear, shut tight, the glass painted black. A bright bulb hung on a drop cord over a kitchen table and a big man sat at the table with a saucer of cigarette butts at his elbow. Two of them still smoked.

A thin loose-lipped man sat on a bed with a Luger beside his left hand. There was a worn carpet on the floor, a few sticks of furniture, a half-opened clapboard door in the corner through which a toilet seat showed, and one end of a big old-fashioned bathtub standing up from the floor on iron legs.

The man at the kitchen table was large but not handsome. He had carroty hair and eyebrows a shade darker, a square aggressive face, a strong jaw. His thick lips held his cigarette brutally. His clothes looked as if they had cost a great deal of money and had been slept in.

He glanced carelessly at Jean Adrian, said around the cigarette: "Park the body, sister. Hi, Carmady. Gimme that rod, Lefty, and you boys drop down below again."

The girl went quietly across the attic and sat down in a straight wooden chair. The man on the bed stood up, put the Luger at the big man's elbow on the kitchen table. The three gunmen went down the stairs, leaving the door open.

The big man touched the Luger, stared at Carmady, said sarcastically: "I'm Doll Conant. Maybe you remember me."

Carmady stood loosely by the kitchen table, with his legs spread wide, his hands in his overcoat pockets, his head tilted back. His half-closed eyes were sleepy, very cold.

He said: "Yeah. I helped my dad hang the only rap on you that ever stuck."

"It didn't stick, mugg. Not with the Court of Appeals."

"Maybe this one will," Carmady said carelessly. "Kidnapping is apt to be a sticky rap in this state."

Conant grinned without opening his lips. His expression was grimly good-humored. He said: "Let's not barber. We got business to do and you know better than that last crack. Sit down—or rather take a look at Exhibit One first. In the bathtub, behind you. Yeah, take a look at that. Then we can get down to tacks."

Carmady turned, went across to the clapboard door, pushed through it. There was a bulb sticking out of the wall, with a key switch. He snapped it on, bent over the tub.

For a moment his body was quite rigid and his breath was held rigidly. Then he let it out very slowly, and reached his left hand back and pushed the door almost shut. He bent farther over the big iron tub.

It was long enough for a man to stretch out in, and a man was stretched out in it, on his back. He was fully dressed even to a hat, although his head didn't look as if he had put it on himself. He had thick, gray-brown curly hair. There was blood on his face and there was a gouged, red-rimmed hole at the inner corner of his left eye.

He was Shenvair and he was long since dead.

Carmady sucked in his breath and straightened slowly, then suddenly bent forward still further until he could see into the space between the tub and the wall. Something blue and metallic glistened down there in the dust. A blue steel gun. A gun like Shenvair's gun.

Carmady glanced back quickly. The not quite shut door showed him a part of the attic, the top of the stairs, one of Doll Conant's feet square and placid on the carpet, under the kitchen table. He reached his arm out slowly down behind the tub, gathered the gun up. The four exposed chambers had steel-jacketed bullets in them.

Carmady opened his coat, slipped the gun down inside the waistband of his trousers, tightened his belt, and buttoned his coat again. He went out of the bathroom, shut the clapboard door carefully.

Doll Conant gestured at a chair across the table from him: "Sit down."

Carmady glanced at Jean Adrian. She was staring at him with a kind of rigid curiosity, her eyes dark and colorless in a stone-white face under the black hat.

He gestured at her, smiled faintly. "It's Mister Shenvair, angel. He met with an accident. He's—dead."

The girl stared at him without any expression at all. Then she shuddered once, violently. She stared at him again, made no sound of any kind.

Carmady sat down in the chair across the table from Conant.

Conant eyed him, added a smoking stub to the collection in the white saucer, lit a fresh cigarette, streaking the match the whole length of the kitchen table.

He puffed, said casually: "Yeah, he's dead. You shot him."

Carmady shook his head very slightly, smiled. "No."

"Skip the baby eyes, feller. You shot him. Perrugini, the wop undertaker across the street, owns this place, rents it out now and then to a right boy for a quick dust. Incidentally, he's a friend of mine, does me a lot of good among the other wops. He rented it to Shenvair. Didn't know him, but Shenvair got a right ticket into him. Perrugini heard shooting over here tonight, took a look out of his window, saw a guy make it to a car. He saw the license number of the car. Your car."

Carmady shook his head again. "But I didn't shoot him, Conant."

"Try and prove it . . . The wop ran over and found Shenvair halfway up the stairs, dead. He dragged him up and stuck him in the bathtub. Some crazy idea about the blood, I suppose. Then he went through him, found a police card, a private-dick license, and that scared him. He got me on the phone and when I got the name, I came steaming."

Conant stopped talking, eyed Carmady steadily. Carmady said very softly: "You hear about the shooting at Cyrano's tonight?"

Conant nodded.

Carmady went on: "I was there, with a kid friend of mine from the hotel. Just before the shooting this Shenvair threw a punch at me. The kid followed Shenvair here and they shot each other. Shenvair was drunk and scared and I'll bet he shot first. I didn't even know the kid had a gun. Shenvair shot him through the stomach. He got home, died there. He left me a note. I have the note."

After a moment Conant said: "You killed Shenvair, or hired that boy to do it. Here's why. He tried to copper his bet on your blackmail racket. He sold out to Courtway."

Carmady looked startled. He snapped his head around to look at Jean Adrian. She was leaning forward staring at him with color in her cheeks, a shine in her eyes. She said very softly: "I'm sorry—angel. I had you wrong."

Carmady smiled a little, turned back to Conant. He said: "She thought I was the one that sold out. Who's Courtway? Your bird dog, the state senator?"

Conant's face turned a little white. He laid his cigarette down very carefully in the saucer, leaned across the table and hit Carmady in the mouth with his fist. Carmady went over backwards in the rickety chair. His head struck the floor.

Jean Adrian stood up quietly and her teeth made a sharp clicking sound. Then she didn't move.

Carmady rolled over on his side and got up and set the chair upright. He got a handkerchief out, patted his mouth, looked at the handkerchief.

Steps clattered on the stairs and the albino poked his narrow head into the room, poked a gun still farther in.

"Need any help, boss?"

Without looking at him, Conant said: "Get out—and shut that door—and stay out!"

The door was shut. The albino's steps died down the stairs.

Carmady put his left hand on the back of the chair and moved it slowly back and forth. His right hand still held the handkerchief. His lips were getting puffed and darkish. His eyes looked at the Luger by Conant's elbow.

Conant picked up his cigarette and put it in his mouth. He said: "Maybe you think I'm going to neck this blackmail racket. I'm not, brother. I'm going to kill it—so it'll stay killed. You're going to spill your guts. I have three boys downstairs who need exercise. Get busy and talk."

Carmady said: "Yeah—but your three boys are downstairs." He slipped the handkerchief inside his coat. His hand came out with the blued gun in it. He said: "Take that Luger by the barrel and push it across the table so I can reach it."

Conant didn't move. His eyes narrowed to slits. His hard mouth jerked the cigarette in it once. He didn't touch the Luger. After a moment he said: "Guess you know what will happen to you now."

Carmady shook his head slightly. He said: "Maybe I'm not particular about that. If it does happen, you won't know anything about it."

Conant stared at him, didn't move. He stared at him for quite a long time, stared at the blue gun. "Where did you get it? Didn't the heels frisk you?"

Carmady said: "They did. This is Shenvair's gun. Your wop friend must have kicked it behind the bathtub. Careless."

Conant reached two thick fingers forward and turned the Luger around and pushed it to the far edge of the table. He nodded and said tonelessly: "I lose this hand. I ought to have thought of that. That makes me do the talking."

Jean Adrian came quickly across the room and stood at the end of the table. Carmady reached forward across the chair and took the Luger in his left hand and slipped it down into his overcoat pocket, kept his hand on it. He rested the hand holding the blue gun on the top of the chair.

Jean Adrian said: "Who is this man?"

"Doll Conant, a local bigtimer. Senator John Myerson Court-

way is his pipe line into the state senate. And Senator Courtway, angel, is the man in your photo frame on your desk. The
man you said was your father, that you said was dead."

The girl said very quietly: "He is my father. I knew he wasn't
dead. I'm blackmailing him—for a hundred grand. Shenvair
and Targo and I. He never married my mother, so I'm illegitimate. But I'm still his child. I have rights and he won't rec-
ognize them. He treated my mother abominably, left her without
a nickel. He had detectives watch me for years. Shenvair was
one of them. He recognized my photos when I came here and
met Targo. He remembered. He went up to San Francisco and
got a copy of my birth certificate. I have it here."

She fumbled at her bag, felt around in it, opened a small
zipper pocket in the lining. Her hand came out with a folded
paper. She tossed it on the table.

Conant stared at her, reached a hand for the paper, spread
it out and studied it. He said slowly: "This doesn't prove anything."

Carmady took his left hand out of his pocket and reached
for the paper. Conant pushed it towards him.

It was a certified copy of a birth certificate, dated originally
in 1912. It recorded the birth of a girl child, Adriana Gianni
Myerson, to John and Antonina Gianni Myerson. Carmady
dropped the paper again.

He said: "Adriana Gianni—Jean Adrian. Was that the tip-
off, Conant?"

Conant shook his head. "Shenvair got cold feet. He tipped
Courtway. He was scared. That's why he had this hideout
lined up. I thought that was why he got killed. Targo couldn't
have done it, because Targo's still in the can. Maybe I had you
wrong, Carmady."

Carmady stared at him woodenly, didn't say anything. Jean
Adrian said: "It's my fault. I'm the one that's to blame. It was
pretty rotten. I see that now. I want to see him and tell him
I'm sorry and that he'll never hear from me again. I want to
make him promise he won't do anything to Duke Targo. May I?"

Carmady said: "You can do anything you want to, angel. I

have two guns that say so. But why did you wait so long? And why didn't you go at him through the courts? You're in show business. The publicity would have made you—even if he beat you out."

The girl bit her lip, said in a low voice: "My mother never really knew who he was, never knew his last name even. He was John Myerson to her. I didn't know until I came here and happened to see a picture in the local paper. He had changed, but I knew the face. And of course the first part of his name—"

Conant said sneeringly: "You didn't go at him openly because you knew damn well you weren't his kid. That your mother just wished you on to him like any cheap broad who sees herself out of a swell meal ticket. Courtway says he can prove it, and that he's going to prove it and put you where you belong. And believe me, sister, he's just the stiff-necked kind of sap who would kill himself in public life raking up a twenty-year-old scandal to do that little thing."

The big man spit his cigarette stub out viciously, added: "It cost me money to put him where he is and I aim to keep him there. That's why I'm in it. No dice, sister. I'm putting the pressure on. You're going to take a lot of air and keep on taking it. As for your two-gun friend—maybe he didn't know, but he knows now and that ties him up in the same package."

Conant banged on the table top, leaned back, looking calmly at the blue gun in Carmady's hand.

Carmady stared into the big man's eyes, said very softly: "That hood at Cyrano's tonight—he wasn't your idea of putting on the pressure by any chance, Conant, was he?"

Conant grinned harshly, shook his head. The door at the top of the stairs opened a little, silently. Carmady didn't see it. He was staring at Conant. Jean Adrian saw it.

Her eyes widened and she stepped back with a startled exclamation, that jerked Carmady's eyes to her.

The albino stepped softly through the door with a gun leveled.

His red eyes glistened, his mouth was drawn wide in a snarling grin. He said: "The door's kind of thin, boss. I listened. Okey? . . . Shed the heater, rube, or I blow you both in half."

Carmady turned slightly and opened his right hand and let the blue gun bounce on the thin carpet. He shrugged, spread his hands out wide, didn't look at Jean Adrian.

The albino stepped clear of the door, came slowly forward and put his gun against Carmady's back.

Conant stood up, came around the table, took the Luger out of Carmady's coat pocket and hefted it. Without a word or change of expression he slammed it against the side of Carmady's jaw.

Carmady sagged drunkenly, then went down on the floor on his side.

Jean Adrian screamed, clawed at Conant. He threw her off, changed the gun to his left hand and slapped the side of her face with a hard palm.

"Pipe down, sister. You've had all your fun."

The albino went to the head of the stairs and called down it. The two other gunmen came up into the room, stood grinning.

Carmady didn't move on the floor. After a little while Conant lit another cigarette and rattled a knuckle on the table top beside the birth certificate. He said gruffly: "She wants to see the old man. Okey, she can see him. We'll all go see him. There's still something in this that stinks." He raised his eyes, looked at the stocky man. "You and Lefty go downtown and spring Targo, get him out to the Senator's place as soon as you can. Step on it."

The two hoods went back down the stairs.

Conant looked down at Carmady, kicked him in the ribs lightly, kept on kicking them until Carmady opened his eyes and stirred.

NINE

The car waited at the top of a hill, before a pair of tall wrought-iron gates, inside which there was a lodge. A door of the lodge stood open and yellow light framed a big man in an overcoat and pulled-down hat. He came forward slowly into the rain, his hands down in his pockets.

The rain slithered about his feet and the albino leaned against the uprights of the gate, clicking his teeth. The big man said: "What yuh want? I can see yuh."

"Shake it up, rube. Mister Conant wants to call on your boss."

The man inside spat into the wet darkness. "So what? Know what time it is?"

Conant opened the car door suddenly and went over to the gates. The rain made noise between the car and the voices.

Carmady turned his head slowly and patted Jean Adrian's hand. She pushed his hand away from her quickly.

Her voice said softly: "You fool—oh, you fool!"

Carmady sighed. "I'm having a swell time, angel. A swell time."

The man inside the gates took out keys on a long chain, unlocked the gates and pushed them back until they clicked on the chocks. Conant and the albino came back to the car.

Conant stood in the rain with a heel hooked on the running board. Carmady took his big flask out of his pocket, felt it over to see if it was dented, then unscrewed the top. He held it out towards the girl, said: "Have a little bottle courage."

She didn't answer him, didn't move. He drank from the flask, put it away, looked past Conant's broad back at acres of dripping trees, a cluster of lighted windows that seemed to hang in the sky.

A car came up the hill stabbing the wet dark with its headlights, pulled behind the sedan and stopped. Conant went over to it, put his head into it and said something. The car backed, turned into the driveway, and its lights splashed on retaining walls, disappeared, reappeared at the top of the drive as a hard white oval against a stone porte-cochère.

Conant got into the sedan and the albino swung it into the driveway after the other car. At the top, in a cement parking circle ringed with cypresses, they all got out.

At the top of steps a big door was open and a man in a bathrobe stood in it. Targo, between two men who leaned hard against him, was halfway up the steps. He was bareheaded and without an overcoat. His big body in the white coat looked enormous between the two gunmen.

The rest of the party went up the steps and into the house and followed the bathrobed butler down a hall lined with portraits of somebody's ancestors, through a still oval foyer to another hall and into a paneled study with soft lights and heavy drapes and deep leather chairs.

A man stood behind a big dark desk that was set in an alcove made by low, outjutting bookcases. He was enormously tall and thin. His white hair was so thick and fine that no single hair was visible in it. He had a small straight bitter mouth, black eyes without depth in a white lined face. He stooped a little and a blue corduroy bathrobe faced with satin was wrapped around his almost freakish thinness.

The butler shut the door and Conant opened it again and jerked his chin at the two men who had come in with Targo. They went out. The albino stepped behind Targo and pushed him down into a chair. Targo looked dazed, stupid. There was a smear of dirt on one side of his face and his eyes had a drugged look.

The girl went over to him quickly, said: "Oh, Duke—are you all right, Duke?"

Targo blinked at her, half-grinned. "So you had to rat, huh? Skip it. I'm fine." His voice had an unnatural sound.

Jean Adrian went away from him and sat down and hunched herself together as if she was cold.

The tall man stared coldly at everyone in the room in turn,

then said lifelessly: "Are these the blackmailers—and was it necessary to bring them here in the middle of the night?"

Conant shook himself out of his coat, threw it on the floor behind a lamp. He lit a fresh cigarette and stood spread-legged in the middle of the room, a big, rough, rugged man very sure of himself. He said: "The girl wanted to see you and tell you she was sorry and wants to play ball. The guy in the ice-cream coat is Targo, the fighter. He got himself in a shooting scrape at a night spot and acted so wild downtown they fed him sleep tablets to quiet him. The other guy is Carmady, old Marcus Carmady's boy. I don't figure him yet."

Carmady said dryly: "I'm a private detective, Senator. I'm here in the interests of my client, Miss Adrian." He laughed.

The girl looked at him suddenly, then looked at the floor.

Conant said gruffly. "Shenvair, the one you know about, got himself bumped off. Not by us. That's still to straighten out."

The tall man nodded coldly. He sat down at his desk and picked up a white quill pen, tickled one ear with it.

"And what is your idea of the way to handle this matter, Conant?" he asked thinly.

Conant shrugged. "I'm a rough boy, but I'd handle this one legal. Talk to the D.A., toss them in a coop on suspicion of extortion. Cook up a story for the papers, then give it time to cool. Then dump these birds across the state line and tell them not to come back—or else."

Senator Courtway moved the quill around to his other ear. "They could attack me again, from a distance," he said icily. "I'm in favor of a showdown, put them where they belong."

"You can't try them, Courtway. It would kill you politically."

"I'm tired of public life, Conant. I'll be glad to retire." The tall thin man curved his mouth into a faint smile.

"The hell you are," Conant growled. He jerked his head around, snapped: "Come here, sister."

Jean Adrian stood up, came slowly across the room, stood in front of the desk.

"Make her?" Conant snarled.

Courtway stared at the girl's set face for a long time, without a trace of expression. He put his quill down on the desk, opened a drawer and took out a photograph. He looked from the photo to the girl, back to the photo, said tonelessly: "This was taken a number of years ago, but there's a very strong resemblance. I don't think I'd hesitate to say it's the same face."

He put the photo down on the desk and with the same unhurried motion took an automatic out of the drawer and put it down on the desk beside the photo.

Conant stared at the gun. His mouth twisted. He said thickly: "You won't need that, Senator. Listen, your showdown idea is all wrong. I'll get detailed confessions from these people and we'll hold them. If they ever act up again, it'll be time enough then to crack down with the big one."

Carmady smiled a little and walked across the carpet until he was near the end of the desk. He said: "I'd like to see that photograph" and leaned over suddenly and took it.

Courtway's thin hand dropped to the gun, then relaxed. He leaned back in his chair and stared at Carmady.

Carmady stared at the photograph, lowered it, said softly to Jean Adrian: "Go sit down."

She turned and went back to her chair, dropped into it wearily.

Carmady said: "I like your showdown idea, Senator. It's clean and straightforward and a wholesome change in policy from Mr. Conant. But it won't work." He snicked a fingernail at the photo. "This has a superficial resemblance, no more. I don't think it's the same girl at all myself. Her ears are differently shaped and lower on her head. Her eyes are closer together than Miss Adrian's eyes, the line of her jaw is longer. Those things don't change. So what have you got? An extortion letter. Maybe, but you can't tie it to anyone or you'd have done it already. The girl's name. Just coincidence. What else?"

Conant's face was granite hard, his mouth bitter. His voice shook a little saying: "And how about that certificate the gal took out of her purse, wise guy?"

Carmady smiled faintly, rubbed the side of his jaw with his

fingertips. "I thought you got that from Shenvair?" he said slyly. "And Shenvair is dead."

Conant's face was a mask of fury. He balled his fist, took a jerky step forward. "Why you—damn louse—"

Jean Adrian was leaning forward staring round-eyed at Carmady. Targo was staring at him, with a loose grin, pale hard eyes. Courtway was staring at him. There was no expression of any kind on Courtway's face. He sat cold, relaxed, distant.

Conant laughed suddenly, snapped his fingers. "Okey, toot your horn," he grunted.

Carmady said slowly: "I'll tell you another reason why there'll be no showdown. That shooting at Cyrano's. Those threats to make Targo drop an unimportant fight. That hood that went to Miss Adrian's hotel room and sapped her, left her lying on her doorway. Can't you tie all that in, Conant? I can."

Courtway leaned forward suddenly and placed his hand on his gun, folded it around the butt. His black eyes were holes in a white frozen face.

Conant didn't move, didn't speak.

Carmady went on: "Why did Targo get those threats, and after he didn't drop the fight, why did a gun go to see him at Cyrano's, a night club, a very bad place for that kind of play? Because at Cyrano's he was with the girl, and Cyrano was his backer, and if anything happened at Cyrano's the law would get the threat story before they had time to think of anything else. That's why. The threats were a build-up for a killing. When the shooting came off Targo was to be with the girl, so the hood could get the girl and it would look as if Targo was the one he was after.

"He would have tried for Targo, too, of course, but above all he would have got the girl. Because she was the dynamite behind this shakedown, without her it meant nothing, and with her it could always be made over into a legitimate paternity suit. If it didn't work the other way. You know about her and about Targo, because Shenvair got cold feet and sold out. And Shenvair knew about the hood—because when the hood showed, and I saw him—and Shenvair knew I knew him, because he had heard me tell Targo about him—then Shenvair tried to pick a drunken fight with me and keep me from trying to interfere."

Carmady stopped, rubbed the side of his head again, very slowly, very gently. He watched Conant with an up-from-under look.

Conant said slowly, very harshly: "I don't play those games, buddy. Believe it or not—I don't."

Carmady said: "Listen. The hood could have killed the girl at the hotel with his sap. He didn't because Targo wasn't there and the fight hadn't been fought, and the build-up would have been all wasted. He went there to have a close look at her, without make-up. And she was scared about something, and had a gun with her. So he sapped her down and ran away. That visit was just a finger."

Conant said again: "I don't play those games, buddy." Then he took the Luger out of his pocket and held it down at his side.

Carmady shrugged, turned his head to stare at Senator Courtway.

"No, but he does," he said softly. "He had the motive, and the play wouldn't look like him. He cooked it up with Shenvair—and if it went wrong, as it did, Shenvair would have breezed and if the law got wise, big tough Doll Conant is the boy whose nose would be in the mud."

Courtway smiled a little and said in an utterly dead voice: "The young man is very ingenious, but surely—"

Targo stood up. His face was a stiff mask. His lips moved slowly and he said: "It sounds pretty good to me. I think I'll twist your goddamn neck, Mister Courtway."

The albino snarled, "Sit down, punk," and lifted his gun. Targo turned slightly and slammed the albino on the jaw. He went over backwards, smashed his head against the wall. The gun sailed along the floor from his limp hand.

Targo started across the room.

Conant looked at him sidewise and didn't move. Targo went

past him, almost touching him. Conant didn't move a muscle. His big face was blank, his eyes narrowed to a faint glitter between the heavy lids.

Nobody moved but Targo. Then Courtway lifted his gun and his finger whitened on the trigger and the gun roared.

Carmady moved across the room very swiftly and stood in front of Jean Adrian, between her and the rest of the room.

Targo looked down at his hands. His face twisted into a silly smile. He sat down on the floor and pressed both his hands against his chest.

Courtway lifted his gun again and then Conant moved. The Luger jerked up, flamed twice. Blood flowed down Courtway's hand. His gun fell behind his desk. His long body seemed to swoop down after the gun. It jackknifed until only his shoulders showed humped above the line of the desk.

Conant said: "Stand up and take it, you goddamn double-crossing swine!"

There was a shot behind the desk. Courtway's shoulders went down out of sight.

After a moment Conant went around behind the desk, stopped, straightened.

"He ate one," he said very calmly. "Through the mouth . . . And I lose me a nice clean senator."

Targo took his hands from his chest and fell over sidewise on the floor and lay still.

The door of the room slammed open. The butler stood in it, tousle-headed, his mouth gaping. He tried to say something, saw the gun in Conant's hand, saw Targo slumped on the floor. He didn't say anything.

The albino was getting to his feet, rubbing his chin, feeling his teeth, shaking his head. He went slowly along the wall and gathered up his gun.

Conant snarled at him: "Swell gut you turned out to be. Get on the phone. Get Malloy, the night captain—and snap it up!"

Carmady turned, put his hand down and lifted Jean Adrian's cold chin.

"It's getting light, angel. And I think the rain has stopped," he said slowly. He pulled his inevitable flask out. "Let's take a drink—to Mister Targo."

The girl shook her head, covered her face with her hands.

After a long time there were sirens.

TEN

The slim, tired-looking kid in the pale and silver of the Carondelet held his white glove in front of the closing doors and said: "Corky's boils is better, but he didn't come to work, Mister Carmady. Tony the bell captain ain't showed this morning neither. Pretty soft for some guys."

Carmady stood close to Jean Adrian in the corner of the car. They were alone in it. He said: "That's what you think."

The boy turned red. Carmady moved over and patted his shoulder, said: "Don't mind me, son. I've been up all night with a sick friend. Here, buy yourself a second breakfast."

"Jeeze, Mister Carmady, I didn't mean—"

The doors opened at nine and they went down the corridor to 914. Carmady took the key and opened the door, put the key on the inside, held the door, said: "Get some sleep and wake up with your fist in your eye. Take my flask and get a mild toot on. Do you good."

The girl went in through the door, said over her shoulder: "I don't want liquor. Come in a minute. There's something I want to tell you."

He shut the door and followed her in. A bright bar of sunlight lay across the carpet all the way to the davenport. He lit a cigarette and stared at it.

Jean Adrian sat down and jerked her hat off and rumpled her hair. She was silent a moment, then she said slowly, carefully: "It was swell of you to go to all that trouble for me. I don't know why you should do it."

Carmady said: "I can think of a couple of reasons, but they

326
▼

didn't keep Targo from getting killed, and that was my fault in a way. Then in another way it wasn't. I didn't ask him to twist Senator Courtway's neck."

The girl said: "You think you're hard-boiled but you're just a big slob that argues himself into a jam for the first tramp he finds in trouble. Forget it. Forget Targo and forget me. Neither of us was worth any part of your time. I wanted to tell you that because I'll be going away as soon as they let me, and I won't be seeing you any more. This is goodbye."

Carmady nodded, stared at the sun on the carpet. The girl went on: "It's a little hard to tell. I'm not looking for sympathy when I say I'm a tramp. I've smothered in too many hall bedrooms, stripped in too many filthy dressing rooms, missed too many meals, told too many lies to be anything else. That's why I wouldn't want to have anything to do with you, ever."

Carmady said: "I like the way you tell it. Go on."

She looked at him quickly, looked away again. "I'm not the Gianni girl. You guessed that. But I knew her. We did a cheap sister act together when they still did sister acts. Ada and Jean Adrian. We made up our names from hers. That flopped, and we went in a road show and that flopped too. In New Orleans. The going was a little too rough for her. She swallowed bichloride. I kept her photos because I knew her story. And looking at that thin cold guy and thinking what he could have done for her I got to hate him. She was his kid all right. Don't ever think she wasn't. I even wrote letters to him, asking for help for her, just a little help, signing her name. But they didn't get any answer. I got to hate him so much I wanted to do something to him, after she took the bichloride. So I came out here when I got a stake."

She stopped talking and laced her fingers together tightly, then pulled them apart violently, as if she wanted to hurt herself. She went on: "I met Targo through Cyrano and Shenvair through him. Shenvair knew the photos. He'd worked once for an agency in Frisco that was hired to watch Ada. You know all the rest of it."

Carmady said: "It sounds pretty good. I wondered why the

touch wasn't made sooner. Do you want me to think you didn't want his money?"

"No. I'd have taken his money all right. But that wasn't what I wanted most. I said I was a tramp."

Carmady smiled very faintly and said: "You don't know a lot about tramps, angel. You made an illegitimate pass and you got caught. That's that, but the money wouldn't have done you any good. It would have been dirty money. I know."

She looked up at him, stared at him. He touched the side of his face and winced and said: "I know because that's the kind of money mine is. My dad made it out of crooked sewerage and paving contracts, out of gambling concessions, appointment pay-offs, even vice, I daresay. He made it every rotten way there is to make money in city politics. And when it was made and there was nothing left to do but sit and look at it, he died and left it to me. It hasn't brought me any fun either. I always hope it's going to, but it never does. Because I'm his pup, his blood, reared in the same gutter. I'm worse than a tramp, angel. I'm a guy that lives on crooked dough and doesn't even do his own stealing."

He stopped, flicked ash on the carpet, straightened his hat on his head.

"Think that over, and don't run too far, because I have all the time in the world and it wouldn't do you any good. It would be so much more fun to run away together."

He went a little way towards the door, stood looking down at the sunlight on the carpet, looked back at her quickly and then went on out.

When the door shut she stood up and went into the bedroom and lay down on the bed just as she was, with her coat on, She stared at the ceiling. After a long time she smiled. In the middle of the smile she fell asleep.

NEVADA
GAS

ONE

Hugo Candless stood in the middle of the squash court bending his big body at the waist, holding the little black ball delicately between left thumb and forefinger. He dropped it near the service line and flicked at it with the long-handled racket.

The black ball hit the front wall a little less than halfway up, floated back in a high, lazy curve, skimmed just below the white ceiling and the lights behind wire protectors. It slid languidly down the back wall, never touching it enough to bounce out.

George Dial made a careless swing at it, whanged the end of his racket against the cement back wall. The ball fell dead.

He said: "That's the story, chief. 12—14. You're just too good for me."

George Dial was tall, dark, handsome, Hollywoodish. He was brown and lean, and had a hard, outdoor look. Everything about him was hard except his full, soft lips and his large, cowlike eyes.

"Yeah. I always was too good for you," Hugo Candless chortled.

He leaned far back from his thick waist and laughed with his mouth wide open. Sweat glistened on his chest and belly.

He was naked except for blue shorts, white wool socks and heavy sneakers with crêpe soles. He had gray hair and a broad moon face with a small nose and mouth, sharp twinkly eyes.

"Want another lickin'?" he asked.

"Not unless I have to."

Hugo Candless scowled. "Okey," he said shortly. He stuck his racket under his arm and got an oilskin pouch out of his shorts, took a cigarette and a match from it. He lit the cigarette with a flourish and threw the match into the middle of the court, where somebody else would have to pick it up.

He threw the door of the squash court open and paraded down the corridor to the locker room with his chest out. Dial walked behind him silently; catlike, soft-footed, with a lithe grace. They went to the showers.

Candless sang in the showers, covered his big body with thick suds, showered dead-cold after the hot, and liked it. He rubbed himself dry with immense leisure, took another towel and stalked out of the shower room yelling for the attendant to bring ice and ginger ale.

A Negro in a stiff white coat came hurrying with a tray. Candless signed the check with a flourish, unlocked his big double locker and planked a bottle of Johnny Walker on the round green table that stood in the locker aisle.

The attendant mixed drinks carefully, two of them, said: "Yes, suh, Mista Candless," and went away palming a quarter.

George Dial, already fully dressed in smart gray flannels, came around the corner and lifted one of the drinks.

"Through for the day, chief?" He looked at the ceiling light through his drink, with tight eyes.

"Guess so," Candless said largely. "Guess I'll go home and give the little woman a treat." He gave Dial a swift, sidewise glance from his little eyes.

"Mind if I don't ride home with you?" Dial asked carelessly.

"With me it's okey. It's tough on Naomi," Candless said unpleasantly.

Dial made a soft sound with his lips, shrugged, said: "You like to burn people up, don't you chief?"

Candless didn't answer, didn't look at him. Dial stood silent with his drink and watched the big man put on monogrammed satin underclothes, purple socks with gray clocks, a monogrammed silk shirt, a suit of tiny black and white checks that made him look as big as a barn.

By the time he got to his purple tie he was yelling for the Negro to come and mix another drink.

Dial refused the second drink, nodded, went away softly along the matting between the tall green lockers.

Candless finished dressing, drank his second highball, locked his liquor away and put a fat brown cigar in his mouth. He had the Negro light the cigar for him. He went off with a strut and several loud greetings here and there.

It seemed very quiet in the locker room after he went out. There were a few snickers.

▼

It was raining outside the Delmar Club. The liveried doorman helped Hugo Candless on with his belted white slicker and went out for his car. When he had it in front of the canopy he held an umbrella over Hugo across the strip of wooden matting to the curb. The car was a royal blue Lincoln limousine, with buff striping. The license number was 5A6.

The chauffeur, in a black slicker turned up high around his ears, didn't look around. The doorman opened the door and Hugo Candless got in and sank heavily on the back seat.

" 'Night, Sam. Tell him to go on home."

The doorman touched his cap, shut the door, and relayed the orders to the driver, who nodded without turning his head. The car moved off in the rain.

The rain came down slantingly and at the intersection sudden gusts blew it rattling against the glass of the limousine. The street corners were clotted with people trying to get across Sunset without being splashed. Hugo Candless grinned out at them, pityingly.

The car went out Sunset, through Sherman, then swung

towards the hills. It began to go very fast. It was on a boulevard where traffic was thin now.

It was very hot in the car. The windows were all shut and the glass partition behind the driver's seat was shut all the way across. The smoke of Hugo's cigar was heavy and choking in the tonneau of the limousine.

Candless scowled and reached out to lower a window. The window lever didn't work. He tried the other side. That didn't work either. He began to get mad. He grabbed for the little telephone dingus to bawl his driver out. There wasn't any little telephone dingus.

The car turned sharply and began to go up a long straight hill with eucalyptus trees on one side and no houses. Candless felt something cold touch his spine, all the way up and down his spine. He bent forward and banged on the glass with his fist. The driver didn't turn his head. The car went very fast up the long dark hill road.

Hugo Candless grabbed viciously for the door handle. The doors didn't have any handles—either side. A sick, incredulous grin broke over Hugo's broad moon face.

The driver bent over to the right and reached for something with his gloved hand. There was a sudden sharp hissing noise. Hugo Candless began to smell the odor of almonds.

Very faint at first—very faint, and rather pleasant. The hissing noise went on. The smell of almonds got bitter and harsh and very deadly. Hugo Candless dropped his cigar and banged with all his strength on the glass of the nearest window. The glass didn't break.

The car was up in the hills now, beyond even the infrequent street lights of the residential sections.

Candless dropped back on the seat and lifted his foot to kick hard at the glass partition in front of him. The kick was never finished. His eyes no longer saw. His face twisted into a snarl and his head went back against the cushions, crushed down against his thick shoulders. His soft white felt hat was shapeless on his big square skull.

The driver looked back quickly, showing a lean, hawklike

face for a brief instant. Then he bent to his right again and
the hissing noise stopped.

He pulled over to the side of the deserted road, stopped the
car, switched off all the lights. The rain made a dull noise
pounding on the roof.

The driver got out in the rain and opened the rear door of
the car, then backed away from it quickly, holding his nose.

He stood a little way off for a while and looked up and down
the road.

In the back of the limousine Hugo Candless didn't move.

TWO

Francine Ley sat in a low red chair beside a small table on
which there was an alabaster bowl. Smoke from the cigarette
she had just discarded into the bowl floated up and made patterns in the still, warm air. Her hands were clasped behind
her head and her smoke-blue eyes were lazy, inviting. She had
dark auburn hair set in loose waves. There were bluish shadows
in the troughs of the waves.

George Dial leaned over and kissed her on the lips, hard.
His own lips were hot when he kissed her, and he shivered.
The girl didn't move. She smiled up at him lazily when he
straightened again.

In a thick, clogged voice Dial said: "Listen, Francy. When
do you ditch this gambler and let me set you up?"

Francine Ley shrugged, without taking her hands from behind her head. "He's a square gambler, George," she drawled.
"That's something nowadays and you don't have enough money."

"I can get it."

"How?" Her voice was low and husky. It moved George Dial
like a cello.

"From Candless. I've got plenty on that bird."

"As for instance?" Francine Ley suggested lazily.

Dial grinned softly down at her. He widened his eyes in a deliberately innocent expression. Francine Ley thought the whites of his eyes were tinged ever so faintly with some color that was not white.

Dial flourished an unlighted cigarette. "Plenty—like he sold out a tough boy from Reno last year. The tough boy's half-brother was under a murder rap here and Candless took twenty-five grand to get him off. He made a deal with the D.A. on another case and let the tough boy's brother go up."

"And what did the tough boy do about all that?" Francine Ley asked gently.

"Nothing—yet. He thinks it was on the up and up, I guess. You can't always win."

"But he might do plenty, if he knew." Francine Ley said, nodding. "Who was the tough boy, Georgie?"

Dial lowered his voice and leaned down over her again. "I'm a sap to tell you that. A man named Zapparty. I've never met him."

"And never want to—if you've got sense, Georgie. No, thanks. I'm not walking myself into any jam like that with you."

Dial smiled lightly, showing even teeth in a dark, smooth face. "Leave it to me, Francy. Just forget the whole thing except how I'm nuts about you."

"Buy us a drink," the girl said.

The room was a living room in a hotel apartment. It was all red and white, with embassy decorations, too stiff. The white walls had red designs painted on them, the white venetian blinds were framed in white box drapes, there was a half-round red rug with a white border in front of the gas fire. There was a kidney-shaped white desk against one wall, between the windows.

Dial went over to the desk and poured Scotch into two glasses, added ice and charged water, carried the glasses back across the room to where a thin wisp of smoke still plumed upward from the alabaster bowl.

"Ditch the gambler," Dial said, handing her a glass. "He's the one will get you in a jam."

She sipped the drink, nodded. Dial took the glass out of her hand, sipped from the same place on the rim, leaned over holding both glasses and kissed her on the lips again.

There were red curtains over a door to a short hallway. They were parted a few inches and a man's face appeared in the opening, cool gray eyes stared in thoughtfully at the kiss. The curtains fell together again without sound.

After a moment a door shut loudly and steps came along the hallway. Johnny De Ruse came through the curtains into the room. By that time Dial was lighting his cigarette.

Johnny De Ruse was tall, lean, quiet, dressed in dark clothes dashingly cut. His cool gray eyes had fine laughter wrinkles at the corners. His thin mouth was delicate but not soft, and his long chin had a cleft in it.

Dial stared at him, made a vague motion with his hand. De Ruse walked over to the desk without speaking, poured some whiskey into a glass and drank it straight.

He stood a moment with his back to the room, tapping on the edge of the desk. Then he turned around, smiled faintly, said: " 'Lo, people," in a gentle, rather drawling voice and went out of the room through an inner door.

He was in a big overdecorated bedroom with twin beds. He went to a closet and got a tan calfskin suitcase out of it, opened it on the nearest bed. He began to rob the drawers of a highboy and put things in the suitcase, arranging them carefully, without haste. He whistled quietly through his teeth while he was doing it.

When the suitcase was packed he snapped it shut and lit a cigarette. He stood for a moment in the middle of the room without moving. His gray eyes looked at the wall without seeing it.

After a little while he went back into the closet and came out with a small gun in a soft leather harness with two short straps. He pulled up the left leg of his trousers and strapped the holster on his leg. Then he picked up the suitcase and went back to the living room.

Francine Ley's eyes narrowed swiftly when she saw the suitcase.

"Going some place?" she asked in her low, husky voice.

"Uh-huh. Where's Dial?"

"He had to leave."

"That's too bad," De Ruse said softly. He put the suitcase down on the floor and stood beside it, moving his cool gray eyes over the girl's face, up and down her slim body, from her ankles to her auburn head. "That's too bad," he said. "I like to see him around. I'm kind of dull for you."

"Maybe you are, Johnny."

He bent to the suitcase, but straightened without touching it and said casually: "Remember Mops Parisi? I saw him in town today."

Her eyes widened and then almost shut. Her teeth clicked lightly. The line of her jawbone stood out very distinctly for a moment.

De Ruse kept moving his glance up and down her face and body.

"Going to do anything about it?" she asked.

"I thought of taking a trip," De Ruse said. "I'm not so scrappy as I was once."

"A powder," Francine Ley said softly. "Where do we go?"

"Not a powder—a trip," De Ruse said tonelessly. "And not we—*me*. I'm going alone."

She sat still, watching his face, not moving a muscle.

De Ruse reached inside his coat and got out a long wallet that opened like a book. He tossed a tight sheaf of bills into the girl's lap, put the wallet away. She didn't touch the bills.

"That'll hold you for longer than you'll need to find a new playmate," he said, without expression. "I wouldn't say I won't send you more, if you need it."

She stood up slowly and the sheaf of bills slid down her skirt to the floor. She held her arms straight down at the sides, the hands clenched so that the tendons on the backs of them were sharp. Her eyes were as dull as slate.

"That means we're through, Johnny?"

He lifted his suitcase. She stepped in front of him swiftly, with two long steps. She put a hand against his coat. He stood quite still, smiling gently with his eyes, but not with his lips. The perfume of Shalimar twitched at his nostrils.

"You know what you are, Johnny?" Her husky voice was almost a lisp.

He waited.

"A pigeon, Johnny. A pigeon."

He nodded slightly. "Check. I called copper on Mops Parisi. I don't like the snatch racket, baby. I'd call copper on it any day. I might even get myself hurt blocking it. That's old stuff. Through?"

"You called copper on Mops Parisi and you don't think he knows it, but maybe he does. So you're running away from him . . . That's a laugh, Johnny. I'm kidding you. That's not why you're leaving me."

"Maybe I'm just tired of you, baby."

She put her head back and laughed sharply, almost with a wild note. De Ruse didn't budge.

"You're not a tough boy, Johnny. You're soft. George Dial is harder than you are. Gawd, how soft you are, Johnny!"

She stepped back, staring at his face. Some flicker of almost unbearable emotion came and went in her eyes.

"You're such a handsome pup, Johnny. Gawd, but you're handsome. It's too bad you're soft."

De Ruse said gently, without moving: "Not soft, baby—just a bit sentimental. I like to clock the ponies and play seven-card stud and mess around with little red cubes with white spots on them. I like games of chance, including women. But when I lose I don't get sore and I don't chisel. I just move on to the next table. Be seein' you."

He stooped, hefted the suitcase, and walked around her. He went across the room and through the red curtains without looking back.

Francine Ley stared with stiff eyes at the floor.

THREE

Standing under the scalloped glass canopy of the side entrance to the Chatterton, De Ruse looked up and down Irolo, towards the flashing lights of Wilshire and towards the dark quiet end of the side street.

The rain fell softly, slantingly. A light drop blew in under the canopy and hit the red end of his cigarette with a sputter. He hefted the suitcase and went along Irolo towards his sedan. It was parked almost at the next corner, a shiny black Packard with a little discreet chromium here and there.

He stopped and opened the door and a gun came up swiftly from inside the car. The gun prodded against his chest. A voice said sharply: "Hold it! The mitts high, sweets!"

De Ruse saw the man dimly inside the car. A lean hawklike face on which some reflected light fell without making it distinct. He felt a gun hard against his chest, hurting his breastbone. Quick steps came up behind him and another gun prodded his back.

"Satisfied?" another voice inquired.

De Ruse dropped the suitcase, lifted his hands and put them against the top of the car.

"Okey," he said wearily. "What is it—a heist?"

A snarling laugh came from the man in the car. A hand smacked De Ruse's hips from behind.

"Back up—slow!"

De Ruse backed up, holding his hands very high in the air.

"Not so high, punk," the man behind said dangerously. "Just shoulder high."

De Ruse lowered them. The man in the car got out, straightened. He put his gun against De Ruse's chest again, put out a long arm and unbuttoned De Ruse's overcoat. De Ruse leaned backwards. The hand belonging to the long arm explored his

338
▼

pockets, his armpits. A .38 in a spring holster ceased to make weight under his arm.

"Got one, Chuck. Anything your side?"

"Nothin' on the hip."

The man in front stepped away and picked up the suitcase.

"March sweets. We'll ride in our heap."

They went farther along Irolo. A big Lincoln limousine loomed up, a blue car with a lighter stripe. The hawk-faced man opened the rear door.

"In."

De Ruse got in listlessly, spitting his cigarette end into the wet darkness, as he stooped under the roof of the car. A faint smell assailed his nose, a smell that might have been overripe peaches or almonds. He got into the car.

"In beside him, Chuck."

"Listen. Let's all ride up front. I can handle——"

"Nix. In beside him, Chuck," the hawk-faced one snapped.

Chuck growled, got into the back seat beside De Ruse. The other man slammed the door hard. His lean face showed through the closed window in a sardonic grin. Then he went around to the driver's seat and started the car, tooled it away from the curb.

DeRuse wrinkled his nose, sniffing at the queer smell.

They spun at the corner, went east on Eighth to Normandie, north on Normandie across Wilshire, across other streets, up over a steep hill and down the other side to Melrose. The big Lincoln slid through the light rain without a whisper. Chuck sat in the corner, held his gun on his knee, scowled. Street lights showed a square, arrogant red face, a face that was not at ease.

The back of the driver's head was motionless beyond the glass partition. They passed Sunset and Hollywood, turned east on Franklin, swung north to Los Feliz and down Los Feliz towards the river bed.

Cars coming up the hill threw sudden brief glares of white light into the interior of the Lincoln. De Ruse tensed, waited.

At the next pair of lights that shot squarely into the car he bent over swiftly and jerked up the left leg of his trousers. He was back against the cushions before the blinding light was gone.

Chuck hadn't moved, hadn't noticed movement.

Down at the bottom of the hill, at the intersection of Riverside Drive, a whole phalanx of cars surged towards them as a light changed. De Ruse waited, timed the impact of the headlights. His body stooped briefly, his hand swooped down, snatched the small gun from the leg holster.

He leaned back once more, the gun against the bulk of his left thigh, concealed behind it from where Chuck sat.

The Lincoln shot over on to Riverside and passed the entrance to Griffith Park.

"Where we going, punk?" De Ruse asked casually.

"Save it," Chuck snarled. "You'll find out."

"Not a stick-up, huh?"

"Save it," Chuck snarled again.

"Mops Parisi's boys?" De Ruse asked thinly, slowly.

The red-faced gunman jerked, lifted the gun off his knee. "I said—save it!"

De Ruse said: "Sorry, punk."

He turned the gun over his thigh, lined it swiftly, squeezed the trigger left-handed. The gun made a small flat sound— almost an unimportant sound.

Chuck yelled and his hand jerked wildly. The gun kicked out of it and fell on the floor of the car. His left hand raced for his right shoulder.

De Ruse shifted the little Mauser to his right hand and put it deep into Chuck's side.

"Steady, boy, steady. Keep your hands out of trouble. Now—kick that cannon over this way—fast!"

Chuck kicked the big automatic along the floor of the car. De Ruse reached down for it swiftly, got it. The lean-faced driver jerked a look back and the car swerved, then straightened again.

De Ruse hefted the big gun. The Mauser was too light for

a sap. He slammed Chuck hard on the side of the head. Chuck groaned, sagged forward, clawing.

"The gas!" he bleated. "The gas! He'll turn on the gas!"

De Ruse hit him again, harder. Chuck was a tumbled heap on the floor of the car.

The Lincoln swung off Riverside, over a short bridge and a bridle path, down a narrow dirt road that split a golf course. It went into darkness and among trees. It went fast, rocketed from side to side, as if the driver wanted it to do just that.

De Ruse steadied himself, felt for the door handle. There wasn't any door handle. His lips curled and he smashed at a window with the gun. The heavy glass was like a wall of stone.

The hawk-faced man leaned over and there was a hissing sound. Then there was a sudden sharp increase of intensity of the smell of almonds.

De Ruse tore a handkerchief out of his pocket and pressed it to his nose. The driver had straightened again now and was driving hunched over, trying to keep his head down.

De Ruse held the muzzle of the big gun close to the glass partition behind the driver's head, who ducked sidewise. He squeezed lead four times quickly, shutting his eyes and turning his head away, like a nervous woman.

No glass flew. When he looked again there was a jagged round hole in the glass and the windshield in a line with it was starred but not broken.

He slammed the gun at the edges of the hole and managed to knock a piece of glass loose. He was getting the gas now, through the handkerchief. His head felt like a balloon. His vision waved and wandered.

The hawk-faced driver, crouched, wrenched the door open at his side, swung the wheel of the car the opposite way and jumped clear.

The car tore over a low embankment, looped a little and smacked sidewise against a tree. The body twisted enough for one of the rear doors to spring open.

De Ruse went through the door in a headlong dive. Soft earth smacked him, knocked some of the wind out of him.

341
▼

Then his lungs breathed clean air. He rolled up on his stomach and elbows, kept his head down, his gun hand up.

The hawk-faced man was on his knees a dozen yards away. De Ruse watched him drag a gun out of his pocket and lift it.

Chuck's gun pulsed and roared in De Ruse's hand until it was empty.

The hawk-faced man folded down slowly and his body merged with the dark shadows and the wet ground. Cars went by distantly on Riverside Drive. Rain dripped off the trees. The Griffith Park beacon turned in the thick sky. The rest was darkness and silence.

De Ruse took a deep breath and got up on his feet. He dropped the empty gun, took a small flash out of his overcoat pocket and pulled his overcoat up against his nose and mouth, pressing the thick cloth hard against his face. He went to the car, switched off the lights and threw the beam of the flash into the driver's compartment. He leaned in quickly and turned a petcock on a copper cylinder like a fire extinguisher. The hissing noise of the gas stopped.

He went over to the hawk-faced man. He was dead. There was some loose money, currency and silver in his pockets, cigarettes, a folder of matches from the Club Egypt, no wallet, a couple of extra clips of cartridges, De Ruse's .38. De Ruse put the last back where it belonged and straightened from the sprawled body.

He looked across the darkness of the Los Angeles river bed towards the lights of Glendale. In the middle distance a green neon sign far from any other light winked on and off: Club Egypt.

De Ruse smiled quietly to himself, and went back to the Lincoln. He dragged Chuck's body out onto the wet ground. Chuck's red face was blue now, under the beam of the small flash. His open eyes held an empty stare. His chest didn't move. De Ruse put the flash down and went through some more pockets.

He found the usual things a man carries, including a wallet

showing a driver's license issued to Charles Le Grand, Hotel Metropole, Los Angeles. He found more Club Egypt matches and a tabbed hotel key marked 809, Hotel Metropole.

He put the key in his pocket, slammed the sprung door of the Lincoln, got in under the wheel. The motor caught. He backed the car away from the tree with a wrench of broken fender metal, swung it around slowly over the soft earth and got it back again on the road.

When he reached Riverside again he turned the lights on and drove back to Hollywood. He put the car under some pepper trees in front of a big brick apartment house on Kenmore half a block north of Hollywood Boulevard, locked the ignition and lifted out his suitcase.

Light from the entrance of the apartment house rested on the front license plate as he walked away. He wondered why gunmen would use a car with plate numbers reading 5A6, almost a privilege number.

In a drugstore he phoned for a taxi. The taxi took him back to the Chatterton.

FOUR

The apartment was empty. The smell of Shalimar and cigarette smoke lingered on the warm air, as if someone had been there not long before. De Ruse pushed into the bedroom, looked at clothes in two closets, articles on a dresser, then went back to the red and white living room and mixed himself a stiff highball.

He put the night latch on the outside door and carried his drink into the bedroom, stripped off his muddy clothes and put on another suit of somber material but dandified cut. He sipped his drink while he knotted a black four-in-hand in the opening of a soft white linen shirt.

He swabbed the barrel of the little Mauser, reassembled it,

and added a shell to the small clip, slipped the gun back into the leg holster. Then he washed his hands and took his drink to the telephone.

The first number he called was the *Chronicle*. He asked for the City Room, Werner.

A drawly voice dripped over the wire: "Werner talkin'. Go ahead. Kid me."

De Ruse said: "This is John De Ruse, Claude. Look up California License 5A6 on your list for me."

"Must be a bloody politician," the drawly voice said, and went away.

De Ruse sat motionless, looking at a fluted white pillar in the corner. It had a red and white bowl of red and white artificial roses on top of it. He wrinkled his nose at it disgustedly.

Werner's voice came back on the wire: "1930 Lincoln limousine registered to Hugo Candless, Casa de Oro Apartments, 2942 Clearwater Street, West Hollywood."

De Ruse said in a tone that meant nothing: "That's the mouthpiece, isn't it?"

"Yeah. The big lip. Mister Take the Witness." Werner's voice came down lower. "Speaking to you, Johnny, and not for publication—a big crooked tub of guts that's not even smart; just been around long enough to know who's for sale . . . Story in it?"

"Hell, no," De Ruse said softly. "He just sideswiped me and didn't stop."

He hung up and finished his drink, stood up to mix another. Then he swept a telephone directory onto the white desk and looked up the number of the Casa de Oro. He dialed it. A switchboard operator told him Mr. Hugo Candless was out of town.

"Give me his apartment," De Ruse said.

A woman's cool voice answered the phone. "Yes. This is Mrs. Hugo Candless speaking. What is it, please?"

De Ruse said: "I'm a client of Mr. Candless, very anxious to get hold of him. Can you help me?"

"I'm very sorry," the cool, almost lazy voice told him. "My husband was called out of town quite suddenly. I don't even know where he went, though I expect to hear from him later this evening. He left his club——"

"What club was that?" De Ruse asked casually.

"The Delmar Club. I say he left there without coming home. If there is any message—"

De Ruse said: "Thank you, Mrs. Candless. Perhaps I may call you again later."

He hung up, smiled slowly and grimly, sipped his fresh drink and looked up the number of the Hotel Metropole. He called it and asked for "Mister Charles Le Grand in Room 809."

"Six-o-nine," the operator said casually. "I'll connect you." A moment later: "There is no answer."

De Ruse thanked her, took the tabbed key out of his pocket, looked at the number on it. The number was 809.

FIVE

Sam, the doorman at the Delmar Club, leaned against the buff stone of the entrance and watched the traffic swish by on Sunset Boulevard. The headlights hurt his eyes. He was tired and he wanted to go home. He wanted a smoke and a big slug of gin. He wished the rain would stop. It was dead inside the club when it rained.

He straightened away from the wall and walked the length of the sidewalk canopy a couple of times, slapping together his big black hands in big white gloves. He tried to whistle the "Skaters Waltz," couldn't get within a block of the tune, whistled "Low Down Lady" instead. That didn't have any tune.

De Ruse came around the corner from Hudson Street and stood beside him near the wall.

"Hugo Candless inside?" he asked, not looking at Sam.

Sam clicked his teeth disapprovingly. "He ain't."

"Been in?"

"Ask at the desk'side, please, mistah."

De Ruse took gloved hands out of his pocket and began to roll a five-dollar bill around his left forefinger.

"What do they know that you don't know?"

Sam grinned slowly, watched the bill being wound tightly around the gloved finger.

"That's a fac', boss. Yeah—he was in. Comes most every day."

"What time he leave?"

"He leave 'bout six-thirty, Ah reckon."

"Drive his blue Lincoln limousine?"

"Shuah. Only he don't drive it hisself. What for you ask?"

"It was raining then," De Ruse said calmly. "Raining pretty hard. Maybe it wasn't the Lincoln."

" 'Twas, too, the Lincoln," Sam protested. "Ain't I tucked him in? He never rides nothin' else."

"License 5A6?" De Ruse bored on relentlessly.

"That's it," Sam chortled. "Just like a councilman's number that number is."

"Know the driver?"

"Shuah—" Sam began, and then stopped cold. He raked a black jaw with a white finger the size of a banana. "Well, Ah'll be a big black slob if he ain't got hisself a new driver again. I ain't *know* that man, sure'nough."

De Ruse poked the rolled bill into Sam's big white paw. Sam grabbed it but his large eyes suddenly got suspicious.

"Say, for what you ask all of them questions, mistah man?"

De Ruse said: "I paid my way, didn't I?"

He went back around the corner to Hudson and got into his black Packard sedan. He drove it out on to Sunset, then west on Sunset almost to Beverly Hills, then turned towards the foothills and began to peer at the signs on street corners. Clearwater Street ran along the flank of a hill and had a view of the entire city. The Casa de Oro, at the corner of Parkinson, was a tricky block of high-class bungalow apartments surrounded by an adobe wall with red tiles on top. It had a lobby in a separate building, a big private garage on Parkinson, opposite one length of the wall.

De Ruse parked across the street from the garage and sat looking through the wide window into a glassed-in office where an attendant in spotless white coveralls sat with his feet on the desk, reading a magazine and spit over his shoulder at an invisible cuspidor.

De Ruse got out of the Packard, crossed the street farther up, came back and slipped into the garage without the attendant seeing him.

The cars were in four rows. Two rows backed against the white walls, two against each other in the middle. There were plenty of vacant stalls, but plenty of cars had gone to bed also. They were mostly big, expensive closed models, with two or three flashy open jobs.

There was only one limousine. It had License No. 5A6.

It was a well-kept car, bright and shiny; royal blue with a buff trimming. De Ruse took a glove off and rested his hand on the radiator shell. Quite cold. He felt the tires, looked at his fingers. A little fine dry dust adhered to the skin. There was no mud in the treads, just bone-dry dust.

He went back along the row of dark car bodies and leaned in the open door of the little office. After a moment the attendant looked up, almost with a start.

"Seen the Candless chauffeur around?" De Ruse asked him.

The man shook his head and spat deftly into a copper spittoon.

"Not since I came on—three o'clock."

"Didn't he go down to the club for the old man?"

"Nope. I guess not. The big hack ain't been out. He always takes that."

"Where does he hang his hat?"

"Who? Mattick? They got servants' quarters in back of the jungle. But I think I heard him say he parks at some hotel. Let's see—" A brow got furrowed.

"The Metropole?" De Ruse suggested.

The garage man thought it over while De Ruse stared at the point of his chin.

"Yeah. I think that's it. I ain't just positive though. Mattick don't open up much."

De Ruse thanked him and crossed the street and got into the Packard again. He drove downtown.

It was twenty-five minutes past nine when he got to the corner of Seventh and Spring, where the Metropole was.

It was an old hotel that had once been exclusive and was now steering a shaky course between a receivership and a bad name at Headquarters. It had too much oily dark wood paneling, too many chipped gilt mirrors. Too much smoke hung below its low beamed lobby ceiling and too many grifters bummed around in its worn leather rockers.

The blonde who looked after the big horseshoe cigar counter wasn't young any more and her eyes were cynical from standing off cheap dates. De Ruse leaned on the glass and pushed his hat back on his crisp black hair.

"Camels, honey," he said in his low-pitched gambler's voice.

The girl smacked the pack in front of him, rang up fifteen cents and slipped the dime change under his elbow, with a faint smile. Her eyes said they liked him. She leaned opposite him and put her head near enough so that he could smell the perfume in her hair.

"Tell me something," De Ruse said.

"What?" she asked softly.

"Find out who lives in eight-o-nine, without telling any answers to the clerk."

The blonde looked disappointed. "Why don't you ask him yourself, mister?"

"I'm too shy," De Ruse said.

"Yes you are!"

She went to her telephone and talked into it with languid grace, came back to De Ruse.

"Name of Mattick. Mean anything?"

"Guess not," De Ruse said. "Thanks a lot. How do you like it in this nice hotel?"

"Who said it was a nice hotel?"

De Ruse smiled, touched his hat, strolled away. Her eyes looked after him sadly. She leaned her sharp elbows on the counter and cupped her chin in her hands to stare after him.

De Ruse crossed the lobby and went up three steps and got into an open-cage elevator that started with a lurch.

"Eight," he said, and leaned against the cage with his hands in his pockets.

Eight was as high as the Metropole went. De Ruse followed a long corridor that smelled of varnish. A turn at the end brought him face to face with 809. He knocked on the dark wood panel. Nobody answered. He bent over, looked through an empty keyhole, knocked again.

Then he took the tabbed key out of his pocket and unlocked the door and went in.

Windows were shut in two walls. The air reeked of whiskey. Lights were on in the ceiling. There was a wide brass bed, a dark bureau, a couple of brown leather rockers, a stiff-looking desk with a flat brown quart of Four Roses on it, nearly empty, without a cap. De Ruse sniffed it and set his hips against the edge of the desk, let his eyes prowl the room.

His glance traversed from the dark bureau across the bed and the wall with the door in it to another door behind which light showed. He crossed to that and opened it.

The man lay on his face, on the yellowish brown woodstone floor of the bathroom. Blood on the floor looked sticky and black. Two soggy patches on the back of the man's head were the points from which rivulets of dark red had run down the side of his neck to the floor. The blood had stopped flowing a long time ago.

De Ruse slipped a glove off and stooped to hold two fingers against the place where an artery would beat. He shook his head and put his hand back into his glove.

He left the bathroom, shut the door and went to open one

of the windows. He leaned out, breathing clean rain-wet air, looking down along slants of thin rain into the dark slit of an alley.

After a little while he shut the window again, switched off the light in the bathroom, took a "Do Not Disturb" sign out of the top bureau drawer, doused the ceiling lights, and went out.

He hung the sign on the knob and went back along the corridor to the elevators and left the Hotel Metropole.

SIX

Francine Ley hummed low down in her throat as she went along the silent corridor of the Chatterton. She hummed unsteadily without knowing what she was humming, and her left hand with its cherry-red fingernails held a green velvet cape from slipping down off her shoulders. There was a wrapped bottle under her other arm.

She unlocked the door, pushed it open and stopped, with a quick frown. She stood still, remembering, trying to remember. She was still a little tight.

She had left the lights on, that was it. They were off now. Could be the maid service, of course. She went on in, fumbled through the red curtains into the living room.

The glow from the heater prowled across the red and white rug and touched shiny black things with a ruddy gleam. The shiny black things were shoes. They didn't move.

Francine Ley said: "Oh—oh," in a sick voice. The hand holding the cape almost tore into her neck with its long, beautifully molded nails.

Something clicked and light glowed in a lamp beside an easy chair. De Ruse sat in the chair, looking at her woodenly.

He had his coat and hat on. His eyes shrouded, far away, filled with a remote brooding.

He said: "Been out, Francy?"

She sat down slowly on the edge of a half-round settee, put the bottle down beside her.

"I got tight," she said. "Thought I'd better eat. Then I thought I'd get tight again." She patted the bottle.

De Ruse said: "I think your friend Dial's boss has been snatched." He said it casually, as if it was of no importance to him.

Francine Ley opened her mouth slowly and as she opened it all the prettiness went out of her face. Her face became a blank haggard mask on which rouge burned violently. Her mouth looked as if it wanted to scream.

After a while it closed again and her face got pretty again and her voice, from far off, said: "Would it do any good to say I don't know what you're talking about?"

De Ruse didn't change his wooden expression. He said: "When I went down to the street from here a couple of hoods jumped me. One of them was stashed in the car. Of course they could have spotted me somewhere else—followed me here."

"They did," Francine Ley said breathlessly. "They did, Johnny."

His long chin moved an inch. "They piled me into a big Lincoln, a limousine. It was quite a car. It had heavy glass that didn't break easily and no door handles and it was all shut up tight. In the front seat it had a tank of Nevada gas, cyanide, which the guy driving could turn into the back part without getting it himself. They took me out Griffith Parkway, towards the Club Egypt. That's that joint on county land, near the airport." He paused, rubbed the end of one eyebrow, went on: "They overlooked the Mauser I sometimes wear on my leg. The driver crashed the car and I got loose."

He spread his hands and looked down at them. A faint metallic smile showed at the corners of his lips.

Francine Ley said: "I didn't have anything to do with it, Johnny." Her voice was as dead as the summer before last.

De Ruse said: "The guy that rode in the car before I did

probably didn't have a gun. He was Hugo Candless. The car was a ringer for his car—same model, same paint job, same plates—but it wasn't his car. Somebody took a lot of trouble. Candless left the Delmar Club in the wrong car about six-thirty. His wife says he's out of town. I talked to her an hour ago. His car hasn't been out of the garage since noon . . . Maybe his wife knows he's snatched by now, maybe not."

Francine Ley's nails clawed at her skirt. Her lips shook.

De Ruse went on calmly, tonelessly: "Somebody gunned the Candless chauffeur in a downtown hotel tonight or this afternoon. The cops haven't found it yet. Somebody took a lot of trouble, Francy. You wouldn't want to be in on that kind of a set-up, would you, precious?"

Francine Ley bent her head forward and stared at the floor. She said thickly: "I need a drink. What I had is dying in me. I feel awful."

De Ruse stood up and went to the white desk. He drained a bottle into a glass and brought it across to her. He stood in front of her, holding the glass out of her reach.

"I only get tough once in a while, baby, but when I get tough I'm not so easy to stop, if I say it myself. If you know anything about all this, now would be a good time to spill it."

He handed her the glass. She gulped the whiskey and a little more light came into her smoke-blue eyes. She said slowly: "I don't know anything about it, Johnny. Not in the way you mean. But George Dial made me a love-nest proposition tonight and he told me he could get money out of Candless by threatening to spill a dirty trick Candless played on some tough boy from Reno."

"Damn clever, these greasers," De Ruse said. "Reno's my town, baby. I know all the tough boys in Reno. Who was it?"

"Somebody named Zapparty."

De Ruse said very softly: "Zapparty is the name of the man who runs the Club Egypt."

Francine Ley stood up suddenly and grabbed his arm. "Stay

out of it, Johnny! For Christ sake, can't you stay out of it for just this once?"

De Ruse shook his head, smiled delicately, lingeringly at her. Then he lifted her hand off his arm and stepped back.

"I had a ride in their gas car, baby, and I didn't like it. I smelled their Nevada gas. I left my lead in somebody's gun punk. That makes me call copper or get jammed up with the law. If someody's snatched and I call copper, there'll be another kidnap victim bumped off, more likely than not. Zapparty's a tough boy from Reno and that could tie in with what Dial told you, and if Mops Parisi is playing with Zapparty, that could make a reason to pull me into it. Parisi loathes my guts."

"You don't have to be a one-man riot squad, Johnny," Francine Ley said desperately.

He kept on smiling, with tight lips and solemn eyes. "There'll be two of us, baby. Get yourself a long coat. It's still raining a little."

She goggled at him. Her outstretched hand, the one that had been on his arm, spread its fingers stiffly, bent back from the palm, straining back. Her voice was hollow with fear.

"Me, Johnny? . . . Oh, please, not . . ."

De Ruse said gently: "Get that coat, honey. Make yourself look nice. It might be the last time we'll go out together."

She staggered past him. He touched her arm softly, held it a moment, said almost in a whisper:

"*You* didn't put the finger on me, did you, Francy?"

She looked back stonily at the pain in his eyes, made a hoarse sound under her breath and jerked her arm loose, went quickly into the bedroom.

After a moment the pain went out of De Ruse's eyes and the metallic smile came back to the corners of his lips.

SEVEN

De Ruse half closed his eyes and watched the croupier's fingers as they slid back across the table and rested on the edge. They were round, plump, tapering fingers, graceful fingers. De Ruse raised his head and looked at the croupier's face. He was a bald-headed man of no particular age, with quiet blue eyes. He had no hair on his head at all, not a single hair.

De Ruse looked down at the croupier's hands again. The right hand turned a little on the edge of the table. The buttons on the sleeve of the croupier's brown velvet coat—cut like a dinner coat—rested on the edge of the table. De Ruse smiled his thin metallic smile.

He had three blue chips on the red. On that play the ball stopped at Black 2. The croupier paid off two of the four other men who were playing.

De Ruse pushed five blue chips forward and settled them on the red diamond. Then he turned his head to the left and watched a huskily built blond young man put three red chips on the zero.

De Ruse licked his lips and turned his head farther, looked towards the side of the rather small room. Francine Ley was sitting on a couch backed to the wall, with her head leaning against it.

"I think I've got it, baby," De Ruse said to her. "I think I've got it."

Francine Ley blinked and lifted her head away from the wall. She reached for a drink on a low round table in front of her.

She sipped the drink, looked at the floor, didn't answer.

De Ruse looked back at the blond man. The three other men had made bets. The croupier looked impatient and at the same time watchful.

354

▼

De Ruse said: "How come you always hit zero when I hit red, and double zero when I hit black?"

The blond young man smiled, shrugged, said nothing.

De Ruse put his hand down on the layout and said very softly: "I asked you a question, mister."

"Maybe I'm Jesse Livermore," the blond young man grunted. "I like to sell short."

"What is this—slow motion?" one of the other men snapped.

"Make your plays, please, gentlemen," the croupier said.

De Ruse looked at him, said: "Let it go."

The croupier spun the wheel left-handed, flicked the ball with the same hand the opposite way. His right hand rested on the edge of the table.

The ball stopped at black 28, next to zero. The blond man laughed. "Close," he said, "close."

De Ruse checked his chips, stacked them carefully. "I'm down six grand," he said. "It's a little raw, but I guess there's money in it. Who runs this clip joint?"

The croupier smiled slowly and stared straight into De Ruse's eyes. He asked quietly: "Did you say clip joint?"

De Ruse nodded. He didn't bother to answer.

"I thought you said clip joint," the croupier said, and moved one foot, put weight on it.

Three of the men who had been playing picked their chips up quickly and went over to a small bar in the corner of the room. They ordered drinks and leaned their backs against the wall by the bar, watching De Ruse and the croupier. The blond man stayed put and smiled sarcastically at De Ruse.

"Tsk, tsk," he said thoughtfully. "Your manners."

Francine Ley finished her drink and leaned her head back against the wall again. Her eyes came down and watched De Ruse furtively, under the long lashes.

A paneled door opened after a moment and a very big man with a black mustache and very rough black eyebrows came in. The croupier moved his eyes to him, then to De Ruse, pointing with his glance.

"Yes, I thought you said clip joint," he repeated tonelessly.

The big man drifted to De Ruse's elbow, touched him with his own elbow.

"Out," he said impassively.

The blond man grinned and put his hands in the pockets of his dark gray suit. The big man didn't look at him.

De Ruse glanced across the layout at the croupier and said: "I'll take back my six grand and call it a day."

"Out," the big man said wearily, jabbing his elbow into De Ruse's side.

The bald-headed croupier smiled politely.

"You," the big man said to De Ruse, "ain't goin' to get tough, are you?"

De Ruse looked at him with sarcastic surprise.

"Well, well, the bouncer," he said softly. "Take him, Nicky."

The blond man took his right hand out of his pocket and swung it. The sap looked black and shiny under the bright lights. It hit the big man on the back of the head with a soft thud. The big man clawed at De Ruse, who stepped away from him quickly and took a gun out from under his arm. The big man clawed at the edge of the roulette table and fell heavily on the floor.

Francine Ley stood up and made a strangled sound in her throat.

The blond man skipped sidewise, whirled and looked at the bartender. The bartender put his hands on top of the bar. The three men who had been playing roulette looked very interested, but they didn't move.

De Ruse said: "The middle button on his right sleeve, Nicky. I think it's copper."

"Yeah." The blond man drifted around the end of the table putting the sap back in his pocket. He went close to the croupier and took hold of the middle of three buttons on his right cuff, jerked it hard. At the second jerk it came away and a thin wire followed it out of the sleeve.

"Correct," the blond man said casually, letting the croupier's arm drop.

"I'll take my six grand now," De Ruse said. "Then we'll go talk to your boss."

The croupier nodded slowly and reached for the rack of chips beside the roulette table.

The big man on the floor didn't move. The blond man put his right hand behind his hip and took a .45 automatic out from inside his waistband at the back.

He swung it in his hand, smiling pleasantly around the room.

EIGHT

They went along a balcony that looked down over the dining room and the dance floor. The lisp of hot jazz came up to them from the lithe, swaying bodies of a high-yaller band. With the lisp of jazz came the smell of food and cigarette smoke and perspiration. The balcony was high and the scene down below had a patterned look, like an overhead camera shot.

The bald-headed croupier opened a door in the corner of the balcony and went through without looking back. The blond man De Ruse had called Nicky went after him. Then De Ruse and Francine Ley.

There was a short hall with a frosted light in the ceiling. The door at the end of that looked like painted metal. The croupier put a plump finger on the small push button at the side, rang it in a certain way. There was a buzzing noise like the sound of an electric door release. The croupier pushed on the edge and opened it.

Inside was a cheerful room, half den and half office. There was a grate fire and a green leather davenport at right angles to it, facing the door. A man sitting on the davenport put a newspaper down and looked up and his face suddenly got livid. He was a small man with a tight round head, a tight round dark face. He had little lightless black eyes like buttons of jet.

There was a big flat desk in the middle of the room and a

very tall man stood at the end of it with a cocktail shaker in his hands. His head turned slowly and he looked over his shoulder at the four people who came into the room while his hands continued to agitate the cocktail shaker in gentle rhythm. He had a cavernous face with sunken eyes, loose grayish skin, and close-cropped reddish hair without shine or parting. A thin crisscross scar like a German *Mensur* scar showed on his left cheek.

The tall man put the cocktail shaker down and turned his body around and stared at the croupier. The man on the davenport didn't move. There was a crouched tensity in his not moving.

The croupier said: "I think it's a stick-up. But I couldn't help myself. They sapped Big George."

The blond man smiled gaily and took his .45 out of his pocket. He pointed it at the floor.

"He thinks it's a stick-up," he said. "Wouldn't that positively slay you?"

De Ruse shut the heavy door. Francine Ley moved away from him, towards the side of the room away from the fire. He didn't look at her. The man on the davenport looked at her, looked at everybody.

De Ruse said quietly: "The tall one is Zapparty. The little one is Mops Parisi."

The blond man stepped to one side, leaving the croupier alone in the middle of the room. The .45 covered the man on the davenport.

"Sure, I'm Zapparty," the tall man said. He looked at De Ruse curiously for a moment.

Then he turned his back and picked the cocktail shaker up again, took out the plug and filled a shallow glass. He drained the glass, wiped his lips with a sheer lawn handkerchief and tucked the handkerchief back into his breast pocket very carefully, so that three points showed.

DeRuse smiled his thin metallic smile and touched one end of his left eyebrow with his forefinger. His right hand was in his jacket pocket.

"Nicky and I put on a little act," he said. "That was so the boys outside would have something to talk about if the going got too noisy when we came in to see you."

"It sounds interesting," Zapparty agreed. "What did you want to see me about?"

"About that gas car you take people for rides in," De Ruse said.

The man on the davenport made a very sudden movement and his hand jumped off his leg as if something had stung it. The blond man said: "No . . . or yes, if you'd rather, Mister Parisi. It's all a matter of taste."

Parisi became motionless again. His hand dropped back to his short thick thigh.

Zapparty widened his deep eyes a little. "Gas car?" His tone was of mild puzzlement.

De Ruse went forward into the middle of the room near the croupier. He stood balanced on the balls of his feet. His gray eyes had a sleepy glitter but his face was drawn and tired, not young.

He said: "Maybe somebody just tossed it in your lap, Zapparty, but I don't think so. I'm talking about the blue Lincoln, License 5A6, with the tank of Nevada gas in front. You know, Zapparty, the stuff they use on killers in our state."

Zapparty swallowed and his large Adam's apple moved in and out. He puffed his lips, then drew them back against his teeth, then puffed them again.

The man on the davenport laughed out loud, seemed to be enjoying himself.

A voice that came from no one in the room said sharply: "Just drop that gat, blondie. The rest of you grab air."

De Ruse looked up towards an opened panel in the wall beyond the desk. A gun showed in the opening, and a hand, but no body or face. Light from the room lit up the hand and the gun.

The gun seemed to point directly at Francine Ley. De Ruse said: "Okey," quickly, and lifted his hands, empty.

The blond man said: "That'll be Big George—all rested and

ready to go." He opened his hand and let the .45 thud to the floor in front of him.

Parisi stood up very swiftly from the davenport and took a gun from under his arm. Zapparty took a revolver out of the desk drawer, leveled it. He spoke towards the panel: "Get out, and stay out."

The panel clicked shut. Zapparty jerked his head at the bald-headed croupier, who had not seemed to move a muscle since he came into the room.

"Back on the job, Louis. Keep the chin up."

The croupier nodded and turned and went out of the room, closing the door carefully behind him.

Francine Ley laughed foolishly. Her hand went up and pulled the collar of her wrap close around her throat, as if it was cold in the room. But there were no windows and it was very warm, from the fire.

Parisi made a whistling sound with his lips and teeth and went quickly to De Ruse and stuck the gun he was holding in De Ruse's face, pushing his head back. He felt in De Ruse's pockets with his left hand, took the Colt, felt under his arms, circled around him, touched his hips, came to the front again.

He stepped back a little and hit De Ruse on the cheek with the flat of one gun. De Ruse stood perfectly still except that his head jerked a little when the hard metal hit his face.

Parisi hit him again the same place. Blood began to run down De Ruse's cheek from the cheekbone, lazily. His head sagged a little and his knees gave way. He went down slowly, leaned with his left hand on the floor, shaking his head. His body was crouched, his legs doubled under him. His right hand dangled loosely beside his left foot.

Zapparty said: "All right, Mops. Don't get blood-hungry. We want words out of these people."

Francine Ley laughed again, rather foolishly. She swayed along the wall, holding one hand up against it.

Parisi breathed hard and backed away from De Ruse with a happy smile on his round swart face.

"I been waitin' a long time for this," he said.

When he was about six feet from De Ruse something small and darkly glistening seemed to slide out of the left leg of De Ruse's trousers into his hand. There was a sharp, snapping explosion, a tiny orange-green flame down on the floor.

Parisi's head jerked back. A round hole appeared under his chin. It got large and red almost instantly. His hands opened laxly and the two guns fell out of them. His body began to sway. He fell heavily.

Zapparty said: "Holy Christ!" and jerked up his revolver.

Francine Ley screamed flatly and hurled herself at him— clawing, kicking, shrilling.

The revolver went off twice with a heavy crash. Two slugs plunked into a wall. Plaster rattled.

Francine Ley slid down to the floor, on her hands and knees. A long slim leg sprawled out from under her dress.

The blond man, down on one knee with his .45 in his hand again, rasped: "She got the bastard's gun!"

Zapparty stood with his hands empty, a terrible expression on his face. There was a long red scratch on the back of his right hand. His revolver lay on the floor beside Francine Ley. His horrified eyes looked down at it unbelievingly.

Parisi coughed once on the floor and after that was still.

De Ruse got up on his feet. The little Mauser looked like a toy in his hand. His voice seemed to come from far away saying: "Watch that panel, Nicky. . . ."

There was no sound outside the room, no sound anywhere. Zapparty stood at the end of the desk, frozen, ghastly.

De Ruse bent down and touched Francine Ley's shoulder. "All right, baby?"

She drew her legs under her and got up, stood looking down at Parisi. Her body shook with a nervous chill.

"I'm sorry, baby," De Ruse said softly beside her. "I guess I had a wrong idea about you."

He took a handkerchief out of his pocket and moistened it with his lips, then rubbed his left cheek lightly and looked at blood on the handkerchief.

Nicky said: "I guess Big George went to sleep again. I was a sap not to blast at him."

De Ruse nodded a little, and said:

"Yeah. The whole play was lousy. Where's your hat and coat, Mister Zapparty? We'd like to have you go riding with us."

NINE

In the shadows under the pepper trees De Ruse said: "There it is, Nicky. Over there. Nobody's bothered it. Better take a look around."

The blond man got out from under the wheel of the Packard and went off under the trees. He stood a little while on the same side of the street as the Packard, then he slipped across to where the big Lincoln was parked in front of the brick apartment house on North Kenmore.

De Ruse leaned forward across the back of the front seat and pinched Francine Ley's cheek. "You're going home now, baby—with this bus. I'll see you later."

"Johnny"—she clutched at his arm—"what are you going to do? For Pete's sake, can't you stop having fun for tonight?"

"Not yet, baby. Mister Zapparty wants to tell us things. I figure a little ride in that gas car will pep him up. Anyway I need it for evidence."

He looked sidewise at Zapparty in the corner of the back seat. Zapparty made a harsh sound in his throat and stared in front of him with a shadowed face.

Nicky came back across the road, stood with one foot on the running board.

"No keys," he said. "Got 'em?"

De Ruse said: "Sure." He took keys out of his pocket and handed them to Nicky. Nicky went around to Zapparty's side of the car and opened the door.

"Out, mister."

Zapparty got out stiffly, stood in the soft, slanting rain, his mouth working. De Ruse got out after him.

"Take it away, baby."

Francine Ley slid along the seat under the steering wheel of the Packard and pushed the starter. The motor caught with a soft whirr.

"So long, baby," De Ruse said gently. "Get my slippers warmed for me. And do me a big favor, honey. Don't phone anyone."

The Packard went off along the dark street, under the big pepper trees. De Ruse watched it turn a corner. He prodded Zapparty with his elbow.

"Let's go. You're going to ride in the back of your gas car. We can't feed you much gas on account of the hole in the glass, but you'll like the smell of it. We'll go off in the country somewhere. We've got all night to play with you."

"I guess you know this is a snatch," Zapparty said harshly.

"Don't I love to think it," De Ruse purred.

They went across the street, three men walking together without haste. Nicky opened the good rear door of the Lincoln. Zapparty got into it. Nicky banged the door shut, got under the wheel and fitted the ignition key in the lock. De Ruse got in beside him and sat with his legs straddling the tank of gas.

The whole car still smelled of the gas.

Nicky started the car, turned it in the middle of the block and drove north to Franklin, back over Los Feliz towards Glendale. After a little while Zapparty leaned forward and banged on the glass. De Ruse put his ear to the hole in the glass behind Nicky's head.

Zapparty's harsh voice said: "Stone house—Castle Road—in the La Crescenta flood area."

"Jeeze, but he's a softy," Nicky grunted, his eyes on the road ahead.

De Ruse nodded, said thoughtfully: "There's more to it than that. With Parisi dead he'd clam up unless he figured he had an out."

Nicky said: "Me, I'd rather take a beating and keep my chin buttoned. Light me a pill, Johnny."

363

▼

De Ruse lit two cigarettes and passed one to the blond man. He glanced back at Zapparty's long body in the corner of the car. Passing light touched up his taut face, made the shadows on it look very deep.

The big car slid noiselessly through Glendale and up the grade towards Montrose. From Montrose over to the Sunland highway and across that into the almost deserted flood area of La Crescenta.

They found Castle Road and followed it towards the mountains. In a few minutes they came to the stone house.

It stood back from the road, across a wide space which might once have been lawn but which was now packed sand, small stones and a few large boulders. The road made a square turn just before they came to it. Beyond it the road ended in a clean edge of concrete chewed off by the flood of New Year's Day, 1934.

Beyond this edge was the main wash of the flood. Bushes grew in it and there were many huge stones. On the very edge a tree grew with half its roots in the air eight feet above the bed of the wash.

Nicky stopped the car and turned off the lights and took a big nickeled flash out of the car pocket. He handed it to De Ruse.

De Ruse got out of the car and stood for a moment with his hand on the open door, holding the flash. He took a gun out of his overcoat pocket and held it down at his side.

"Looks like a stall," he said. "I don't think there's anything stirring here."

He glanced in at Zapparty, smiled sharply and walked off across the ridges of sand, towards the house. The front door stood half open, wedged that way by sand. De Ruse went towards the corner of the house, keeping out of line with the door as well as he could. He went along the side wall, looking at boarded-up windows behind which there was no trace of light.

At the back of the house was what had been a chicken house. A piece of rusted junk in a squashed garage was all that remained of the family sedan. The back door was nailed up like the windows. De Ruse stood silent in the rain, wondering why the front door was open. Then he remembered that there had been another flood a few months before, not such a bad one. There might have been enough water to break open the door on the side towards the mountains.

Two stucco houses, both abandoned, loomed on the adjoining lots. Farther away from the wash, on a bit of higher ground, there was a lighted window. It was the only light anywhere in the range of De Ruse's vision.

He went back to the front of the house and slipped through the open door, stood inside it and listened. After quite a long time he snapped the flash on.

The house didn't smell like a house. It smelled like out of doors. There was nothing in the front room but sand, a few pieces of smashed furniture, some marks on the walls, above the dark line of the flood water, where pictures had hung.

De Ruse went through a short hall into a kitchen that had a hole in the floor where the sink had been and a rusty gas stove stuck in the hole. From the kitchen he went into a bedroom. He had not heard any whisper of sound in the house so far.

The bedroom was square and dark. A carpet stiff with old mud was plastered to the floor. There was a metal bed with a rusted spring, and a waterstained mattress over part of the spring.

Feet stuck out from under the bed.

They were large feet in walnut brown brogues, with purple socks above them. The socks had gray clocks down the sides. Above the socks were trousers of black and white check.

De Ruse stood very still and played the flash down on the feet. He made a soft sucking sound with his lips. He stood like that for a couple of minutes, without moving at all. Then he stood the flash on the floor, on its end, so that the light it shot against the ceiling was reflected down to make dim light all over the room.

He took hold of the mattress and pulled it off the bed. He

reached down and touched one of the hands of the man who was under the bed. The hand was ice cold. He took hold of the ankles and pulled, but the man was large and heavy.

It was easier to move the bed from over him.

TEN

Zapparty leaned his head back against the upholstery and shut his eyes and turned his head away a little. His eyes were shut very tight and he tried to turn his head far enough so that the light from the big flash wouldn't shine through his eyelids.

Nicky held the flash close to his face and snapped it on, off again, on, off again, monotonously, in a kind of rhythm.

De Ruse stood with one foot on the running board by the open door and looked off through the rain. On the edge of the murky horizon an airplane beacon flashed weakly.

Nicky said carelessly: "You never know what'll get a guy. I saw one break once because a cop held his fingernail against the dimple in his chin."

De Ruse laughed under his breath. "This one is tough," he said. "You'll have to think of something better than a flashlight."

Nicky snapped the flash on, off, on, off. "I could," he said, "But I don't want to get my hands dirty."

After a little while Zapparty raised his hands in front of him and let them fall slowly and began to talk. He talked in a low monotonous voice, keeping his eyes shut against the flash.

"Parisi worked the snatch. I didn't know anything about it until it was done. Parisi muscled in on me about a month ago, with a couple of tough boys to back him up. He had found out somehow that Candless beat me out of twenty-five grand to defend my half-brother on a murder rap, then sold the kid out. I didn't tell Parisi that. I didn't know he knew until tonight.

"He came into the club about seven or a little after and said: 'We've got a friend of yours, Hugo Candless. It's a hundred-grand job, a quick turnover. All you have to do is help spread the pay-off across the tables here, get it mixed up with a bunch of other money. You have to do that because we give you a cut—and because the caper is right up your alley, if anything goes sour.' That's about all. Parisi sat around then and chewed his fingers and waited for his boys. He got pretty jumpy when they didn't show. He went out once to make a phone call from a beer parlor."

De Ruse drew on a cigarette he held cupped inside a hand.

He said: "Who fingered the job, and how did you know Candless was up here?"

Zapparty said: "Mops told me. But I didn't know he was dead."

Nicky laughed and snapped the flash several times quickly.

De Ruse said: "Hold it steady for a minute." Nicky held the beam steady on Zapparty's white face. Zapparty moved his lips in and out. He opened his eyes once. They were blind eyes, like the eyes of a dead fish.

Nicky said: "It's damn cold up here. What do we do with his nibs?"

De Ruse said: "We'll take him into the house and tie him to Candless. They can keep each other warm. We'll come up again in the morning and see if he's got any fresh ideas."

Zapparty shuddered. The gleam of something like a tear showed in the corner of his nearest eye. After a moment of silence he said: "Okey. I planned the whole thing. The gas car was my idea. I didn't want the money. I wanted Candless, and I wanted him dead. My kid brother was hanged in Quentin a week ago Friday."

There was a little silence. Nicky said something under his breath. De Ruse didn't move or make a sound.

Zapparty went on: "Mattick, the Candless driver, was in on it. He hated Candless. He was supposed to drive the ringer car to make everything look good and then take a powder. But he lapped up too much corn getting set for the job and Parisi got leery of him, had him knocked off. Another boy drove the car. It was raining and that helped."

De Ruse said: "Better—but still not all of it, Zapparty."

Zapparty shrugged quickly, slightly opened his eyes against the flash, almost grinned.

"What the hell do you want? Jam on both sides?"

De Ruse said: "I want a finger put on the bird that had me grabbed . . . Let it go. I'll do it myself."

He took his foot off the running board and snapped his butt away into the darkness. He slammed the car door shut, got in the front. Nicky put the flash away and slid around under the wheel, started the engine.

De Ruse said: "Somewhere where I can phone for a cab, Nicky. Then you take this riding for another hour and then call Francy. I'll have a word for you there."

The blond man shook his head slowly from side to side. "You're a good pal, Johnny, and I like you. But this has gone far enough this way. I'm taking it down to Headquarters. Don't forget I've got a private-dick license under my old shirts at home.

De Ruse said: "Give me an hour, Nicky. Just an hour."

The car slid down the hill and crossed the Sunland Highway, started down another hill towards Montrose. After a while Nicky said: "Check."

ELEVEN

It was twelve minutes past one by the stamping clock on the end of the desk in the lobby of the Casa de Oro. The lobby was antique Spanish, with black and red Indian rugs, nail-studded chairs with leather cushions and leather tassels on the corners of the cushions; the gray-green olivewood doors were fitted with clumsy wrought-iron strap hinges.

A thin, dapper clerk with a waxed blond mustache and a blond pompadour leaned on the desk and looked at the clock and yawned, tapping his teeth with the backs of his bright fingernails.

The door opened from the street and De Ruse came in. He took off his hat and shook it, put it on again and yanked the brim down. His eyes looked slowly around the deserted lobby and he went to the desk, slapped a gloved palm on it.

"What's the number of the Hugo Candless bungalow?" he asked.

The clerk looked annoyed. He glanced at the clock, at De Ruse's face, back at the clock. He smiled superciliously, spoke a slight accent.

"Twelve C. Do you wish to be announced—at this hour?"

De Ruse said: "No."

He turned away from the desk and went towards a large door with a diamond of glass in it. It looked like the door of a very high-class privy.

As he put his hand out to the door a bell rang sharply behind him.

De Ruse looked back over his shoulder, turned and went back to the desk. The clerk took his hand away from the bell, rather quickly.

His voice was cold, sarcastic, insolent, saying: "It's not that kind of apartment house, if you please."

Two patches above De Ruse's cheekbones got a dusky red. He leaned across the counter and took hold of the braided lapel of the clerk's jacket, pulled the man's chest against the edge of the desk.

"What was that crack, nance?"

The clerk paled but managed to bang his bell again with a flailing hand.

A pudgy man in a baggy suit and a seal-brown toupee came around the corner of the desk, put out a plump finger and said: "Hey."

De Ruse let the clerk go. He looked expressionlessly at cigar ash on the front of the pudgy man's coat.

The pudgy man said: "I'm the house man. You gotta see me if you want to get tough."

De Ruse said: "You speak my language. Come over in the corner."

They went over in the corner and sat down beside a palm. The pudgy man yawned amiably and lifted the edge of his toupee and scratched under it.

"I'm Kuvalick," he said. "Times I could bop that Swiss myself. What's the beef?"

De Ruse said: "Are you a guy that can stay clammed?"

"No. I like to talk. It's all the fun I get around this dude ranch." Kuvalick got half of a cigar out of a pocket and burned his nose lighting it.

De Ruse said: "This is one time you stay clammed."

He reached inside his coat, got his wallet out, took out two tens. He rolled them around his forefinger, then slipped them off in a tube and tucked the tube into the outside pocket of the pudgy man's coat.

Kuvalick blinked, but didn't say anything.

De Ruse said: "There's a man in the Candless apartment named George Dial. His car's outside, and that's where he would be. I want to see him and I don't want to send a name in. You can take me in and stay with me."

The pudgy man said cautiously: "It's kind of late. Maybe he's in bed."

"If he is, he's in the wrong bed," De Ruse said. "He ought to get up."

The pudgy man stood up. "I don't like what I'm thinkin', but I like your tens," he said. "I'll go in and see if they're up. You stay put."

De Ruse nodded. Kuvalick went along the wall and slipped through a door in the corner. The clumsy square butt of a hip holster showed under the back of his coat as he walked. The clerk looked after him, then looked contemptuously towards De Ruse and got out a nail file.

Ten minutes went by, fifteen. Kuvalick didn't come back. De Ruse stood up suddenly, scowled and marched towards the door in the corner. The clerk at the desk stiffened, and his eyes went to the telephone on the desk, but he didn't touch it.

De Ruse went through the door and found himself under a roofed gallery. Rain dripped softly off the slanting tiles of the roof. He went along a patio the middle of which was an oblong pool framed in a mosaic of gaily colored tiles. At the end of that, other patios branched off. There was a window light at the far end of the one to the left. He went towards it, at a venture, and when he came close to it made out the number 12C on the door.

He went up two flat steps and punched a bell that rang in the distance. Nothing happened. In a little while he rang again, then tried the door. It was locked. Somewhere inside he thought he heard a faint muffled thumping sound.

He stood in the rain a moment, then went around the corner of the bungalow, down a narrow, very wet passage to the back. He tried the service door; locked also. De Ruse swore, took his gun out from under his arm, held his hat against the glass panel of the service door and smashed the pane with the butt of the gun. Glass fell tinkling lightly inside.

He put the gun away, straightened his hat on his head and reached in through the broken pane to unlock the door.

The kitchen was large and bright with black and yellow tiling, looked as if it was used mostly for mixing drinks. Two bottles of Haig and Haig, a bottle of Hennessy, three or four kinds of fancy cordial bottles stood on the tiled drainboard. A short hall with a closed door led to the living room. There was a grand piano in the corner with a lamp lit beside it. Another lamp on a low table with drinks and glasses. A wood fire was dying on the hearth.

The thumping noise got louder.

De Ruse went across the living room and through a door framed in a valance into another hallway, thence into a beautifully paneled bedroom. The thumping noise came from a closet. De Ruse opened the door of the closet and saw a man.

He was sitting on the floor with his back in a forest of dresses on hangers. A towel was tied around his face. Another held

371

▼

his ankles together. His wrists were tied behind him. He was a very bald man, as bald as the croupier at the Club Egypt.

De Ruse stared down at him harshly, then suddenly grinned, bent and cut him loose.

The man spit a washcloth out of his mouth, swore hoarsely and dived into the clothes at the back of the closet. He came up with something furry clutched in his hand, straightened it out, and put it on his hairless head.

That made him Kuvalick, the house dick.

He got up still swearing and backed away from De Ruse, with a stiff alert grin on his fat face. His right hand shot to his hip holster.

De Ruse spread his hands, said: "Tell it," and sat down in a small chintz-covered slipper chair.

Kuvalick stared at him quietly for a moment, then took his hand away from his gun.

"There's lights," he said, "So I push the buzzer. A tall dark guy opens. I seen him around here a lot. That's Dial. I say to him there's a guy outside in the lobby wants to see him hush-hush, won't give a name."

"That made you a sap," De Ruse commented dryly.

"Not yet, but soon," Kuvalick grinned, and spit a shred of cloth out of his mouth. "I describe you. *That* makes me a sap. He smiled kind of funny and asks me to come in a minute. I go in past him and he shuts the door and sticks a gun in my kidney. He says: 'Did you say he wore all dark clothes?' I say: 'Yes. And what's that gat for?' He says: 'Does he have gray eyes and sort of crinkly black hair and is he hard around the teeth?' I say: 'Yes, you bastard and what's the gat for?'

"He says: 'For this,' and lets me have it on the back of the head. I go down, groggy, but not out. Then the Candless broad comes out from a doorway and they tie me up and shove me in the closet and that's that. I hear them fussin' around for a little while and then I hear silence. That's all until you ring the bell."

De Ruse smiled lazily, pleasantly. His whole body was lax in the chair. His manner had become indolent and unhurried.

"They faded," he said softly. "They got tipped off. I don't think that was very bright."

Kuvalick said: "I'm an old Wells Fargo dick and I can stand a shock. What they been up to?"

"What kind of woman is Mrs. Candless?"

"Dark, a looker, Sex hungry, as the fellow says. Kind of worn and tight. They get a new chauffeur every three months. There's a couple guys in the Casa she likes too. I guess there's this gigolo that bopped me."

De Ruse looked at his watch, nodded, leaned forward to get up. "I guess it's about time for some law. Got any friends downtown you'd like to give a snatch story to?"

A voice said: "Not quite yet."

George Dial came quickly into the room from the hallway and stood quietly inside it with a long, thin, silenced automatic in his hand. His eyes were bright and mad, but his lemon-colored finger was very steady on the trigger of the small gun.

"We didn't fade," he said. "We weren't quite ready. But it might not have been a bad idea—for you two."

Kuvalick's pudgy hand swept for his hip holster.

The small automatic with the black tube on it made two flat dull sounds.

A puff of dust jumped from the front of Kuvalick's coat. His hands jerked sharply away from the sides and his small eyes snapped very wide open, like seeds bursting from a pod. He fell heavily on his side against the wall, lay quite still on his left side, with his eyes half open and his back against the wall. His toupee was tipped over rakishly.

De Ruse looked at him swiftly, looked back at Dial. No emotion showed in his face, not even excitement.

He said: "You're a crazy fool, Dial. That kills your last chance. You could have bluffed it out. But that's not your only mistake."

Dial said calmly: "No. I see that now. I shouldn't have sent the boys after you. I did that just for the hell of it. That comes of not being a professional."

De Ruse nodded slightly, looked at Dial almost with friendliness. "Just for the fun of it—who tipped you off the game had gone smash?"

"Francy—and she took her damn time about it," Dial said savagely. "I'm leaving, so I won't be able to thank her for a while."

"Not ever," De Ruse said. "You won't get out of the state. You won't ever touch a nickel of the big boy's money. Not you or your sidekicks or your woman. The cops are getting the story—right now."

Dial said: "We'll get clear. We have enough to tour on, Johnny. So long."

Dial's face tightened and his hand jerked up, with the gun in it. De Ruse half closed his eyes, braced himself for the shock. The little gun didn't go off. There was a rustle behind Dial and a tall dark woman in a gray fur coat slid into the room. A small hat was balanced on dark hair knotted on the nape of her neck. She was pretty, in a thin, haggard sort of way. The lip rouge on her mouth was as black as soot; there was no color in her cheeks.

She had a cool lazy voice that didn't match with her taut expression. "Who is Francy?" she asked coldly.

De Ruse opened his eyes wide and his body got stiff in the chair and his right hand began to slide up towards his chest.

"Francy is my girl friend," he said. "Mister Dial has been trying to get her away from me. But that's all right. He's a handsome lad and ought to be able to pick his spots."

The tall woman's face suddenly became dark and wild and furious. She grabbed fiercely at Dial's arm, the one that held the gun.

De Ruse snatched for his shoulder holster, got his .38 loose. But it wasn't his gun that went off. It wasn't the silenced automatic in Dial's hand. It was a huge frontier Colt with an eight-inch barrel and a boom like an exploding bomb. It went off from the floor, from beside Kuvalick's right hip, where Kuvalick's plump hand held it.

It went off just once. Dial was thrown back against the wall as if by a giant hand. His head crashed against the wall and instantly his darkly handsome face was a mask of blood.

He fell laxly down the wall and the little automatic with the black tube on it fell in front of him. The dark woman dived for it, down on her hands and knees in front of Dial's sprawled body.

She got it, began to bring it up. Her face was convulsed, her lips were drawn back over thin wolfish teeth that shimmered.

Kuvalick's voice said: "I'm a tough guy. I used to be a Wells Fargo dick."

His great cannon slammed again. A shrill scream was torn from the woman's lips. Her body was flung against Dial's. Her eyes opened and shut, opened and shut. Her face got white and vacant.

"Shoulder shot. She's okay," Kuvalick said, and got up on his feet. He jerked open his coat and patted his chest.

"Bullet-proof vest," he said proudly. "But I thought I'd better lie quiet for a while or he'd popped me in the face."

TWELVE

Francine Ley yawned and stretched out a long green pajama-clad leg and looked at a slim green slipper on her bare foot. She yawned again, got up and walked nervously across the room to the kidney-shaped desk. She poured a drink, drank it quickly, with a sharp nervous shudder. Her face was drawn and tired, her eyes hollow; there were dark smudges under her eyes.

She looked at the tiny watch on her wrist. It was almost four o'clock in the morning. Still with her wrist up she whirled at a sound, put her back to the desk and began to breathe very quickly, pantingly.

De Ruse came in through the red curtains. He stopped and

looked at her without expression, then slowly took off his hat and overcoat and dropped them on a chair. He took off his suit coat and his tan shoulder harness and walked over to the drinks.

He sniffed at a glass, filled it a third full of whiskey, put it down in a gulp.

"So you had to tip the louse off," he said somberly, looking down into the empty glass he held.

Francine Ley said: "Yes. I had to phone him. What happened?"

"You had to phone the louse," De Ruse said in exactly the same tone. "You knew damn well he was mixed up in it. You'd rather he got loose, even if he cooled me off doing it."

"You're all right, Johnny?" She asked softly, tiredly.

De Ruse didn't speak, didn't look at her. He put the glass down slowly and poured some more whiskey into it, added charged water, looked around for some ice. Not finding any he began to sip the drink with his eyes on the white top of the desk.

Francine Ley said: "There isn't a guy in the world that doesn't rate a start on you, Johnny. It wouldn't do him any good, but he'd have to have it, if I knew him."

De Ruse said slowly: "That's swell. Only I'm not quite that good. I'd be a stiff right now except for a comic hotel dick that wears a Buntline Special and a bullet-proof vest to work."

After a little while Francine Ley said: "Do you want me to blow?"

De Ruse looked at her quickly, looked away again. He put his glass down and walked away from the desk. Over his shoulder he said: "Not so long as you keep on telling me the truth."

He sat down in a deep chair and leaned his elbows on the arms of it, cupped his face in his hands. Francine Ley watched him for a moment, then went over and sat on an arm of the chair. She pulled his head back gently until it was against the back of the chair. She began to stroke his forehead.

De Ruse closed his eyes. His body became loose and relaxed. His voice began to sound sleepy.

"You saved my life over at the Club Egypt maybe. I guess that gave you the right to let handsome have a shot at me."

Francine Ley stroked his head, without speaking.

"Handsome is dead," De Ruse went on. "The peeper shot his face off."

Francine Ley's hand stopped. In a moment it began again, stroking his head.

"The Candless frau was in on it. Seems she's a hot number. She wanted Hugo's dough, and she wanted all the men in the world except Hugo. Thank heaven she didn't get bumped. She talked plenty. So did Zapparty."

"Yes, honey," Francine Ley said quietly.

De Ruse yawned. "Candless is dead. He was dead before we started. They never wanted him anything else but dead. Parisi didn't care one way or the other, as long as he got paid."

Francine Ley said: "Yes, honey."

"Tell you the rest in the morning," De Ruse said thickly. "I guess Nicky and I are all square with the law . . . Let's go to Reno, get married . . . I'm sick of this tomcat life . . . Get me 'nother drink, baby."

Francine Ley didn't move except to draw her fingers softly and soothingly across his forehead and back over his temples. De Ruse moved lower in the chair. His head rolled to one side.

"Yes, honey."

"Don't call me honey," De Ruse said thickly. "Just call me pigeon."

When he was quite asleep she got off the arm of the chair and went and sat down near him. She sat very still and watched him, her face cupped in her long delicate hands with the cherry-colored nails.

ABOUT THE AUTHOR

RAYMOND CHANDLER was born in Chicago, Illinois, on July 23, 1888, but spent most of his boyhood and youth in England, where he attended Dulwich College and later worked as a free-lance journalist for *The Westminster Gazette* and *The Spectator*. During World War I, he served in France with the First Division of the Canadian Expeditionary Force, transferring later to the Royal Flying Corps (R.A.F.). In 1919 he returned to the United States, settling in California, where he eventually became director of a number of independent oil companies. The Depression put an end to his business career, and in 1933, at the age of forty-five, he turned to writing, publishing his first stories in *Black Mask*. His first novel, *The Big Sleep*, was published in 1939. Never a prolific writer, he published only one collection of stories and seven novels in his lifetime. In the last year of his life he was elected president of the Mystery Writers of America. He died in La Jolla, California, on March 26, 1959.